CHAPTER ONE

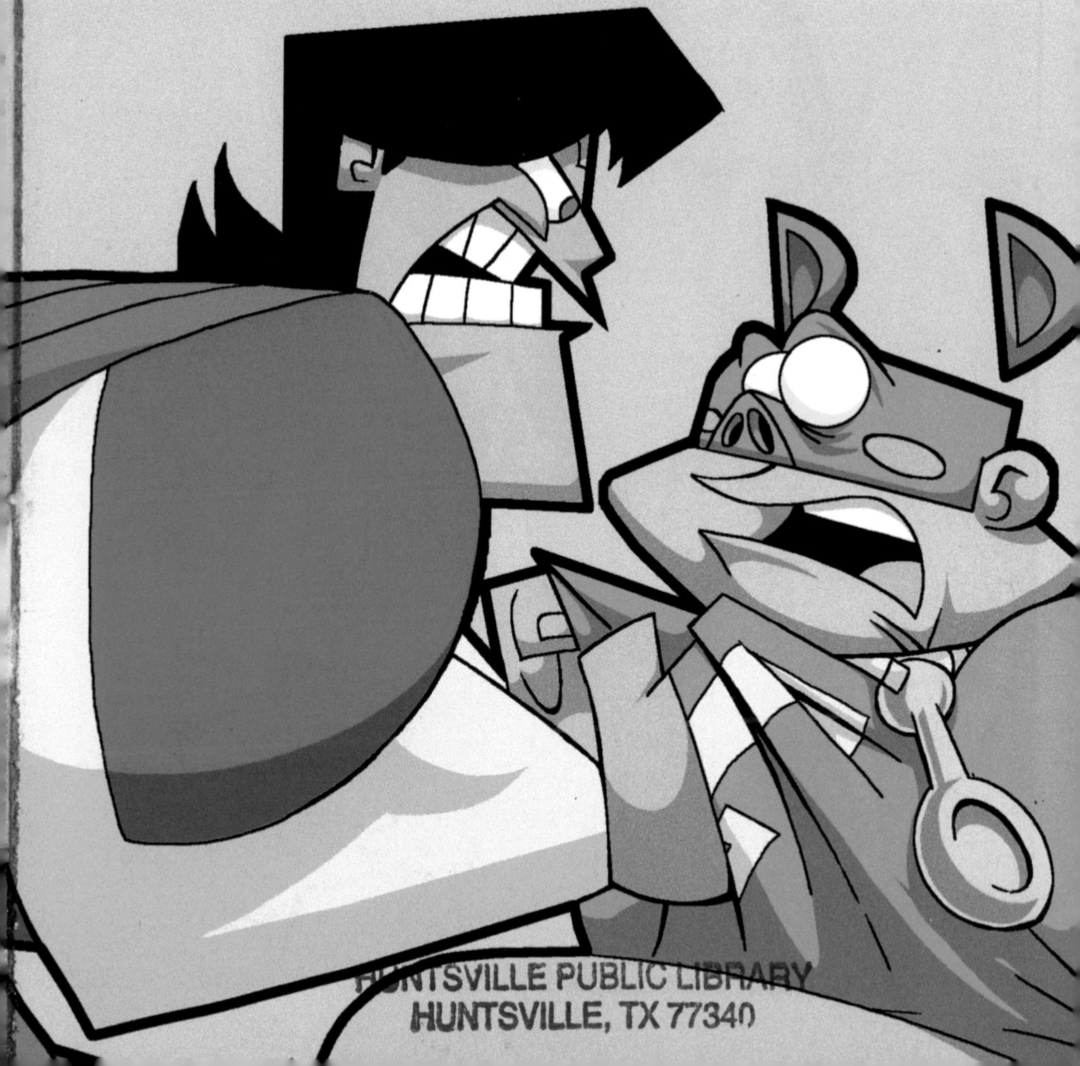

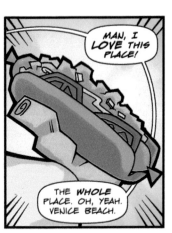

MAN, I *LOVE* THIS PLACE!

THE *WHOLE* PLACE. OH, YEAH. VENICE BEACH.

BEST GIRLS AND BEST FOOD ON THE ENTIRE PLANET.

CHICAGO STYLE. 'NO BETTER WAY TO MAKE A HOT DOG.

YOU KNOW WHAT? YOU'RE BECOMING MORE DISGUSTING BY THE DAY.

I THINK YOU'VE FALLEN TOO MUCH IN *LOVE* WITH THIS PLANET.

YEAH ≈MUNCH≈ IT'S ALL ≈SLOBBER≈ SO TASTY.

I GUESS WE ALL HAVE A WEAKNESS, ATLAS. AND YOURS... WELL, IT HAPPENS TO BE A FOOD MADE FROM ENTRAILS.

DOESN'T RANK UP THERE WITH *KRYPTONITE*, DOES IT?

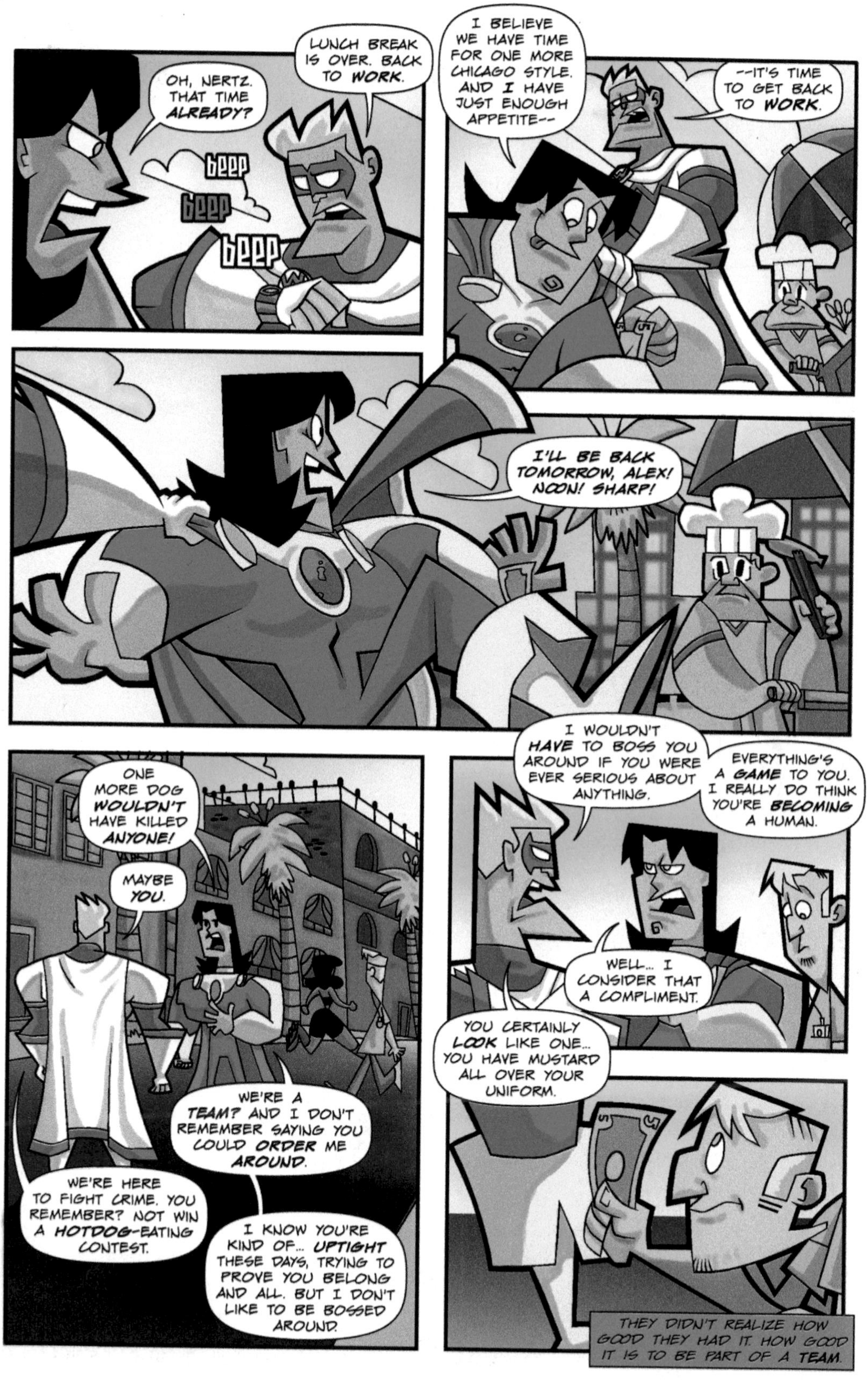
OH, NERTZ. THAT TIME ALREADY?
LUNCH BREAK IS OVER. BACK TO WORK.
BEEP
BEEP
BEEP
I BELIEVE WE HAVE TIME FOR ONE MORE CHICAGO STYLE. AND I HAVE JUST ENOUGH APPETITE--
--IT'S TIME TO GET BACK TO WORK.
I'LL BE BACK TOMORROW, ALEX! NOON! SHARP!
ONE MORE DOG WOULDN'T HAVE KILLED ANYONE!
MAYBE YOU.
WE'RE HERE TO FIGHT CRIME. YOU REMEMBER? NOT WIN A HOTDOG-EATING CONTEST.
WE'RE A TEAM? AND I DON'T REMEMBER SAYING YOU COULD ORDER ME AROUND.
I KNOW YOU'RE KIND OF... UPTIGHT THESE DAYS, TRYING TO PROVE YOU BELONG AND ALL. BUT I DON'T LIKE TO BE BOSSED AROUND.
I WOULDN'T HAVE TO BOSS YOU AROUND IF YOU WERE EVER SERIOUS ABOUT ANYTHING.
EVERYTHING'S A GAME TO YOU. I REALLY DO THINK YOU'RE BECOMING A HUMAN.
WELL... I CONSIDER THAT A COMPLIMENT.
YOU CERTAINLY LOOK LIKE ONE... YOU HAVE MUSTARD ALL OVER YOUR UNIFORM.
THEY DIDN'T REALIZE HOW GOOD THEY HAD IT. HOW GOOD IT IS TO BE PART OF A TEAM.

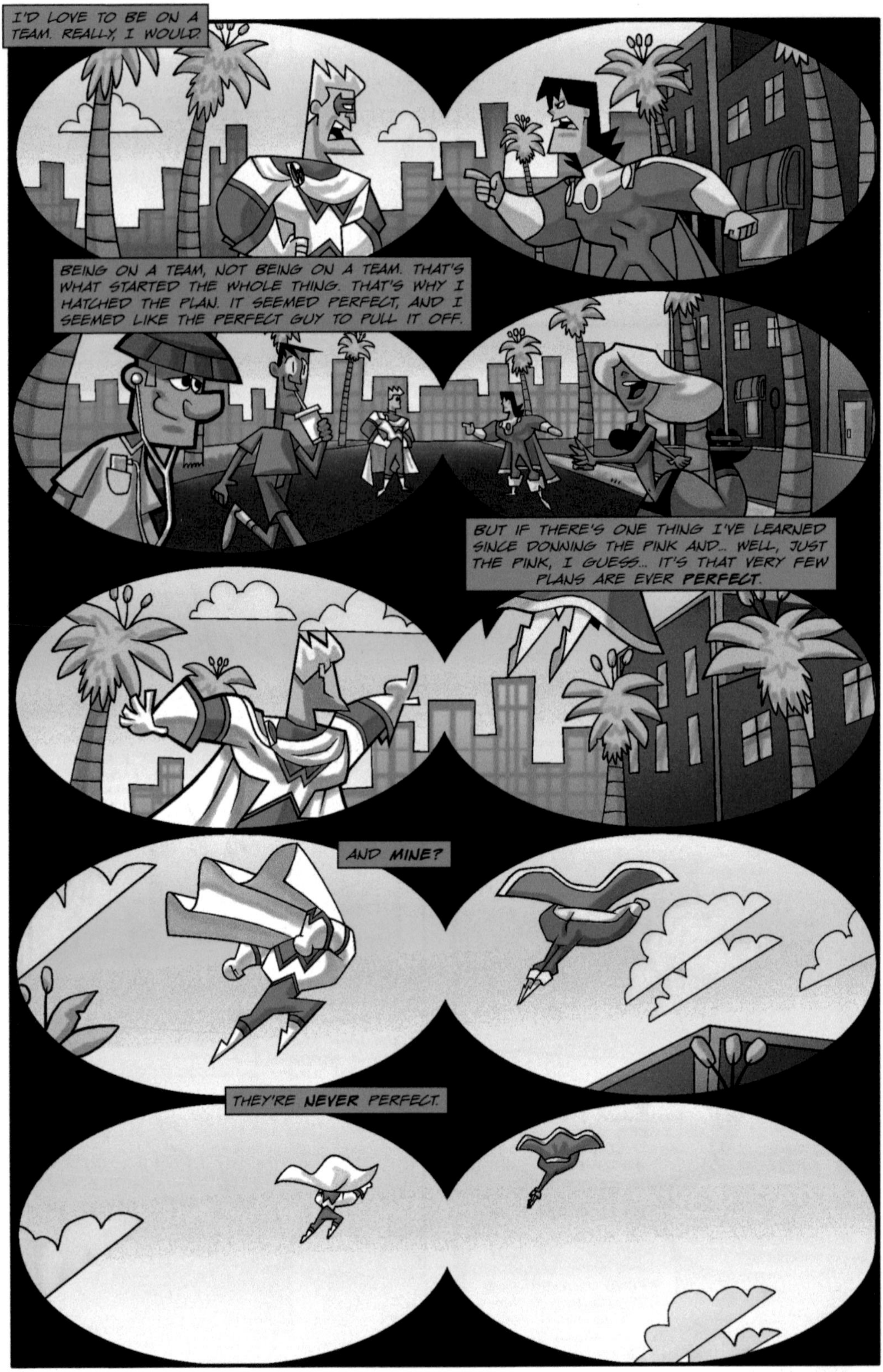
I'D LOVE TO BE ON A TEAM. REALLY, I WOULD.
BEING ON A TEAM, NOT BEING ON A TEAM. THAT'S WHAT STARTED THE WHOLE THING. THAT'S WHY I HATCHED THE PLAN. IT SEEMED PERFECT, AND I SEEMED LIKE THE PERFECT GUY TO PULL IT OFF.
BUT IF THERE'S ONE THING I'VE LEARNED SINCE DONNING THE PINK AND... WELL, JUST THE PINK, I GUESS... IT'S THAT VERY FEW PLANS ARE EVER **PERFECT**.
AND **MINE**?
THEY'RE **NEVER** PERFECT.

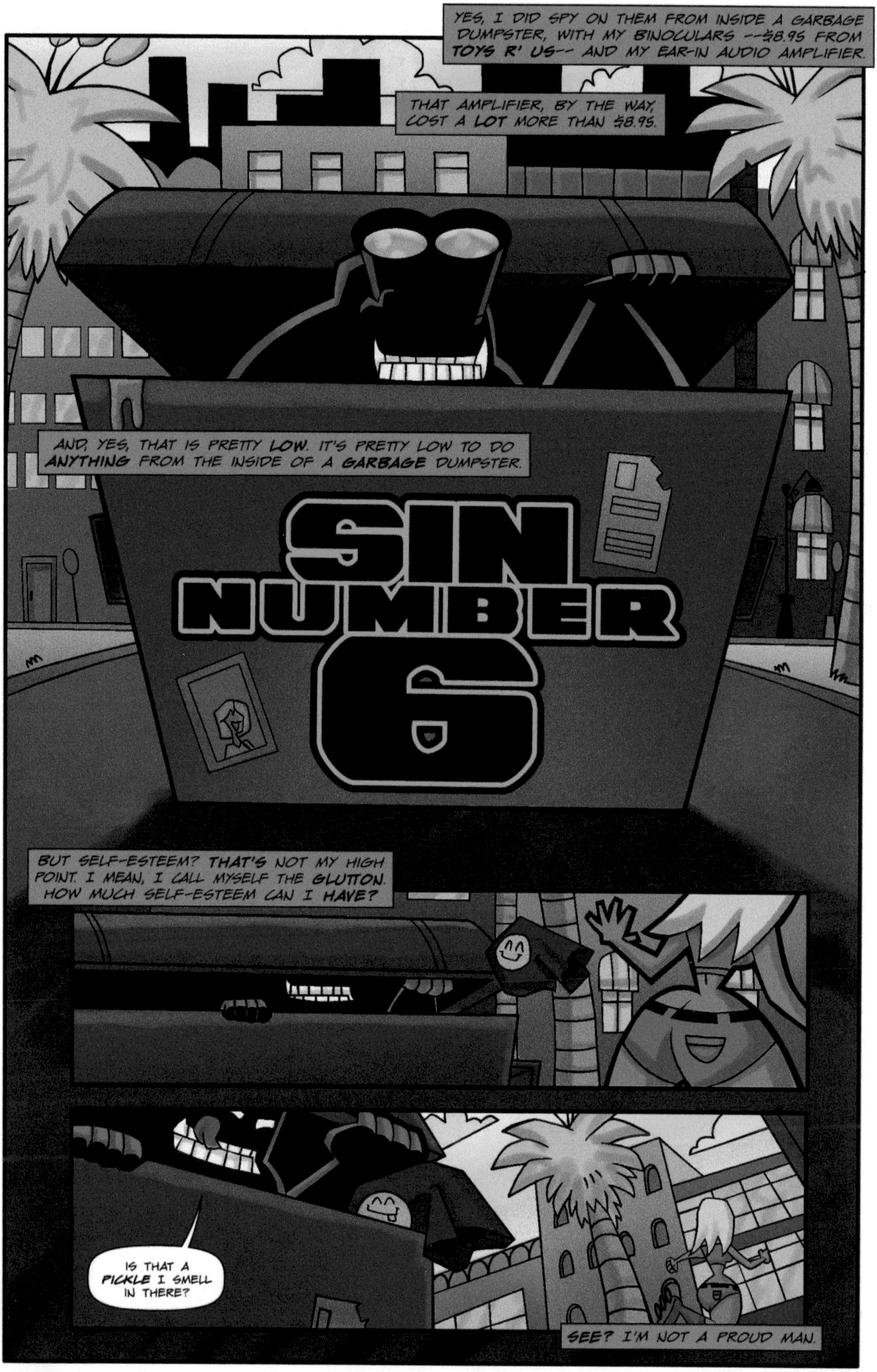
YES, I DID SPY ON THEM FROM INSIDE A GARBAGE DUMPSTER, WITH MY BINOCULARS --$8.95 FROM TOYS R' US-- AND MY EAR-IN AUDIO AMPLIFIER.
THAT AMPLIFIER, BY THE WAY, COST A LOT MORE THAN $8.95.
AND, YES, THAT IS PRETTY LOW. IT'S PRETTY LOW TO DO ANYTHING FROM THE INSIDE OF A GARBAGE DUMPSTER.
SIN NUMBER 6
BUT SELF-ESTEEM? THAT'S NOT MY HIGH POINT. I MEAN, I CALL MYSELF THE GLUTTON. HOW MUCH SELF-ESTEEM CAN I HAVE?
IS THAT A PICKLE I SMELL IN THERE?
SEE? I'M NOT A PROUD MAN.

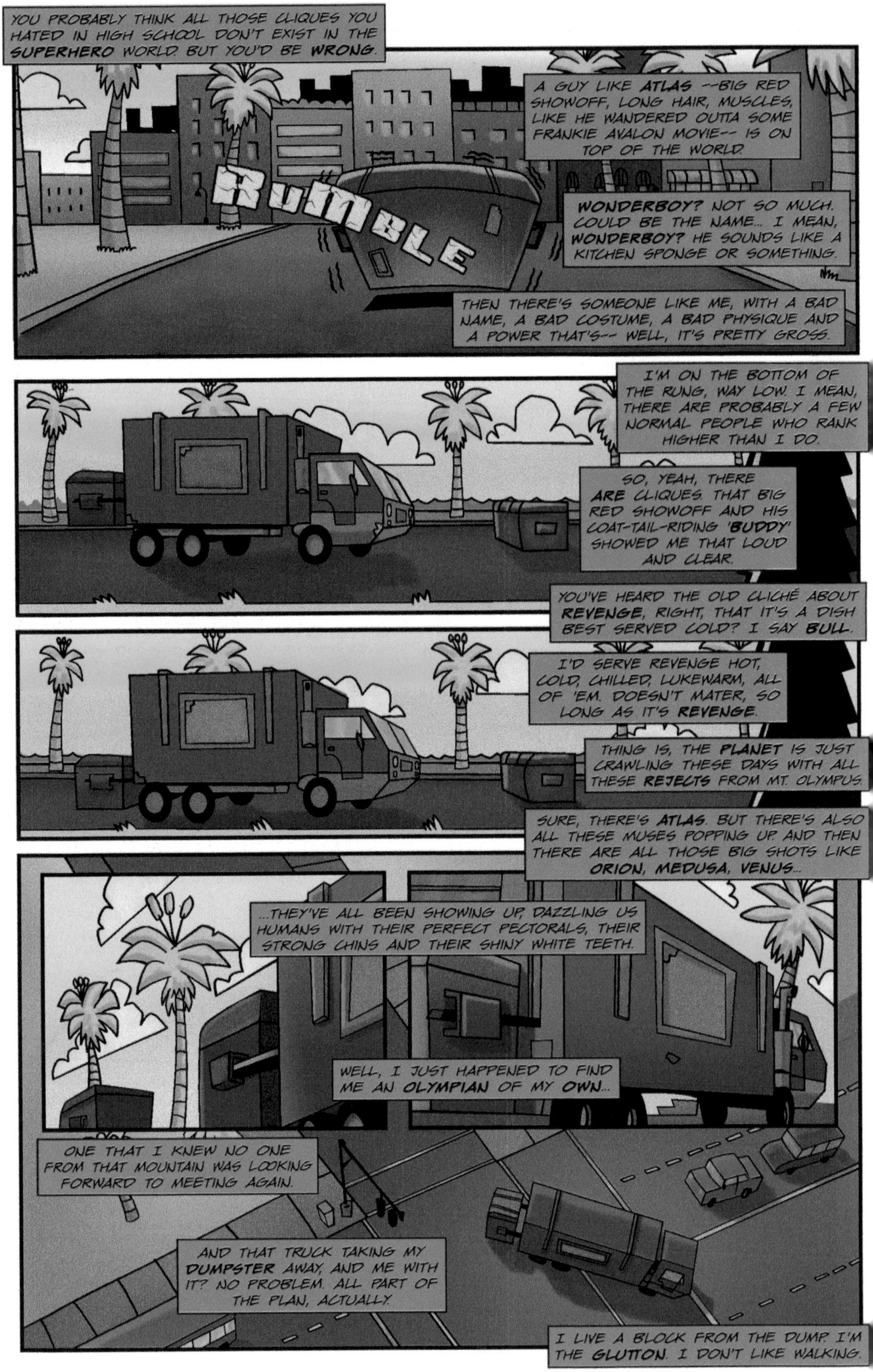
YOU PROBABLY THINK ALL THOSE CLIQUES YOU HATED IN HIGH SCHOOL DON'T EXIST IN THE SUPERHERO WORLD. BUT YOU'D BE WRONG.
A GUY LIKE ATLAS --BIG RED SHOWOFF, LONG HAIR, MUSCLES, LIKE HE WANDERED OUTTA SOME FRANKIE AVALON MOVIE-- IS ON TOP OF THE WORLD.
RUMBLE
WONDERBOY? NOT SO MUCH. COULD BE THE NAME... I MEAN, WONDERBOY? HE SOUNDS LIKE A KITCHEN SPONGE OR SOMETHING.
THEN THERE'S SOMEONE LIKE ME, WITH A BAD NAME, A BAD COSTUME, A BAD PHYSIQUE AND A POWER THAT'S-- WELL, IT'S PRETTY GROSS.
I'M ON THE BOTTOM OF THE RUNG, WAY LOW. I MEAN, THERE ARE PROBABLY A FEW NORMAL PEOPLE WHO RANK HIGHER THAN I DO.
SO, YEAH, THERE ARE CLIQUES. THAT BIG RED SHOWOFF AND HIS COAT-TAIL-RIDING 'BUDDY' SHOWED ME THAT LOUD AND CLEAR.
YOU'VE HEARD THE OLD CLICHÉ ABOUT REVENGE, RIGHT, THAT IT'S A DISH BEST SERVED COLD? I SAY BULL.
I'D SERVE REVENGE HOT, COLD, CHILLED, LUKEWARM, ALL OF 'EM. DOESN'T MATER, SO LONG AS IT'S REVENGE.
THING IS, THE PLANET IS JUST CRAWLING THESE DAYS WITH ALL THESE REJECTS FROM MT. OLYMPUS.
SURE, THERE'S ATLAS. BUT THERE'S ALSO ALL THESE MUSES POPPING UP. AND THEN THERE ARE ALL THOSE BIG SHOTS LIKE ORION, MEDUSA, VENUS...
...THEY'VE ALL BEEN SHOWING UP, DAZZLING US HUMANS WITH THEIR PERFECT PECTORALS, THEIR STRONG CHINS AND THEIR SHINY WHITE TEETH.
WELL, I JUST HAPPENED TO FIND ME AN OLYMPIAN OF MY OWN...
ONE THAT I KNEW NO ONE FROM THAT MOUNTAIN WAS LOOKING FORWARD TO MEETING AGAIN.
AND THAT TRUCK TAKING MY DUMPSTER AWAY, AND ME WITH IT? NO PROBLEM. ALL PART OF THE PLAN, ACTUALLY.
I LIVE A BLOCK FROM THE DUMP. I'M THE GLUTTON. I DON'T LIKE WALKING.

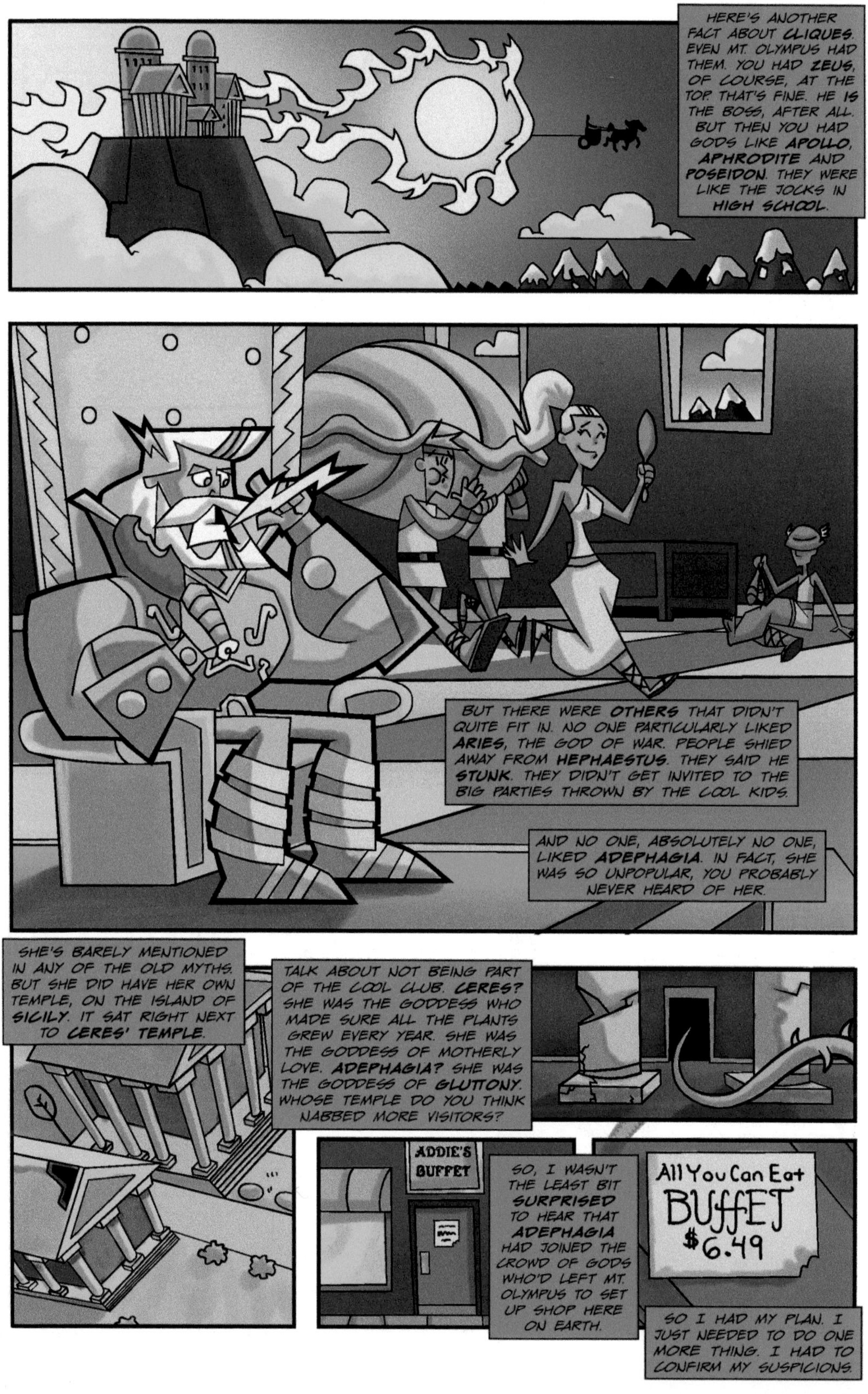

HERE'S ANOTHER FACT ABOUT CLIQUES. EVEN MT. OLYMPUS HAD THEM. YOU HAD ZEUS, OF COURSE, AT THE TOP. THAT'S FINE. HE IS THE BOSS, AFTER ALL. BUT THEN YOU HAD GODS LIKE APOLLO, APHRODITE AND POSEIDON. THEY WERE LIKE THE JOCKS IN HIGH SCHOOL.
BUT THERE WERE OTHERS THAT DIDN'T QUITE FIT IN. NO ONE PARTICULARLY LIKED ARIES, THE GOD OF WAR. PEOPLE SHIED AWAY FROM HEPHAESTUS. THEY SAID HE STUNK. THEY DIDN'T GET INVITED TO THE BIG PARTIES THROWN BY THE COOL KIDS.
AND NO ONE, ABSOLUTELY NO ONE, LIKED ADEPHAGIA. IN FACT, SHE WAS SO UNPOPULAR, YOU PROBABLY NEVER HEARD OF HER.
SHE'S BARELY MENTIONED IN ANY OF THE OLD MYTHS. BUT SHE DID HAVE HER OWN TEMPLE, ON THE ISLAND OF SICILY. IT SAT RIGHT NEXT TO CERES' TEMPLE.
TALK ABOUT NOT BEING PART OF THE COOL CLUB. CERES? SHE WAS THE GODDESS WHO MADE SURE ALL THE PLANTS GREW EVERY YEAR. SHE WAS THE GODDESS OF MOTHERLY LOVE. ADEPHAGIA? SHE WAS THE GODDESS OF GLUTTONY. WHOSE TEMPLE DO YOU THINK NABBED MORE VISITORS?
ADDIE'S BUFFET
SO, I WASN'T THE LEAST BIT SURPRISED TO HEAR THAT ADEPHAGIA HAD JOINED THE CROWD OF GODS WHO'D LEFT MT. OLYMPUS TO SET UP SHOP HERE ON EARTH.
All You Can Eat BUFFET $6.49
SO I HAD MY PLAN. I JUST NEEDED TO DO ONE MORE THING. I HAD TO CONFIRM MY SUSPICIONS.

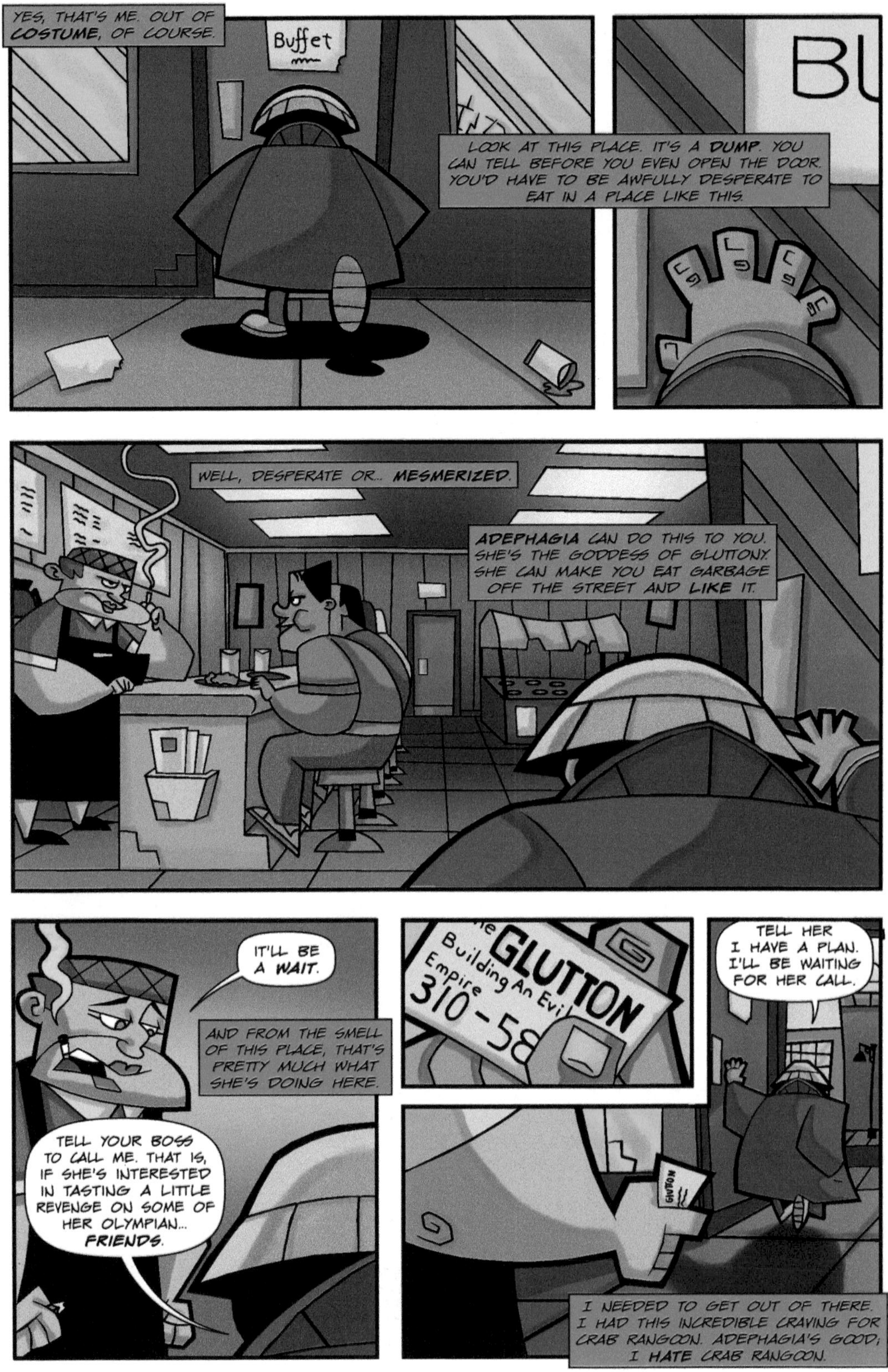
YES, THAT'S ME. OUT OF COSTUME, OF COURSE.
Buffet
BU
LOOK AT THIS PLACE. IT'S A DUMP. YOU CAN TELL BEFORE YOU EVEN OPEN THE DOOR. YOU'D HAVE TO BE AWFULLY DESPERATE TO EAT IN A PLACE LIKE THIS.
WELL, DESPERATE OR... MESMERIZED.
ADEPHAGIA CAN DO THIS TO YOU. SHE'S THE GODDESS OF GLUTTONY. SHE CAN MAKE YOU EAT GARBAGE OFF THE STREET AND LIKE IT.
IT'LL BE A WAIT.
AND FROM THE SMELL OF THIS PLACE, THAT'S PRETTY MUCH WHAT SHE'S DOING HERE.
TELL YOUR BOSS TO CALL ME. THAT IS, IF SHE'S INTERESTED IN TASTING A LITTLE REVENGE ON SOME OF HER OLYMPIAN... FRIENDS.
GLUTTON
Building An Evil
Empire
310-58
TELL HER I HAVE A PLAN. I'LL BE WAITING FOR HER CALL.
GLUTTON
I NEEDED TO GET OUT OF THERE. I HAD THIS INCREDIBLE CRAVING FOR CRAB RANGOON. ADEPHAGIA'S GOOD; I HATE CRAB RANGOON.

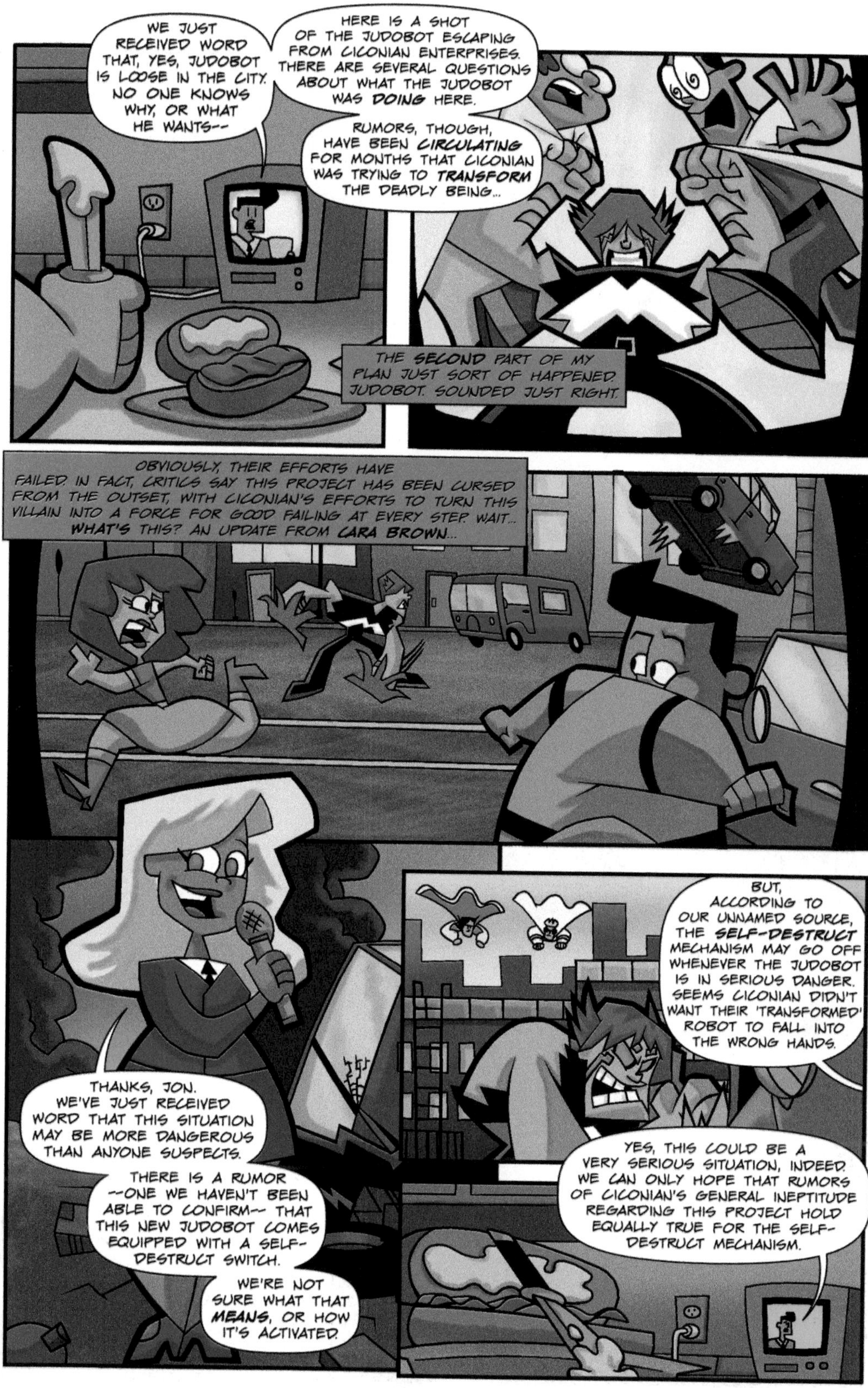
WE JUST RECEIVED WORD THAT, YES, JUDOBOT IS LOOSE IN THE CITY. NO ONE KNOWS WHY, OR WHAT HE WANTS--
HERE IS A SHOT OF THE JUDOBOT ESCAPING FROM CICONIAN ENTERPRISES. THERE ARE SEVERAL QUESTIONS ABOUT WHAT THE JUDOBOT WAS DOING HERE.
RUMORS, THOUGH, HAVE BEEN CIRCULATING FOR MONTHS THAT CICONIAN WAS TRYING TO TRANSFORM THE DEADLY BEING...
THE SECOND PART OF MY PLAN JUST SORT OF HAPPENED. JUDOBOT. SOUNDED JUST RIGHT.
OBVIOUSLY, THEIR EFFORTS HAVE FAILED. IN FACT, CRITICS SAY THIS PROJECT HAS BEEN CURSED FROM THE OUTSET, WITH CICONIAN'S EFFORTS TO TURN THIS VILLAIN INTO A FORCE FOR GOOD FAILING AT EVERY STEP. WAIT... WHAT'S THIS? AN UPDATE FROM CARA BROWN...
THANKS, JON. WE'VE JUST RECEIVED WORD THAT THIS SITUATION MAY BE MORE DANGEROUS THAN ANYONE SUSPECTS.
THERE IS A RUMOR --ONE WE HAVEN'T BEEN ABLE TO CONFIRM-- THAT THIS NEW JUDOBOT COMES EQUIPPED WITH A SELF-DESTRUCT SWITCH.
WE'RE NOT SURE WHAT THAT MEANS, OR HOW IT'S ACTIVATED.
BUT, ACCORDING TO OUR UNNAMED SOURCE, THE SELF-DESTRUCT MECHANISM MAY GO OFF WHENEVER THE JUDOBOT IS IN SERIOUS DANGER. SEEMS CICONIAN DIDN'T WANT THEIR 'TRANSFORMED' ROBOT TO FALL INTO THE WRONG HANDS.
YES, THIS COULD BE A VERY SERIOUS SITUATION, INDEED. WE CAN ONLY HOPE THAT RUMORS OF CICONIAN'S GENERAL INEPTITUDE REGARDING THIS PROJECT HOLD EQUALLY TRUE FOR THE SELF-DESTRUCT MECHANISM.

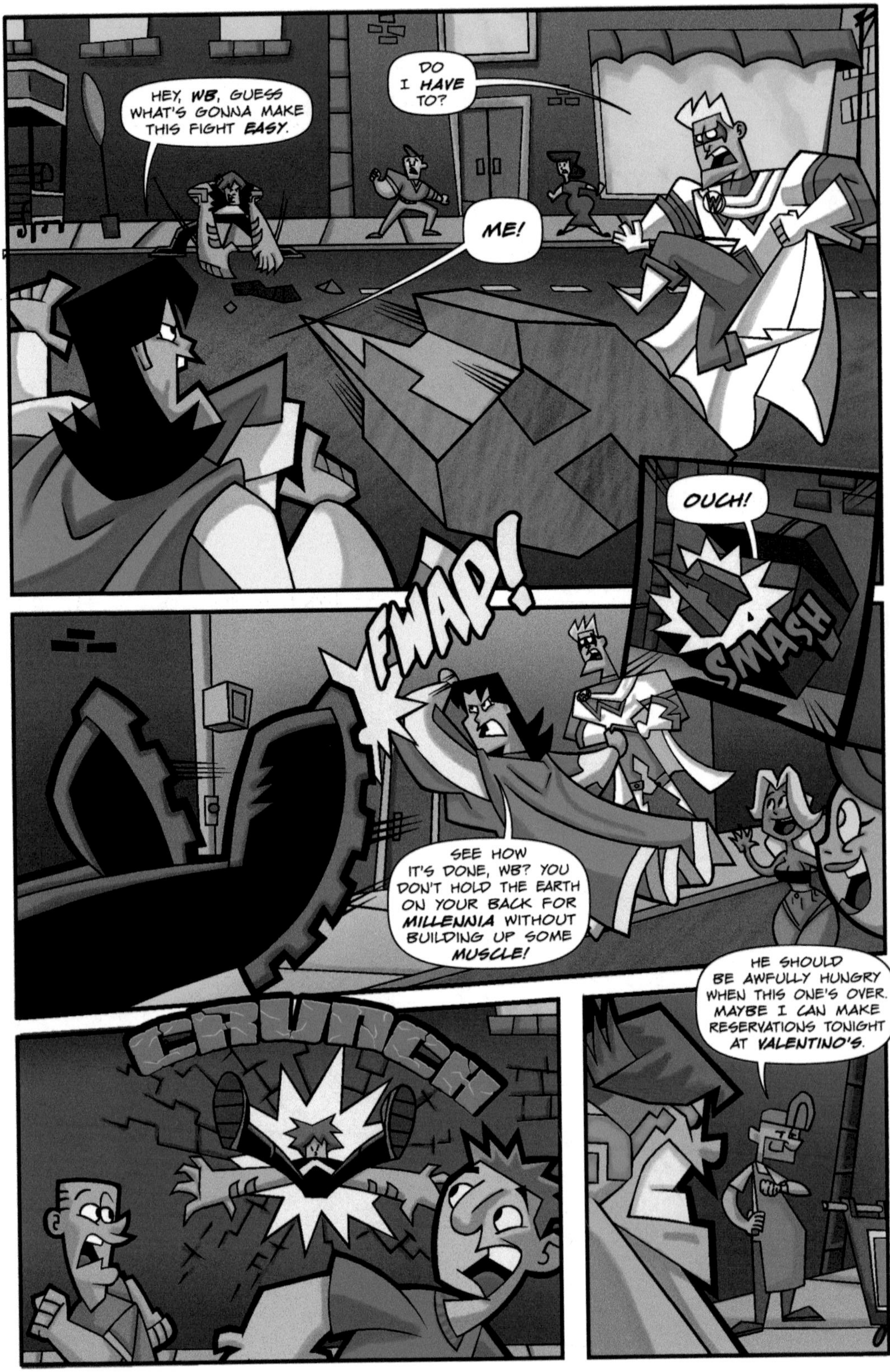
HEY, WB, GUESS WHAT'S GONNA MAKE THIS FIGHT EASY.
DO I HAVE TO?
ME!
OUCH!
SMASH
FWAP!
SEE HOW IT'S DONE, WB? YOU DON'T HOLD THE EARTH ON YOUR BACK FOR MILLENNIA WITHOUT BUILDING UP SOME MUSCLE!
CRUNCH
HE SHOULD BE AWFULLY HUNGRY WHEN THIS ONE'S OVER. MAYBE I CAN MAKE RESERVATIONS TONIGHT AT VALENTINO'S.

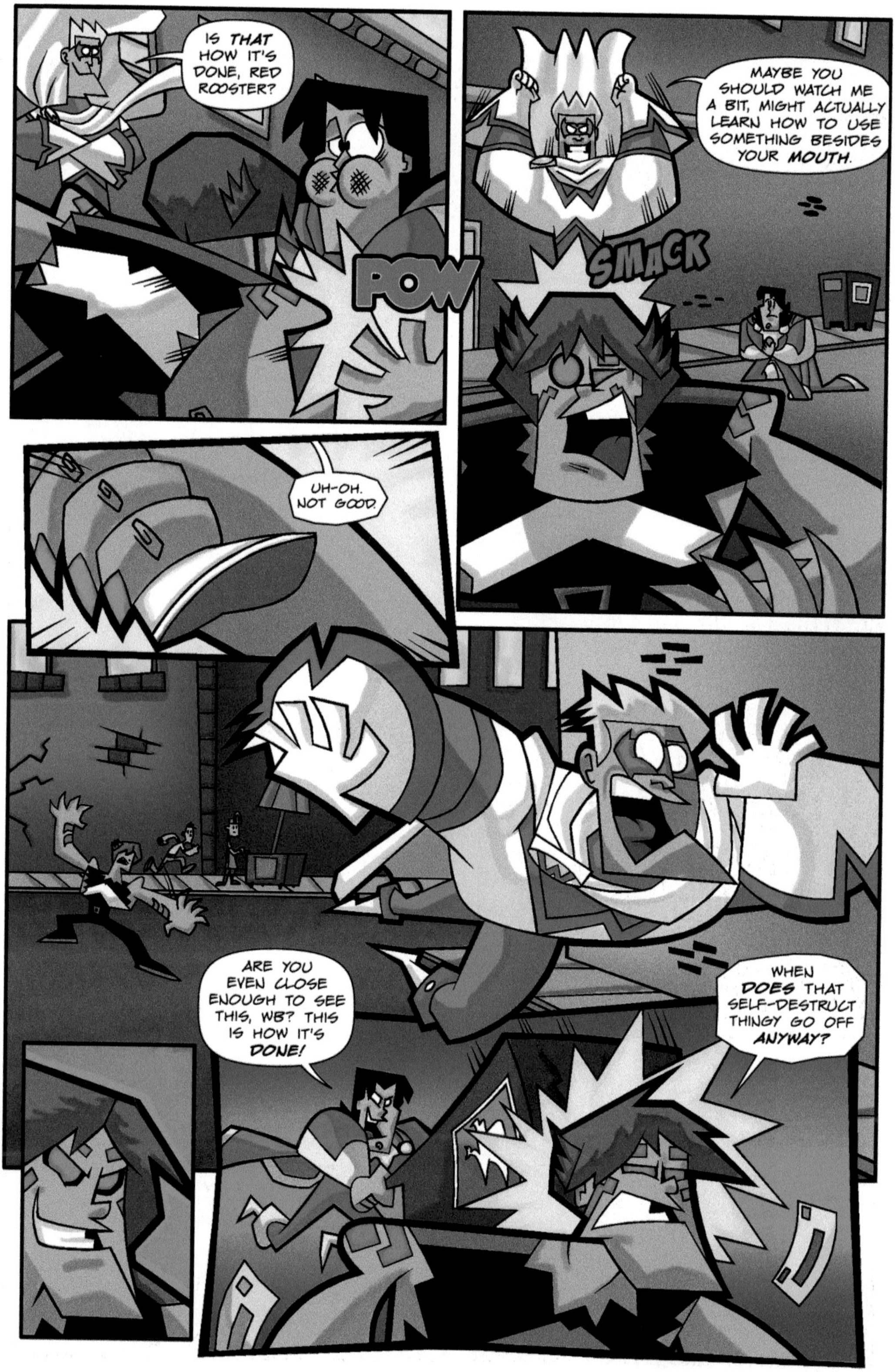
IS THAT HOW IT'S DONE, RED ROOSTER?
POW
MAYBE YOU SHOULD WATCH ME A BIT, MIGHT ACTUALLY LEARN HOW TO USE SOMETHING BESIDES YOUR MOUTH.
SMACK
UH-OH. NOT GOOD.
ARE YOU EVEN CLOSE ENOUGH TO SEE THIS, WB? THIS IS HOW IT'S DONE!
WHEN DOES THAT SELF-DESTRUCT THINGY GO OFF ANYWAY?

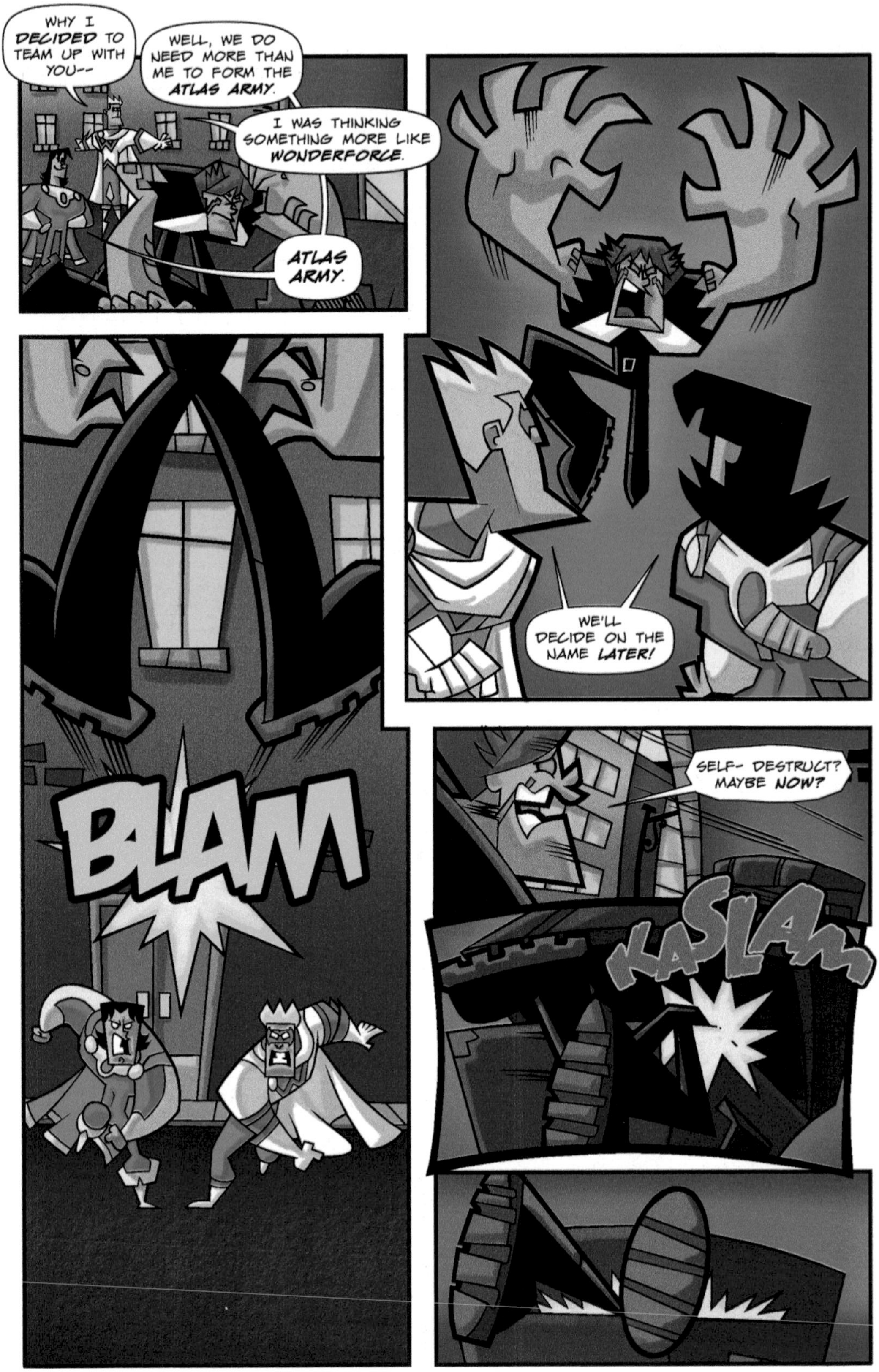
WHY I DECIDED TO TEAM UP WITH YOU--
WELL, WE DO NEED MORE THAN ME TO FORM THE ATLAS ARMY.
I WAS THINKING SOMETHING MORE LIKE WONDERFORCE.
ATLAS ARMY.
WE'LL DECIDE ON THE NAME LATER!
BLAM
SELF- DESTRUCT? MAYBE NOW?
KASLAM

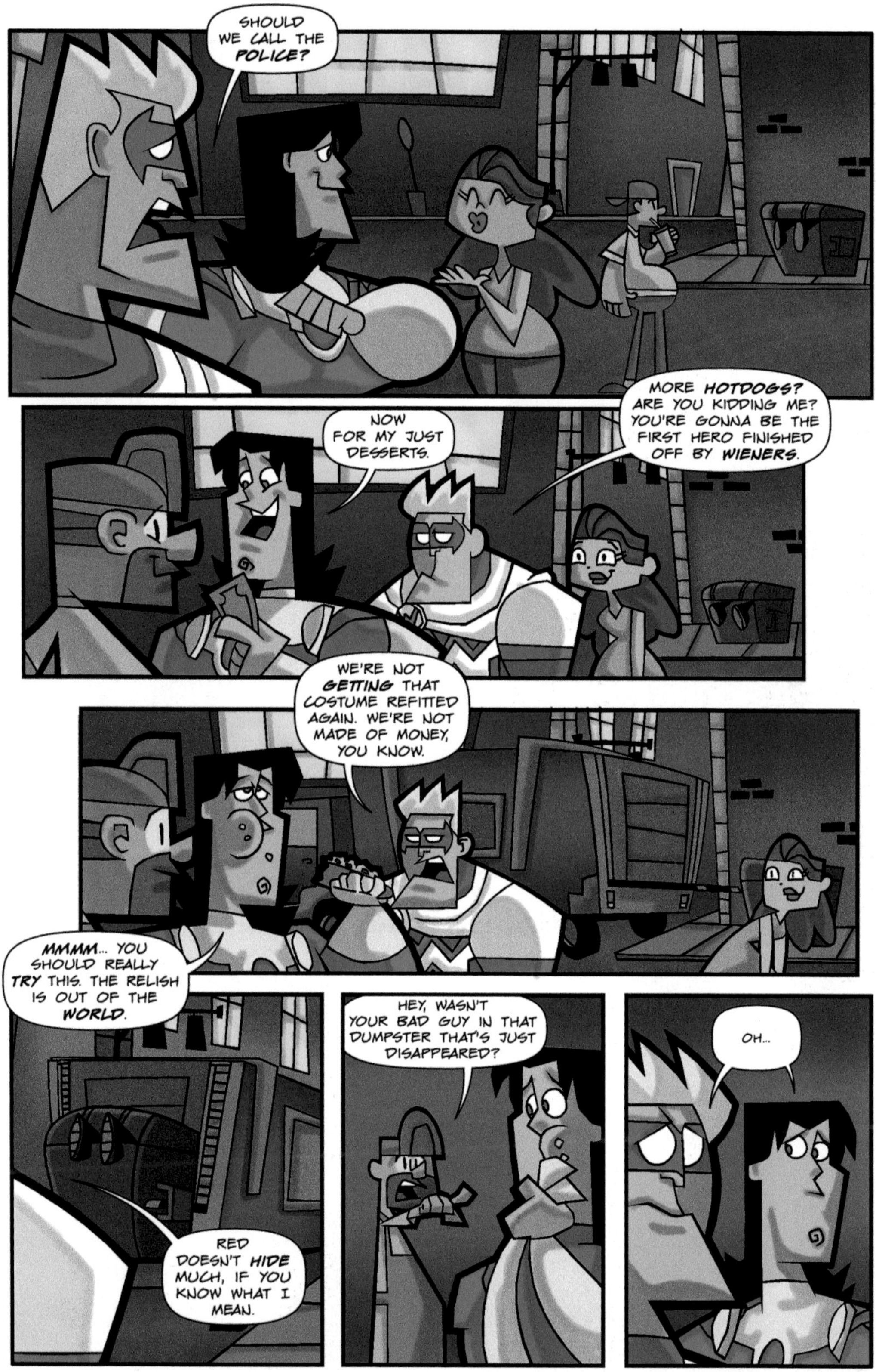
SHOULD WE CALL THE POLICE?
NOW FOR MY JUST DESSERTS.
MORE HOTDOGS? ARE YOU KIDDING ME? YOU'RE GONNA BE THE FIRST HERO FINISHED OFF BY WIENERS.
WE'RE NOT GETTING THAT COSTUME REFITTED AGAIN. WE'RE NOT MADE OF MONEY, YOU KNOW.
MMMM... YOU SHOULD REALLY TRY THIS. THE RELISH IS OUT OF THE WORLD.
RED DOESN'T HIDE MUCH, IF YOU KNOW WHAT I MEAN.
HEY, WASN'T YOUR BAD GUY IN THAT DUMPSTER THAT'S JUST DISAPPEARED?
OH...

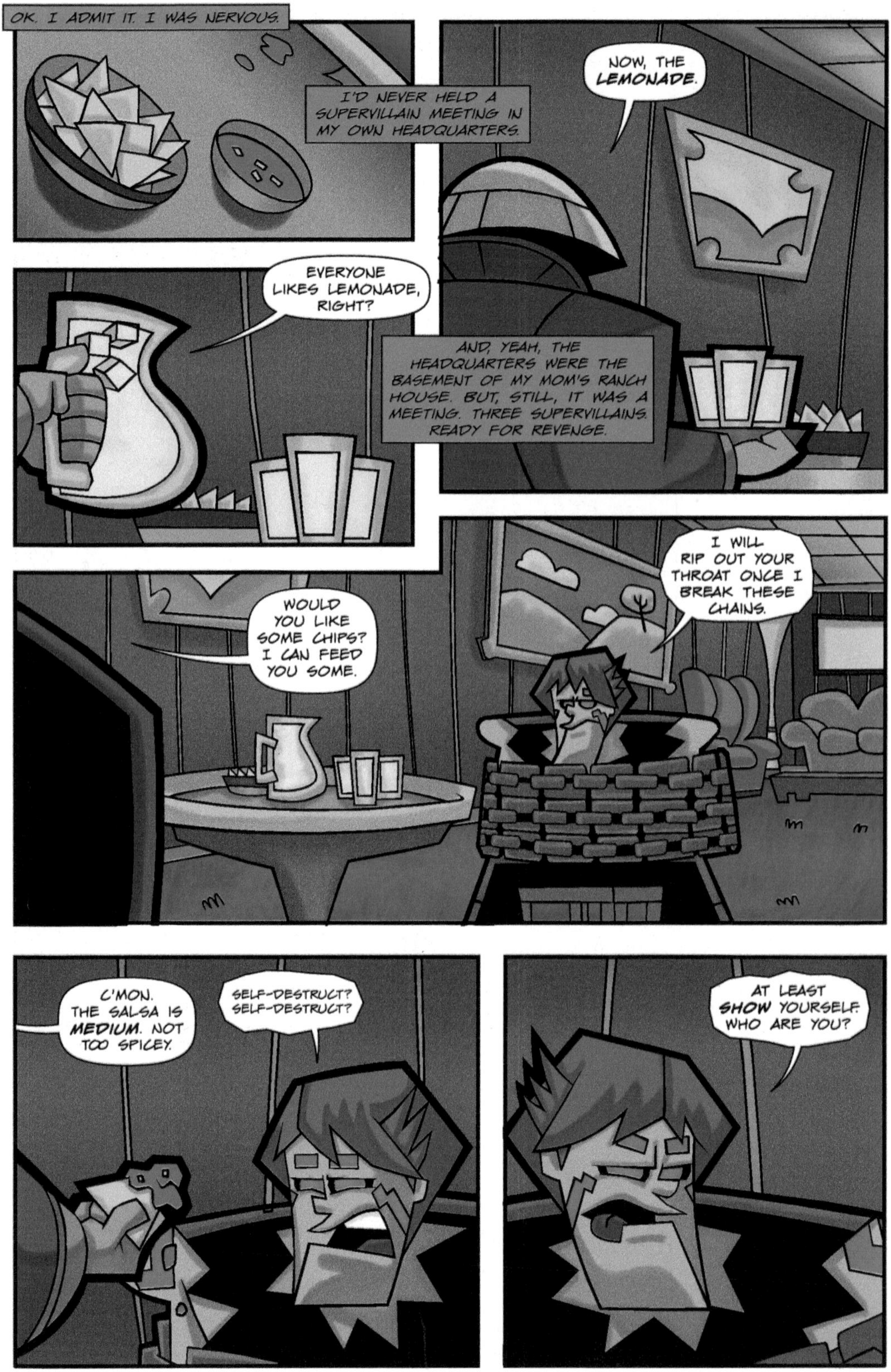
OK. I ADMIT IT. I WAS NERVOUS.
I'D NEVER HELD A SUPERVILLAIN MEETING IN MY OWN HEADQUARTERS.
NOW, THE LEMONADE.
AND, YEAH, THE HEADQUARTERS WERE THE BASEMENT OF MY MOM'S RANCH HOUSE. BUT, STILL, IT WAS A MEETING. THREE SUPERVILLAINS. READY FOR REVENGE.
EVERYONE LIKES LEMONADE, RIGHT?
WOULD YOU LIKE SOME CHIPS? I CAN FEED YOU SOME.
I WILL RIP OUT YOUR THROAT ONCE I BREAK THESE CHAINS.
C'MON. THE SALSA IS MEDIUM. NOT TOO SPICEY.
SELF-DESTRUCT? SELF-DESTRUCT?
AT LEAST SHOW YOURSELF. WHO ARE YOU?

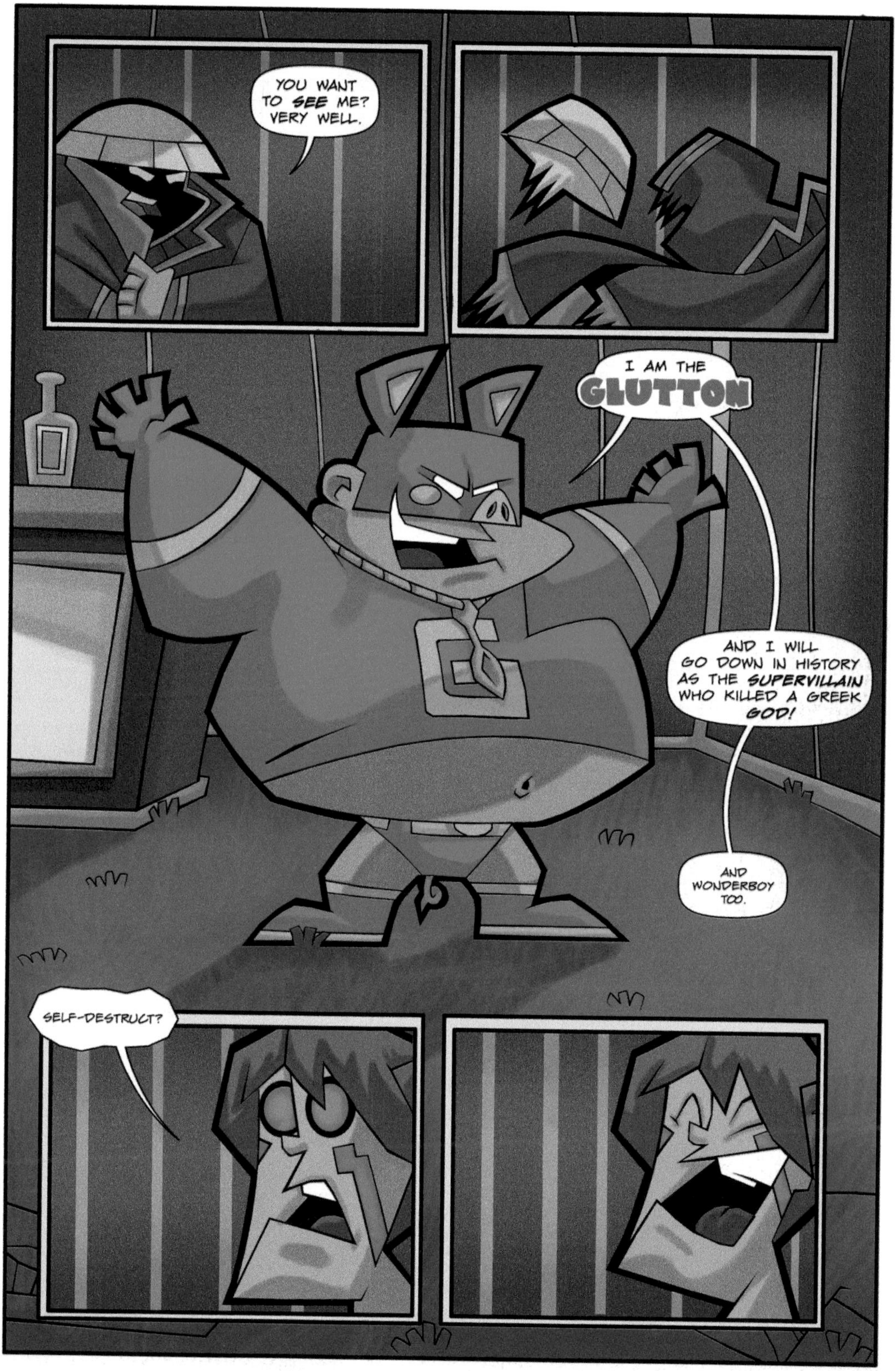
YOU WANT TO SEE ME? VERY WELL.
I AM THE GLUTTON
AND I WILL GO DOWN IN HISTORY AS THE SUPERVILLAIN WHO KILLED A GREEK GOD!
AND WONDERBOY TOO.
SELF-DESTRUCT?

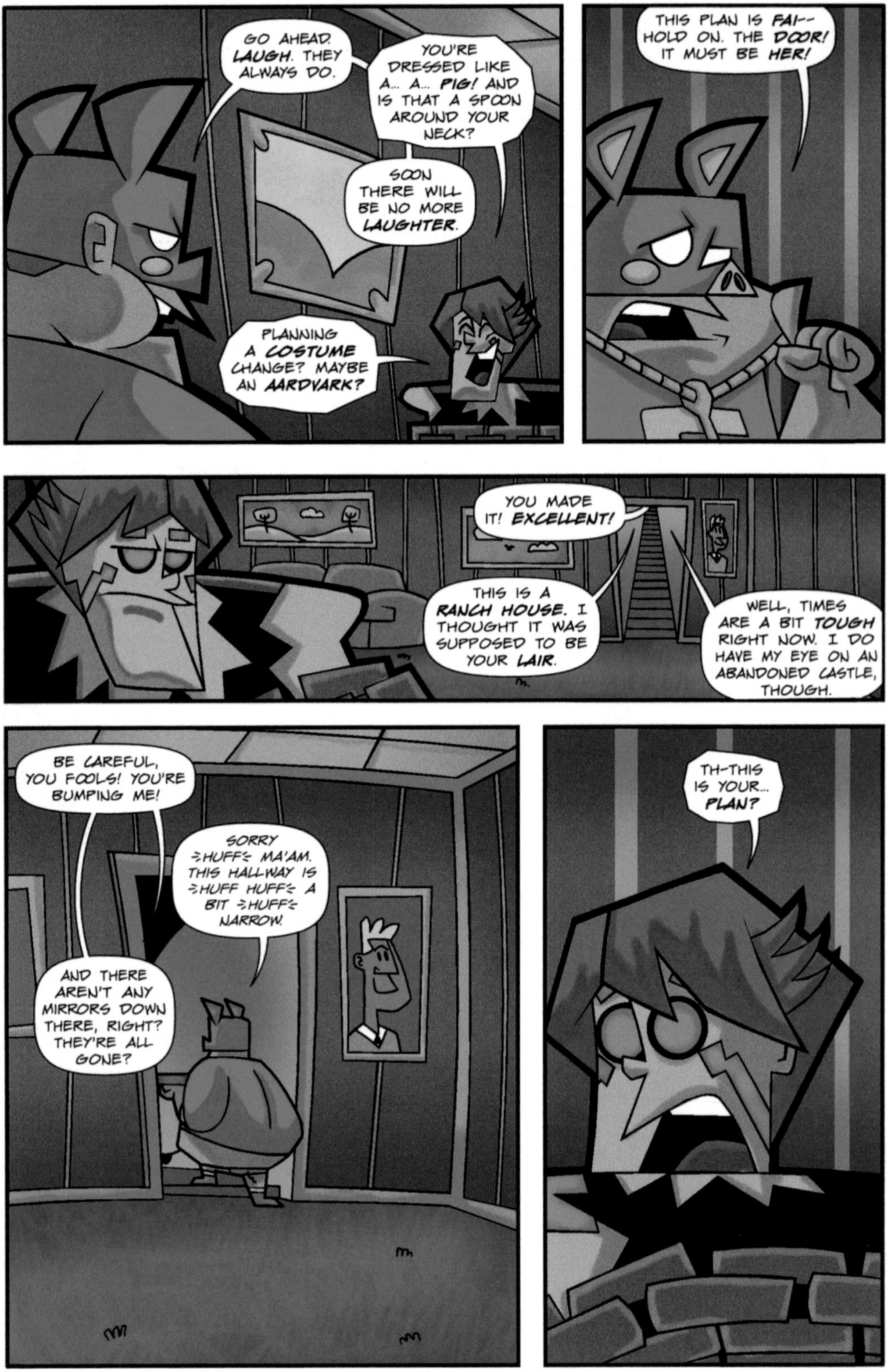
GO AHEAD. LAUGH. THEY ALWAYS DO.
YOU'RE DRESSED LIKE A... A... PIG! AND IS THAT A SPOON AROUND YOUR NECK?
SOON THERE WILL BE NO MORE LAUGHTER.
PLANNING A COSTUME CHANGE? MAYBE AN AARDVARK?
THIS PLAN IS FAI-- HOLD ON. THE DOOR! IT MUST BE HER!
YOU MADE IT! EXCELLENT!
THIS IS A RANCH HOUSE. I THOUGHT IT WAS SUPPOSED TO BE YOUR LAIR.
WELL, TIMES ARE A BIT TOUGH RIGHT NOW. I DO HAVE MY EYE ON AN ABANDONED CASTLE, THOUGH.
BE CAREFUL, YOU FOOLS! YOU'RE BUMPING ME!
SORRY =HUFF= MA'AM. THIS HALLWAY IS =HUFF HUFF= A BIT =HUFF= NARROW.
AND THERE AREN'T ANY MIRRORS DOWN THERE, RIGHT? THEY'RE ALL GONE?
TH-THIS IS YOUR... PLAN?

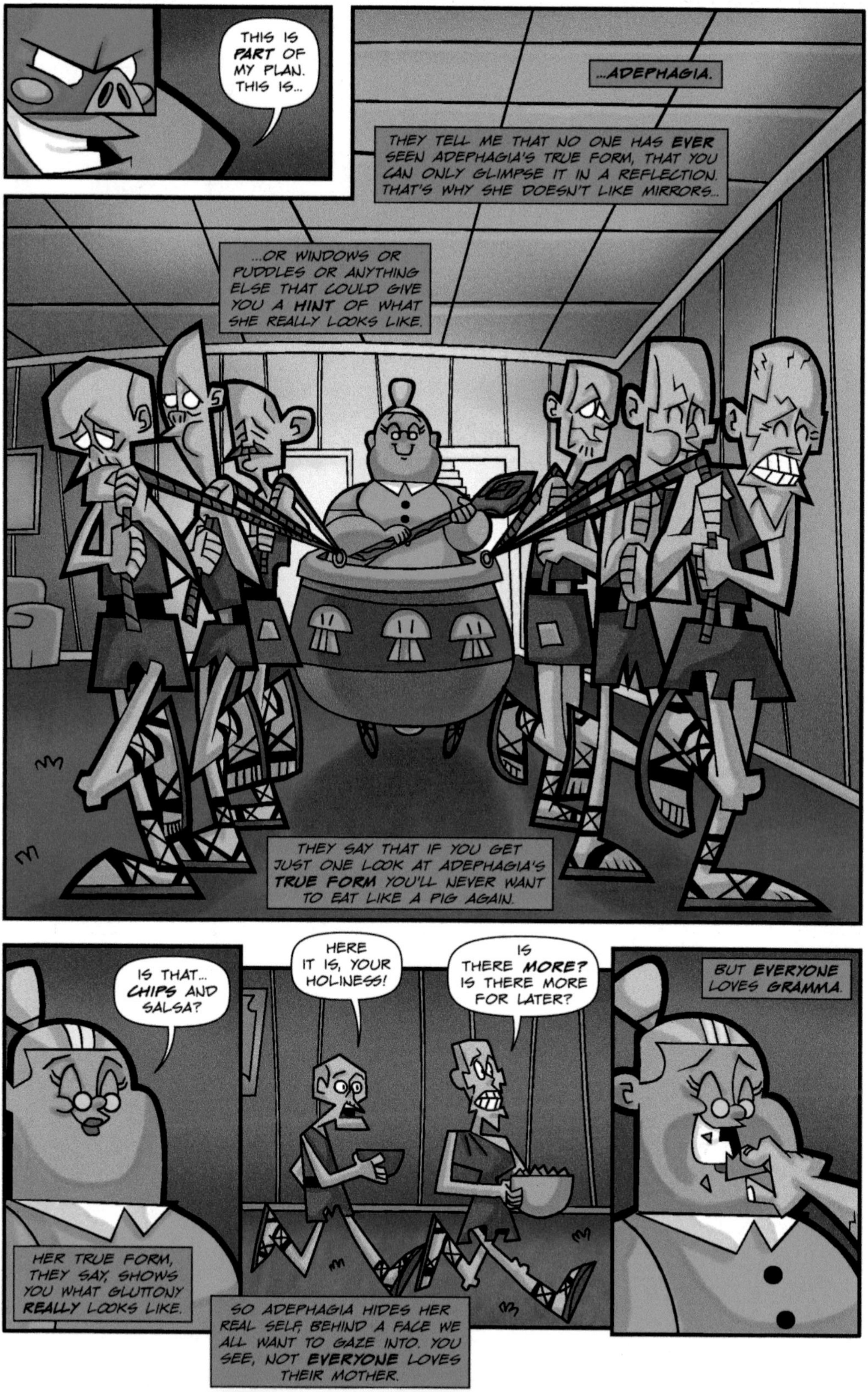

THIS IS PART OF MY PLAN. THIS IS...
...ADEPHAGIA.
THEY TELL ME THAT NO ONE HAS EVER SEEN ADEPHAGIA'S TRUE FORM, THAT YOU CAN ONLY GLIMPSE IT IN A REFLECTION. THAT'S WHY SHE DOESN'T LIKE MIRRORS...
...OR WINDOWS OR PUDDLES OR ANYTHING ELSE THAT COULD GIVE YOU A HINT OF WHAT SHE REALLY LOOKS LIKE.
THEY SAY THAT IF YOU GET JUST ONE LOOK AT ADEPHAGIA'S TRUE FORM YOU'LL NEVER WANT TO EAT LIKE A PIG AGAIN.
IS THAT... CHIPS AND SALSA?
HER TRUE FORM, THEY SAY, SHOWS YOU WHAT GLUTTONY REALLY LOOKS LIKE.
HERE IT IS, YOUR HOLINESS!
IS THERE MORE? IS THERE MORE FOR LATER?
SO ADEPHAGIA HIDES HER REAL SELF, BEHIND A FACE WE ALL WANT TO GAZE INTO. YOU SEE, NOT EVERYONE LOVES THEIR MOTHER.
BUT EVERYONE LOVES GRAMMA.

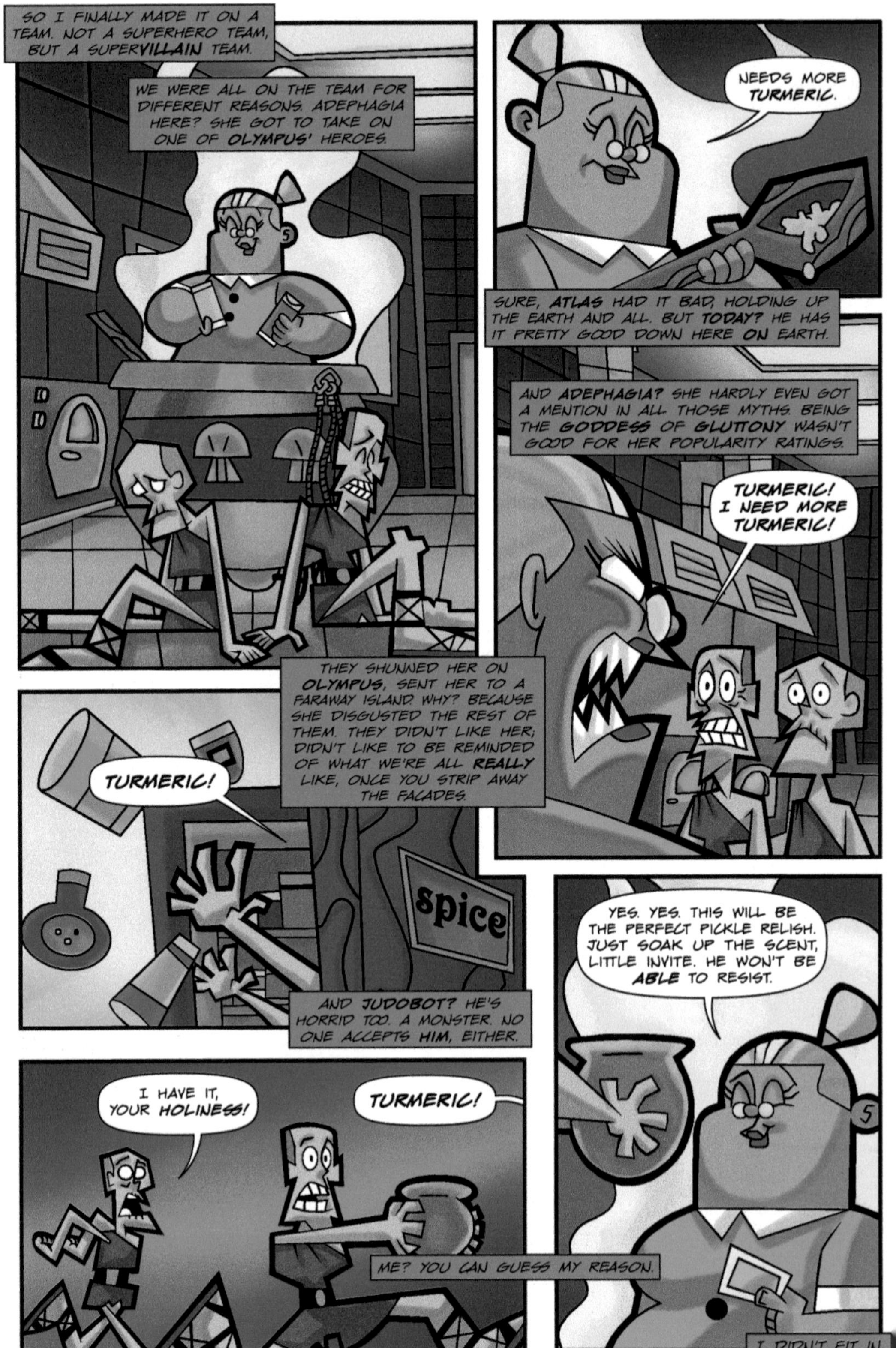
SO I FINALLY MADE IT ON A TEAM. NOT A SUPERHERO TEAM, BUT A SUPERVILLAIN TEAM.
WE WERE ALL ON THE TEAM FOR DIFFERENT REASONS. ADEPHAGIA HERE? SHE GOT TO TAKE ON ONE OF OLYMPUS' HEROES.
NEEDS MORE TURMERIC.
SURE, ATLAS HAD IT BAD, HOLDING UP THE EARTH AND ALL. BUT TODAY? HE HAS IT PRETTY GOOD DOWN HERE ON EARTH.
AND ADEPHAGIA? SHE HARDLY EVEN GOT A MENTION IN ALL THOSE MYTHS. BEING THE GODDESS OF GLUTTONY WASN'T GOOD FOR HER POPULARITY RATINGS.
TURMERIC! I NEED MORE TURMERIC!
THEY SHUNNED HER ON OLYMPUS, SENT HER TO A FARAWAY ISLAND. WHY? BECAUSE SHE DISGUSTED THE REST OF THEM. THEY DIDN'T LIKE HER; DIDN'T LIKE TO BE REMINDED OF WHAT WE'RE ALL REALLY LIKE, ONCE YOU STRIP AWAY THE FACADES.
TURMERIC!
spice
AND JUDOBOT? HE'S HORRID TOO. A MONSTER. NO ONE ACCEPTS HIM, EITHER.
I HAVE IT, YOUR HOLINESS!
TURMERIC!
ME? YOU CAN GUESS MY REASON.
YES. YES. THIS WILL BE THE PERFECT PICKLE RELISH. JUST SOAK UP THE SCENT, LITTLE INVITE. HE WON'T BE ABLE TO RESIST.
I DIDN'T FIT IN, EITHER. NEVER.

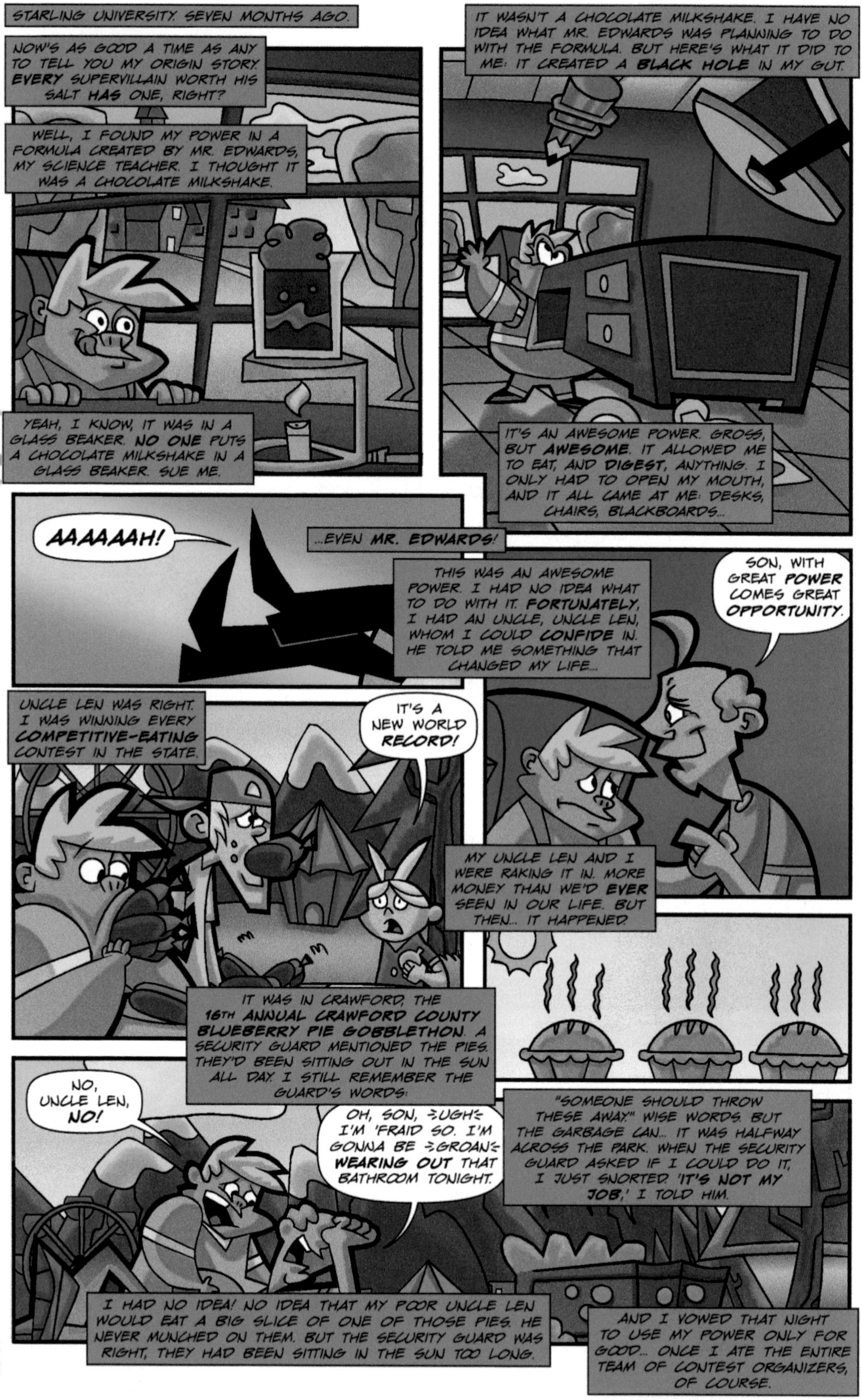
STARLING UNIVERSITY. SEVEN MONTHS AGO.
NOW'S AS GOOD A TIME AS ANY TO TELL YOU MY ORIGIN STORY. EVERY SUPERVILLAIN WORTH HIS SALT HAS ONE, RIGHT?
WELL, I FOUND MY POWER IN A FORMULA CREATED BY MR. EDWARDS, MY SCIENCE TEACHER. I THOUGHT IT WAS A CHOCOLATE MILKSHAKE.
YEAH, I KNOW, IT WAS IN A GLASS BEAKER. NO ONE PUTS A CHOCOLATE MILKSHAKE IN A GLASS BEAKER. SUE ME.
IT WASN'T A CHOCOLATE MILKSHAKE. I HAVE NO IDEA WHAT MR. EDWARDS WAS PLANNING TO DO WITH THE FORMULA. BUT HERE'S WHAT IT DID TO ME: IT CREATED A BLACK HOLE IN MY GUT.
IT'S AN AWESOME POWER. GROSS, BUT AWESOME. IT ALLOWED ME TO EAT, AND DIGEST, ANYTHING. I ONLY HAD TO OPEN MY MOUTH, AND IT ALL CAME AT ME: DESKS, CHAIRS, BLACKBOARDS...
AAAAAAH!
...EVEN MR. EDWARDS!
THIS WAS AN AWESOME POWER. I HAD NO IDEA WHAT TO DO WITH IT. FORTUNATELY, I HAD AN UNCLE, UNCLE LEN, WHOM I COULD CONFIDE IN. HE TOLD ME SOMETHING THAT CHANGED MY LIFE...
SON, WITH GREAT POWER COMES GREAT OPPORTUNITY.
UNCLE LEN WAS RIGHT. I WAS WINNING EVERY COMPETITIVE-EATING CONTEST IN THE STATE.
IT'S A NEW WORLD RECORD!
MY UNCLE LEN AND I WERE RAKING IT IN. MORE MONEY THAN WE'D EVER SEEN IN OUR LIFE. BUT THEN... IT HAPPENED.
IT WAS IN CRAWFORD, THE 16TH ANNUAL CRAWFORD COUNTY BLUEBERRY PIE GOBBLETHON. A SECURITY GUARD MENTIONED THE PIES. THEY'D BEEN SITTING OUT IN THE SUN ALL DAY. I STILL REMEMBER THE GUARD'S WORDS:
"SOMEONE SHOULD THROW THESE AWAY." WISE WORDS. BUT THE GARBAGE CAN... IT WAS HALFWAY ACROSS THE PARK. WHEN THE SECURITY GUARD ASKED IF I COULD DO IT, I JUST SNORTED. 'IT'S NOT MY JOB,' I TOLD HIM.
NO, UNCLE LEN, NO!
OH, SON, =UGH= I'M 'FRAID SO. I'M GONNA BE =GROAN= WEARING OUT THAT BATHROOM TONIGHT.
I HAD NO IDEA! NO IDEA THAT MY POOR UNCLE LEN WOULD EAT A BIG SLICE OF ONE OF THOSE PIES. HE NEVER MUNCHED ON THEM. BUT THE SECURITY GUARD WAS RIGHT, THEY HAD BEEN SITTING IN THE SUN TOO LONG.
AND I VOWED THAT NIGHT TO USE MY POWER ONLY FOR GOOD... ONCE I ATE THE ENTIRE TEAM OF CONTEST ORGANIZERS, OF COURSE.

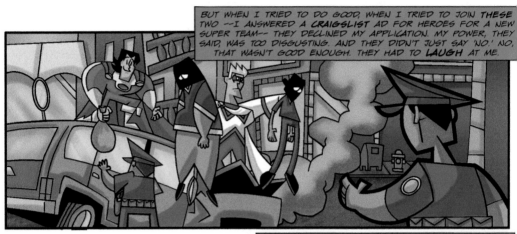

BUT WHEN I TRIED TO DO GOOD, WHEN I TRIED TO JOIN THESE TWO --I ANSWERED A CRAIGSLIST AD FOR HEROES FOR A NEW SUPER TEAM-- THEY DECLINED MY APPLICATION. MY POWER, THEY SAID, WAS TOO DISGUSTING. AND THEY DIDN'T JUST SAY 'NO.' NO, THAT WASN'T GOOD ENOUGH. THEY HAD TO LAUGH AT ME.

I'M TELLING YOU, WB, THEY'RE GONNA BE LINING UP TO JOIN US NOW.

NO MORE ADS FOR US. ANOTHER CATCH. WE'RE GONNA BE BIG TIME SOON.

THEY'VE BEEN LAUGHING AT ME ALL MY LIFE. YOU GET POWERS AND YOU THINK THE LAUGHTER'S GOING TO STOP? WELL, THAT DEPENDS ON WHAT POWERS YOU GET. STICK TO WALLS, PUNCH THROUGH TANKS, HECK, EVEN BREATH UNDERWATER AND YOU'RE A STAR.

JUST TWO COMMON CROOKS. WE NEED TO NAB A SUPERVILLAIN...

...AND NOT LET HIM DISAPPEAR ONCE WE'VE CAUGHT HIM.

MAYBE WE'LL GET SOMEONE LIKE MEGAWATT TO JOIN UP. I HEARD A RUMOR THAT HE'S TIRED OF FLYING SOLO.

HE GAVE ME A PHONE NUMBER! AN ACTUAL NUMBER!

THINK OF THE MONEY WE'D SAVE ON LIGHTBULBS.

EAT ANYTHING YOU WANT? YOU'RE STILL A LAUGHINGSTOCK.

WHAT'S THAT?

THIS CARD... THIS INVITATION... IT SMELLS... WELL, IT SMELLS DELICIOUS, LIKE, LIKE... DODGER'S STADIUM!

FREE ALL YOU CAN EAT!
CHICAGO HOT DOG BUFFET!
ONE NIGHT ONLY, TONIGHT!
DODIE'S BUFFET!
MUST HAVE TICKET TO EAT. TRY OUR CHICAGO HOT DOG! IT'S LOADED!

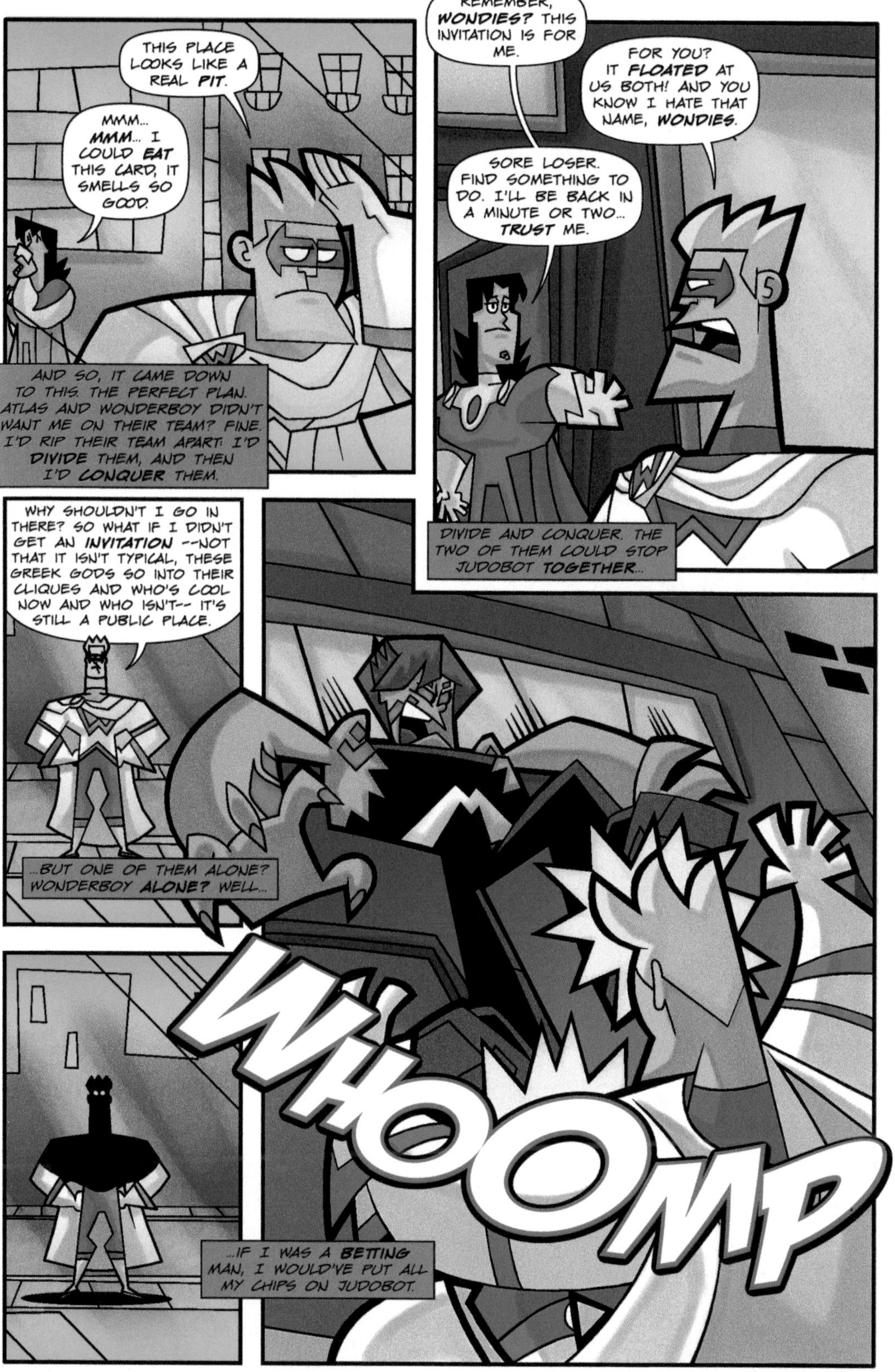
THIS PLACE LOOKS LIKE A REAL PIT.
MMM... MMM... I COULD EAT THIS CARD, IT SMELLS SO GOOD.
AND SO, IT CAME DOWN TO THIS. THE PERFECT PLAN. ATLAS AND WONDERBOY DIDN'T WANT ME ON THEIR TEAM? FINE. I'D RIP THEIR TEAM APART: I'D DIVIDE THEM, AND THEN I'D CONQUER THEM.
REMEMBER, WONDIES? THIS INVITATION IS FOR ME.
FOR YOU? IT FLOATED AT US BOTH! AND YOU KNOW I HATE THAT NAME, WONDIES.
SORE LOSER. FIND SOMETHING TO DO. I'LL BE BACK IN A MINUTE OR TWO... TRUST ME.
DIVIDE AND CONQUER. THE TWO OF THEM COULD STOP JUDOBOT TOGETHER...
WHY SHOULDN'T I GO IN THERE? SO WHAT IF I DIDN'T GET AN INVITATION --NOT THAT IT ISN'T TYPICAL, THESE GREEK GODS SO INTO THEIR CLIQUES AND WHO'S COOL NOW AND WHO ISN'T-- IT'S STILL A PUBLIC PLACE.
...BUT ONE OF THEM ALONE? WONDERBOY ALONE? WELL...
WHOOMP
...IF I WAS A BETTING MAN, I WOULD'VE PUT ALL MY CHIPS ON JUDOBOT.

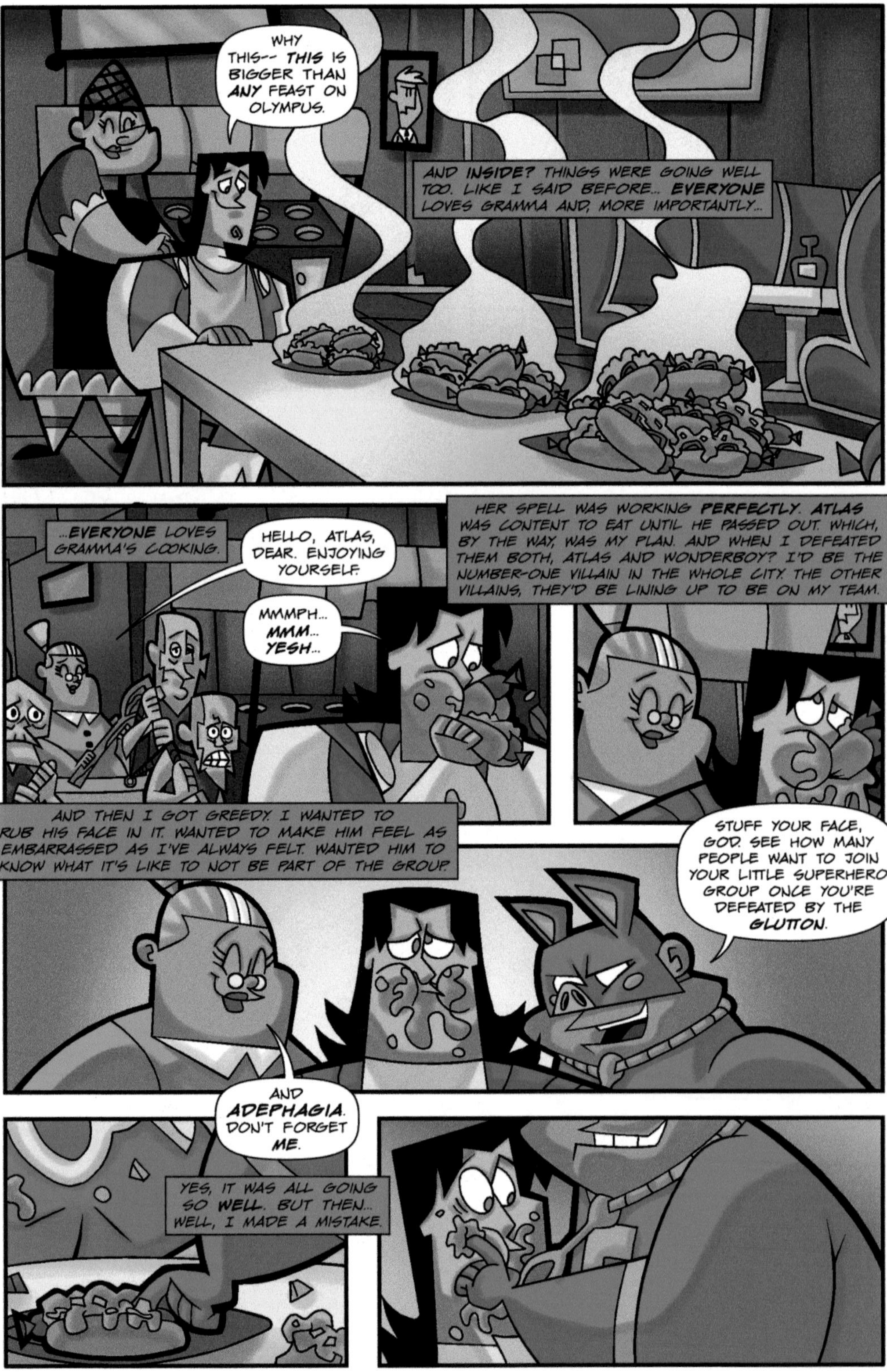

WHY THIS-- THIS IS BIGGER THAN ANY FEAST ON OLYMPUS.
AND INSIDE? THINGS WERE GOING WELL TOO. LIKE I SAID BEFORE... EVERYONE LOVES GRAMMA AND, MORE IMPORTANTLY...
...EVERYONE LOVES GRAMMA'S COOKING.
HELLO, ATLAS, DEAR. ENJOYING YOURSELF.
MMMPH... MMM... YESH...
HER SPELL WAS WORKING PERFECTLY. ATLAS WAS CONTENT TO EAT UNTIL HE PASSED OUT. WHICH, BY THE WAY, WAS MY PLAN. AND WHEN I DEFEATED THEM BOTH, ATLAS AND WONDERBOY? I'D BE THE NUMBER-ONE VILLAIN IN THE WHOLE CITY. THE OTHER VILLAINS, THEY'D BE LINING UP TO BE ON MY TEAM.
AND THEN I GOT GREEDY. I WANTED TO RUB HIS FACE IN IT. WANTED TO MAKE HIM FEEL AS EMBARRASSED AS I'VE ALWAYS FELT. WANTED HIM TO KNOW WHAT IT'S LIKE TO NOT BE PART OF THE GROUP.
STUFF YOUR FACE, GOD. SEE HOW MANY PEOPLE WANT TO JOIN YOUR LITTLE SUPERHERO GROUP ONCE YOU'RE DEFEATED BY THE GLUTTON.
AND ADEPHAGIA. DON'T FORGET ME.
YES, IT WAS ALL GOING SO WELL. BUT THEN... WELL, I MADE A MISTAKE.

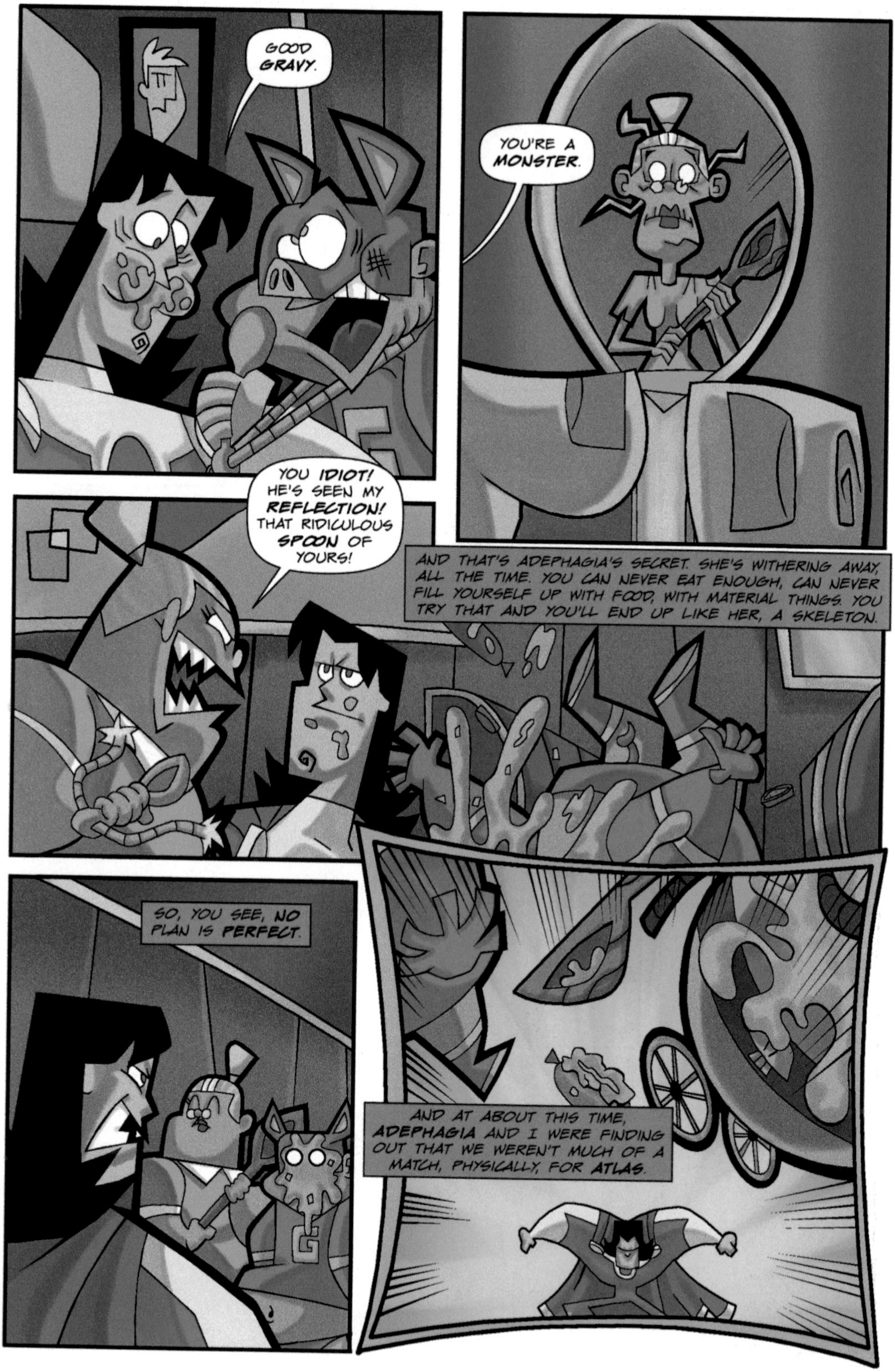
GOOD GRAVY.
YOU'RE A MONSTER.
YOU IDIOT! HE'S SEEN MY REFLECTION! THAT RIDICULOUS SPOON OF YOURS!
AND THAT'S ADEPHAGIA'S SECRET. SHE'S WITHERING AWAY, ALL THE TIME. YOU CAN NEVER EAT ENOUGH, CAN NEVER FILL YOURSELF UP WITH FOOD, WITH MATERIAL THINGS. YOU TRY THAT AND YOU'LL END UP LIKE HER, A SKELETON.
SO, YOU SEE, NO PLAN IS PERFECT.
AND AT ABOUT THIS TIME, ADEPHAGIA AND I WERE FINDING OUT THAT WE WEREN'T MUCH OF A MATCH, PHYSICALLY, FOR ATLAS.

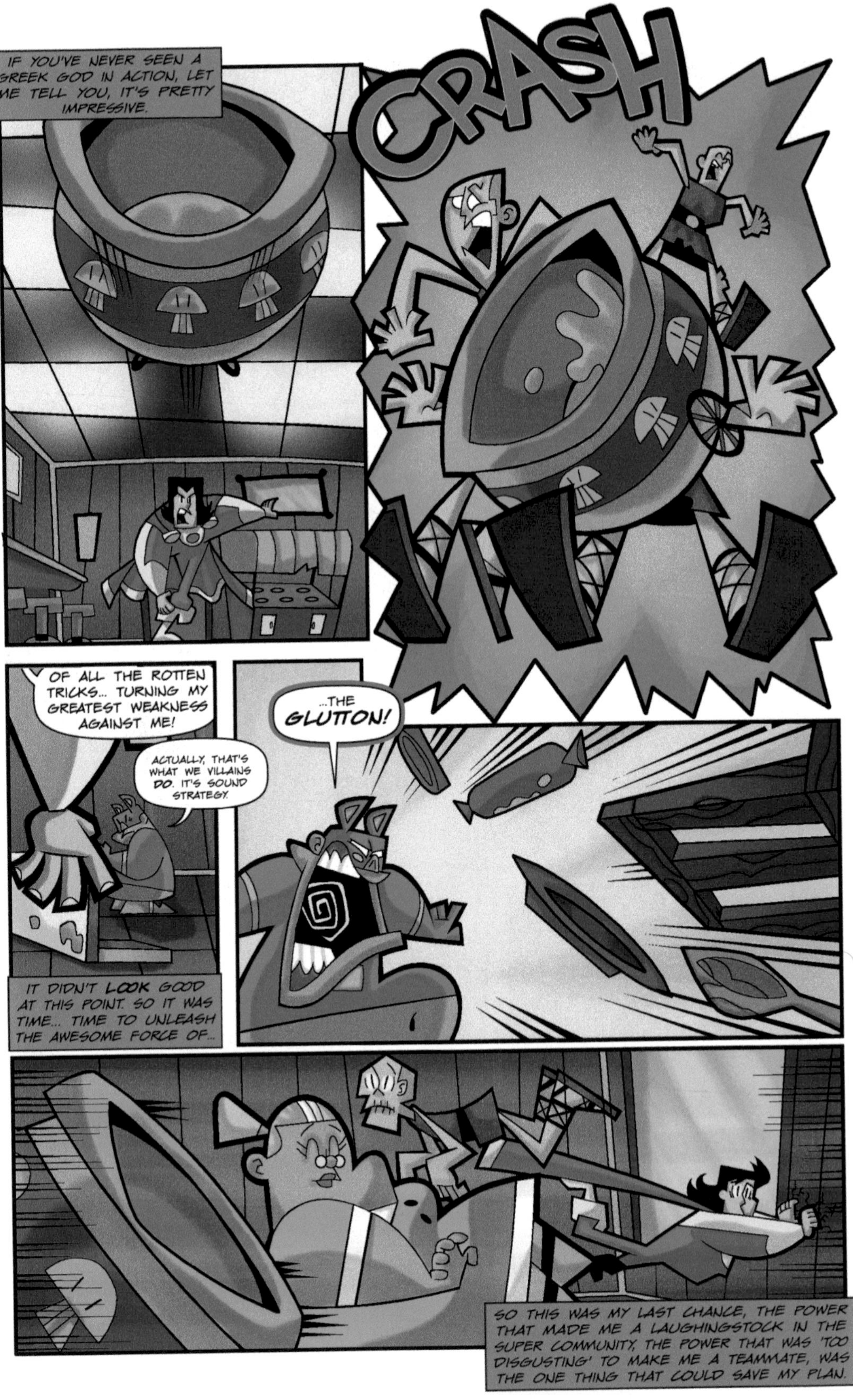

IF YOU'VE NEVER SEEN A GREEK GOD IN ACTION, LET ME TELL YOU, IT'S PRETTY IMPRESSIVE.
CRASH
OF ALL THE ROTTEN TRICKS... TURNING MY GREATEST WEAKNESS AGAINST ME!
ACTUALLY, THAT'S WHAT WE VILLAINS DO. IT'S SOUND STRATEGY.
IT DIDN'T LOOK GOOD AT THIS POINT. SO IT WAS TIME... TIME TO UNLEASH THE AWESOME FORCE OF...
...THE GLUTTON!
SO THIS WAS MY LAST CHANCE, THE POWER THAT MADE ME A LAUGHINGSTOCK IN THE SUPER COMMUNITY, THE POWER THAT WAS 'TOO DISGUSTING' TO MAKE ME A TEAMMATE, WAS THE ONE THING THAT COULD SAVE MY PLAN.

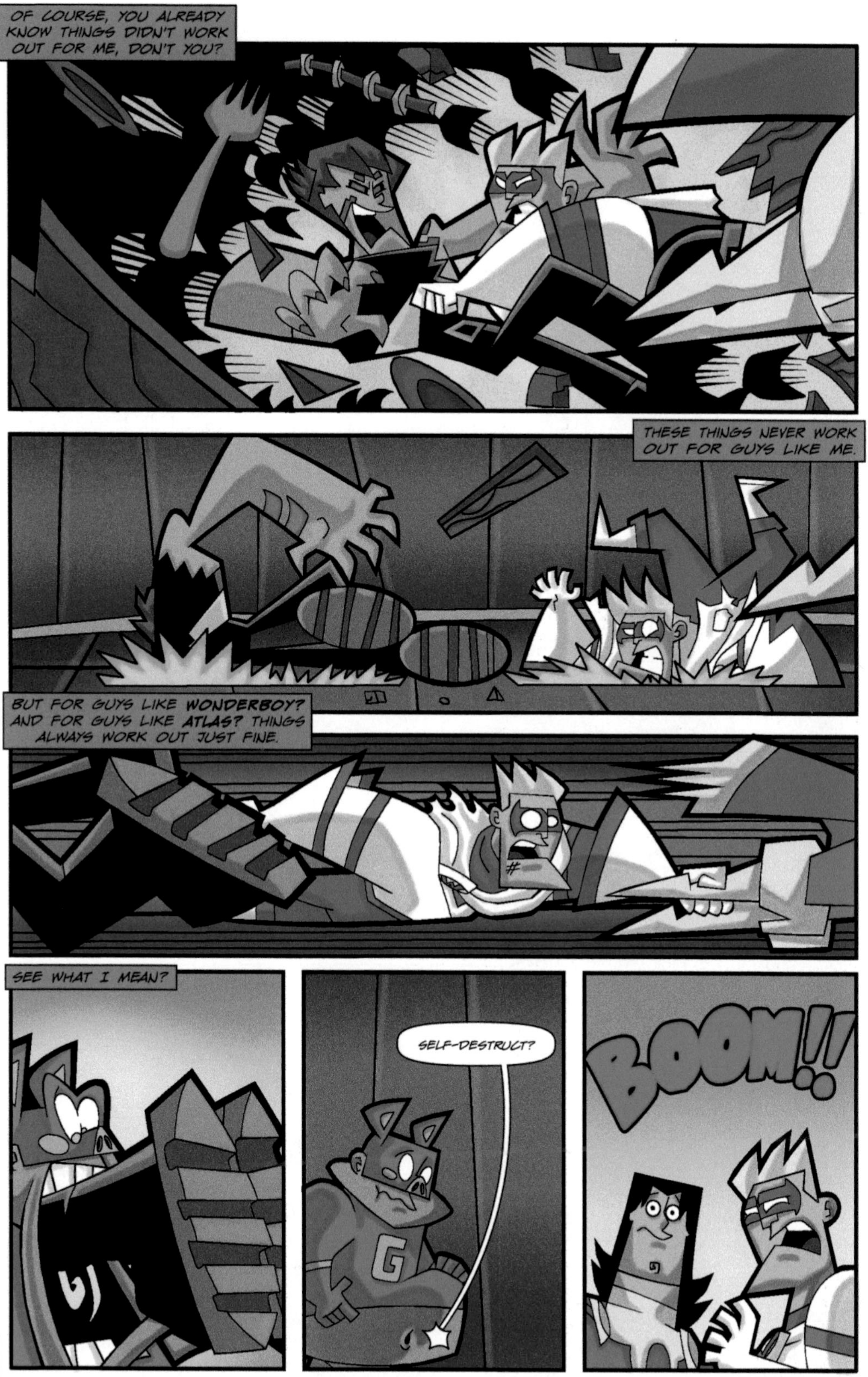
OF COURSE, YOU ALREADY KNOW THINGS DIDN'T WORK OUT FOR ME, DON'T YOU?
THESE THINGS NEVER WORK OUT FOR GUYS LIKE ME.
BUT FOR GUYS LIKE WONDERBOY? AND FOR GUYS LIKE ATLAS? THINGS ALWAYS WORK OUT JUST FINE.
SEE WHAT I MEAN?
SELF-DESTRUCT?
BOOM!!

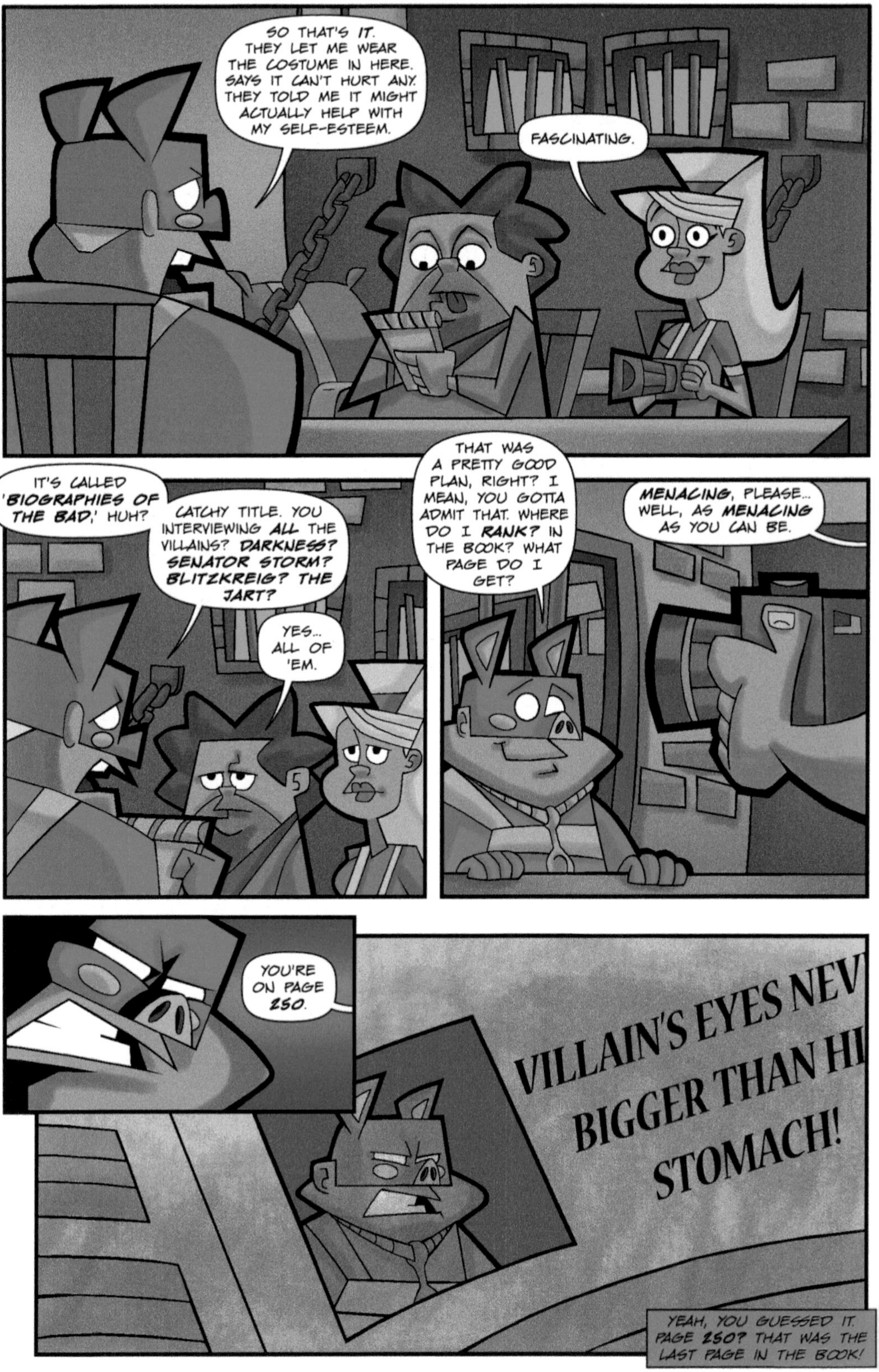
SO THAT'S IT. THEY LET ME WEAR THE COSTUME IN HERE. SAYS IT CAN'T HURT ANY. THEY TOLD ME IT MIGHT ACTUALLY HELP WITH MY SELF-ESTEEM.
FASCINATING.
IT'S CALLED 'BIOGRAPHIES OF THE BAD,' HUH?
CATCHY TITLE. YOU INTERVIEWING ALL THE VILLAINS? DARKNESS? SENATOR STORM? BLITZKREIG? THE JART?
YES... ALL OF 'EM.
THAT WAS A PRETTY GOOD PLAN, RIGHT? I MEAN, YOU GOTTA ADMIT THAT. WHERE DO I RANK? IN THE BOOK? WHAT PAGE DO I GET?
MENACING, PLEASE... WELL, AS MENACING AS YOU CAN BE.
YOU'RE ON PAGE 250.
VILLAIN'S EYES NEV
BIGGER THAN HI
STOMACH!
YEAH, YOU GUESSED IT. PAGE 250? THAT WAS THE LAST PAGE IN THE BOOK!

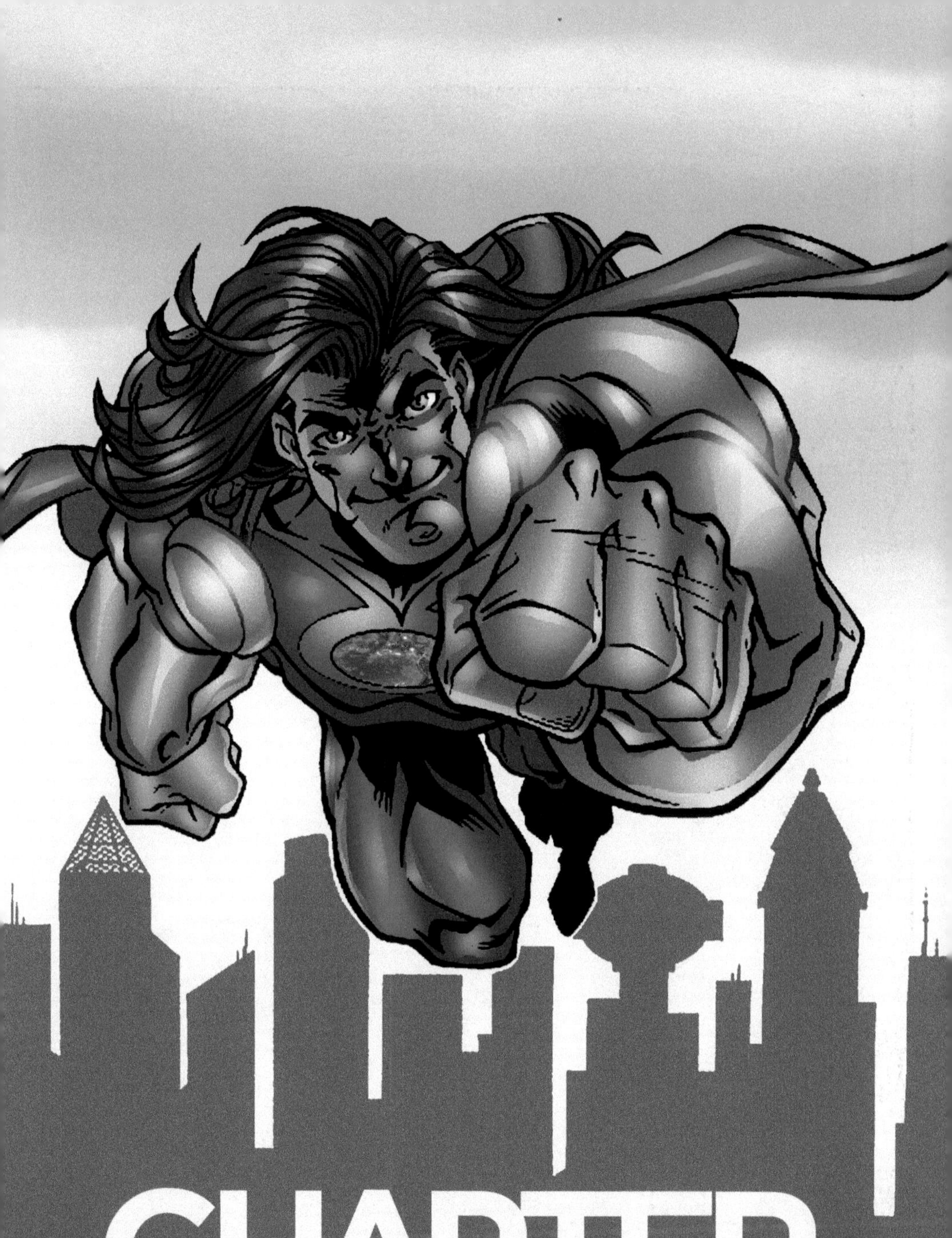

CHAPTER TWO

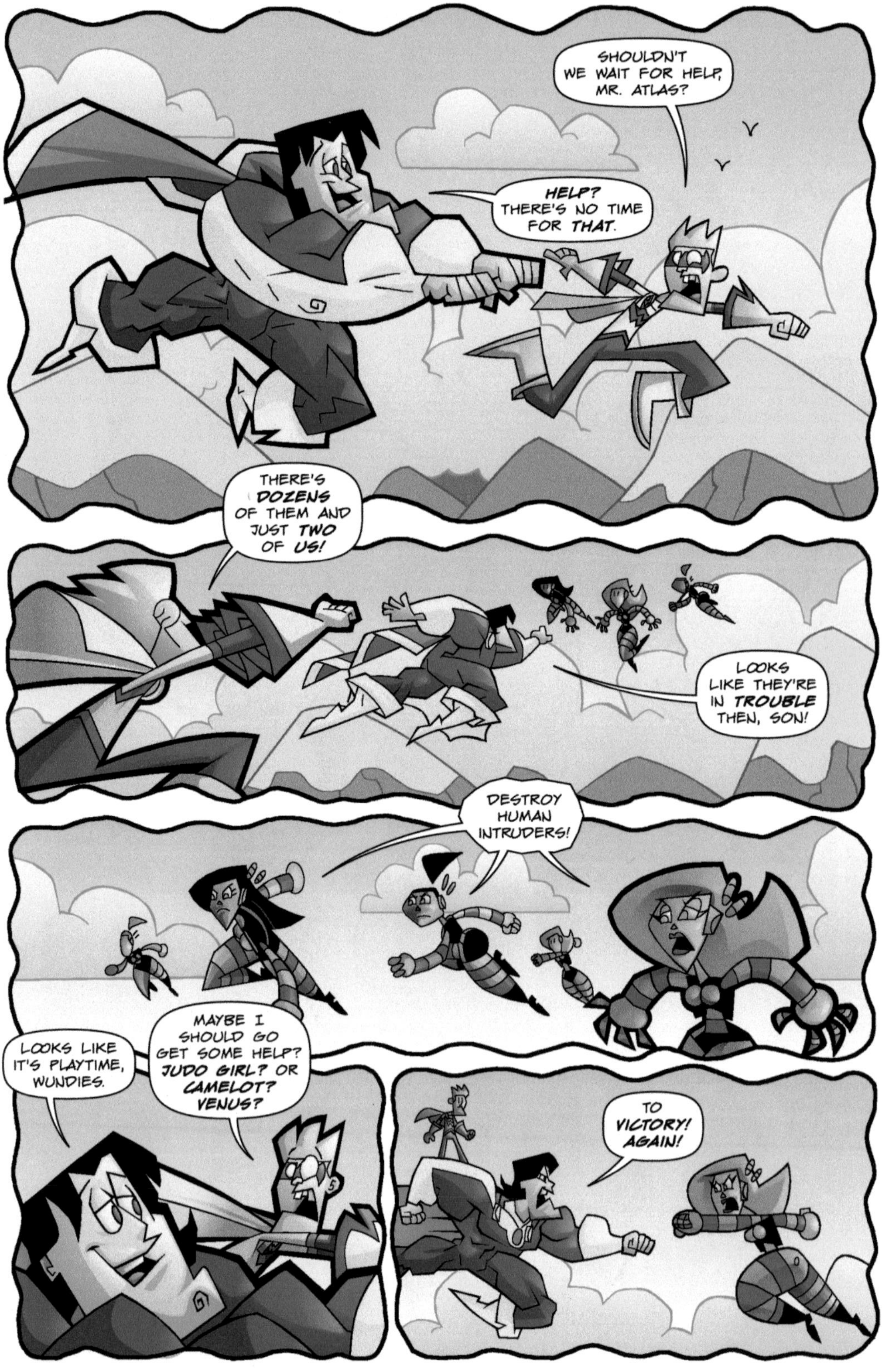
SHOULDN'T WE WAIT FOR HELP, MR. ATLAS?
HELP? THERE'S NO TIME FOR THAT.
THERE'S DOZENS OF THEM AND JUST TWO OF US!
LOOKS LIKE THEY'RE IN TROUBLE THEN, SON!
DESTROY HUMAN INTRUDERS!
LOOKS LIKE IT'S PLAYTIME, WUNDIES.
MAYBE I SHOULD GO GET SOME HELP? JUDO GIRL? OR CAMELOT? VENUS?
TO VICTORY! AGAIN!

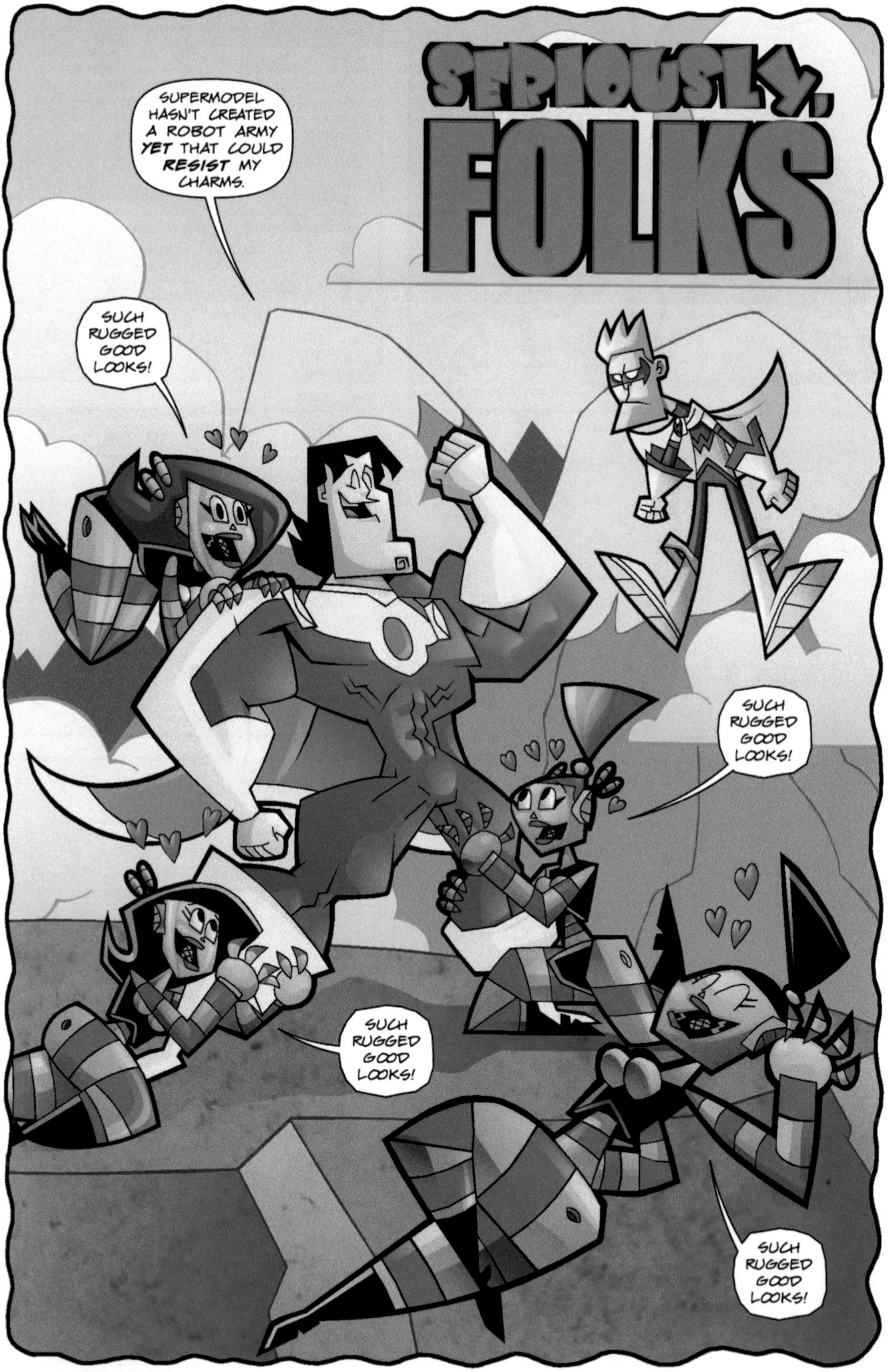
SERIOUSLY, FOLKS
SUPERMODEL HASN'T CREATED A ROBOT ARMY YET THAT COULD RESIST MY CHARMS.
SUCH RUGGED GOOD LOOKS!
SUCH RUGGED GOOD LOOKS!
SUCH RUGGED GOOD LOOKS!
SUCH RUGGED GOOD LOOKS!

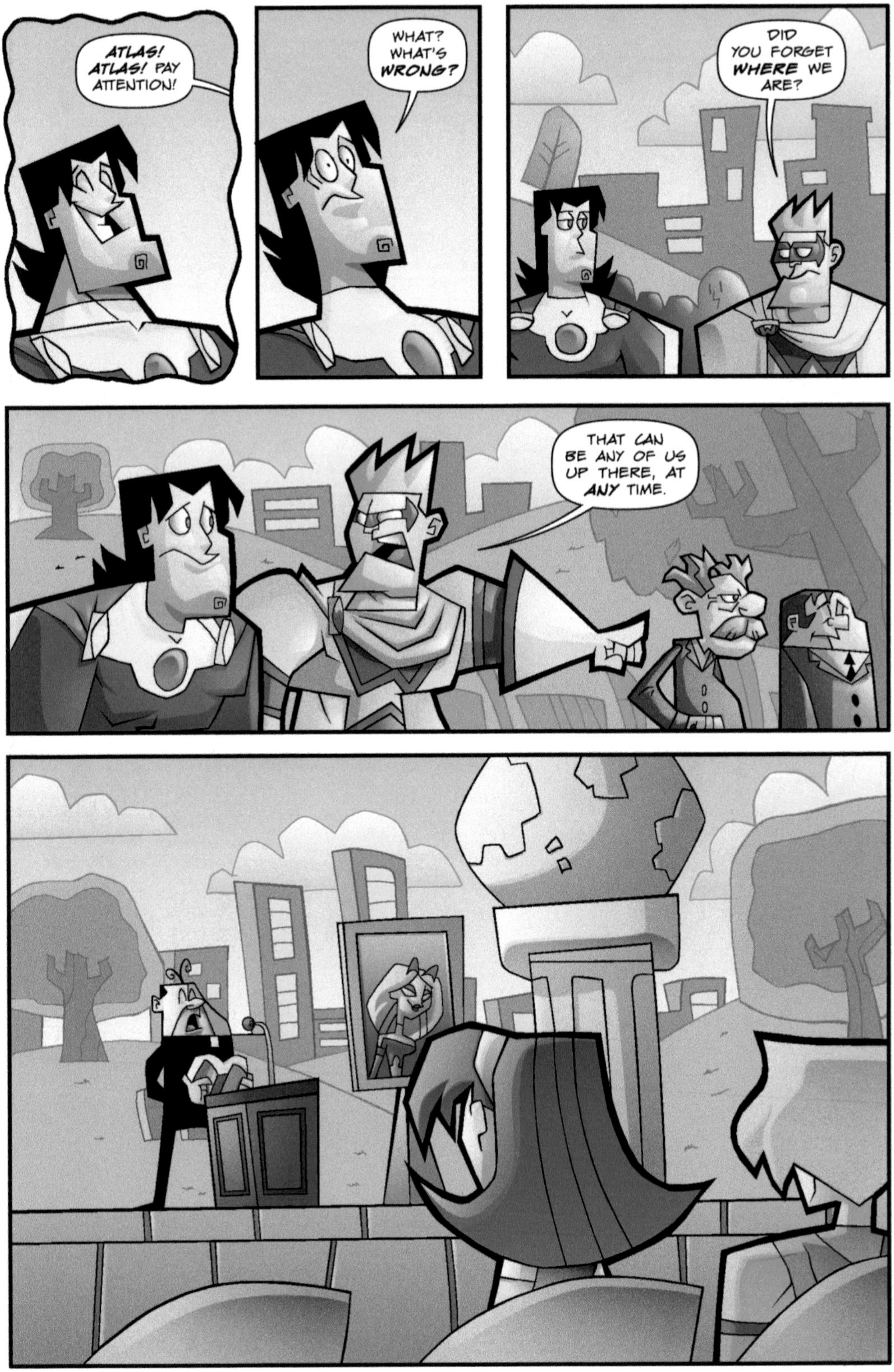
ATLAS! ATLAS! PAY ATTENTION!
WHAT? WHAT'S WRONG?
DID YOU FORGET WHERE WE ARE?
THAT CAN BE ANY OF US UP THERE, AT ANY TIME.

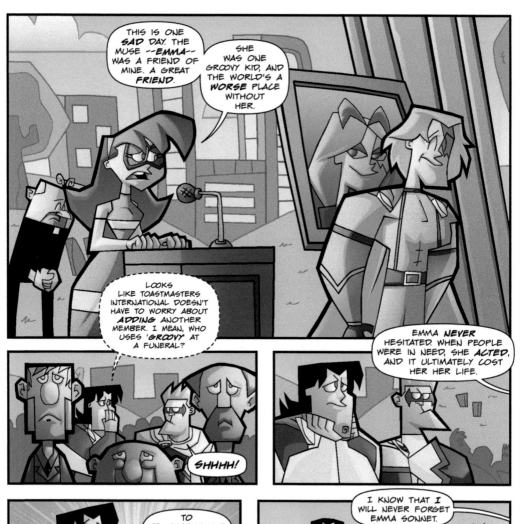

THIS IS ONE **SAD** DAY. THE MUSE --**EMMA**-- WAS A FRIEND OF MINE. A GREAT **FRIEND**.

SHE WAS ONE **GROOVY** KID, AND THE WORLD'S A **WORSE** PLACE WITHOUT HER.

LOOKS LIKE TOASTMASTERS INTERNATIONAL DOESN'T HAVE TO WORRY ABOUT **ADDING** ANOTHER MEMBER. I MEAN, WHO USES '**GROOVY**' AT A FUNERAL?

EMMA **NEVER** HESITATED. WHEN PEOPLE WERE IN NEED, SHE **ACTED**, AND IT ULTIMATELY COST HER HER LIFE.

SHHHH!

TO ME, THAT IS THE **TRUE** DEFINITION OF A HERO. **AND** A FRIEND.

I KNOW THAT **I** WILL NEVER FORGET EMMA SONNET.

POP

AND THE PEOPLE SHE SAVED --THE **MANY** PEOPLE-- WILL NOT, EITHER.

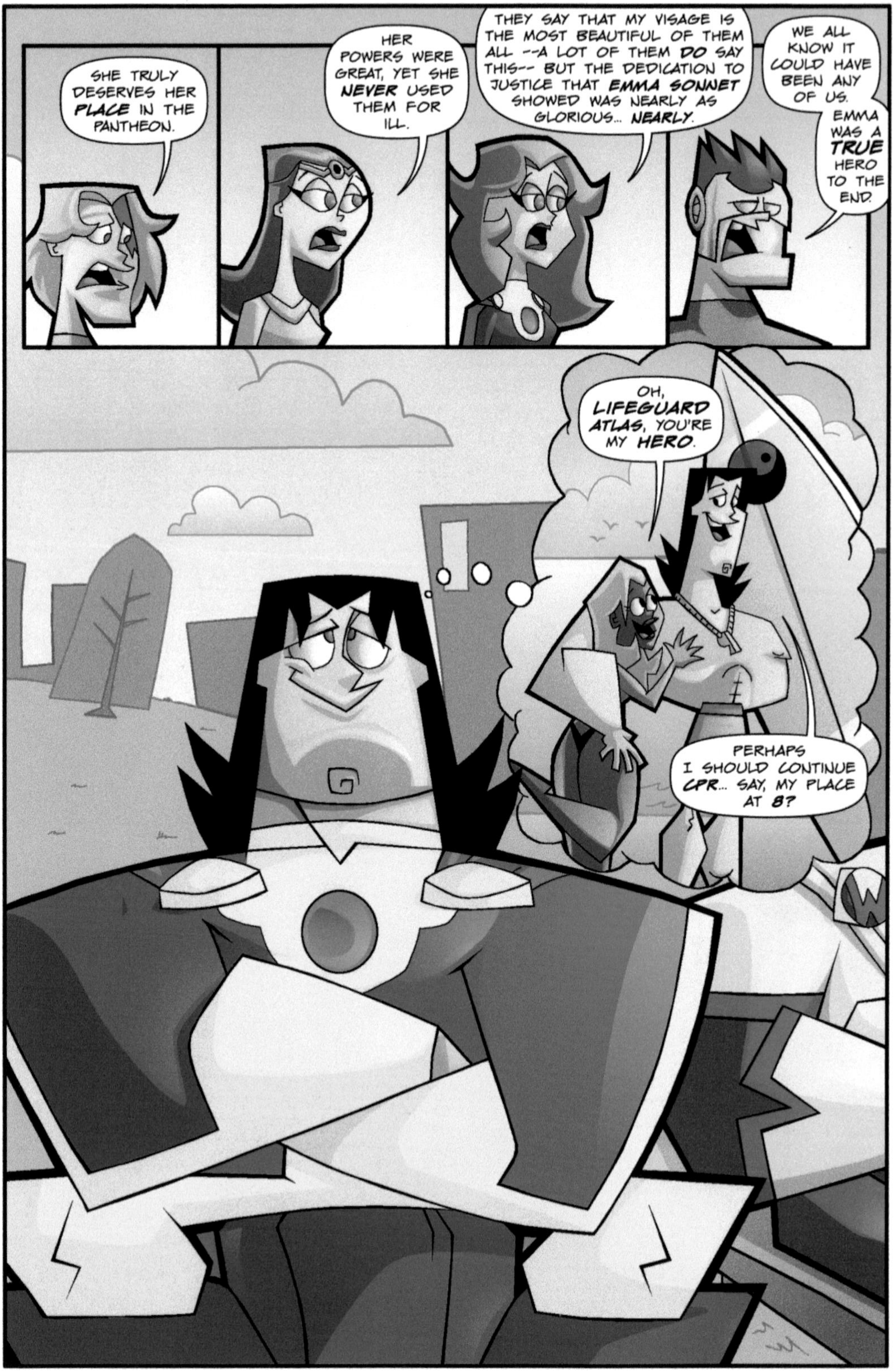
SHE TRULY DESERVES HER PLACE IN THE PANTHEON.
HER POWERS WERE GREAT, YET SHE NEVER USED THEM FOR ILL.
THEY SAY THAT MY VISAGE IS THE MOST BEAUTIFUL OF THEM ALL --A LOT OF THEM DO SAY THIS-- BUT THE DEDICATION TO JUSTICE THAT EMMA SONNET SHOWED WAS NEARLY AS GLORIOUS... NEARLY.
WE ALL KNOW IT COULD HAVE BEEN ANY OF US.
EMMA WAS A TRUE HERO TO THE END.
OH, LIFEGUARD ATLAS, YOU'RE MY HERO.
PERHAPS I SHOULD CONTINUE CPR... SAY, MY PLACE AT 8?

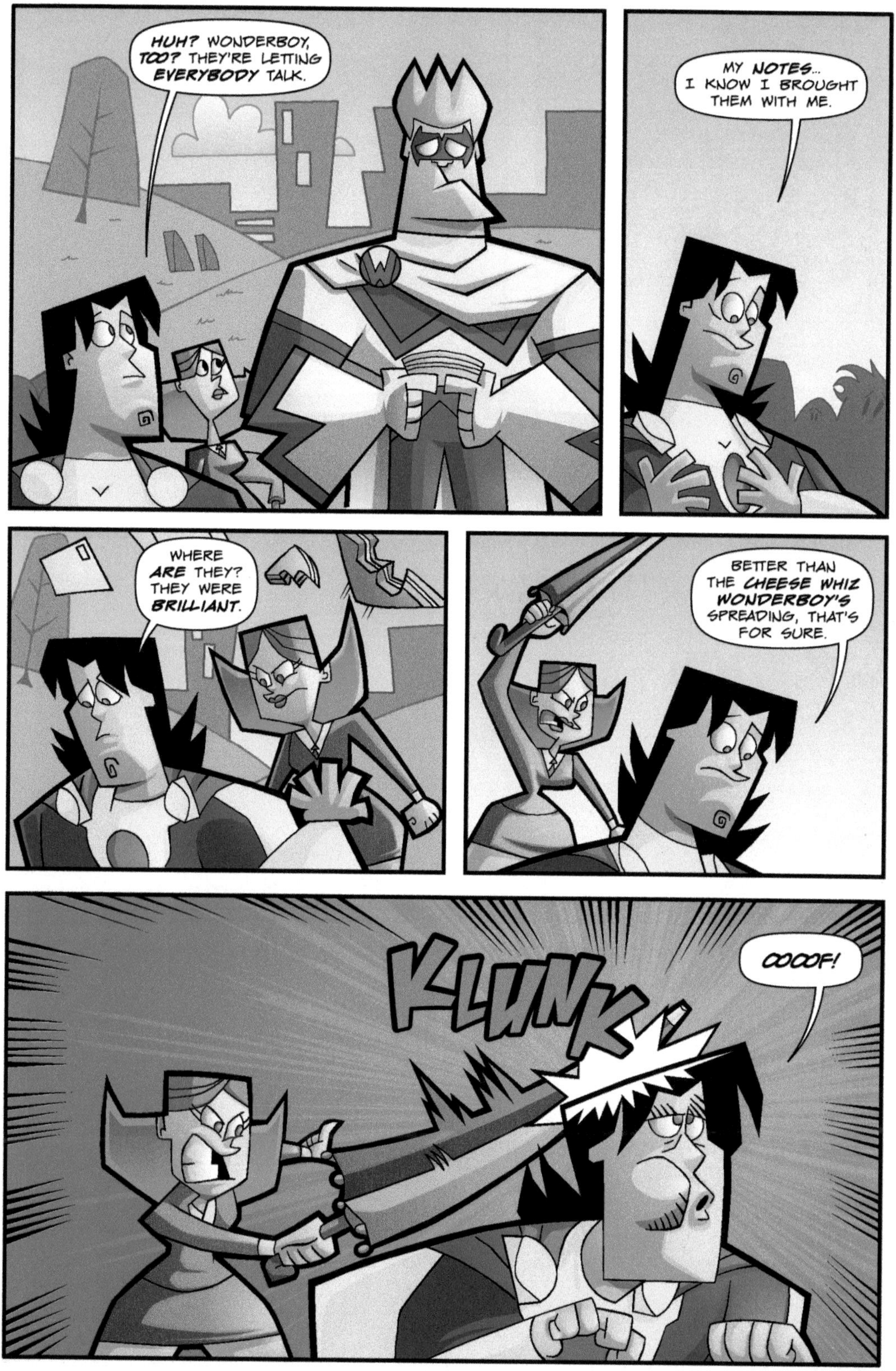
HUH? WONDERBOY, TOO? THEY'RE LETTING EVERYBODY TALK.
MY NOTES... I KNOW I BROUGHT THEM WITH ME.
WHERE ARE THEY? THEY WERE BRILLIANT.
BETTER THAN THE CHEESE WHIZ WONDERBOY'S SPREADING, THAT'S FOR SURE.
KLUNK!
OOOOF!

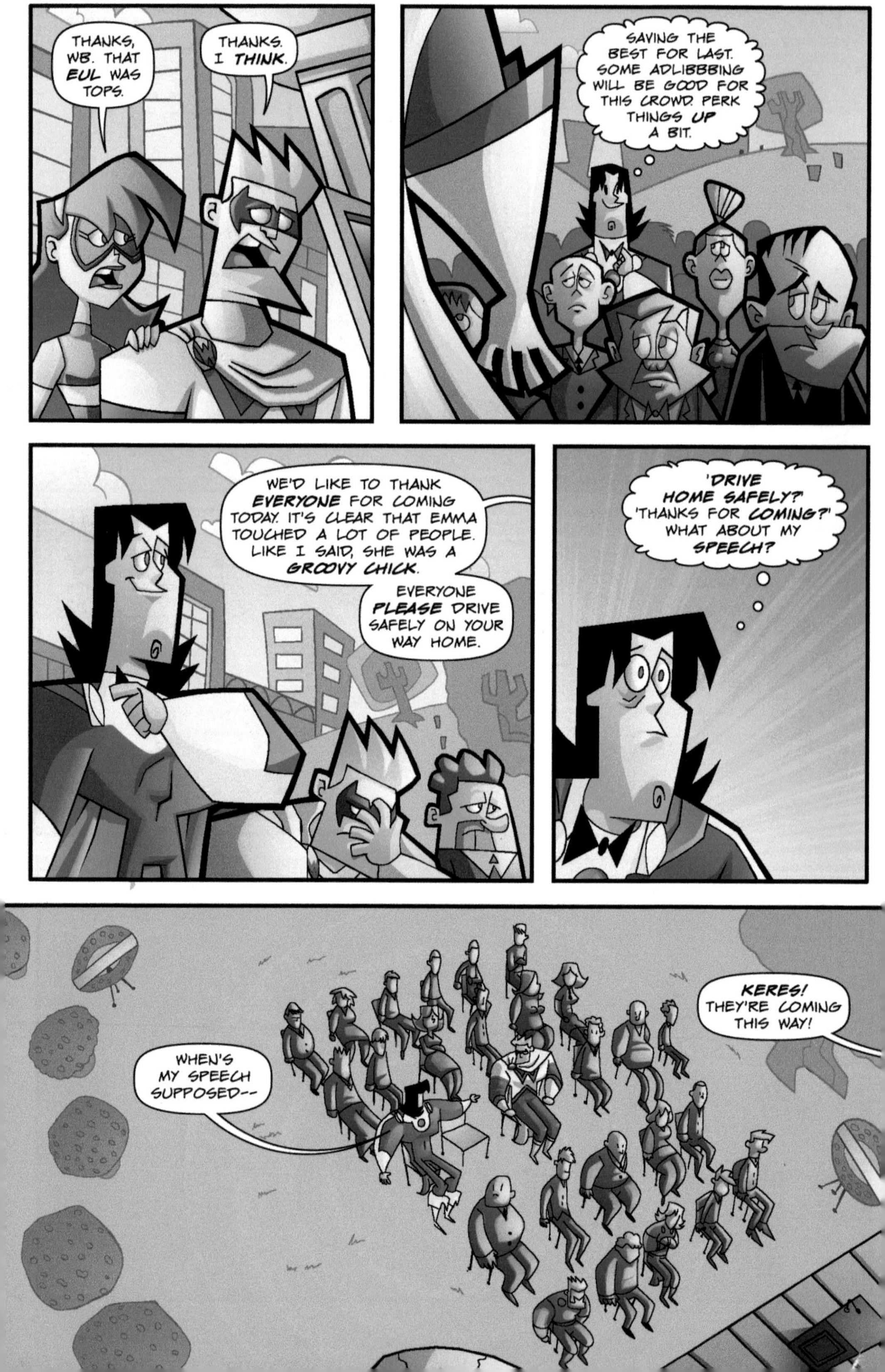
THANKS, WB. THAT EUL WAS TOPS.
THANKS. I THINK.
SAVING THE BEST FOR LAST. SOME ADLIBBBING WILL BE GOOD FOR THIS CROWD. PERK THINGS UP A BIT.
WE'D LIKE TO THANK EVERYONE FOR COMING TODAY. IT'S CLEAR THAT EMMA TOUCHED A LOT OF PEOPLE. LIKE I SAID, SHE WAS A GROOVY CHICK.
EVERYONE PLEASE DRIVE SAFELY ON YOUR WAY HOME.
'DRIVE HOME SAFELY?' 'THANKS FOR COMING?' WHAT ABOUT MY SPEECH?
WHEN'S MY SPEECH SUPPOSED--
KERES! THEY'RE COMING THIS WAY!

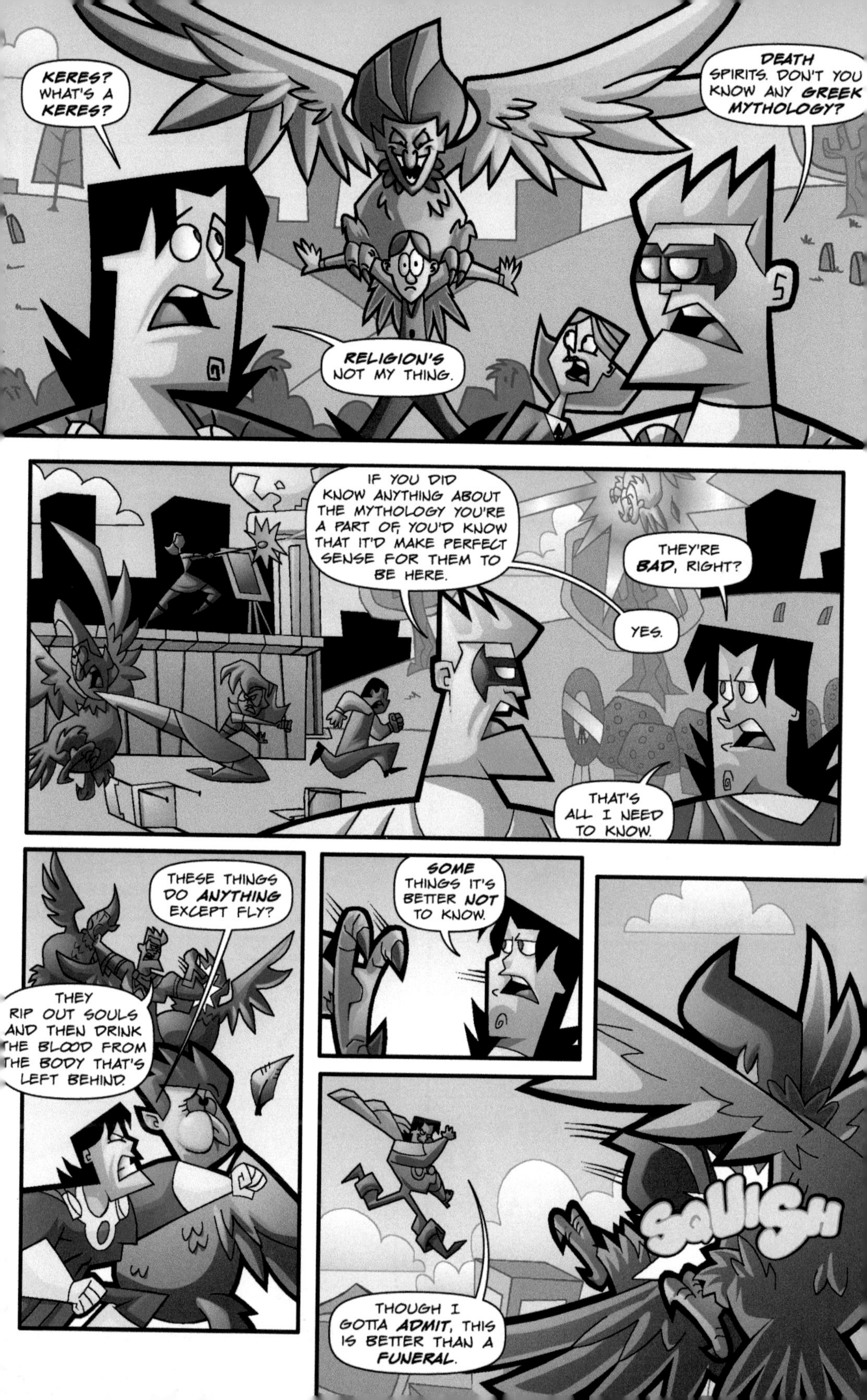
KERES? WHAT'S A KERES?
DEATH SPIRITS. DON'T YOU KNOW ANY GREEK MYTHOLOGY?
RELIGION'S NOT MY THING.
IF YOU DID KNOW ANYTHING ABOUT THE MYTHOLOGY YOU'RE A PART OF, YOU'D KNOW THAT IT'D MAKE PERFECT SENSE FOR THEM TO BE HERE.
THEY'RE BAD, RIGHT?
YES.
THAT'S ALL I NEED TO KNOW.
THESE THINGS DO ANYTHING EXCEPT FLY?
THEY RIP OUT SOULS AND THEN DRINK THE BLOOD FROM THE BODY THAT'S LEFT BEHIND.
SOME THINGS IT'S BETTER NOT TO KNOW.
SQUISH
THOUGH I GOTTA ADMIT, THIS IS BETTER THAN A FUNERAL.

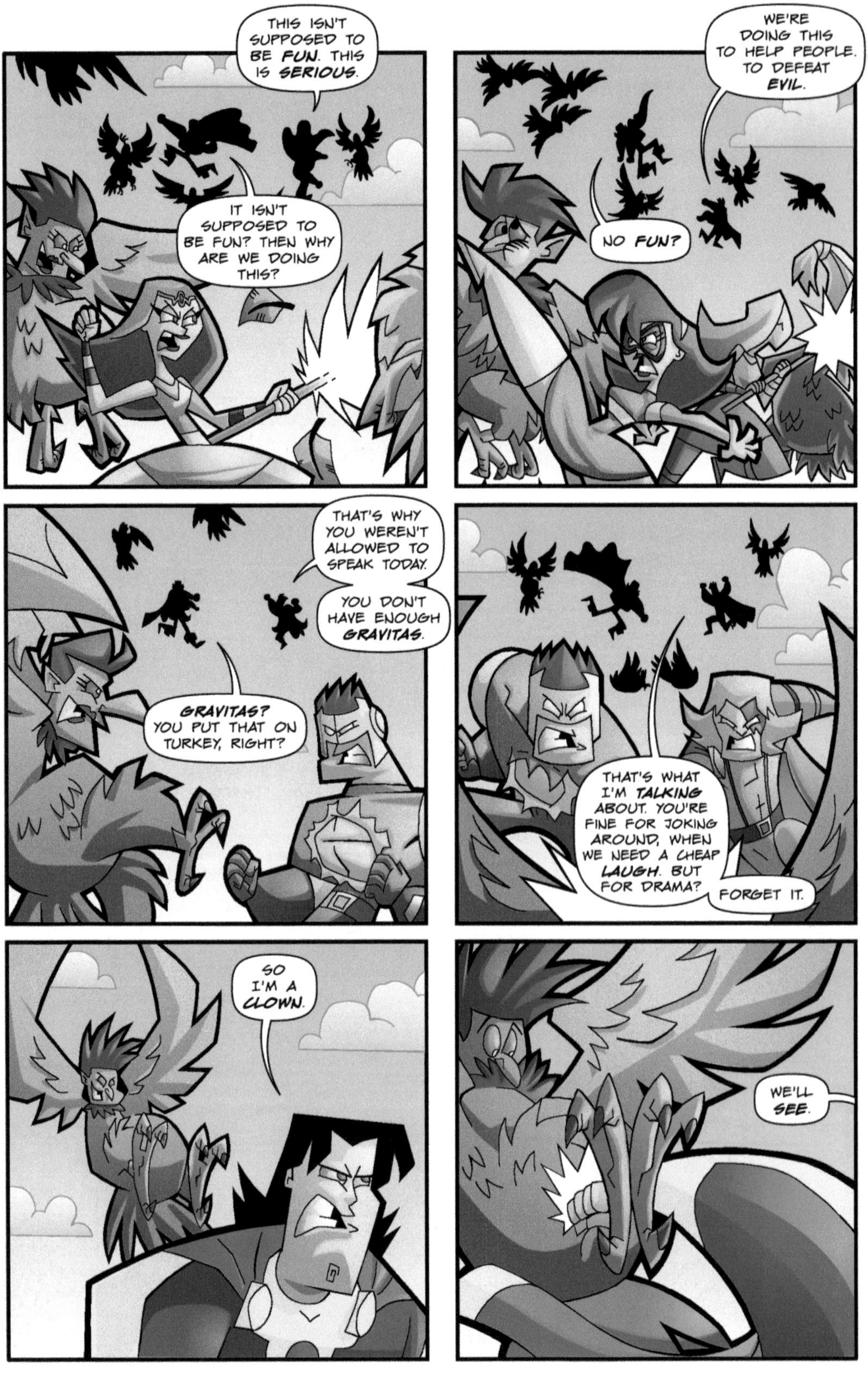
THIS ISN'T SUPPOSED TO BE FUN. THIS IS SERIOUS.
IT ISN'T SUPPOSED TO BE FUN? THEN WHY ARE WE DOING THIS?
WE'RE DOING THIS TO HELP PEOPLE. TO DEFEAT EVIL.
NO FUN?
THAT'S WHY YOU WEREN'T ALLOWED TO SPEAK TODAY.
YOU DON'T HAVE ENOUGH GRAVITAS.
GRAVITAS? YOU PUT THAT ON TURKEY, RIGHT?
THAT'S WHAT I'M TALKING ABOUT. YOU'RE FINE FOR JOKING AROUND, WHEN WE NEED A CHEAP LAUGH. BUT FOR DRAMA?
FORGET IT.
SO I'M A CLOWN.
WE'LL SEE.

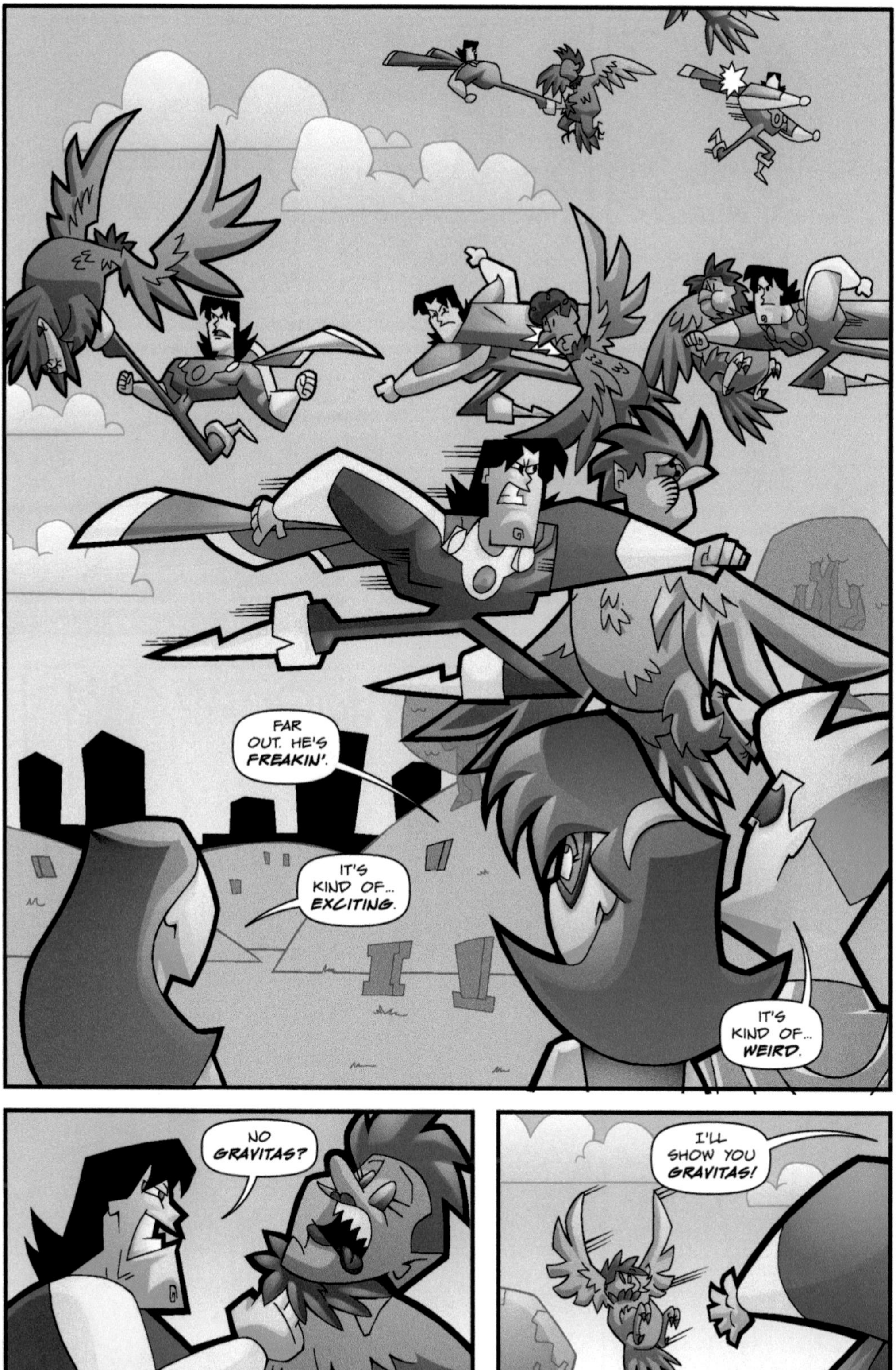
FAR OUT. HE'S FREAKIN'.
IT'S KIND OF... EXCITING.
IT'S KIND OF... WEIRD.
NO GRAVITAS?
I'LL SHOW YOU GRAVITAS!

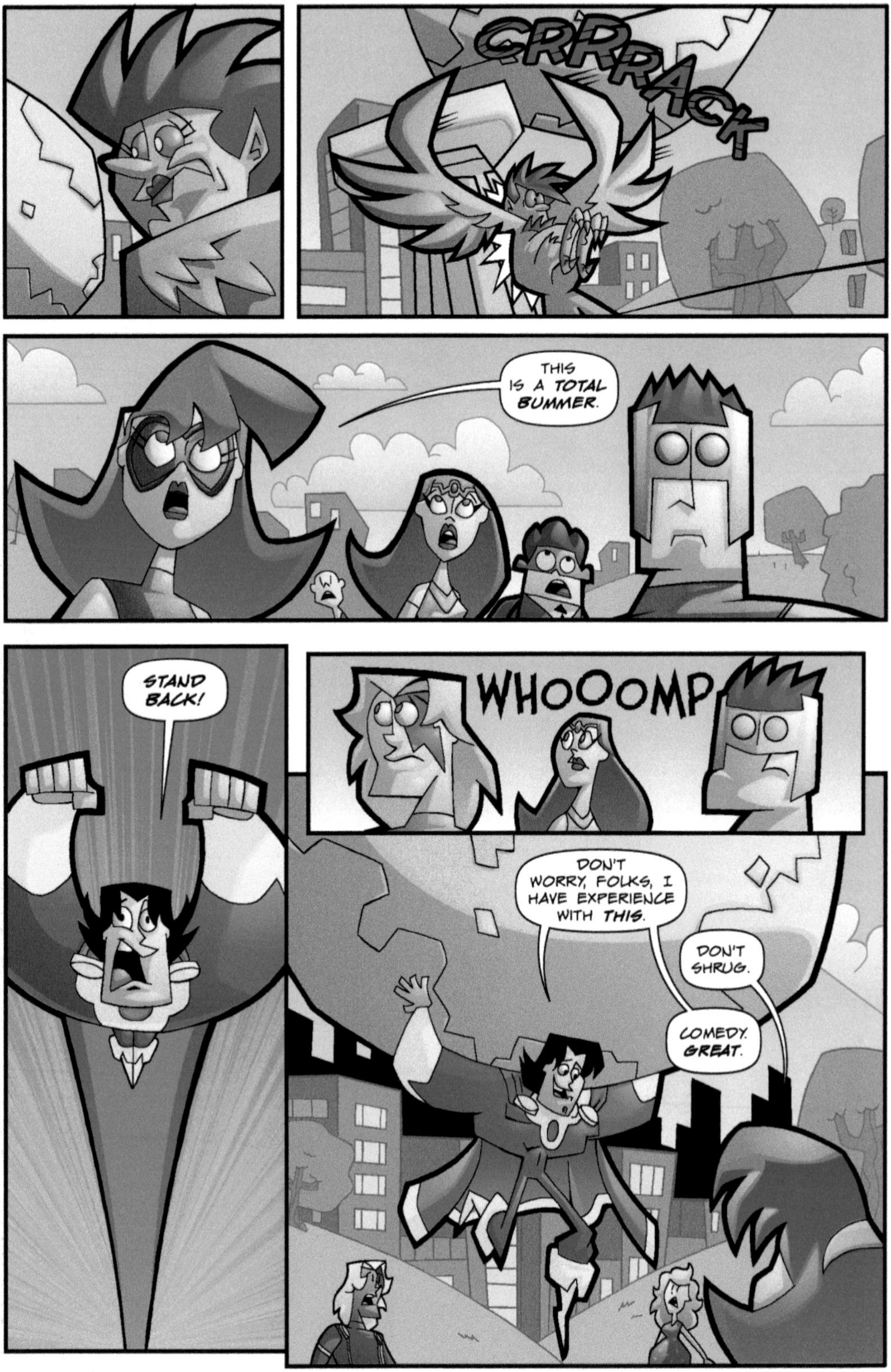
CRRRACK
THIS IS A TOTAL BUMMER.
STAND BACK!
WHOOOMP
DON'T WORRY, FOLKS, I HAVE EXPERIENCE WITH THIS.
DON'T SHRUG.
COMEDY. GREAT.

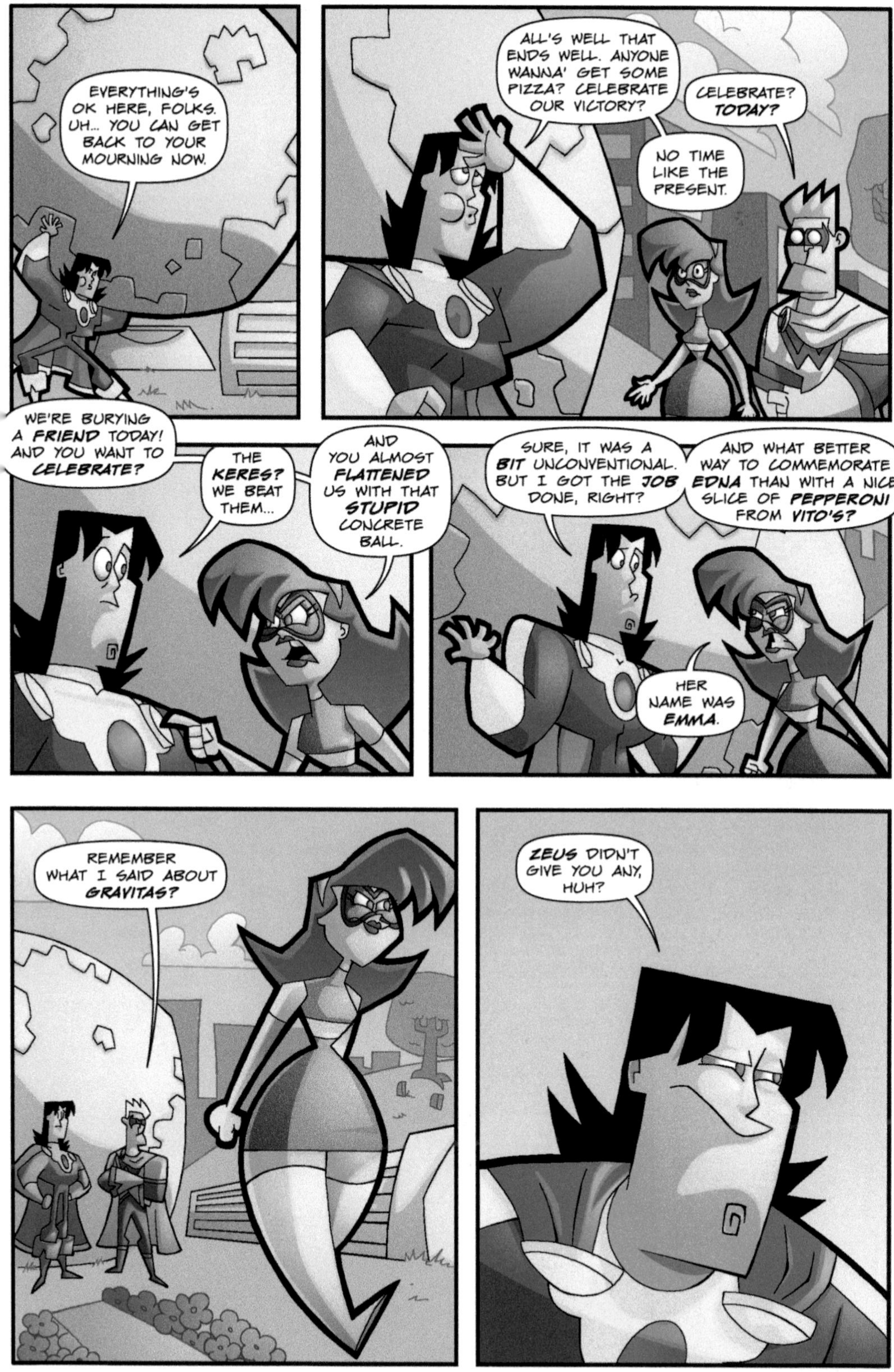
EVERYTHING'S OK HERE, FOLKS. UH... YOU CAN GET BACK TO YOUR MOURNING NOW.
ALL'S WELL THAT ENDS WELL. ANYONE WANNA' GET SOME PIZZA? CELEBRATE OUR VICTORY?
CELEBRATE? TODAY?
NO TIME LIKE THE PRESENT.
WE'RE BURYING A FRIEND TODAY! AND YOU WANT TO CELEBRATE?
THE KERES? WE BEAT THEM...
AND YOU ALMOST FLATTENED US WITH THAT STUPID CONCRETE BALL.
SURE, IT WAS A BIT UNCONVENTIONAL. BUT I GOT THE JOB DONE, RIGHT?
AND WHAT BETTER WAY TO COMMEMORATE EDNA THAN WITH A NICE SLICE OF PEPPERONI FROM VITO'S?
HER NAME WAS EMMA.
REMEMBER WHAT I SAID ABOUT GRAVITAS?
ZEUS DIDN'T GIVE YOU ANY, HUH?

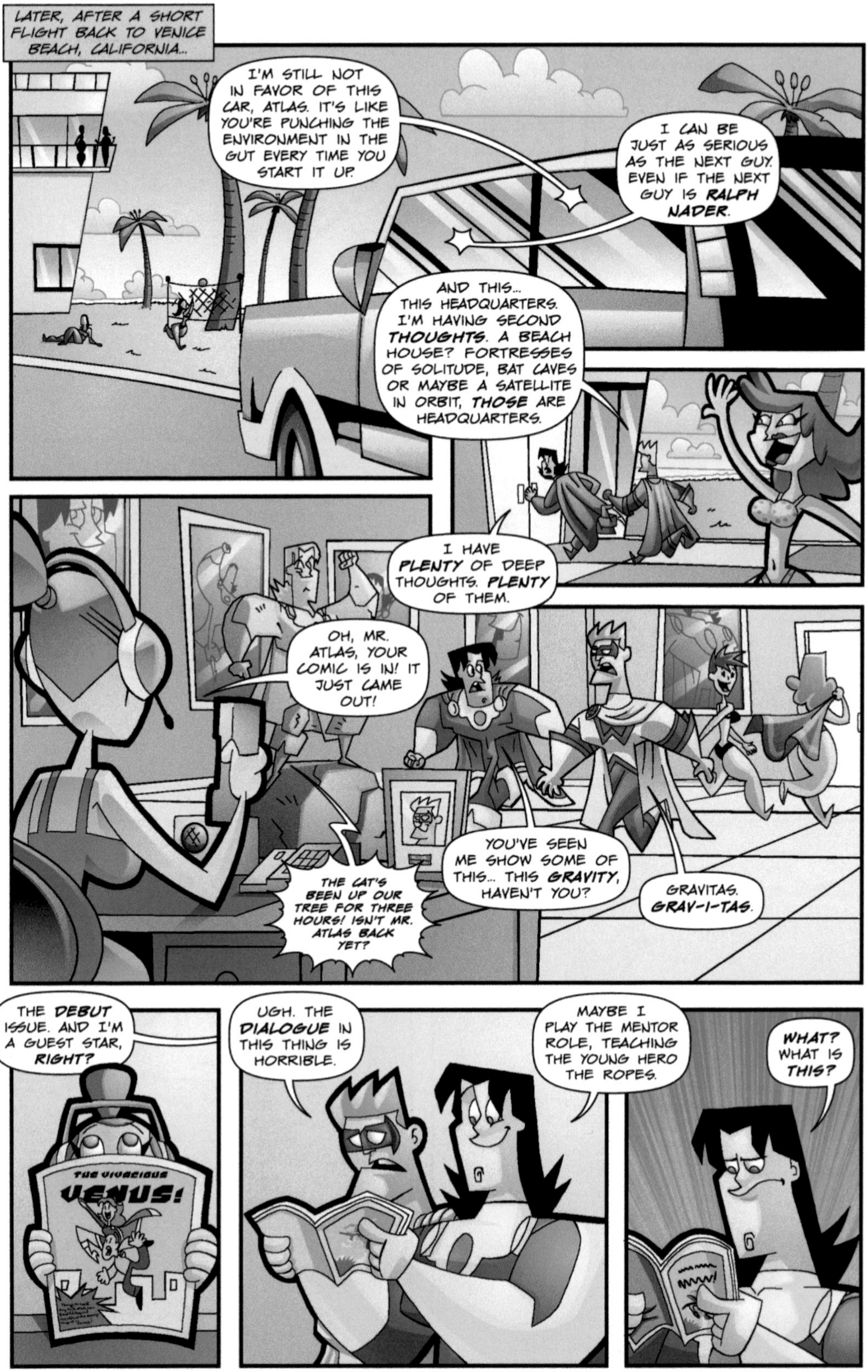
LATER, AFTER A SHORT FLIGHT BACK TO VENICE BEACH, CALIFORNIA...
I'M STILL NOT IN FAVOR OF THIS CAR, ATLAS. IT'S LIKE YOU'RE PUNCHING THE ENVIRONMENT IN THE GUT EVERY TIME YOU START IT UP.
I CAN BE JUST AS SERIOUS AS THE NEXT GUY. EVEN IF THE NEXT GUY IS RALPH NADER.
AND THIS... THIS HEADQUARTERS. I'M HAVING SECOND THOUGHTS. A BEACH HOUSE? FORTRESSES OF SOLITUDE, BAT CAVES OR MAYBE A SATELLITE IN ORBIT, THOSE ARE HEADQUARTERS.
I HAVE PLENTY OF DEEP THOUGHTS. PLENTY OF THEM.
OH, MR. ATLAS, YOUR COMIC IS IN! IT JUST CAME OUT!
THE CAT'S BEEN UP OUR TREE FOR THREE HOURS! ISN'T MR. ATLAS BACK YET?
YOU'VE SEEN ME SHOW SOME OF THIS... THIS GRAVITY, HAVEN'T YOU?
GRAVITAS. GRAV-I-TAS.
THE DEBUT ISSUE. AND I'M A GUEST STAR, RIGHT?
THE VIVACIOUS
VENUS!
UGH. THE DIALOGUE IN THIS THING IS HORRIBLE.
MAYBE I PLAY THE MENTOR ROLE, TEACHING THE YOUNG HERO THE ROPES.
WHAT? WHAT IS THIS?

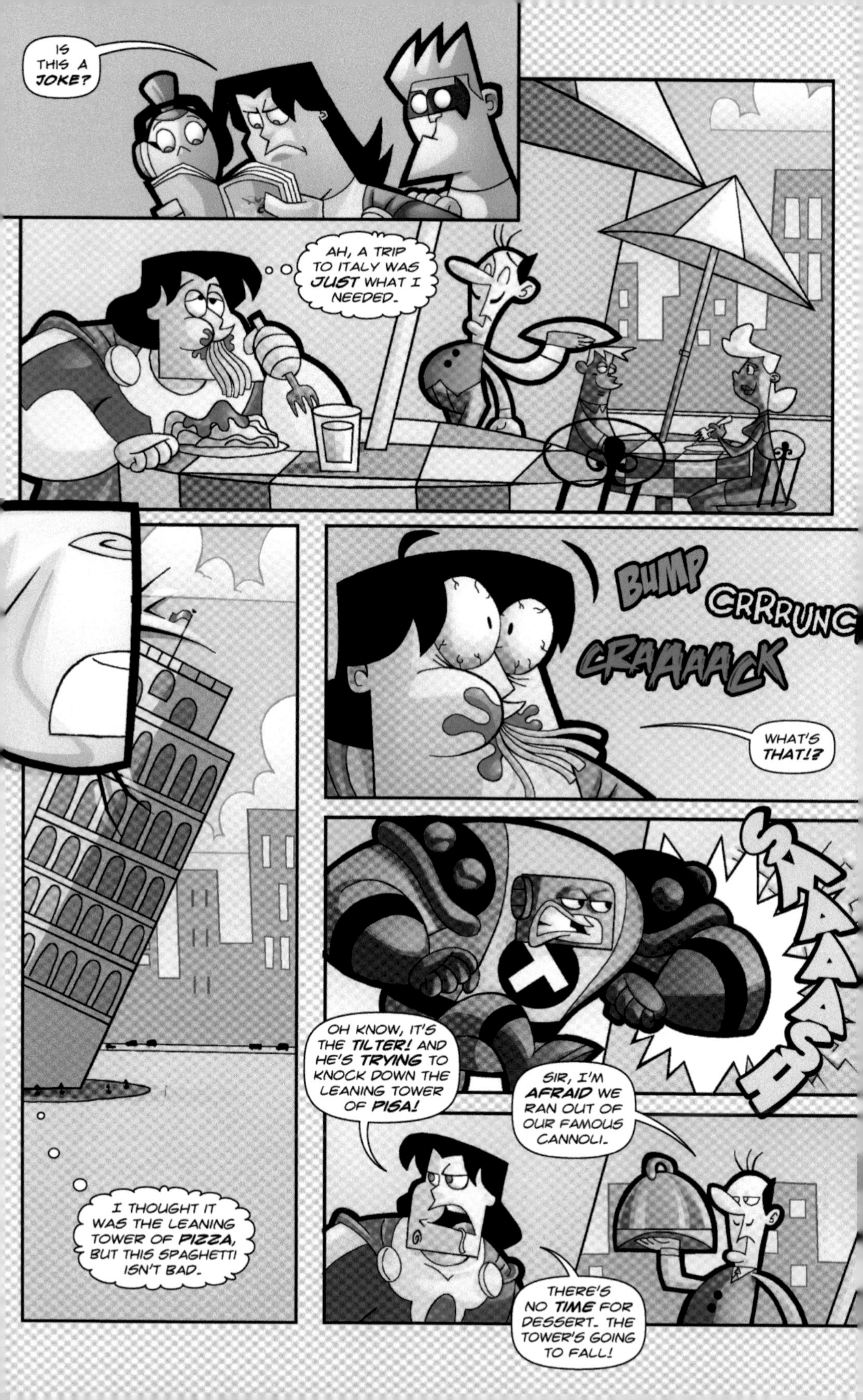

IS THIS A JOKE?
AH, A TRIP TO ITALY WAS JUST WHAT I NEEDED.
I THOUGHT IT WAS THE LEANING TOWER OF PIZZA, BUT THIS SPAGHETTI ISN'T BAD.
BUMP
CRRRUNC
CRAAAACK
WHAT'S THAT!?
SMAAASH
OH KNOW, IT'S THE TILTER! AND HE'S TRYING TO KNOCK DOWN THE LEANING TOWER OF PISA!
SIR, I'M AFRAID WE RAN OUT OF OUR FAMOUS CANNOLI.
THERE'S NO TIME FOR DESSERT. THE TOWER'S GOING TO FALL!

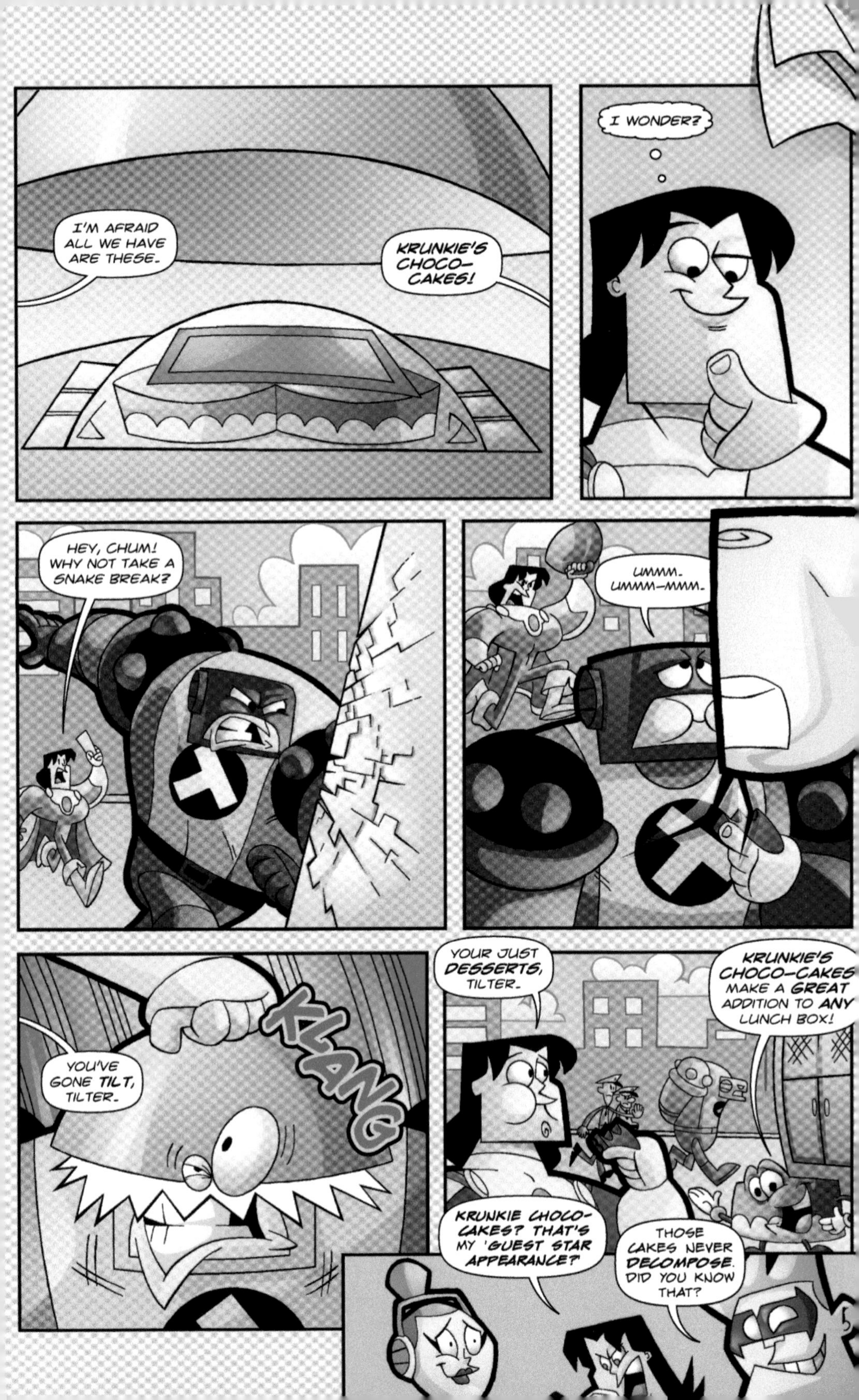
I'M AFRAID ALL WE HAVE ARE THESE...
KRUNKIE'S CHOCO-CAKES!
I WONDER?
HEY, CHUM! WHY NOT TAKE A SNAKE BREAK?
UMMM... UMMM-MMM...
YOU'VE GONE TILT, TILTER...
KLANG
YOUR JUST DESSERTS, TILTER...
KRUNKIE'S CHOCO-CAKES MAKE A GREAT ADDITION TO ANY LUNCH BOX!
KRUNKIE CHOCO-CAKES? THAT'S MY 'GUEST STAR APPEARANCE?'
THOSE CAKES NEVER DECOMPOSE. DID YOU KNOW THAT?

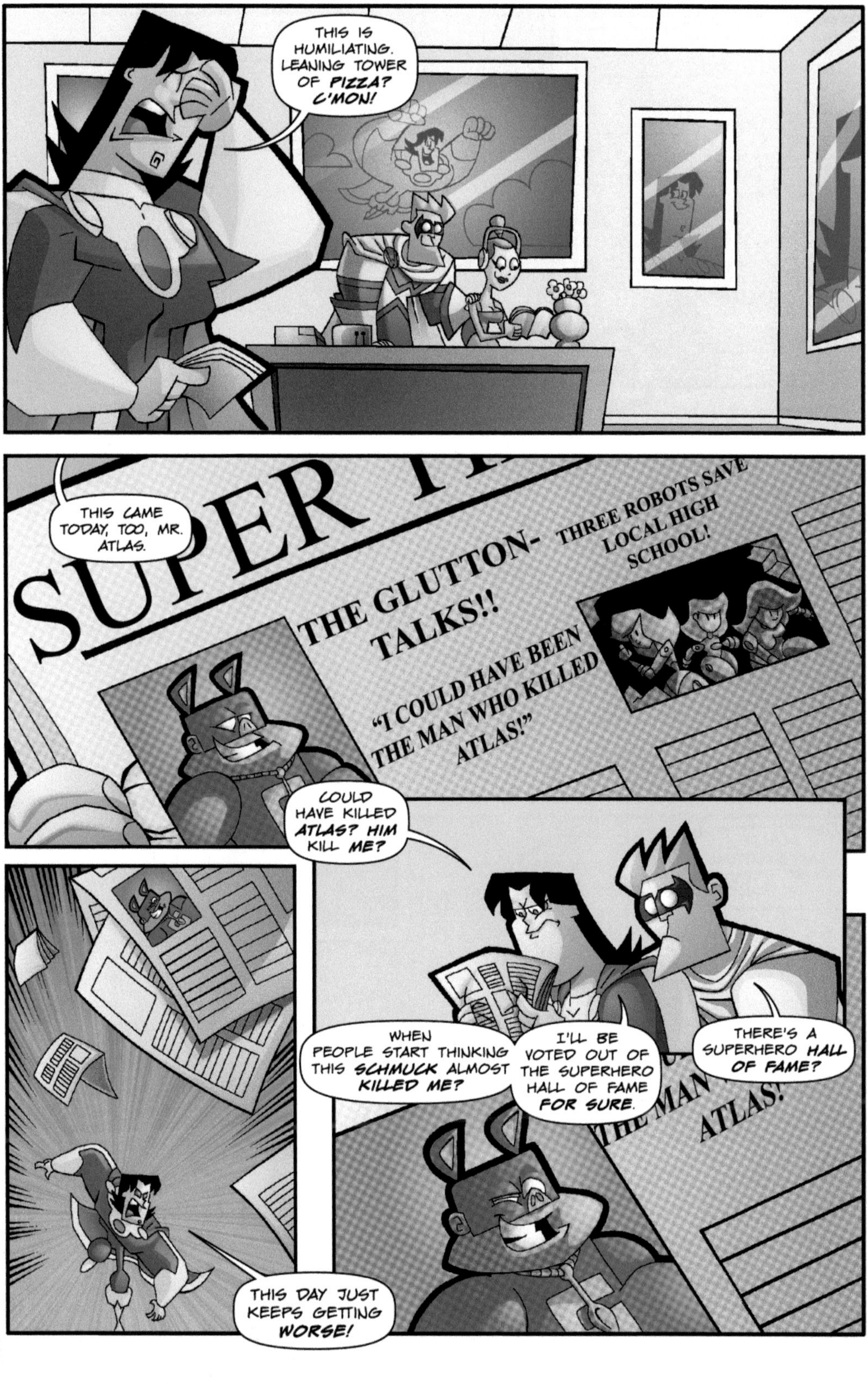

THIS IS HUMILIATING. LEANING TOWER OF PIZZA? C'MON!
SUPER
THIS CAME TODAY, TOO, MR. ATLAS.
THREE ROBOTS SAVE LOCAL HIGH SCHOOL!
THE GLUTTON-TALKS!!
"I COULD HAVE BEEN THE MAN WHO KILLED ATLAS!"
COULD HAVE KILLED ATLAS? HIM KILL ME?
WHEN PEOPLE START THINKING THIS SCHMUCK ALMOST KILLED ME?
I'LL BE VOTED OUT OF THE SUPERHERO HALL OF FAME FOR SURE.
THERE'S A SUPERHERO HALL OF FAME?
THIS DAY JUST KEEPS GETTING WORSE!

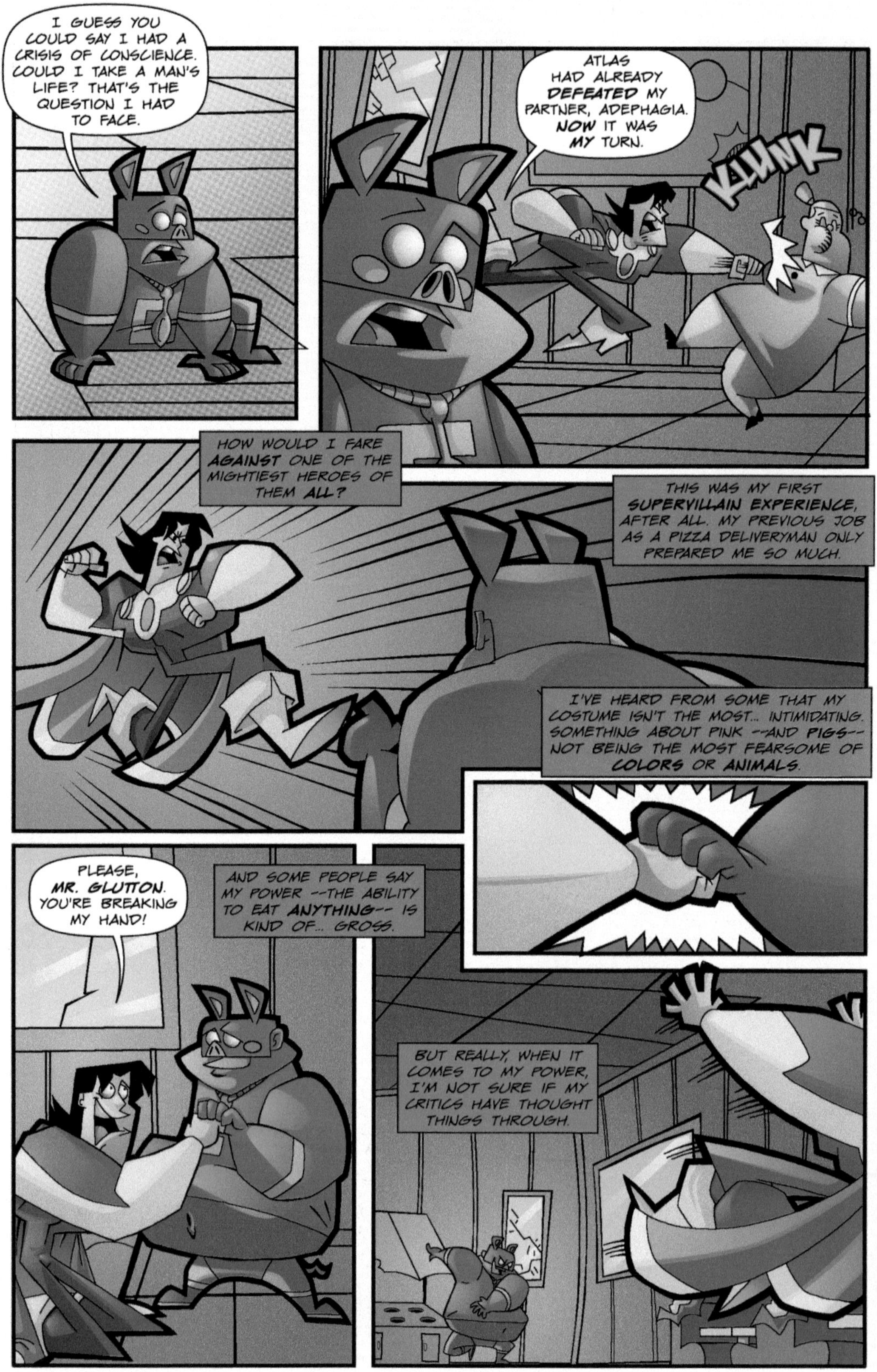
I GUESS YOU COULD SAY I HAD A CRISIS OF CONSCIENCE. COULD I TAKE A MAN'S LIFE? THAT'S THE QUESTION I HAD TO FACE.
ATLAS HAD ALREADY DEFEATED MY PARTNER, ADEPHAGIA. NOW IT WAS MY TURN.
KLUNK
HOW WOULD I FARE AGAINST ONE OF THE MIGHTIEST HEROES OF THEM ALL?
THIS WAS MY FIRST SUPERVILLAIN EXPERIENCE, AFTER ALL. MY PREVIOUS JOB AS A PIZZA DELIVERYMAN ONLY PREPARED ME SO MUCH.
I'VE HEARD FROM SOME THAT MY COSTUME ISN'T THE MOST... INTIMIDATING. SOMETHING ABOUT PINK --AND PIGS-- NOT BEING THE MOST FEARSOME OF COLORS OR ANIMALS.
PLEASE, MR. GLUTTON. YOU'RE BREAKING MY HAND!
AND SOME PEOPLE SAY MY POWER --THE ABILITY TO EAT ANYTHING-- IS KIND OF... GROSS.
BUT REALLY, WHEN IT COMES TO MY POWER, I'M NOT SURE IF MY CRITICS HAVE THOUGHT THINGS THROUGH.

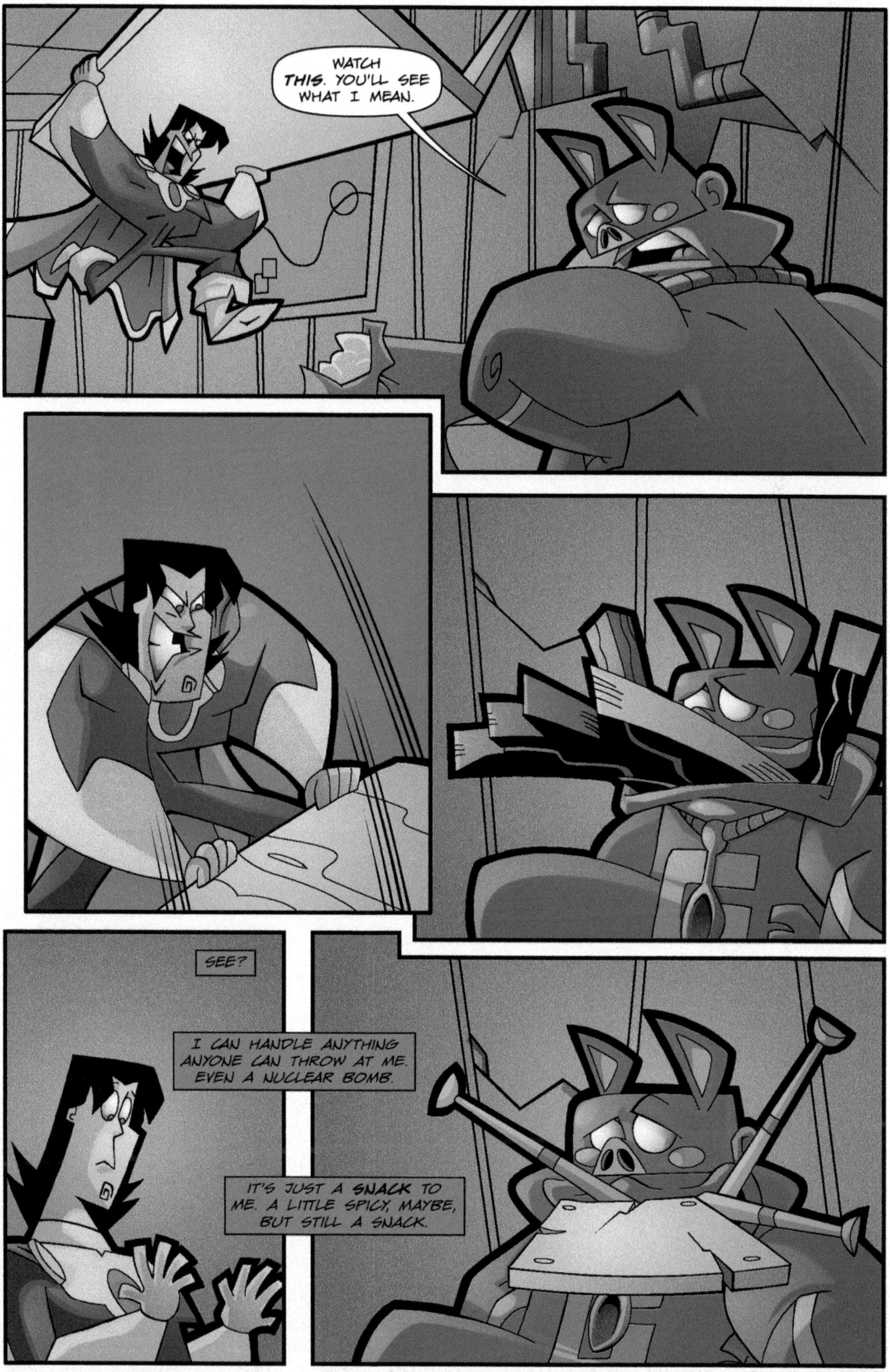
WATCH
THIS. YOU'LL SEE
WHAT I MEAN.
SEE?
I CAN HANDLE ANYTHING
ANYONE CAN THROW AT ME.
EVEN A NUCLEAR BOMB.
IT'S JUST A SNACK TO
ME. A LITTLE SPICY, MAYBE,
BUT STILL A SNACK.

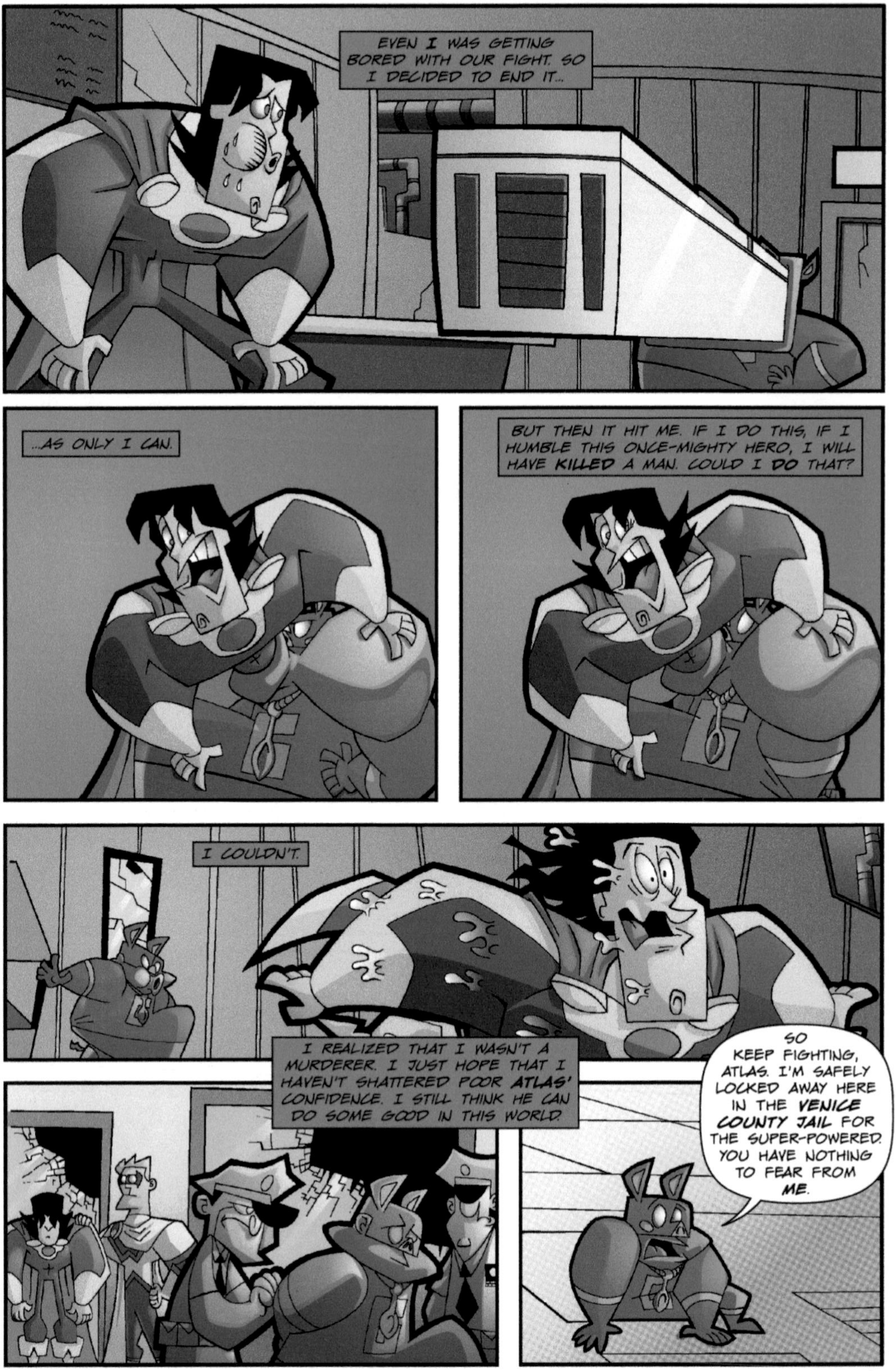
EVEN I WAS GETTING BORED WITH OUR FIGHT. SO I DECIDED TO END IT...
...AS ONLY I CAN.
BUT THEN IT HIT ME. IF I DO THIS, IF I HUMBLE THIS ONCE-MIGHTY HERO, I WILL HAVE KILLED A MAN. COULD I DO THAT?
I COULDN'T.
I REALIZED THAT I WASN'T A MURDERER. I JUST HOPE THAT I HAVEN'T SHATTERED POOR ATLAS' CONFIDENCE. I STILL THINK HE CAN DO SOME GOOD IN THIS WORLD.
SO KEEP FIGHTING, ATLAS. I'M SAFELY LOCKED AWAY HERE IN THE VENICE COUNTY JAIL FOR THE SUPER-POWERED. YOU HAVE NOTHING TO FEAR FROM ME.

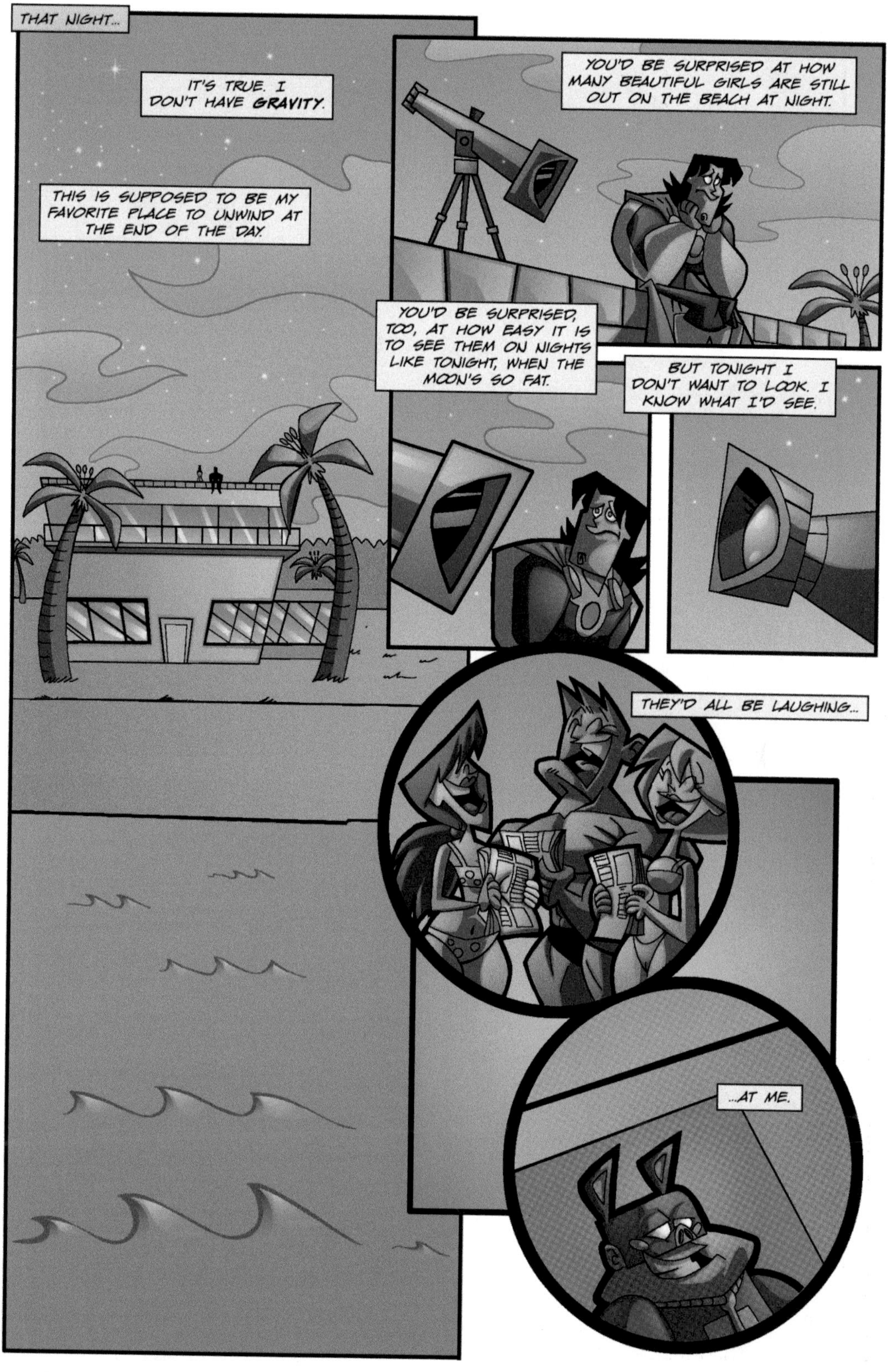
THAT NIGHT...
IT'S TRUE. I DON'T HAVE GRAVITY.
THIS IS SUPPOSED TO BE MY FAVORITE PLACE TO UNWIND AT THE END OF THE DAY.
YOU'D BE SURPRISED AT HOW MANY BEAUTIFUL GIRLS ARE STILL OUT ON THE BEACH AT NIGHT.
YOU'D BE SURPRISED, TOO, AT HOW EASY IT IS TO SEE THEM ON NIGHTS LIKE TONIGHT, WHEN THE MOON'S SO FAT.
BUT TONIGHT I DON'T WANT TO LOOK. I KNOW WHAT I'D SEE.
THEY'D ALL BE LAUGHING...
...AT ME.

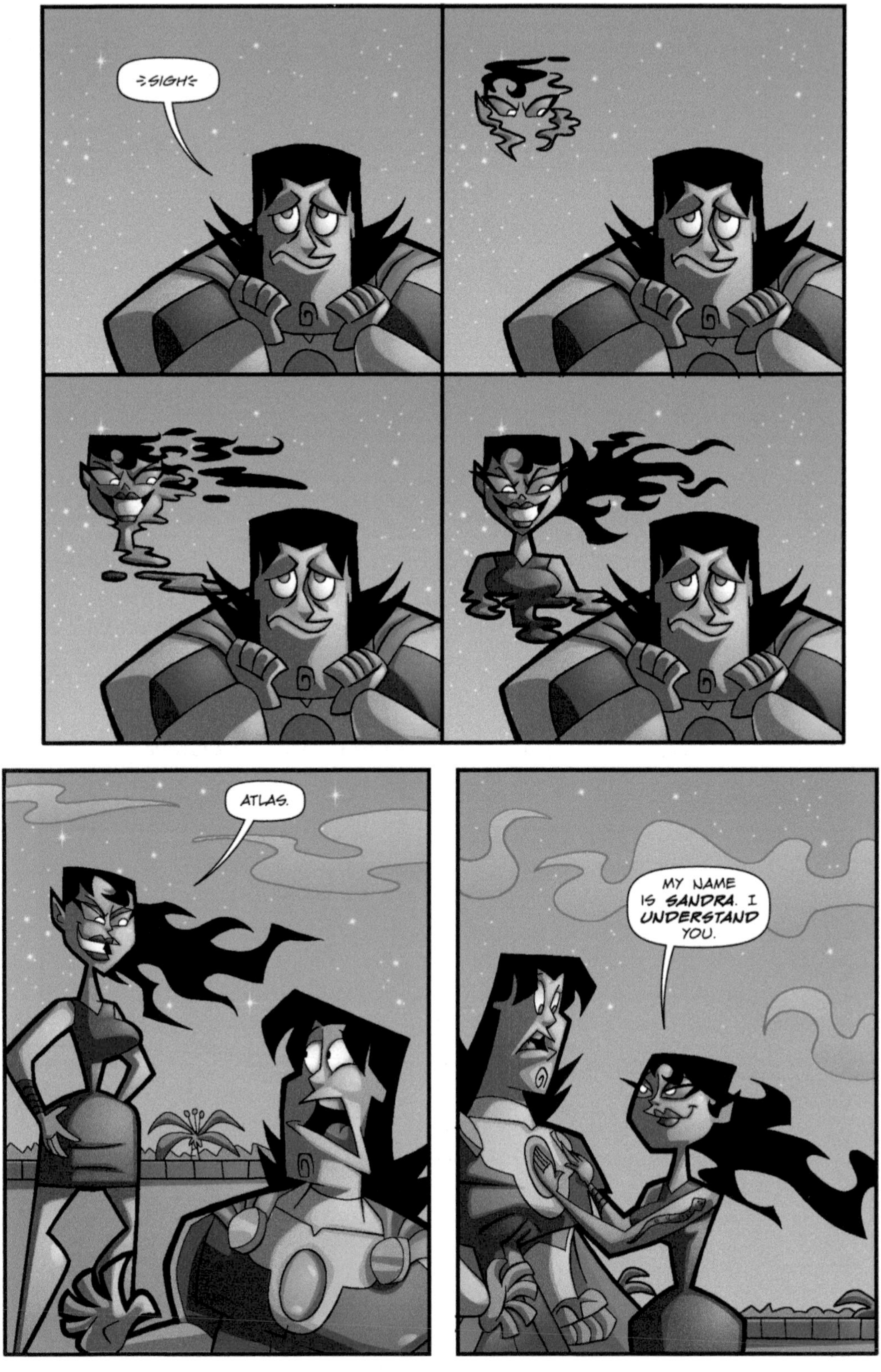

=SIGH=
ATLAS.
MY NAME IS SANDRA. I UNDERSTAND YOU.

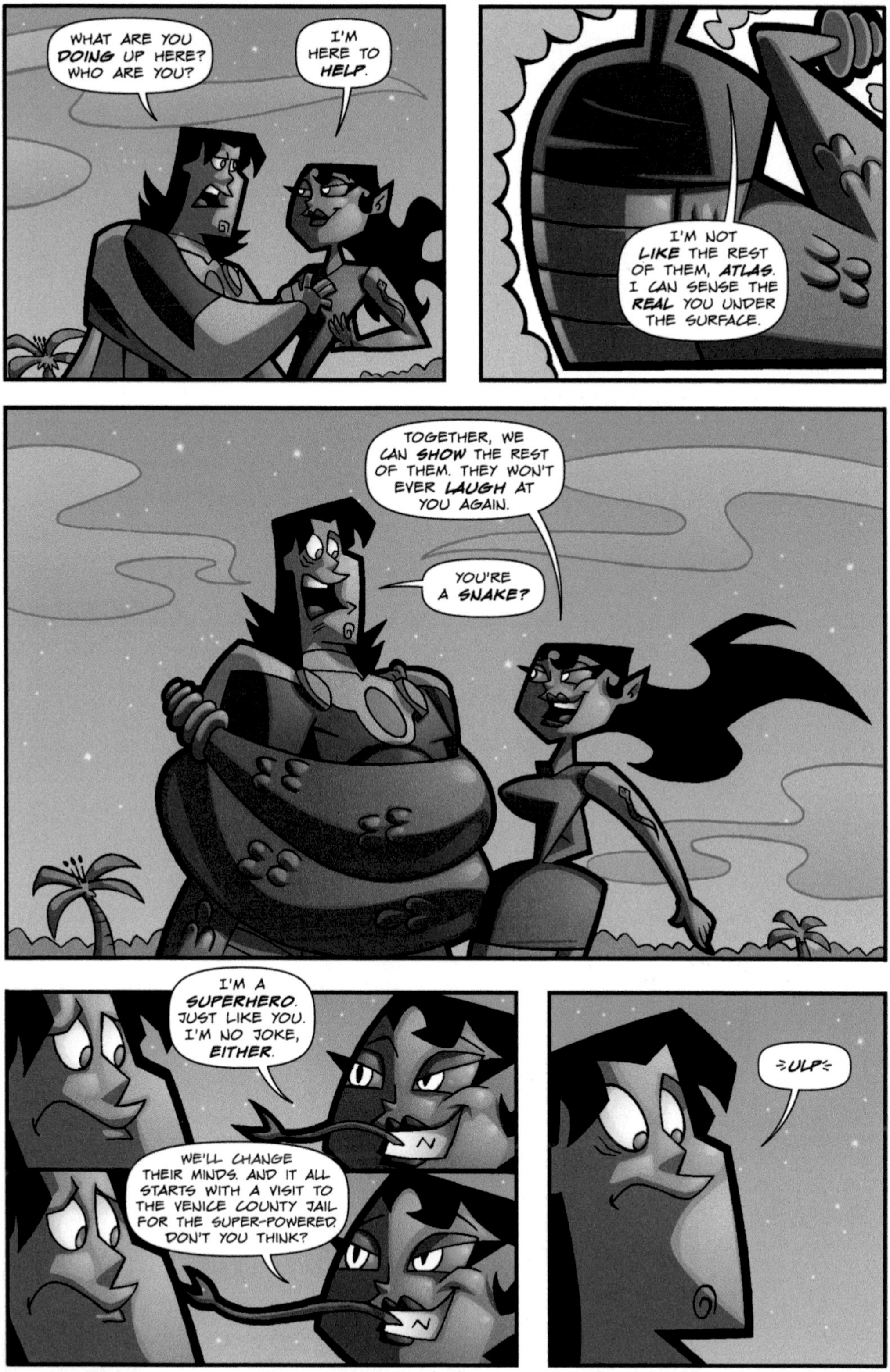
WHAT ARE YOU DOING UP HERE? WHO ARE YOU?
I'M HERE TO HELP.
I'M NOT LIKE THE REST OF THEM, ATLAS. I CAN SENSE THE REAL YOU UNDER THE SURFACE.
TOGETHER, WE CAN SHOW THE REST OF THEM. THEY WON'T EVER LAUGH AT YOU AGAIN.
YOU'RE A SNAKE?
I'M A SUPERHERO. JUST LIKE YOU. I'M NO JOKE, EITHER.
WE'LL CHANGE THEIR MINDS. AND IT ALL STARTS WITH A VISIT TO THE VENICE COUNTY JAIL FOR THE SUPER-POWERED. DON'T YOU THINK?
ULP

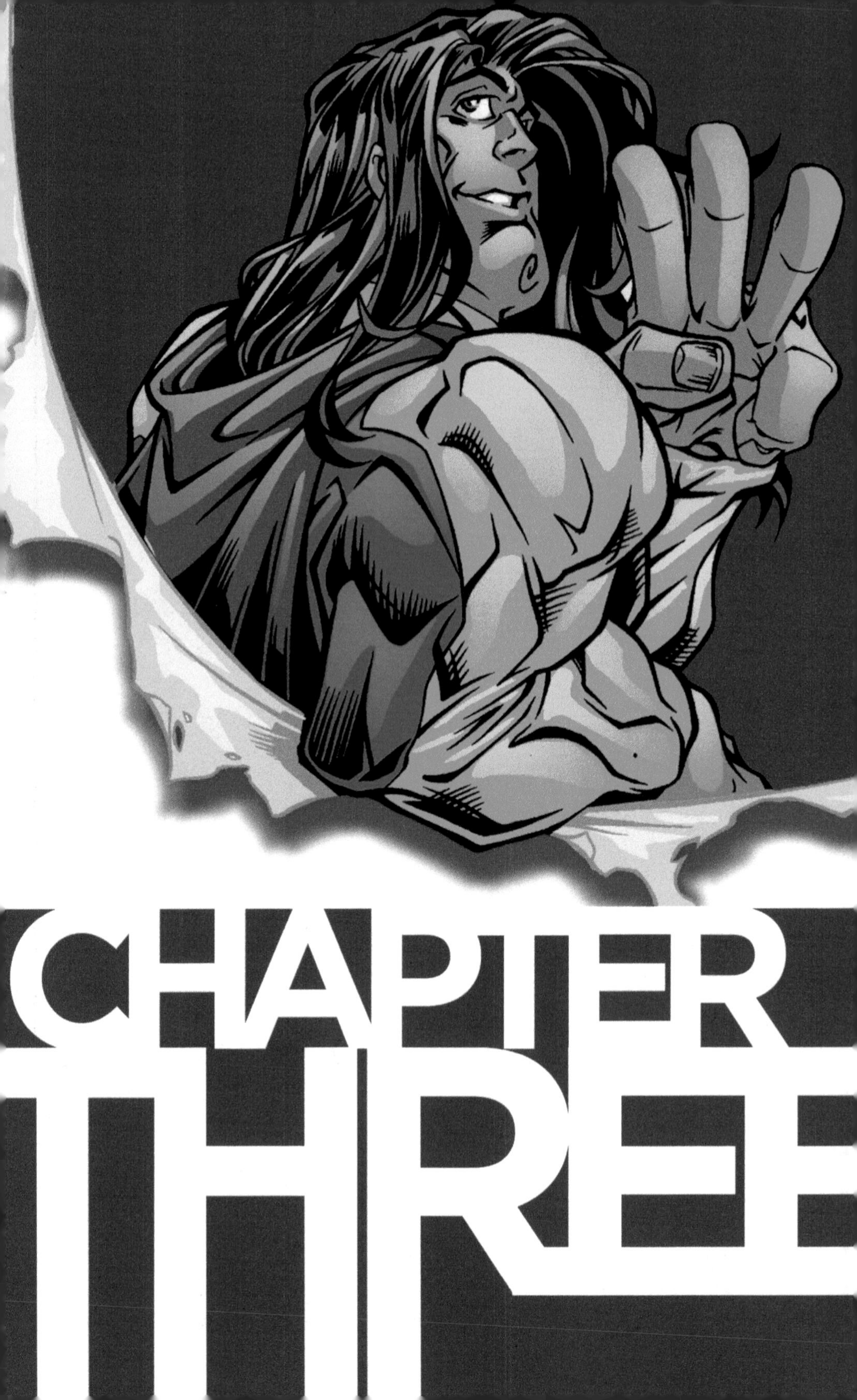

CHAPTER THREE

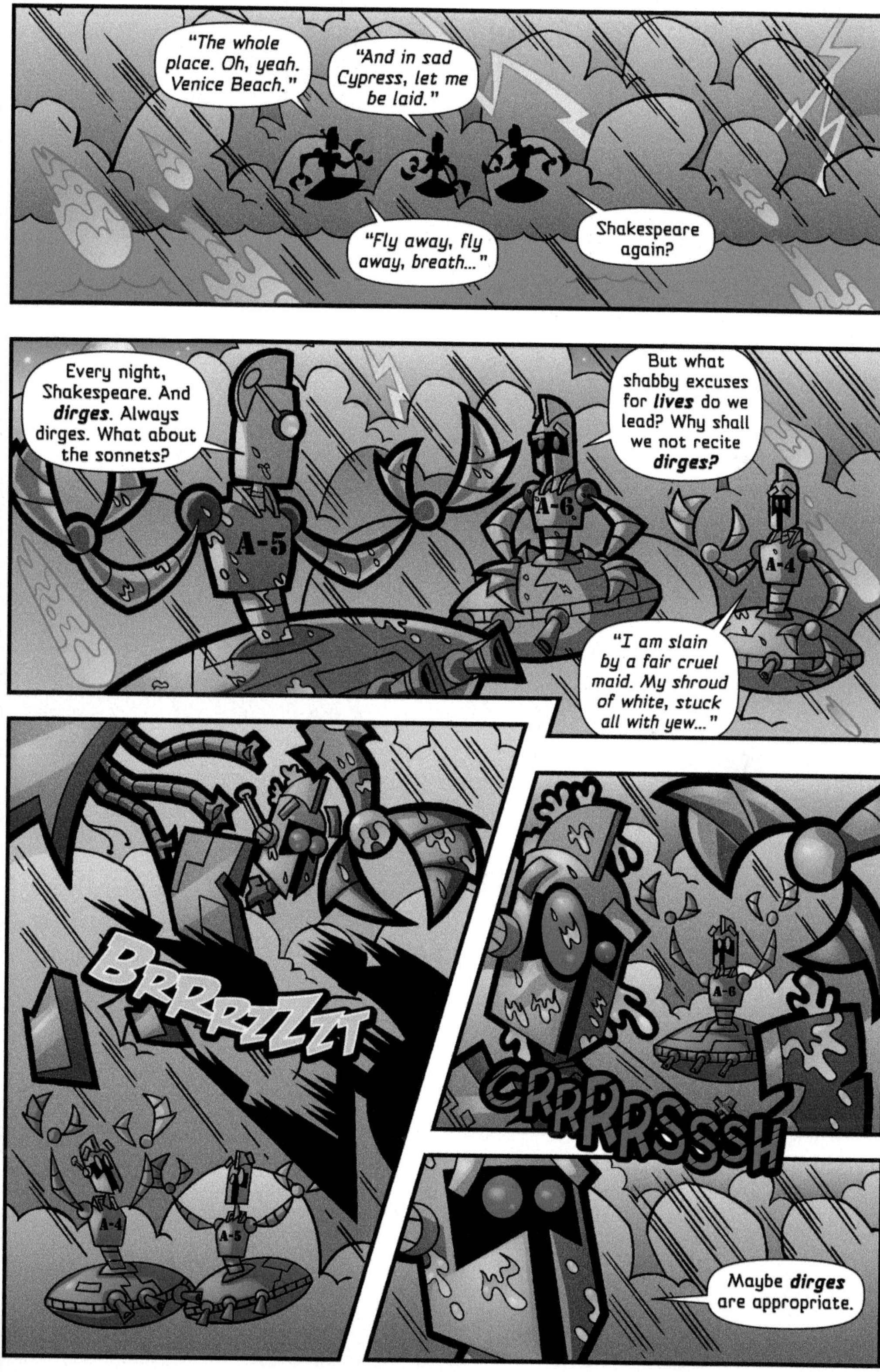
"The whole place. Oh, yeah. Venice Beach."
"And in sad Cypress, let me be laid."
"Fly away, fly away, breath..."
Shakespeare again?
Every night, Shakespeare. And **dirges**. Always dirges. What about the sonnets?
But what shabby excuses for **lives** do we lead? Why shall we not recite **dirges?**
"I am slain by a fair cruel maid. My shroud of white, stuck all with yew..."
A-5
A-6
A-4
BRRRZZZT
A-4
A-5
CRRRRSSSH
A-6
Maybe **dirges** are appropriate.

This is a **restricted area!** Defensive actions will be taken...

...**Now!**

ZAP

A-5

BLASSSZT

ZIZZZZZ

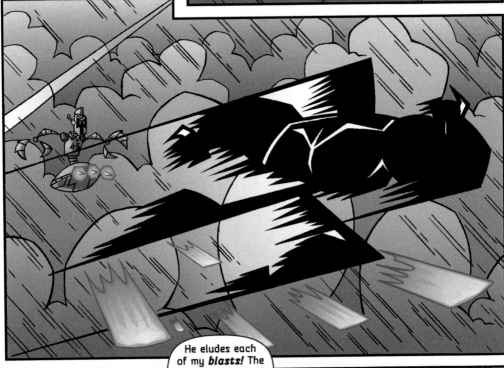

He eludes each of my **blasts!** The outcome is logically pre-ordained: the probability of a hit is near nill!

"Not a flower, not a flower **sweet** on my black coffin let there be strewn."

Thanks, Will. **"Twelfth Night"** was awewsome!

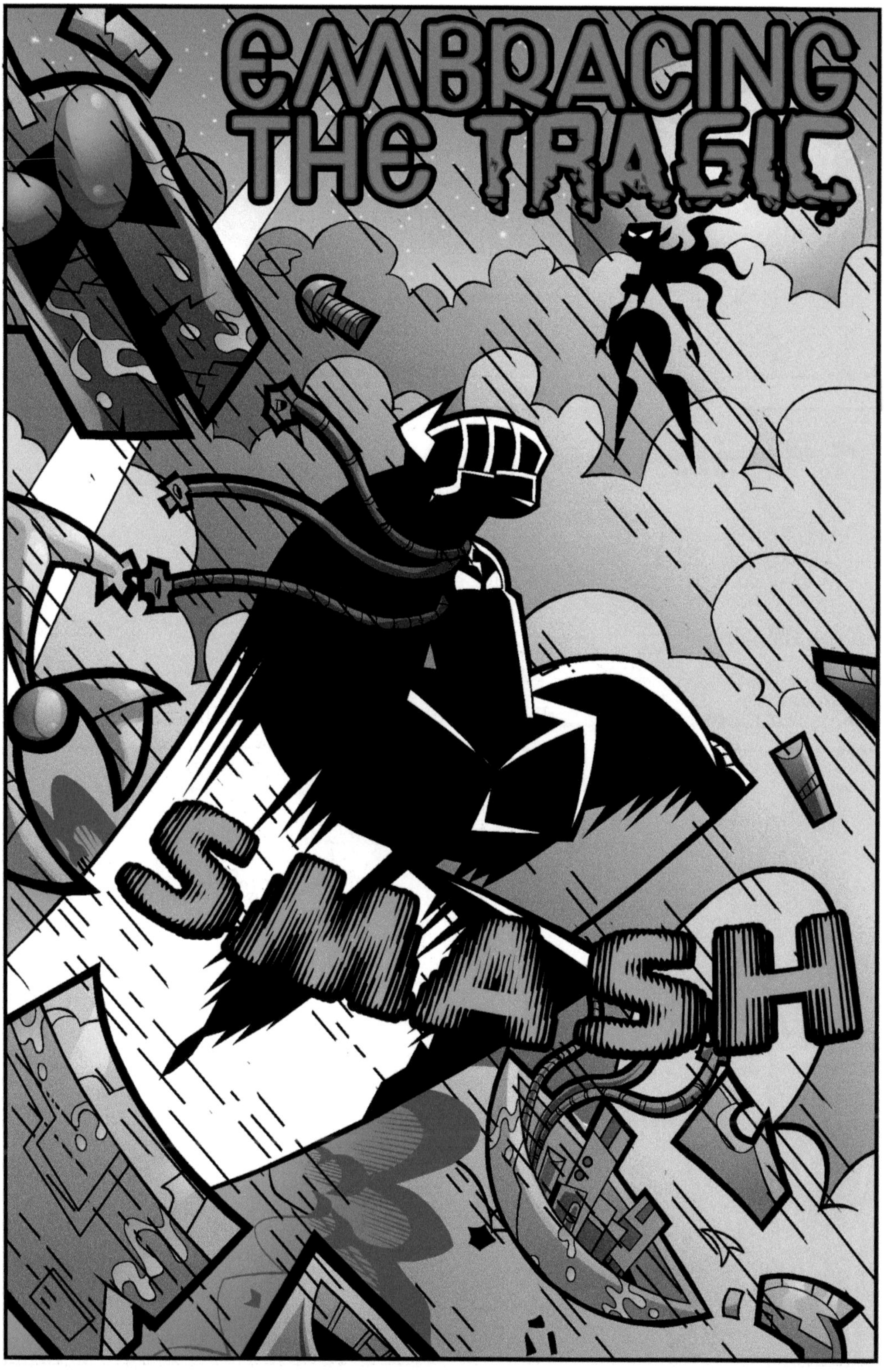
EMBRACING
THE TRAGIC
SMASH

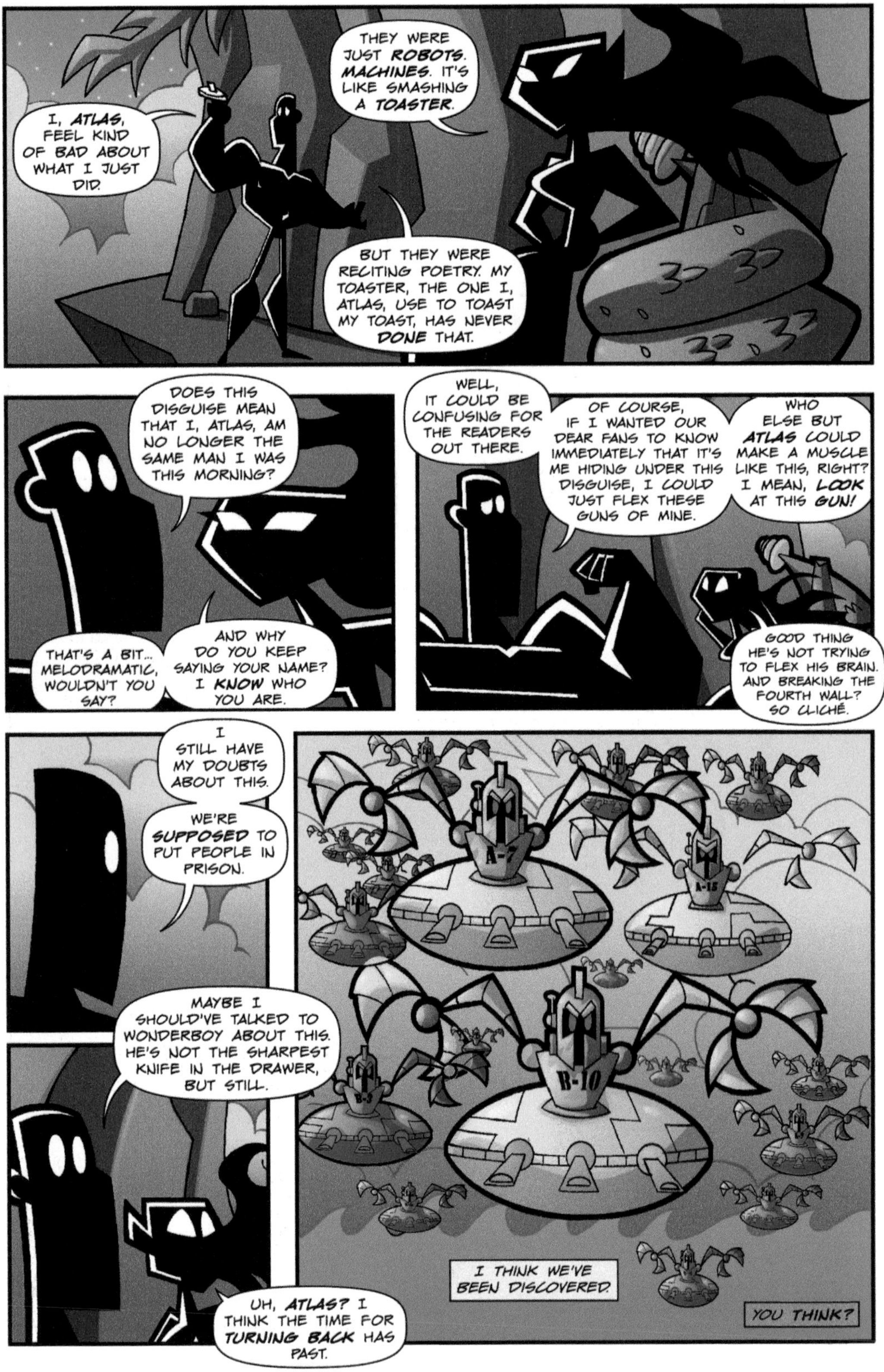
I, ATLAS, FEEL KIND OF BAD ABOUT WHAT I JUST DID.
THEY WERE JUST ROBOTS. MACHINES. IT'S LIKE SMASHING A TOASTER.
BUT THEY WERE RECITING POETRY. MY TOASTER, THE ONE I, ATLAS, USE TO TOAST MY TOAST, HAS NEVER DONE THAT.
DOES THIS DISGUISE MEAN THAT I, ATLAS, AM NO LONGER THE SAME MAN I WAS THIS MORNING?
THAT'S A BIT... MELODRAMATIC, WOULDN'T YOU SAY?
AND WHY DO YOU KEEP SAYING YOUR NAME? I KNOW WHO YOU ARE.
WELL, IT COULD BE CONFUSING FOR THE READERS OUT THERE.
OF COURSE, IF I WANTED OUR DEAR FANS TO KNOW IMMEDIATELY THAT IT'S ME HIDING UNDER THIS DISGUISE, I COULD JUST FLEX THESE GUNS OF MINE.
WHO ELSE BUT ATLAS COULD MAKE A MUSCLE LIKE THIS, RIGHT? I MEAN, LOOK AT THIS GUN!
GOOD THING HE'S NOT TRYING TO FLEX HIS BRAIN. AND BREAKING THE FOURTH WALL? SO CLICHÉ.
I STILL HAVE MY DOUBTS ABOUT THIS.
WE'RE SUPPOSED TO PUT PEOPLE IN PRISON.
MAYBE I SHOULD'VE TALKED TO WONDERBOY ABOUT THIS. HE'S NOT THE SHARPEST KNIFE IN THE DRAWER, BUT STILL.
UH, ATLAS? I THINK THE TIME FOR TURNING BACK HAS PAST.
A-7
A-15
B-10
B-3
I THINK WE'VE BEEN DISCOVERED.
YOU THINK?

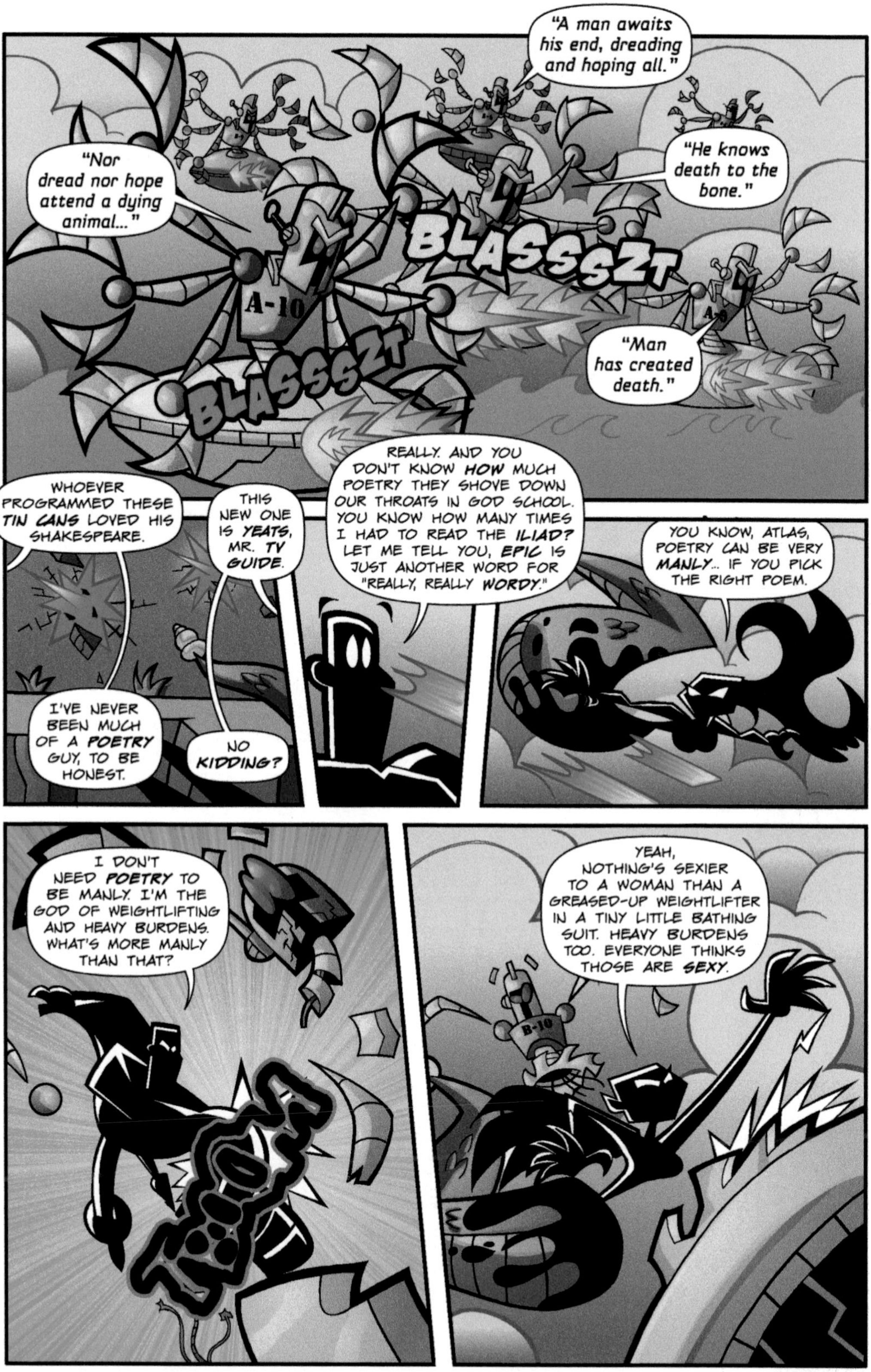
"Nor dread nor hope attend a dying animal..."
"A man awaits his end, dreading and hoping all."
"He knows death to the bone."
BLASSSSZT
"Man has created death."
BLASSSSZT
WHOEVER PROGRAMMED THESE TIN CANS LOVED HIS SHAKESPEARE.
THIS NEW ONE IS YEATS, MR. TV GUIDE.
I'VE NEVER BEEN MUCH OF A POETRY GUY, TO BE HONEST.
NO KIDDING?
REALLY. AND YOU DON'T KNOW HOW MUCH POETRY THEY SHOVE DOWN OUR THROATS IN GOD SCHOOL. YOU KNOW HOW MANY TIMES I HAD TO READ THE ILIAD? LET ME TELL YOU, EPIC IS JUST ANOTHER WORD FOR "REALLY, REALLY WORDY."
YOU KNOW, ATLAS, POETRY CAN BE VERY MANLY... IF YOU PICK THE RIGHT POEM.
I DON'T NEED POETRY TO BE MANLY. I'M THE GOD OF WEIGHTLIFTING AND HEAVY BURDENS. WHAT'S MORE MANLY THAN THAT?
YEAH, NOTHING'S SEXIER TO A WOMAN THAN A GREASED-UP WEIGHTLIFTER IN A TINY LITTLE BATHING SUIT. HEAVY BURDENS TOO. EVERYONE THINKS THOSE ARE SEXY.

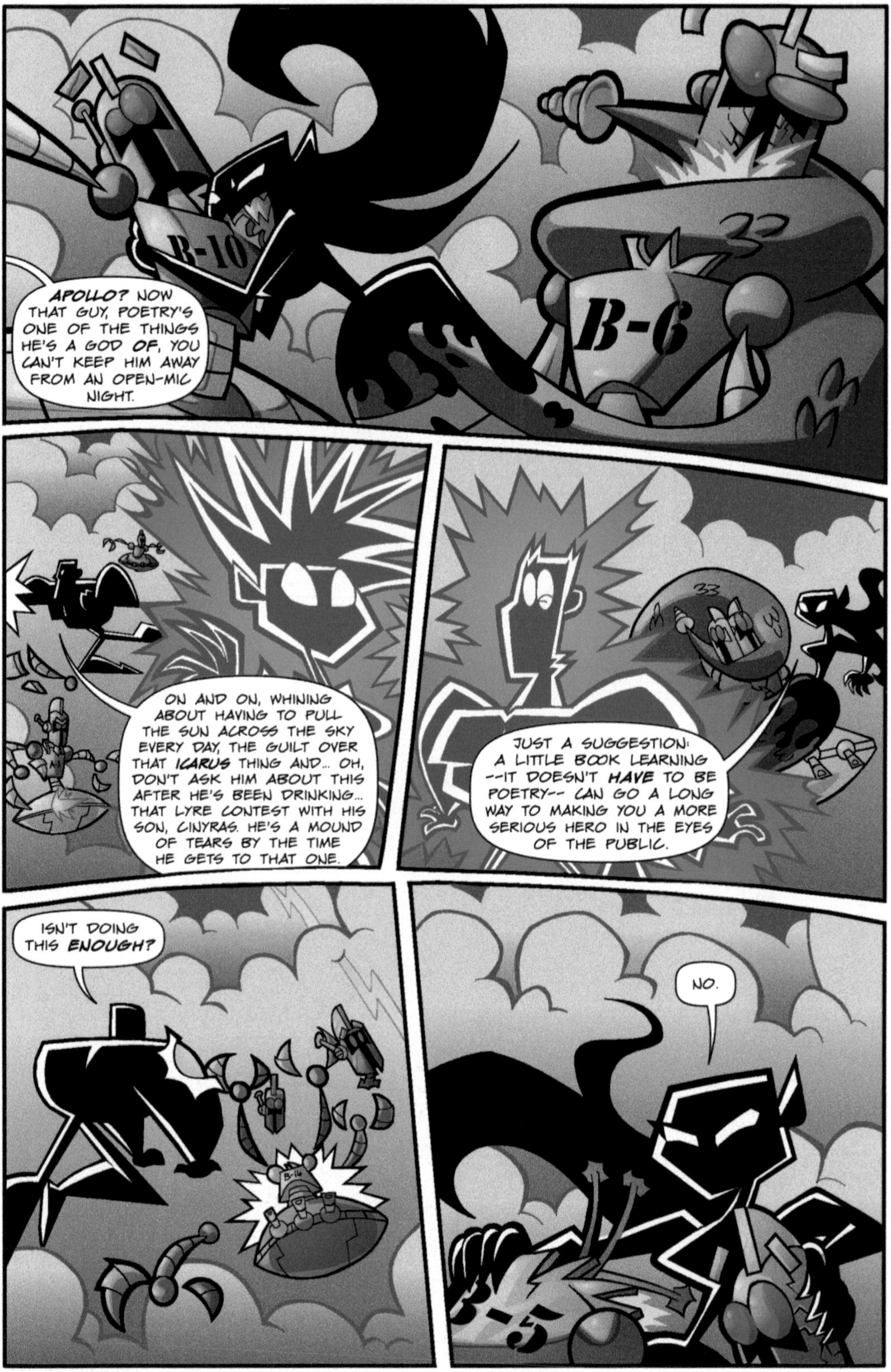

B-10
B-6
APOLLO? NOW THAT GUY, POETRY'S ONE OF THE THINGS HE'S A GOD OF, YOU CAN'T KEEP HIM AWAY FROM AN OPEN-MIC NIGHT.
ON AND ON, WHINING ABOUT HAVING TO PULL THE SUN ACROSS THE SKY EVERY DAY, THE GUILT OVER THAT ICARUS THING AND... OH, DON'T ASK HIM ABOUT THIS AFTER HE'S BEEN DRINKING... THAT LYRE CONTEST WITH HIS SON, CINYRAS. HE'S A MOUND OF TEARS BY THE TIME HE GETS TO THAT ONE.
JUST A SUGGESTION: A LITTLE BOOK LEARNING --IT DOESN'T HAVE TO BE POETRY-- CAN GO A LONG WAY TO MAKING YOU A MORE SERIOUS HERO IN THE EYES OF THE PUBLIC.
ISN'T DOING THIS ENOUGH?
NO.

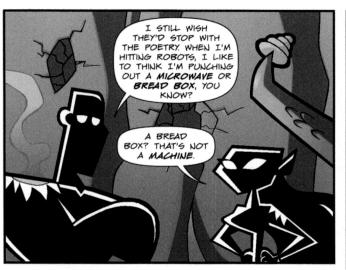

I STILL WISH THEY'D STOP WITH THE POETRY. WHEN I'M HITTING ROBOTS, I LIKE TO THINK I'M PUNCHING OUT A *MICROWAVE* OR *BREAD BOX*, YOU KNOW?

A BREAD BOX? THAT'S NOT A *MACHINE*.

WE'LL LEAVE THAT ARGUMENT FOR ANOTHER DAY --AND MAYBE A TRIP TO *WIKIPEDIA*-- BUT FOR NOW, I GUESS IT'S TIME TO GET THIS OVER WITH.

THE PRISON'S RIGHT UP THERE... THROUGH THE FORBIDDING FOG... OF *COURSE*.

THE MOST POWERFUL OF ALL THE WORLD'S SUPERVILLAINS, THE MOST HATED TERRORISTS, MONSTERS FROM OTHER WORLDS, THEY'RE ALL IN THERE.

AND GLUTTON *TOO?*

YES. HIM TOO.

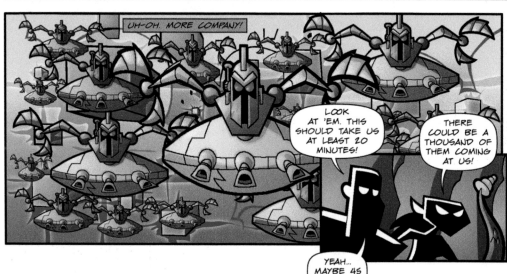

UH-OH. MORE COMPANY!

LOOK AT 'EM. THIS SHOULD TAKE US AT LEAST 20 MINUTES!

THERE COULD BE A THOUSAND OF THEM COMING AT US!

YEAH... MAYBE 45 MINUTES.

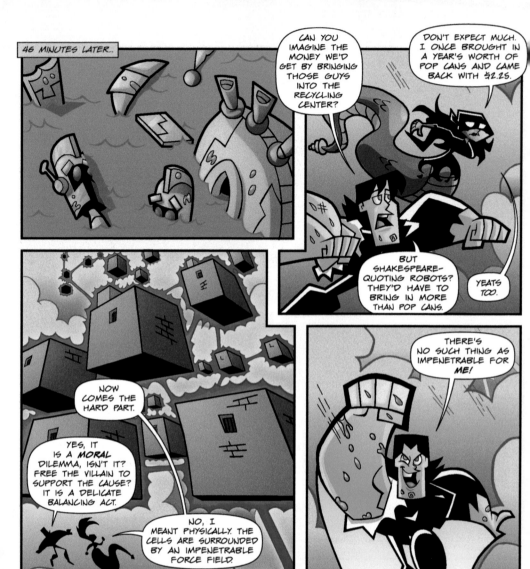

46 MINUTES LATER...

CAN YOU IMAGINE THE MONEY WE'D GET BY BRINGING THOSE GUYS INTO THE RECYCLING CENTER?

DON'T EXPECT MUCH. I ONCE BROUGHT IN A YEAR'S WORTH OF POP CANS AND CAME BACK WITH $2.25.

BUT SHAKESPEARE-QUOTING ROBOTS? THEY'D HAVE TO BRING IN MORE THAN POP CANS.

YEATS TOO.

NOW COMES THE HARD PART.

YES, IT IS A *MORAL* DILEMMA, ISN'T IT? FREE THE VILLAIN TO SUPPORT THE CAUSE? IT IS A DELICATE BALANCING ACT.

NO, I MEANT PHYSICALLY. THE CELLS ARE SURROUNDED BY AN IMPENETRABLE FORCE FIELD.

THERE'S NO SUCH THING AS IMPENETRABLE FOR *ME!*

ZZZZAP

WELL, MAYBE THERE'S *ONE* IMPENETRABLE THING. JUST ONE.

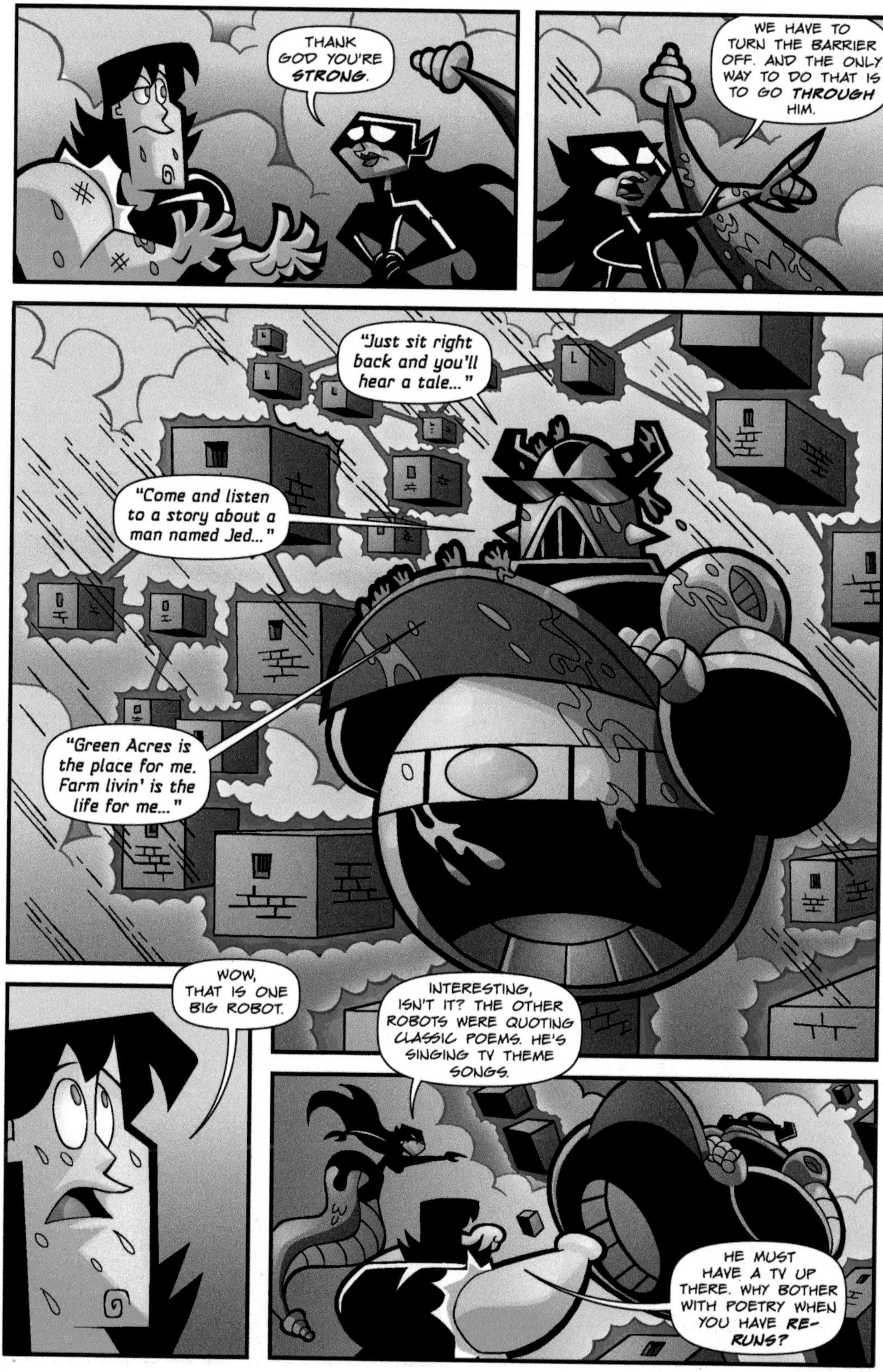
THANK GOD YOU'RE STRONG.
WE HAVE TO TURN THE BARRIER OFF. AND THE ONLY WAY TO DO THAT IS TO GO THROUGH HIM.
"Just sit right back and you'll hear a tale..."
"Come and listen to a story about a man named Jed..."
"Green Acres is the place for me. Farm livin' is the life for me..."
WOW, THAT IS ONE BIG ROBOT.
INTERESTING, ISN'T IT? THE OTHER ROBOTS WERE QUOTING CLASSIC POEMS. HE'S SINGING TV THEME SONGS.
HE MUST HAVE A TV UP THERE. WHY BOTHER WITH POETRY WHEN YOU HAVE RE-RUNS?

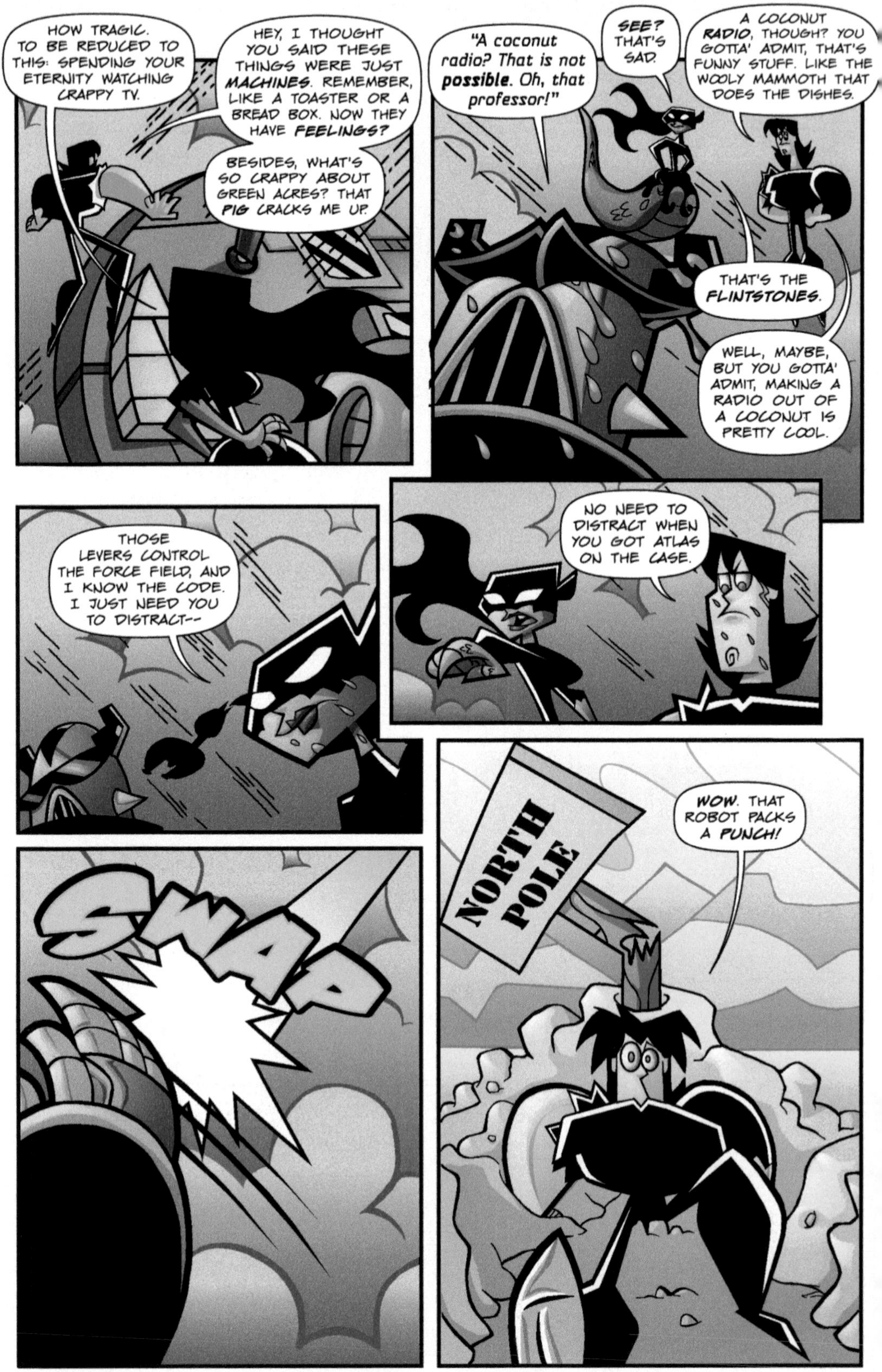
HOW TRAGIC. TO BE REDUCED TO THIS: SPENDING YOUR ETERNITY WATCHING CRAPPY TV.
HEY, I THOUGHT YOU SAID THESE THINGS WERE JUST MACHINES. REMEMBER, LIKE A TOASTER OR A BREAD BOX. NOW THEY HAVE FEELINGS?
BESIDES, WHAT'S SO CRAPPY ABOUT GREEN ACRES? THAT PIG CRACKS ME UP.
"A coconut radio? That is not possible. Oh, that professor!"
SEE? THAT'S SAD.
A COCONUT RADIO, THOUGH? YOU GOTTA' ADMIT, THAT'S FUNNY STUFF. LIKE THE WOOLY MAMMOTH THAT DOES THE DISHES.
THAT'S THE FLINTSTONES.
WELL, MAYBE, BUT YOU GOTTA' ADMIT, MAKING A RADIO OUT OF A COCONUT IS PRETTY COOL.
THOSE LEVERS CONTROL THE FORCE FIELD, AND I KNOW THE CODE. I JUST NEED YOU TO DISTRACT--
NO NEED TO DISTRACT WHEN YOU GOT ATLAS ON THE CASE.
SWAP
NORTH POLE
WOW. THAT ROBOT PACKS A PUNCH!

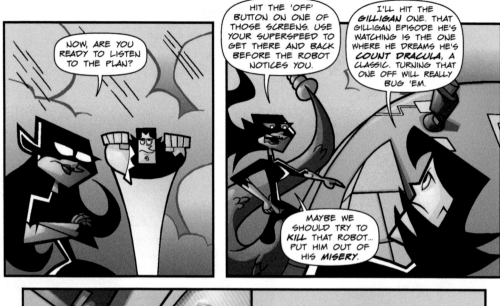

NOW, ARE YOU READY TO LISTEN TO THE PLAN?

HIT THE 'OFF' BUTTON ON ONE OF THOSE SCREENS. USE YOUR SUPERSPEED TO GET THERE AND BACK BEFORE THE ROBOT NOTICES YOU.

I'LL HIT THE *GILLIGAN* ONE. THAT GILLIGAN EPISODE HE'S WATCHING IS THE ONE WHERE HE DREAMS HE'S *COUNT DRACULA*, A CLASSIC. TURNING THAT ONE OFF WILL REALLY BUG 'EM.

MAYBE WE SHOULD TRY TO *KILL* THAT ROBOT... PUT HIM OUT OF HIS *MISERY*.

IT WORKED. HE DIDN'T EVEN NOTICE I TURNED OFF THE FORCE FIELD. SOMETIMES, ATLAS, STEALTH AND BRAINS TRUMP BRAWN AND FORCE.

OH, THAT BEVERLY HILLBILLIES ONE ISN'T BAD, EITHER. IT'S THE ONE WHERE JETRHO GOES TO SCHOOL. GREAT STUFF. HUMANS DON'T REALIZE HOW LUCKY THEY ARE TO HAVE TV.

"Get that bat, Skipper! Ha-ha-ha!"

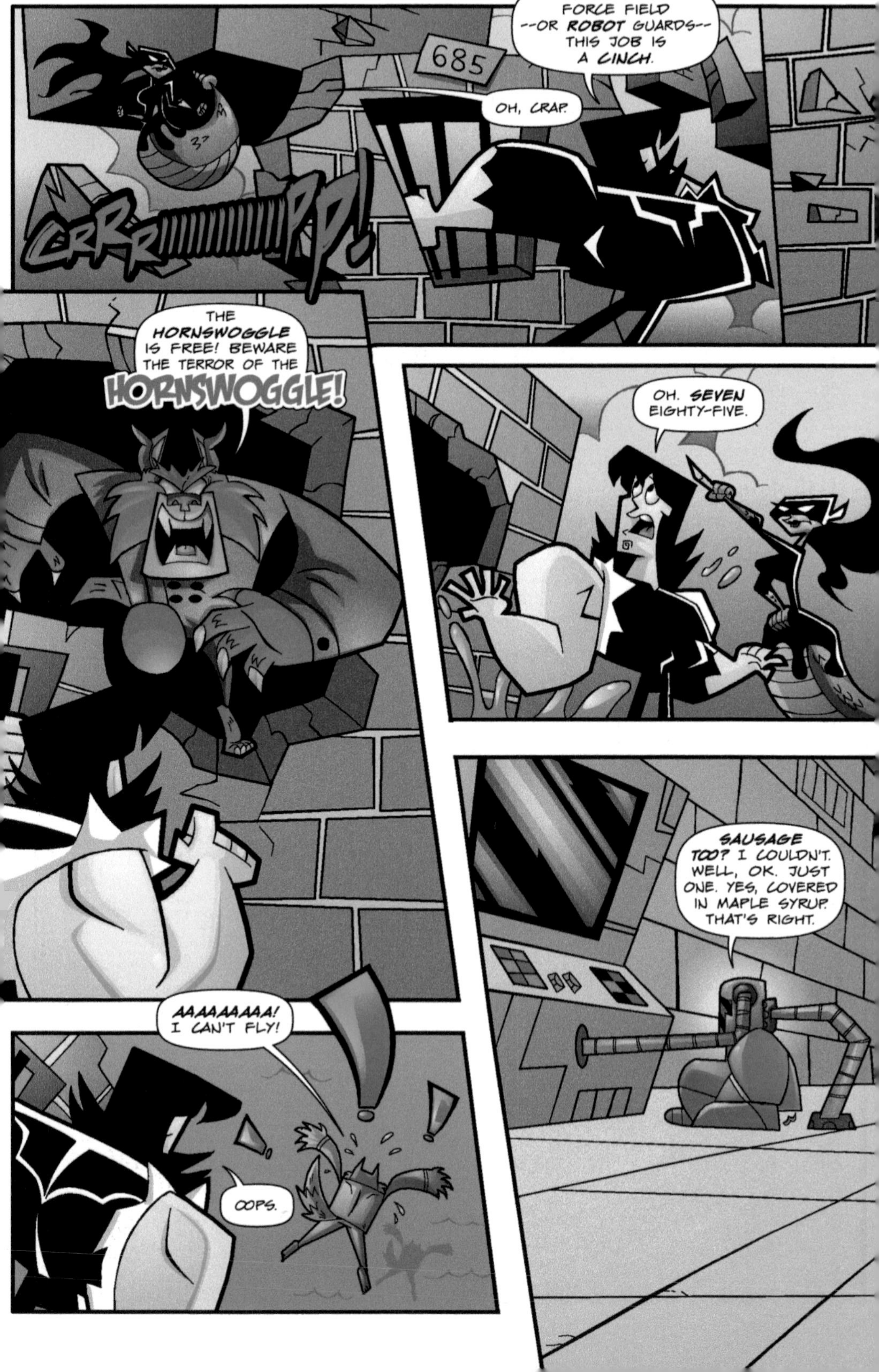
685
WITHOUT A FORCE FIELD --OR ROBOT GUARDS-- THIS JOB IS A CINCH.
OH, CRAP.
CRRRIIIIIIIIIIPP!
THE HORNSWOGGLE IS FREE! BEWARE THE TERROR OF THE HORNSWOGGLE!
OH. SEVEN EIGHTY-FIVE.
SAUSAGE TOO? I COULDN'T. WELL, OK. JUST ONE. YES, COVERED IN MAPLE SYRUP. THAT'S RIGHT.
AAAAAAAAA! I CAN'T FLY!
OOPS.

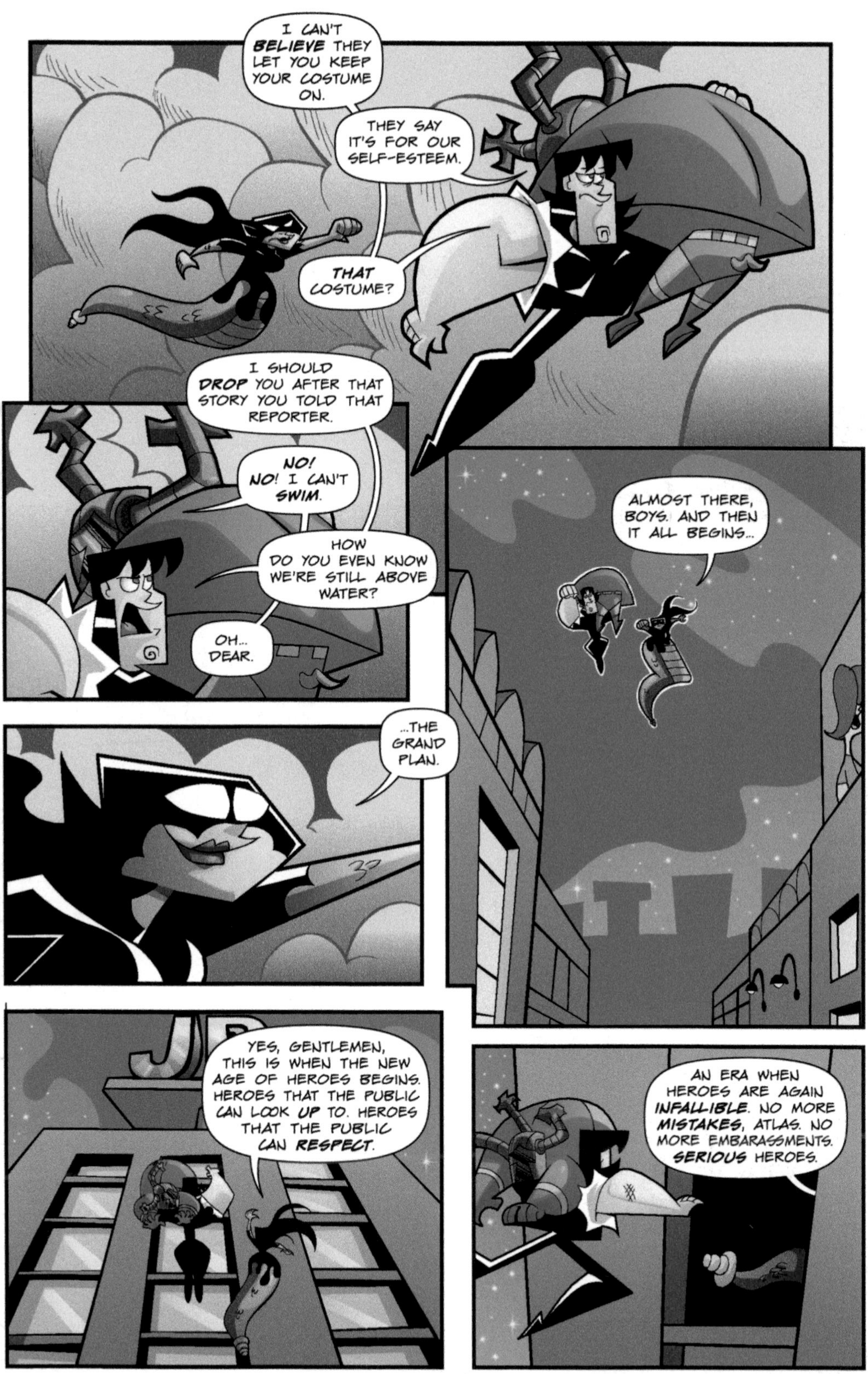
I CAN'T BELIEVE THEY LET YOU KEEP YOUR COSTUME ON.
THEY SAY IT'S FOR OUR SELF-ESTEEM.
THAT COSTUME?
I SHOULD DROP YOU AFTER THAT STORY YOU TOLD THAT REPORTER.
NO! NO! I CAN'T SWIM.
HOW DO YOU EVEN KNOW WE'RE STILL ABOVE WATER?
OH... DEAR.
ALMOST THERE, BOYS. AND THEN IT ALL BEGINS...
...THE GRAND PLAN.
YES, GENTLEMEN, THIS IS WHEN THE NEW AGE OF HEROES BEGINS. HEROES THAT THE PUBLIC CAN LOOK UP TO. HEROES THAT THE PUBLIC CAN RESPECT.
AN ERA WHEN HEROES ARE AGAIN INFALLIBLE. NO MORE MISTAKES, ATLAS. NO MORE EMBARASSMENTS. SERIOUS HEROES.

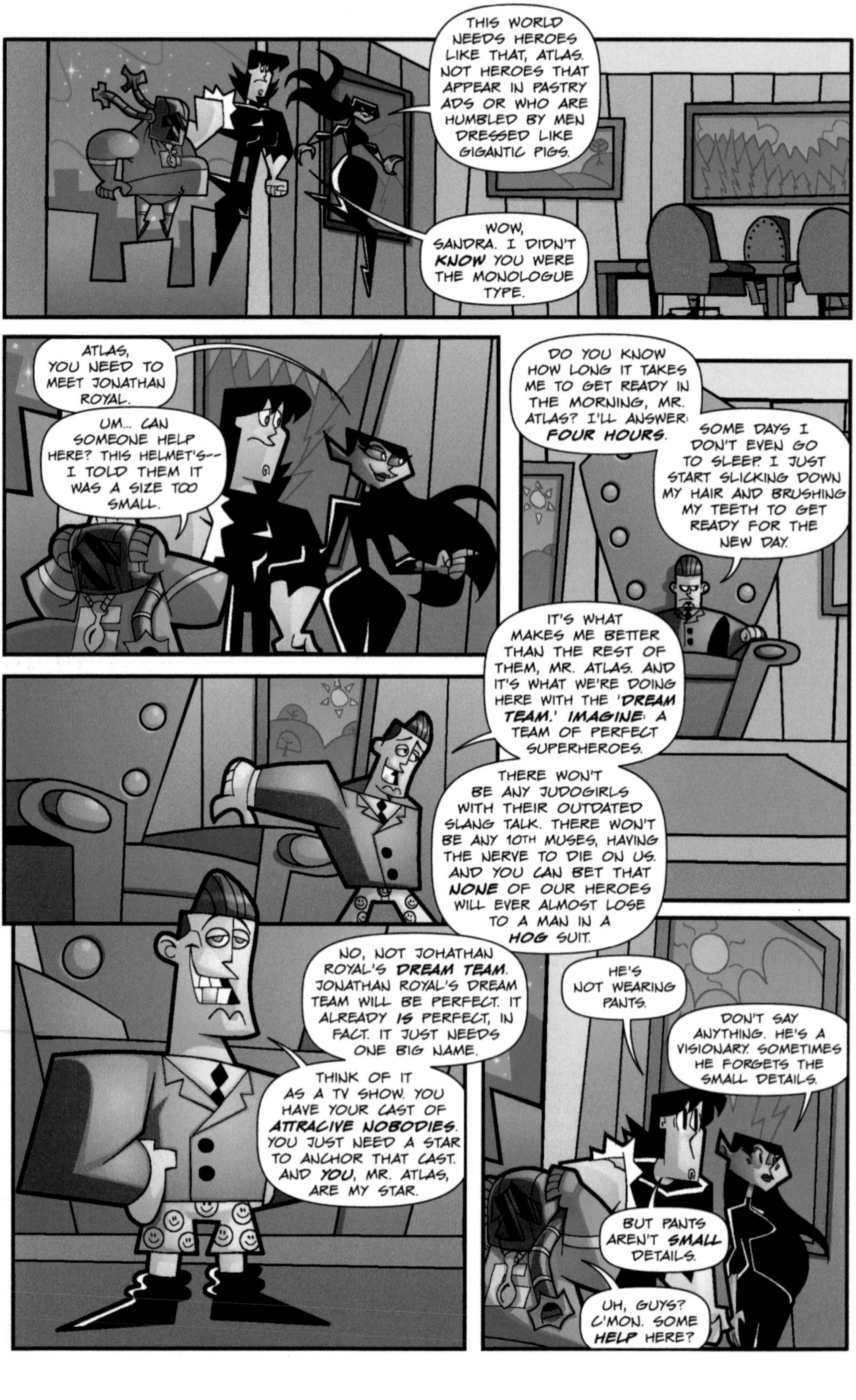

THIS WORLD NEEDS HEROES LIKE THAT, ATLAS. NOT HEROES THAT APPEAR IN PASTRY ADS OR WHO ARE HUMBLED BY MEN DRESSED LIKE GIGANTIC PIGS.
WOW, SANDRA. I DIDN'T **KNOW** YOU WERE THE MONOLOGUE TYPE.
ATLAS, YOU NEED TO MEET JONATHAN ROYAL.
UM... CAN SOMEONE HELP HERE? THIS HELMET'S-- I TOLD THEM IT WAS A SIZE TOO SMALL.
DO YOU KNOW HOW LONG IT TAKES ME TO GET READY IN THE MORNING, MR. ATLAS? I'LL ANSWER: **FOUR HOURS**.
SOME DAYS I DON'T EVEN GO TO SLEEP. I JUST START SLICKING DOWN MY HAIR AND BRUSHING MY TEETH TO GET READY FOR THE NEW DAY.
IT'S WHAT MAKES ME BETTER THAN THE REST OF THEM, MR. ATLAS. AND IT'S WHAT WE'RE DOING HERE WITH THE '**DREAM TEAM.**' **IMAGINE**: A TEAM OF PERFECT SUPERHEROES.
THERE WON'T BE ANY JUDOGIRLS WITH THEIR OUTDATED SLANG TALK. THERE WON'T BE ANY 10TH MUSES, HAVING THE NERVE TO DIE ON US. AND YOU CAN BET THAT **NONE** OF OUR HEROES WILL EVER ALMOST LOSE TO A MAN IN A **HOG** SUIT.
NO, NOT JOHATHAN ROYAL'S **DREAM TEAM**. JONATHAN ROYAL'S DREAM TEAM WILL BE PERFECT. IT ALREADY **IS** PERFECT, IN FACT. IT JUST NEEDS ONE BIG NAME.
THINK OF IT AS A TV SHOW. YOU HAVE YOUR CAST OF **ATTRACIVE NOBODIES**. YOU JUST NEED A STAR TO ANCHOR THAT CAST. AND **YOU**, MR. ATLAS, ARE MY STAR.
HE'S NOT WEARING PANTS.
DON'T SAY ANYTHING. HE'S A VISIONARY. SOMETIMES HE FORGETS THE SMALL DETAILS.
BUT PANTS AREN'T **SMALL** DETAILS.
UH, GUYS? C'MON. SOME **HELP** HERE?

WHAT DO YOU SAY, *MR. ATLAS*. YOU WANT TO BE THE STAR OF JONATHAN ROYAL'S DREAM TEAM?

THAT IS HOW WE REFER TO THE DREAM TEAM, BY THE WAY: JONATHAN ROYAL'S DREAM TEAM. *ALWAYS*. THAT'S COPYRIGHTED.

YOU WANT TO MEET JONATHAN ROYAL'S DREAM TEAM? MEET THE *FUTURE SUPERSTARS* OF THIS CITY?

SURE?

WELL, YOU CAN'T... *YET*. WE HAVEN'T FILLED THE ROLES YET. WE HAVE THE NAMES DOWN, THOUGH, DUSTBUSTER, REPO, FROSTBITE, POWERPUNCH. WE'RE STILL LOOKING FOR THE RIGHT... *PERFORMERS*. IN THE MEANTIME, THOUGH...

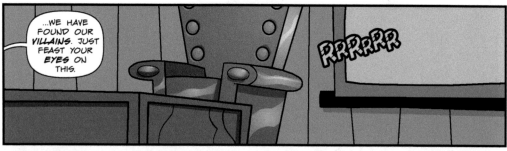

...WE HAVE FOUND OUR *VILLAINS*. JUST FEAST YOUR *EYES* ON THIS.

RRRRR

BEHOLD, THE GROTESQUE *GLUTTON* AND HIS ARMY OF METAL FOOD-BOTS! GUARANTEED TO GIVE THE WORLD A FIRST-CLASS *STOMACH ACHE!*

SORRY ABOUT "GROTESQUE." I COULDN'T THINK OF ANOTHER FITTING WORD THAT STARTED WITH "G."

METAL *FOOD-BOTS?* I DON'T HAVE METAL *FOOD-BOTS.*

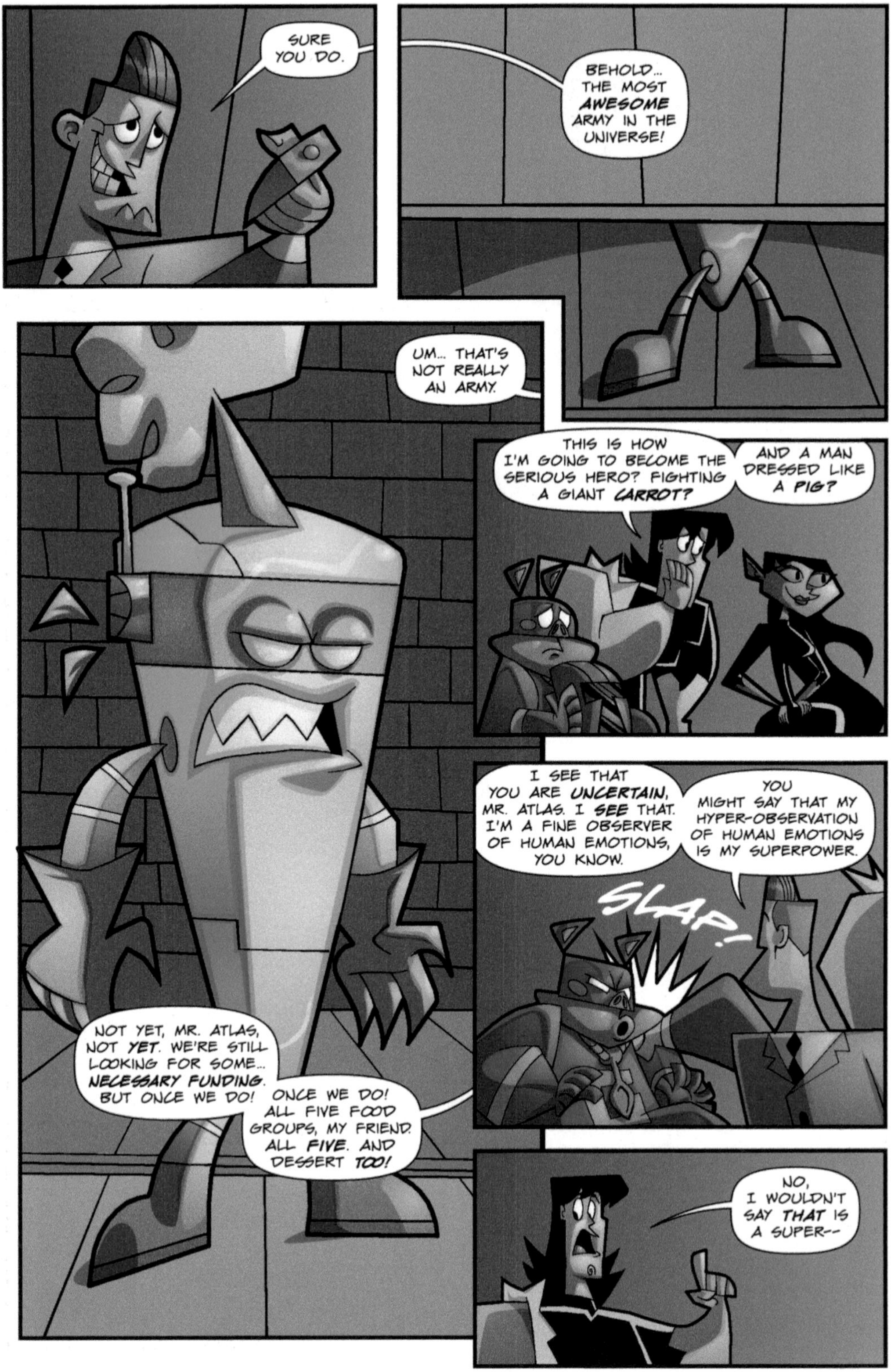
SURE YOU DO.
BEHOLD... THE MOST AWESOME ARMY IN THE UNIVERSE!
UM... THAT'S NOT REALLY AN ARMY.
THIS IS HOW I'M GOING TO BECOME THE SERIOUS HERO? FIGHTING A GIANT CARROT?
AND A MAN DRESSED LIKE A PIG?
NOT YET, MR. ATLAS, NOT YET. WE'RE STILL LOOKING FOR SOME... NECESSARY FUNDING. BUT ONCE WE DO!
ONCE WE DO! ALL FIVE FOOD GROUPS, MY FRIEND. ALL FIVE. AND DESSERT TOO!
I SEE THAT YOU ARE UNCERTAIN, MR. ATLAS. I SEE THAT. I'M A FINE OBSERVER OF HUMAN EMOTIONS, YOU KNOW.
YOU MIGHT SAY THAT MY HYPER-OBSERVATION OF HUMAN EMOTIONS IS MY SUPERPOWER.
SLAP!
NO, I WOULDN'T SAY THAT IS A SUPER--

HOW MANY OF THESE THINGS DOES HE HAVE IN HERE?

IT'S ONE OF THE REASONS WHY WE ONLY HAVE ONE *CARROT*.

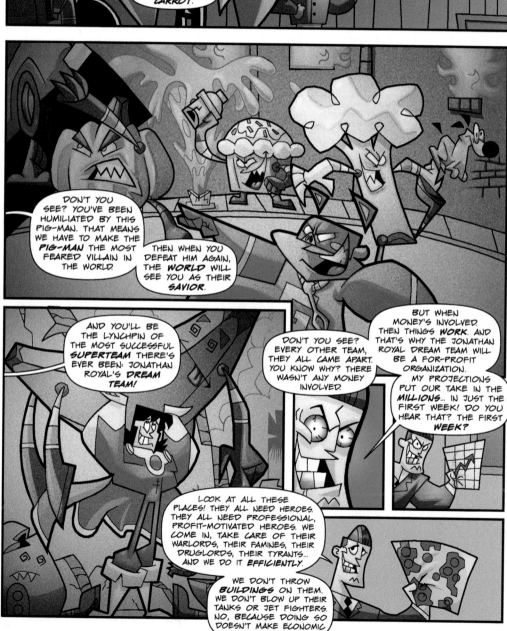

DON'T YOU SEE? YOU'VE BEEN HUMILIATED BY THIS *PIG-MAN*. THAT MEANS WE HAVE TO MAKE THE *PIG-MAN* THE MOST FEARED VILLAIN IN THE WORLD.

THEN WHEN YOU DEFEAT HIM AGAIN, THE *WORLD* WILL SEE YOU AS THEIR *SAVIOR*.

AND YOU'LL BE THE LYNCHPIN OF THE MOST SUCCESSFUL *SUPERTEAM* THERE'S EVER BEEN: JONATHAN ROYAL'S *DREAM TEAM!*

DON'T YOU SEE? EVERY OTHER TEAM, THEY ALL CAME APART. YOU KNOW WHY? THERE WASN'T ANY MONEY INVOLVED.

BUT WHEN MONEY'S INVOLVED, THEN THINGS *WORK*. AND THAT'S WHY THE JONATHAN ROYAL DREAM TEAM WILL BE A FOR-PROFIT ORGANIZATION. MY PROJECTIONS PUT OUR TAKE IN THE *MILLIONS*... IN JUST THE FIRST WEEK! DO YOU HEAR THAT? THE FIRST *WEEK?*

LOOK AT ALL THESE PLACES! THEY ALL NEED HEROES. THEY ALL NEED PROFESSIONAL, PROFIT-MOTIVATED HEROES. WE COME IN, TAKE *CARE* OF THEIR WARLORDS, THEIR FAMINES, THEIR DRUGLORDS, THEIR TYRANTS... AND WE DO IT *EFFICIENTLY*.

WE DON'T THROW *BUILDINGS* ON THEM. WE DON'T BLOW UP THEIR TANKS OR JET FIGHTERS. NO, BECAUSE DOING SO DOESN'T MAKE ECONOMIC SENSE. *SEE?*

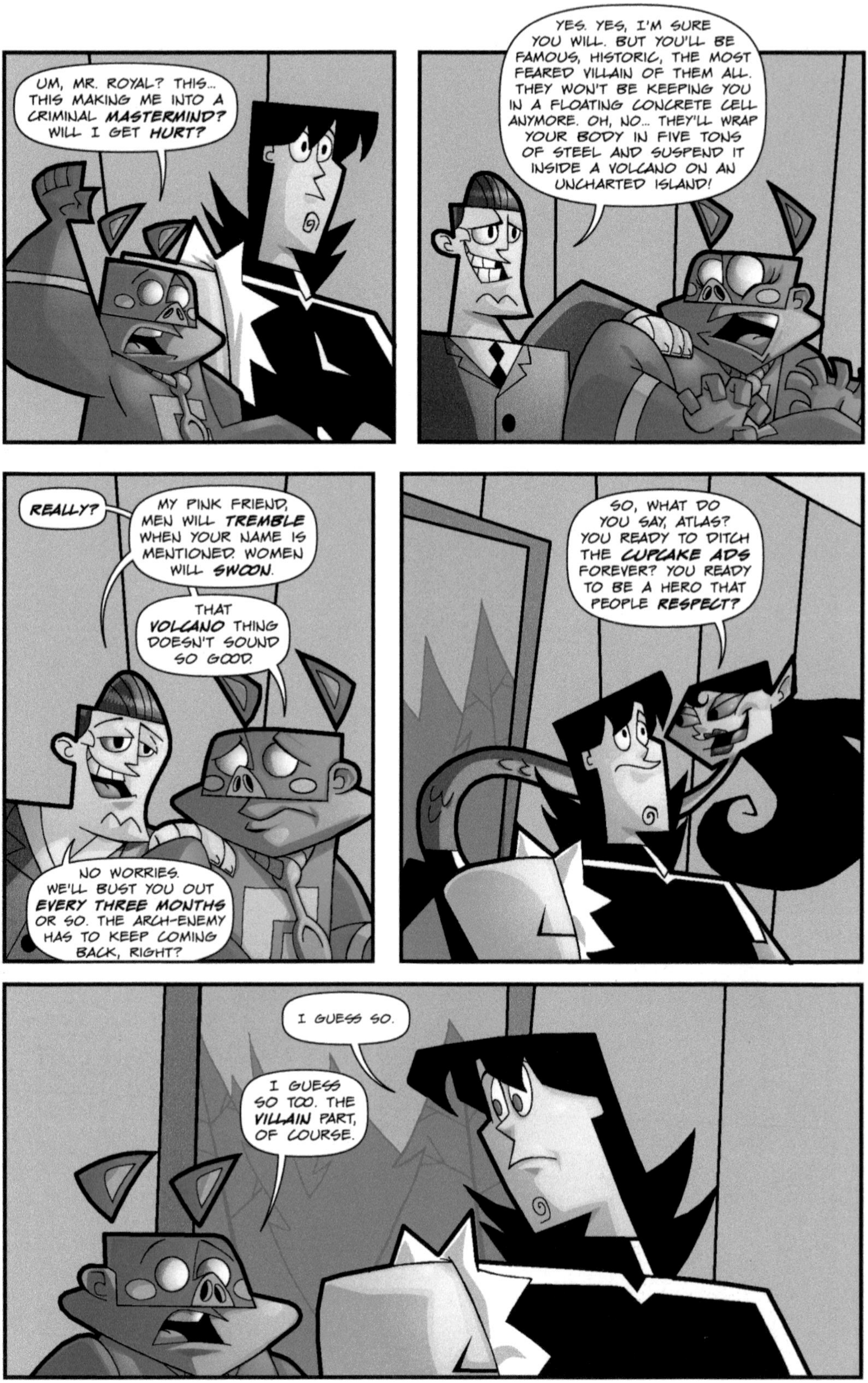
UM, MR. ROYAL? THIS... THIS MAKING ME INTO A CRIMINAL MASTERMIND? WILL I GET HURT?
YES. YES, I'M SURE YOU WILL. BUT YOU'LL BE FAMOUS, HISTORIC, THE MOST FEARED VILLAIN OF THEM ALL. THEY WON'T BE KEEPING YOU IN A FLOATING CONCRETE CELL ANYMORE. OH, NO... THEY'LL WRAP YOUR BODY IN FIVE TONS OF STEEL AND SUSPEND IT INSIDE A VOLCANO ON AN UNCHARTED ISLAND!
REALLY?
MY PINK FRIEND, MEN WILL TREMBLE WHEN YOUR NAME IS MENTIONED. WOMEN WILL SWOON.
THAT VOLCANO THING DOESN'T SOUND SO GOOD.
NO WORRIES. WE'LL BUST YOU OUT EVERY THREE MONTHS OR SO. THE ARCH-ENEMY HAS TO KEEP COMING BACK, RIGHT?
SO, WHAT DO YOU SAY, ATLAS? YOU READY TO DITCH THE CUPCAKE ADS FOREVER? YOU READY TO BE A HERO THAT PEOPLE RESPECT?
I GUESS SO.
I GUESS SO TOO. THE VILLAIN PART, OF COURSE.

WELL, THEN, I THINK WE NEED YOUR NEW COSTUME!

OOOPS, SORRY. THAT WAS PLAN '*A*.' THAT... *AHEM*... DIDN'T WORK OUT. LET'S SEE... AH, YES, PLAN '*B*.'

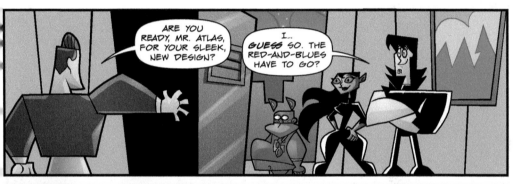

ARE YOU READY, MR. ATLAS, FOR YOUR SLEEK, NEW DESIGN?

I... *GUESS* SO. THE RED-AND-BLUES HAVE TO GO?

AND... HERE IT IS!

I... I... LOVE IT!

HEY, CAN I GET A NEW OUTFIT TOO?

LATER THAT DAY...

FWWOOOSH

RUN, FOOLS! RUN! AND TELL THE WORLD THAT *GLUTTON* IS ON THE *LOOSE!*

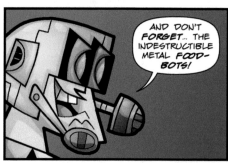

AND DON'T *FORGET...* THE INDESTRUCTIBLE METAL *FOOD-BOTS!*

FFFF-SMAAASH

AND THE *INDESTRUCTIBLE* METAL FOOD-BOT ARMY!

METAL *FOOD-BOT?* OF *COURSE* THEY'RE METAL!

I'VE NEVER SEEN A *NON-METAL* ROBOT.

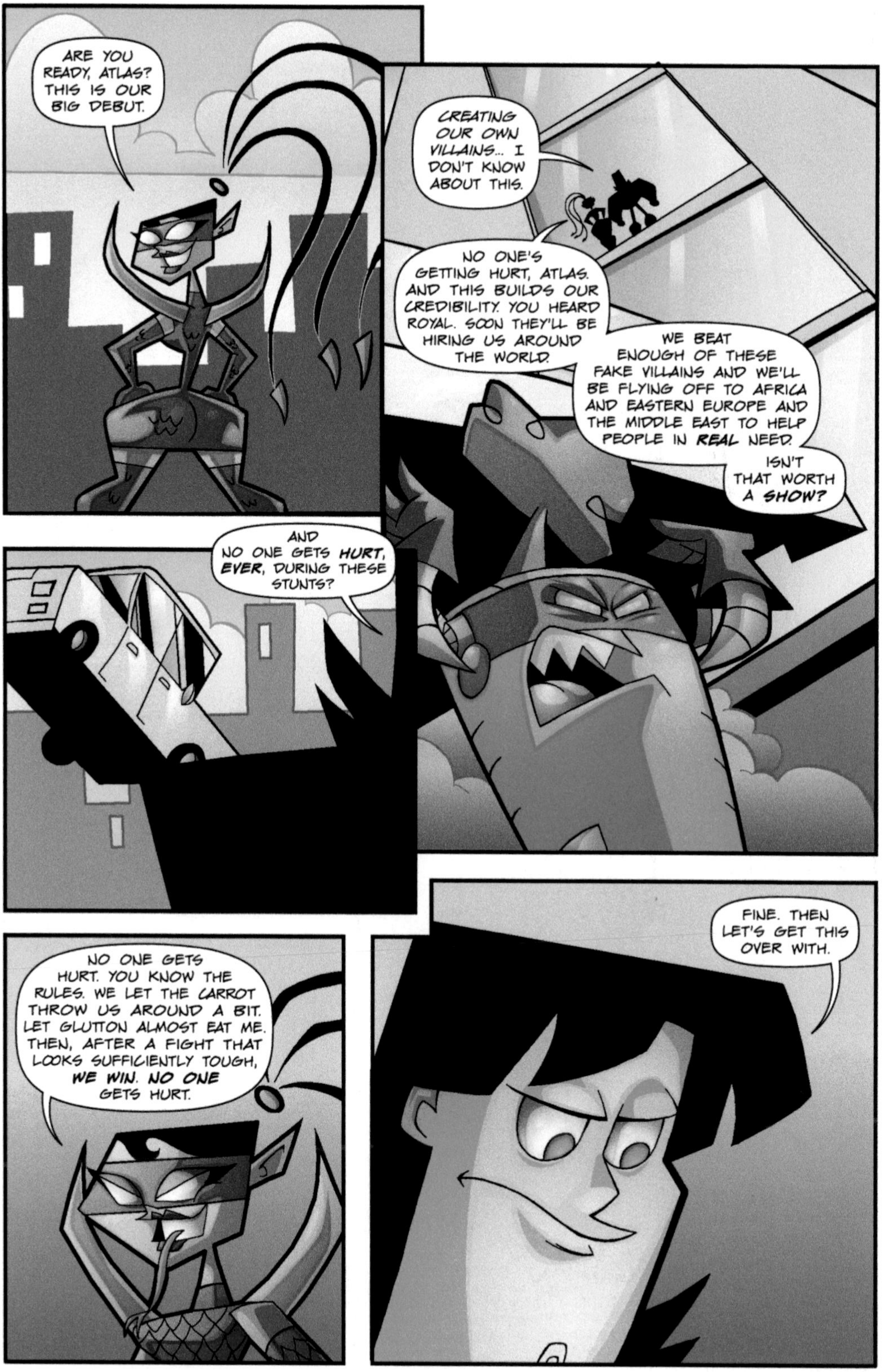
ARE YOU READY, ATLAS? THIS IS OUR BIG DEBUT.
CREATING OUR OWN VILLAINS... I DON'T KNOW ABOUT THIS.
NO ONE'S GETTING HURT, ATLAS. AND THIS BUILDS OUR CREDIBILITY. YOU HEARD ROYAL. SOON THEY'LL BE HIRING US AROUND THE WORLD.
WE BEAT ENOUGH OF THESE FAKE VILLAINS AND WE'LL BE FLYING OFF TO AFRICA AND EASTERN EUROPE AND THE MIDDLE EAST TO HELP PEOPLE IN REAL NEED.
ISN'T THAT WORTH A SHOW?
AND NO ONE GETS HURT, EVER, DURING THESE STUNTS?
NO ONE GETS HURT. YOU KNOW THE RULES. WE LET THE CARROT THROW US AROUND A BIT. LET GLUTTON ALMOST EAT ME. THEN, AFTER A FIGHT THAT LOOKS SUFFICIENTLY TOUGH, WE WIN. NO ONE GETS HURT.
FINE. THEN LET'S GET THIS OVER WITH.

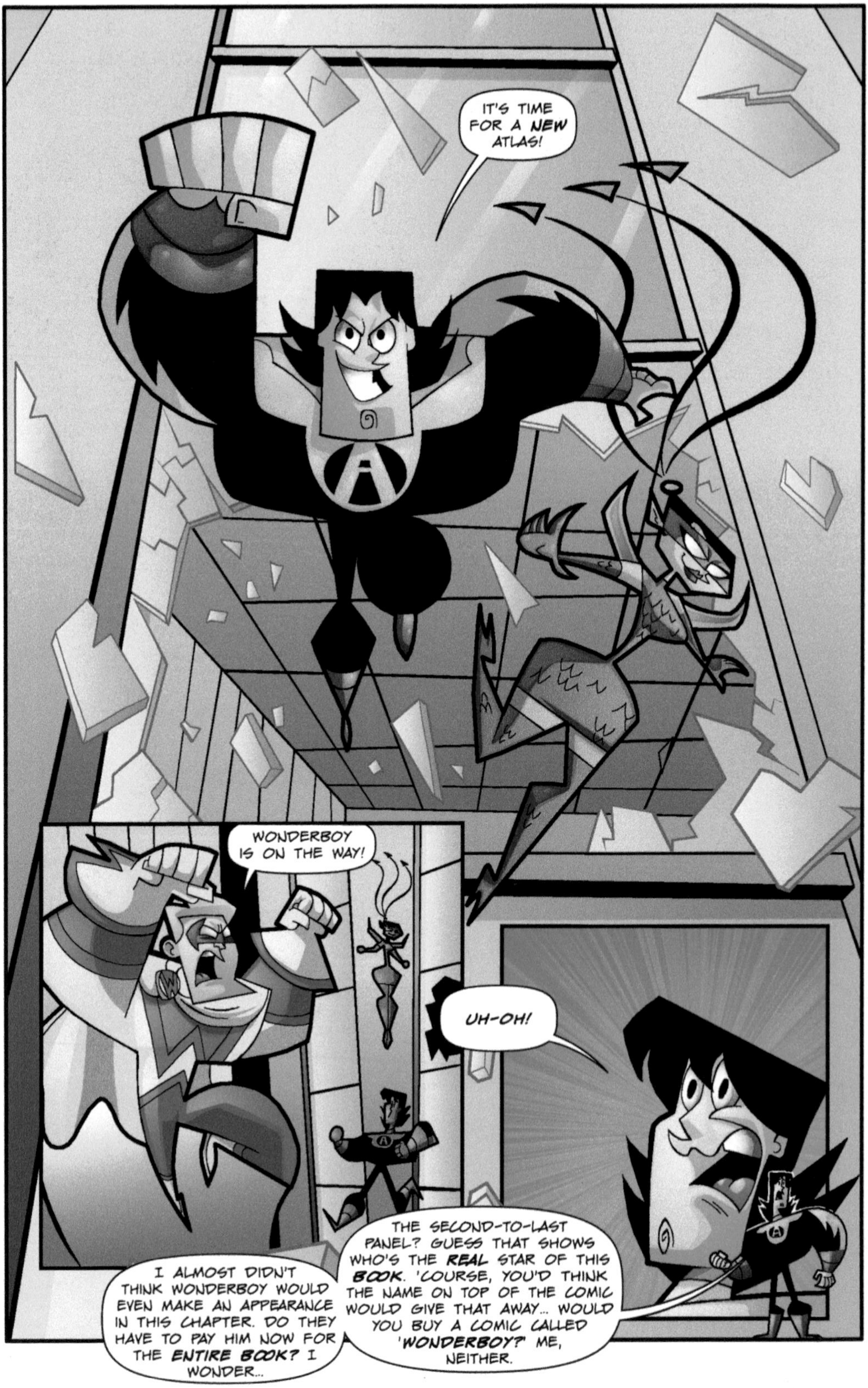
IT'S TIME FOR A NEW ATLAS!
WONDERBOY IS ON THE WAY!
UH-OH!
I ALMOST DIDN'T THINK WONDERBOY WOULD EVEN MAKE AN APPEARANCE IN THIS CHAPTER. DO THEY HAVE TO PAY HIM NOW FOR THE ENTIRE BOOK? I WONDER...
THE SECOND-TO-LAST PANEL? GUESS THAT SHOWS WHO'S THE REAL STAR OF THIS BOOK. 'COURSE, YOU'D THINK THE NAME ON TOP OF THE COMIC WOULD GIVE THAT AWAY... WOULD YOU BUY A COMIC CALLED 'WONDERBOY?' ME, NEITHER.

CHAPTER FOUR

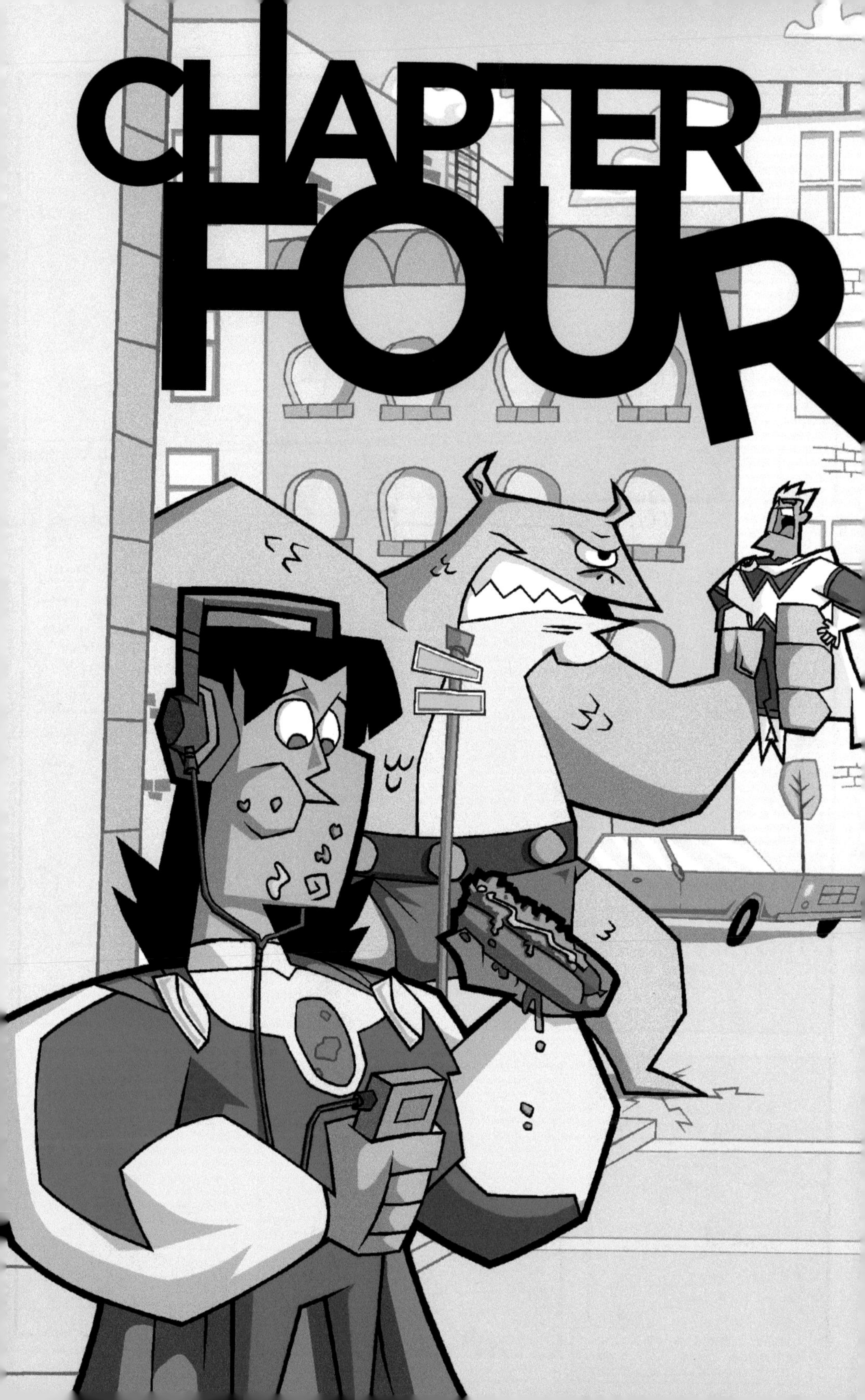

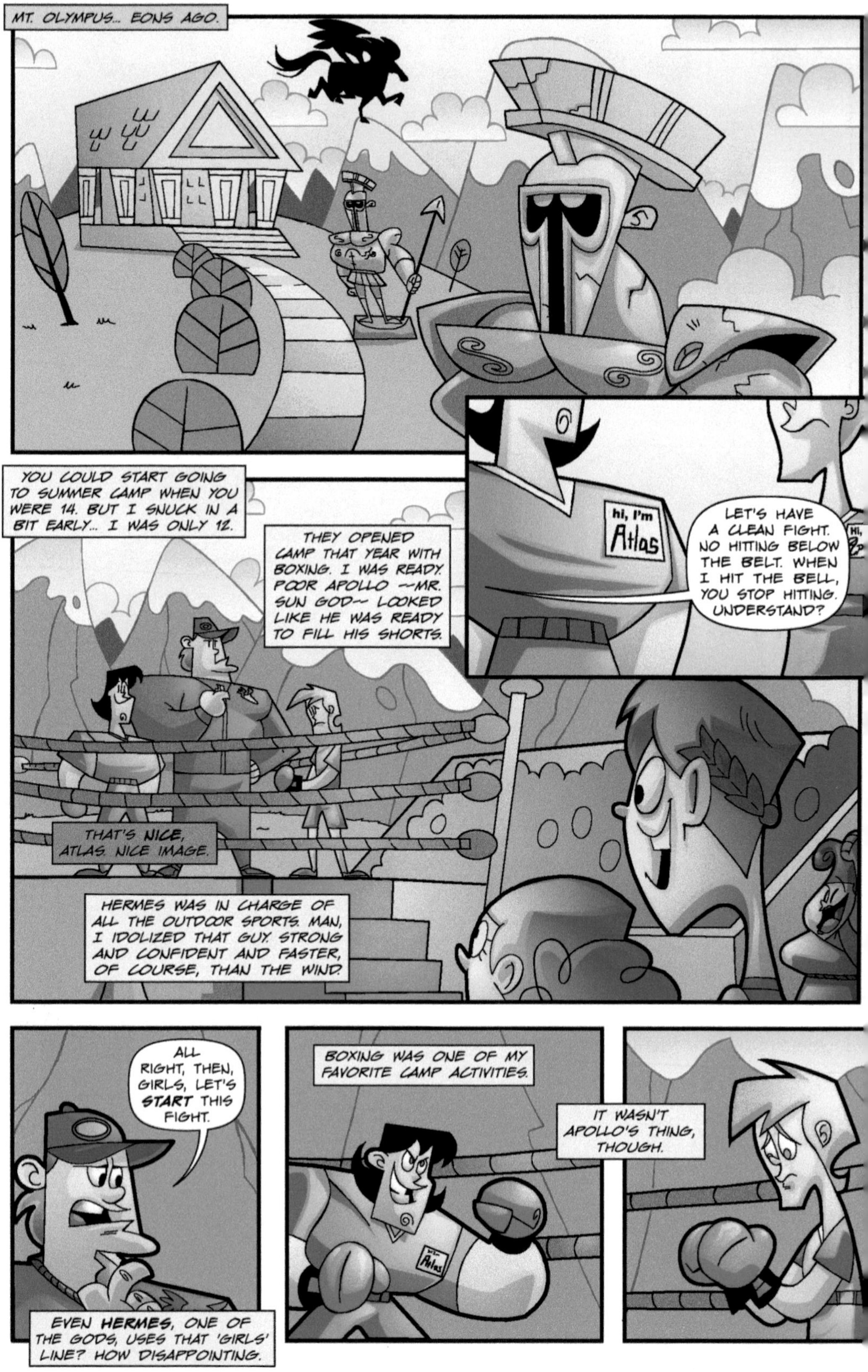
MT. OLYMPUS... EONS AGO.
hi, I'm Atlas
LET'S HAVE A CLEAN FIGHT. NO HITTING BELOW THE BELT. WHEN I HIT THE BELL, YOU STOP HITTING. UNDERSTAND?
YOU COULD START GOING TO SUMMER CAMP WHEN YOU WERE 14. BUT I SNUCK IN A BIT EARLY... I WAS ONLY 12.
THEY OPENED CAMP THAT YEAR WITH BOXING. I WAS READY. POOR APOLLO --MR. SUN GOD-- LOOKED LIKE HE WAS READY TO FILL HIS SHORTS.
THAT'S NICE, ATLAS. NICE IMAGE.
HERMES WAS IN CHARGE OF ALL THE OUTDOOR SPORTS. MAN, I IDOLIZED THAT GUY. STRONG AND CONFIDENT AND FASTER, OF COURSE, THAN THE WIND.
ALL RIGHT, THEN, GIRLS, LET'S START THIS FIGHT.
EVEN HERMES, ONE OF THE GODS, USES THAT 'GIRLS' LINE? HOW DISAPPOINTING.
BOXING WAS ONE OF MY FAVORITE CAMP ACTIVITIES.
Atlas
IT WASN'T APOLLO'S THING, THOUGH.

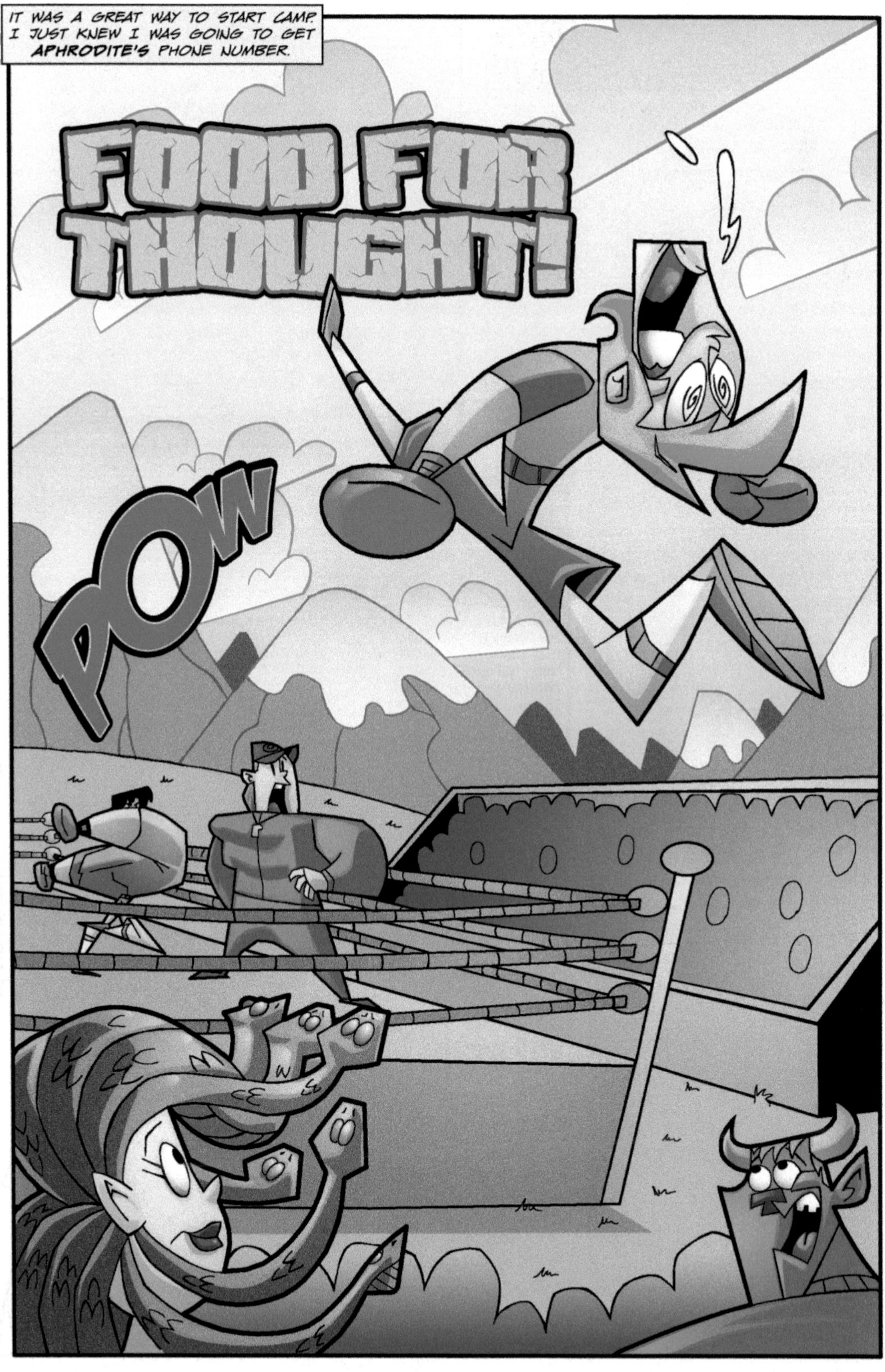

IT WAS A GREAT WAY TO START CAMP. I JUST KNEW I WAS GOING TO GET APHRODITE'S PHONE NUMBER.
FOOD FOR THOUGHT!
POW

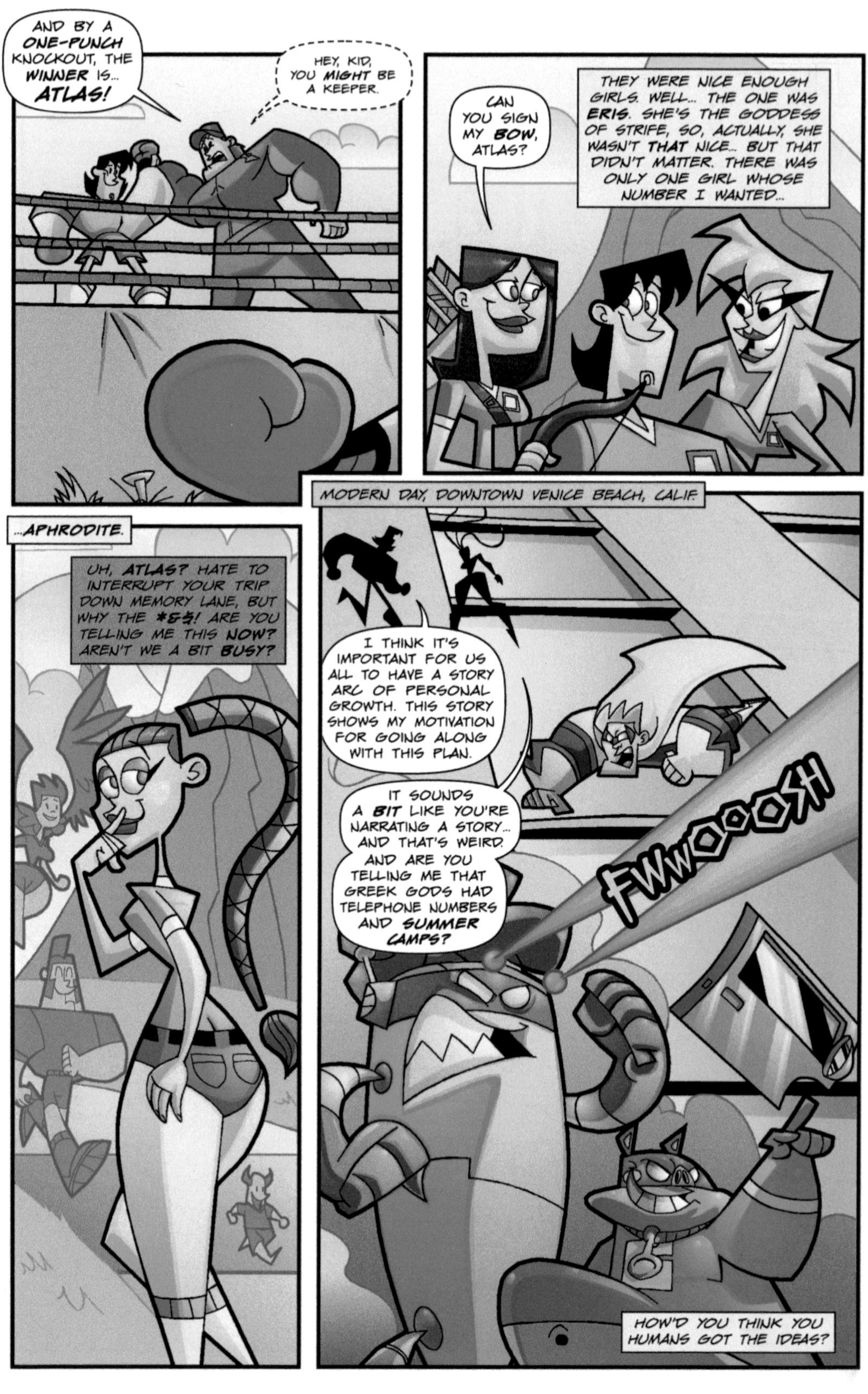
AND BY A ONE-PUNCH KNOCKOUT, THE WINNER IS... ATLAS!
HEY, KID, YOU MIGHT BE A KEEPER.
CAN YOU SIGN MY BOW, ATLAS?
THEY WERE NICE ENOUGH GIRLS. WELL... THE ONE WAS ERIS. SHE'S THE GODDESS OF STRIFE, SO, ACTUALLY, SHE WASN'T THAT NICE... BUT THAT DIDN'T MATTER. THERE WAS ONLY ONE GIRL WHOSE NUMBER I WANTED...
...APHRODITE.
UH, ATLAS? HATE TO INTERRUPT YOUR TRIP DOWN MEMORY LANE, BUT WHY THE *&$! ARE YOU TELLING ME THIS NOW? AREN'T WE A BIT BUSY?
MODERN DAY, DOWNTOWN VENICE BEACH, CALIF.
I THINK IT'S IMPORTANT FOR US ALL TO HAVE A STORY ARC OF PERSONAL GROWTH. THIS STORY SHOWS MY MOTIVATION FOR GOING ALONG WITH THIS PLAN.
IT SOUNDS A BIT LIKE YOU'RE NARRATING A STORY... AND THAT'S WEIRD.
AND ARE YOU TELLING ME THAT GREEK GODS HAD TELEPHONE NUMBERS AND SUMMER CAMPS?
FWWOOOSH
HOW'D YOU THINK YOU HUMANS GOT THE IDEAS?

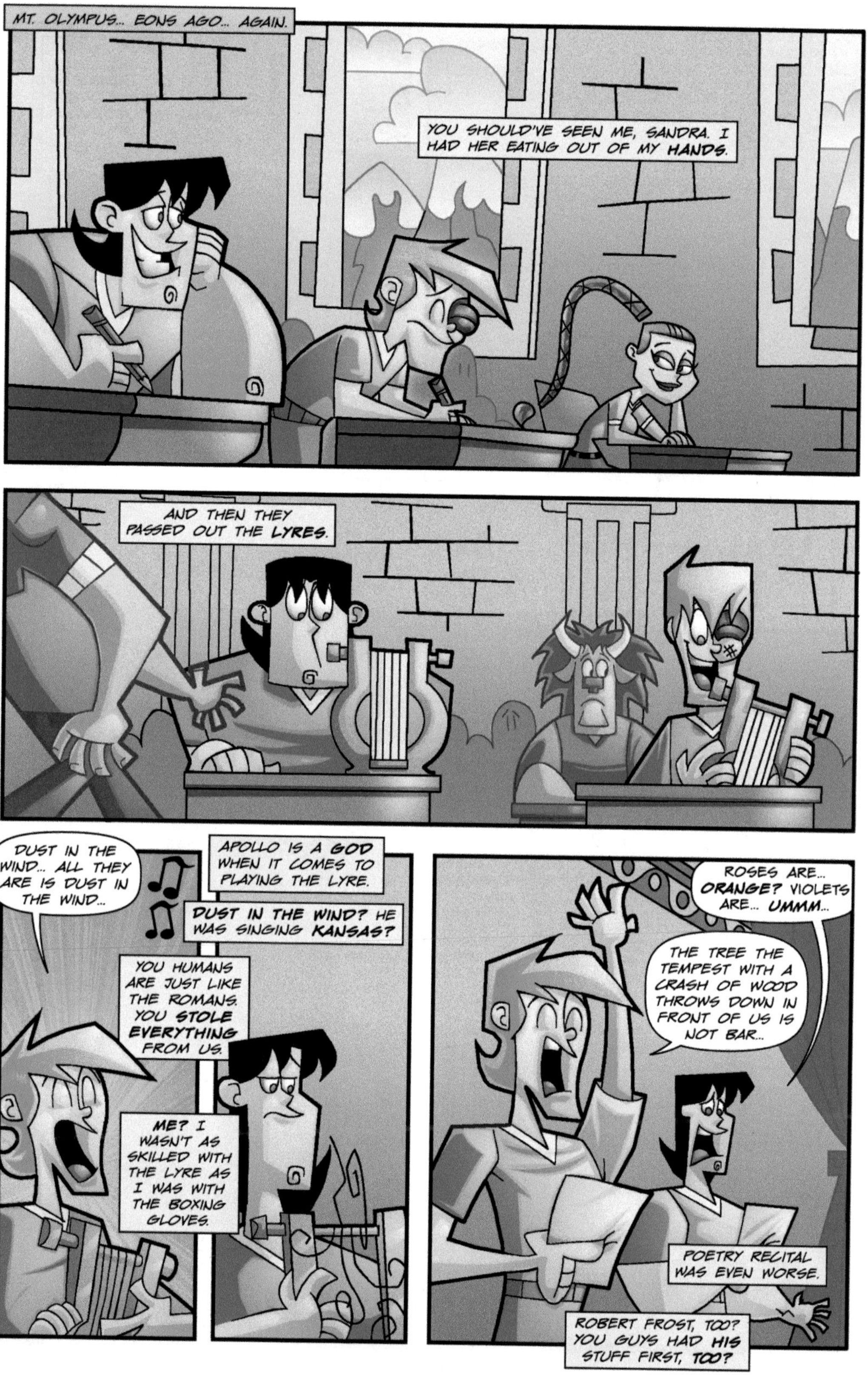
MT. OLYMPUS... EONS AGO... AGAIN.
YOU SHOULD'VE SEEN ME, SANDRA. I HAD HER EATING OUT OF MY **HANDS**.
AND THEN THEY PASSED OUT THE **LYRES**.
DUST IN THE WIND... ALL THEY ARE IS DUST IN THE WIND...
APOLLO IS A **GOD** WHEN IT COMES TO PLAYING THE LYRE.
DUST IN THE WIND? HE WAS SINGING **KANSAS?**
YOU HUMANS ARE JUST LIKE THE ROMANS. YOU **STOLE EVERYTHING** FROM US.
ME? I WASN'T AS SKILLED WITH THE LYRE AS I WAS WITH THE BOXING GLOVES.
ROSES ARE... **ORANGE?** VIOLETS ARE... **UMMM**...
THE TREE THE TEMPEST WITH A CRASH OF WOOD THROWS DOWN IN FRONT OF US IS NOT BAR...
POETRY RECITAL WAS EVEN WORSE.
ROBERT FROST, TOO? YOU GUYS HAD **HIS** STUFF FIRST, **TOO?**

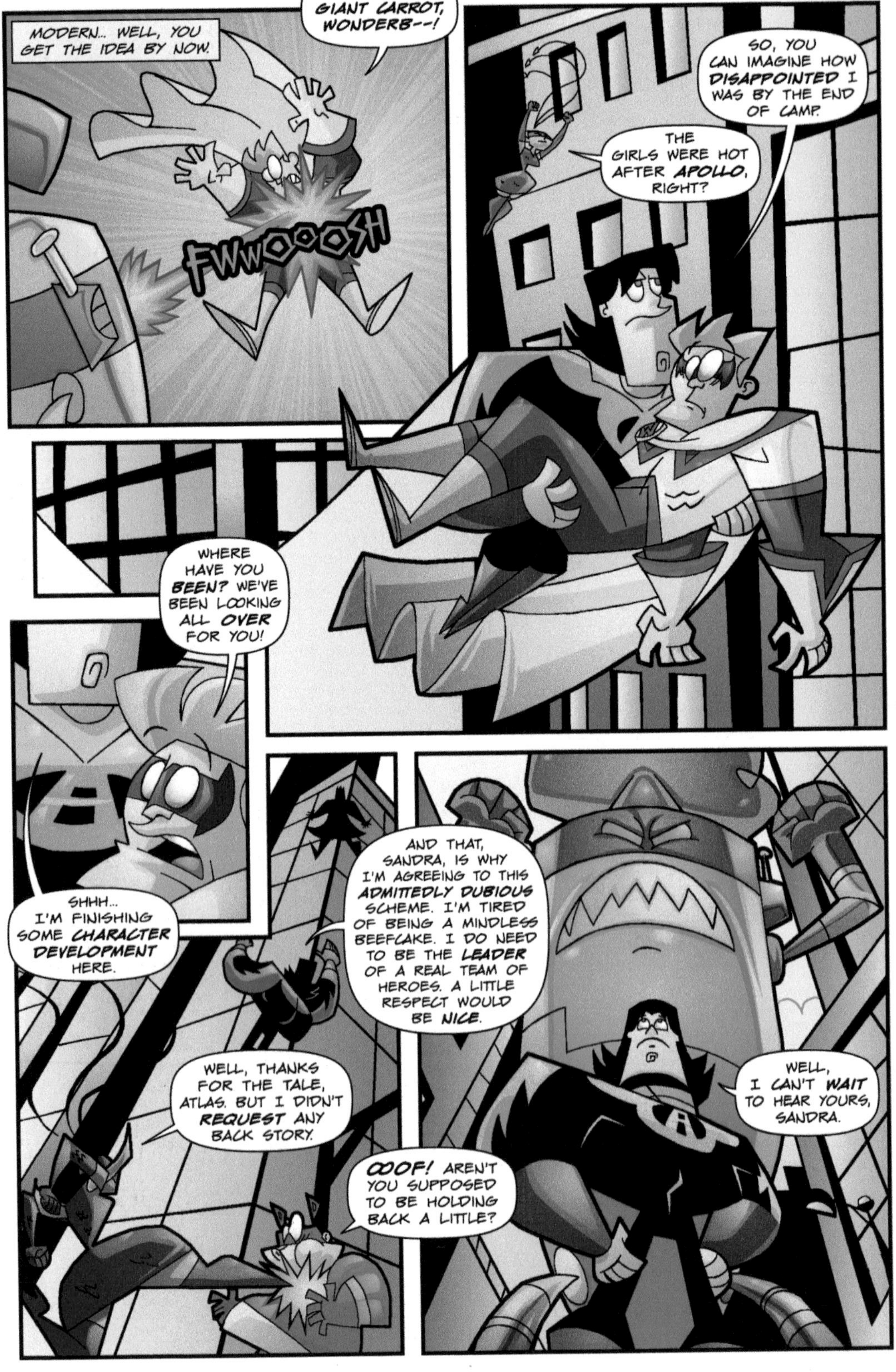
MODERN... WELL, YOU GET THE IDEA BY NOW.
HALT GIANT CARROT, WONDERB--!
FWWOOOSH
SO, YOU CAN IMAGINE HOW DISAPPOINTED I WAS BY THE END OF CAMP.
THE GIRLS WERE HOT AFTER APOLLO, RIGHT?
WHERE HAVE YOU BEEN? WE'VE BEEN LOOKING ALL OVER FOR YOU!
SHHH... I'M FINISHING SOME CHARACTER DEVELOPMENT HERE.
AND THAT, SANDRA, IS WHY I'M AGREEING TO THIS ADMITTEDLY DUBIOUS SCHEME. I'M TIRED OF BEING A MINDLESS BEEFCAKE. I DO NEED TO BE THE LEADER OF A REAL TEAM OF HEROES. A LITTLE RESPECT WOULD BE NICE.
WELL, THANKS FOR THE TALE, ATLAS. BUT I DIDN'T REQUEST ANY BACK STORY.
OOOF! AREN'T YOU SUPPOSED TO BE HOLDING BACK A LITTLE?
WELL, I CAN'T WAIT TO HEAR YOURS, SANDRA.

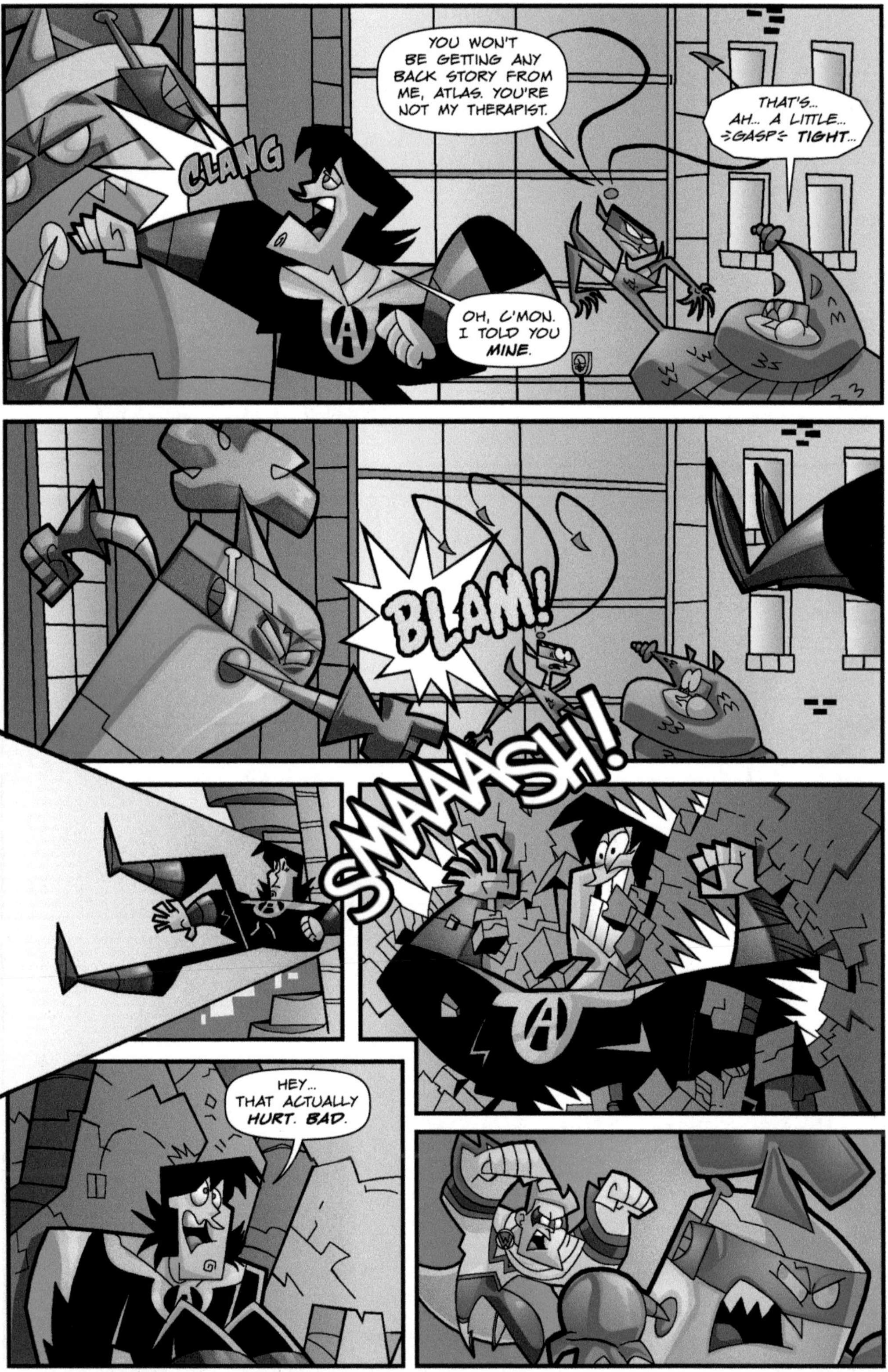

CLANG
YOU WON'T BE GETTING ANY BACK STORY FROM ME, ATLAS. YOU'RE NOT MY THERAPIST.
OH, C'MON. I TOLD YOU MINE.
THAT'S... AH... A LITTLE... GASP TIGHT...
BLAM!
SMAAASH!
HEY... THAT ACTUALLY HURT. BAD.

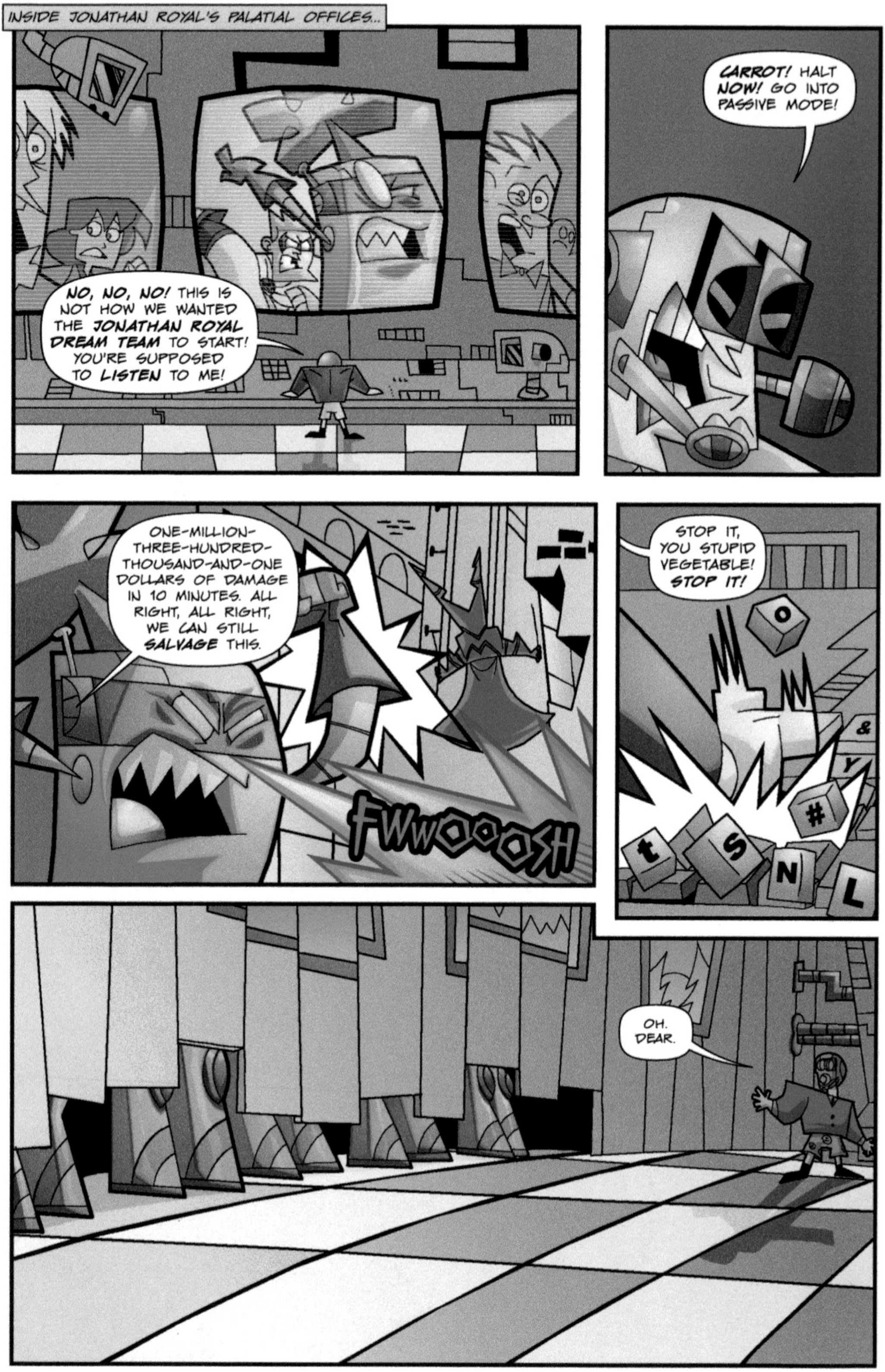
INSIDE JONATHAN ROYAL'S PALATIAL OFFICES...
NO, NO, NO! THIS IS NOT HOW WE WANTED THE JONATHAN ROYAL DREAM TEAM TO START! YOU'RE SUPPOSED TO LISTEN TO ME!
CARROT! HALT NOW! GO INTO PASSIVE MODE!
ONE-MILLION-THREE-HUNDRED-THOUSAND-AND-ONE DOLLARS OF DAMAGE IN 10 MINUTES. ALL RIGHT, ALL RIGHT, WE CAN STILL SALVAGE THIS.
FWWOOOOSH
STOP IT, YOU STUPID VEGETABLE! STOP IT!
OH. DEAR.

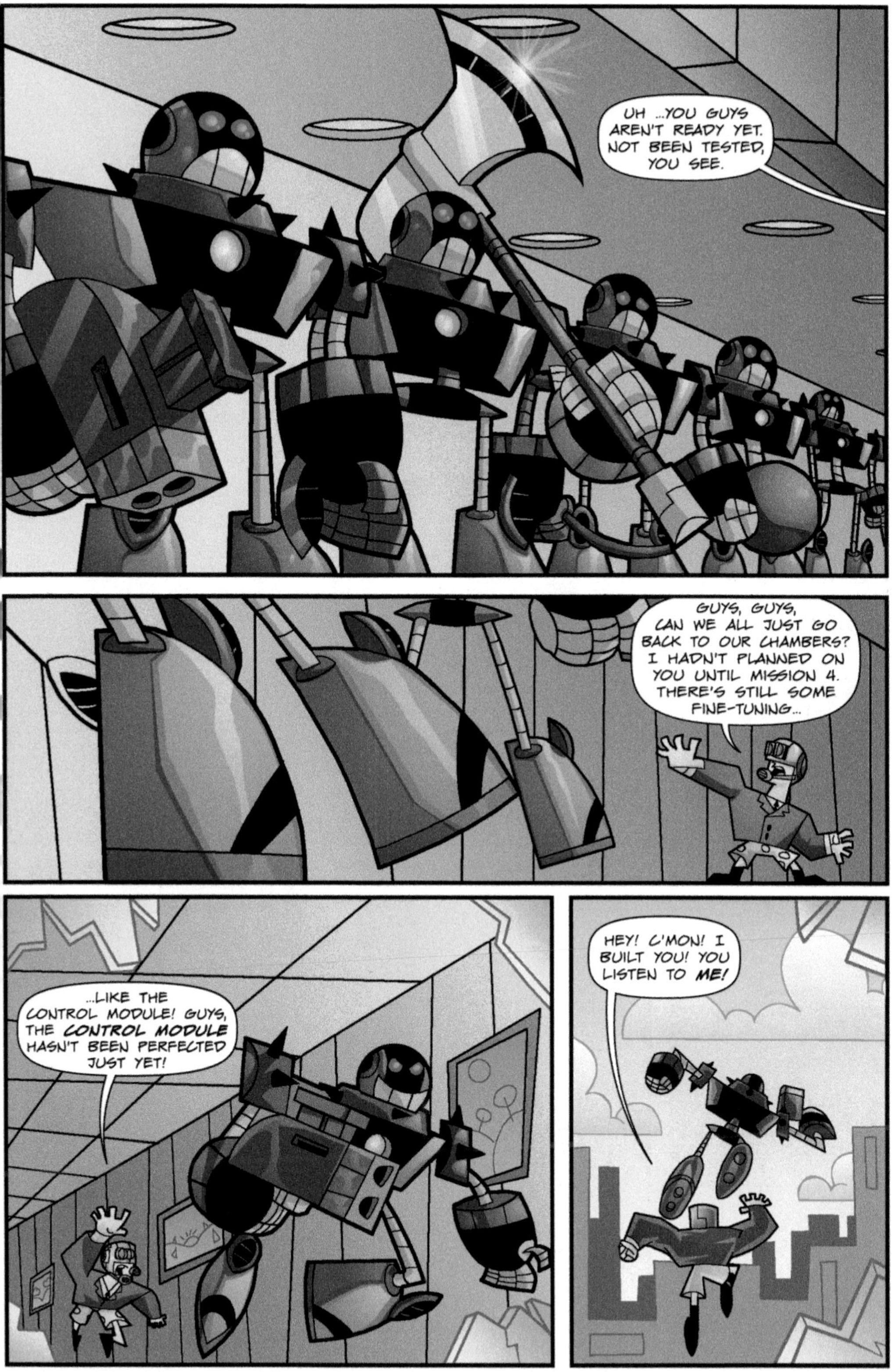
UH ...YOU GUYS AREN'T READY YET. NOT BEEN TESTED, YOU SEE.
GUYS, GUYS, CAN WE ALL JUST GO BACK TO OUR CHAMBERS? I HADN'T PLANNED ON YOU UNTIL MISSION 4. THERE'S STILL SOME FINE-TUNING...
...LIKE THE CONTROL MODULE! GUYS, THE ***CONTROL MODULE*** HASN'T BEEN PERFECTED JUST YET!
HEY! C'MON! I BUILT YOU! YOU LISTEN TO ***ME!***

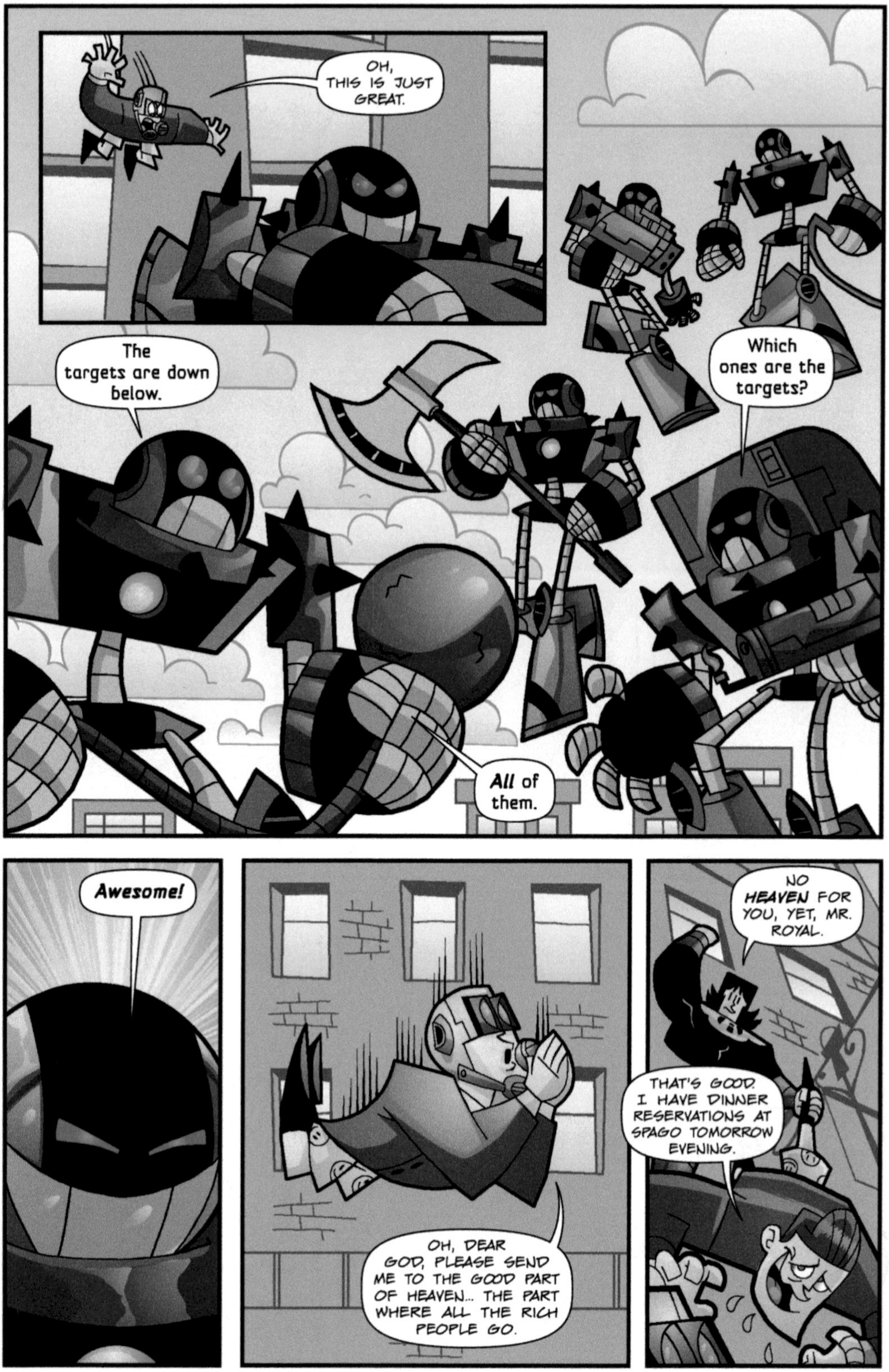
OH, THIS IS JUST GREAT.
The targets are down below.
Which ones are the targets?
All of them.
Awesome!
OH, DEAR GOD, PLEASE SEND ME TO THE GOOD PART OF HEAVEN... THE PART WHERE ALL THE RICH PEOPLE GO.
NO HEAVEN FOR YOU, YET, MR. ROYAL.
THAT'S GOOD. I HAVE DINNER RESERVATIONS AT SPAGO TOMORROW EVENING.

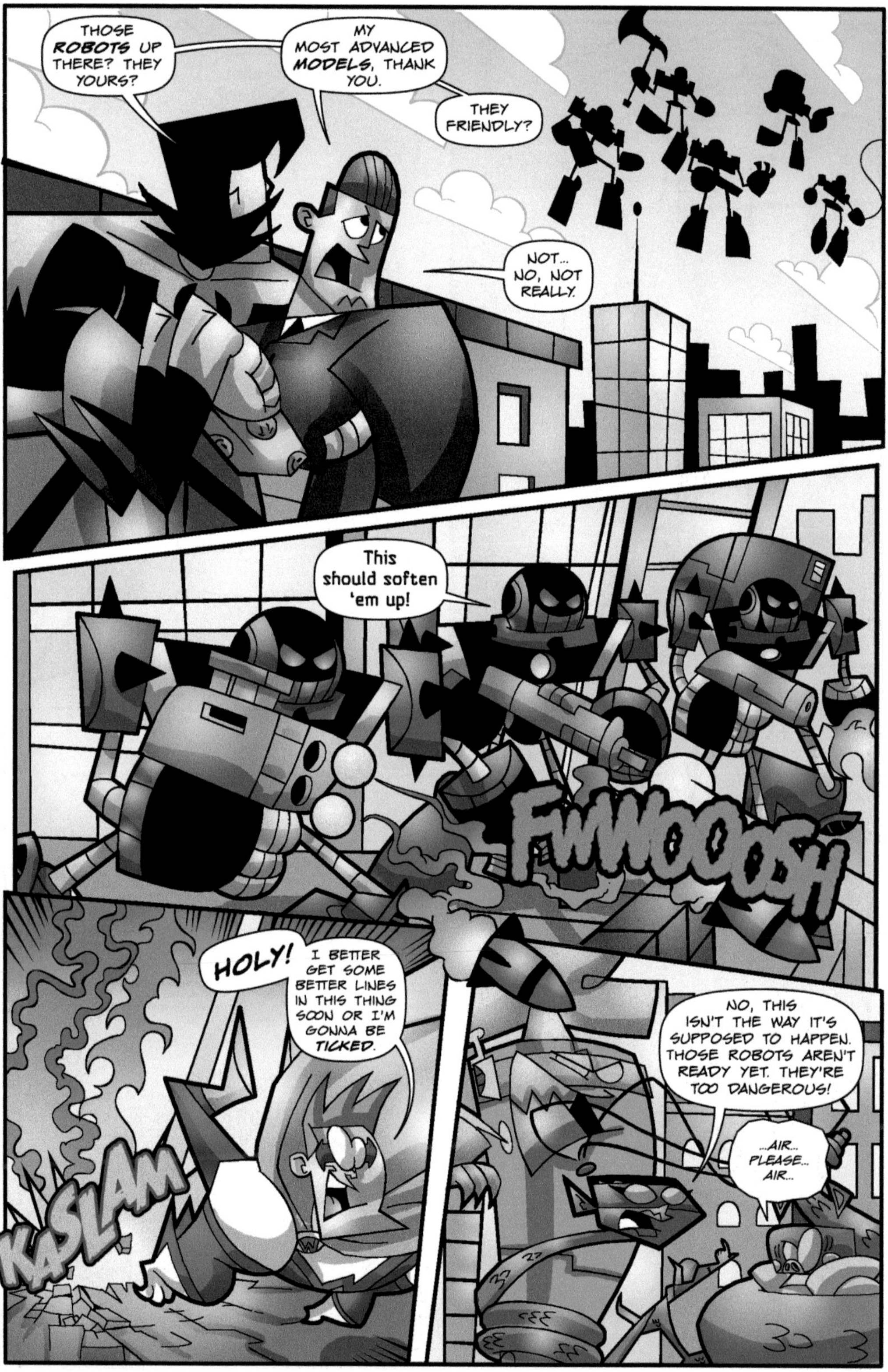
THOSE ROBOTS UP THERE? THEY YOURS?
MY MOST ADVANCED MODELS, THANK YOU.
THEY FRIENDLY?
NOT... NO, NOT REALLY.
This should soften 'em up!
FWWOOOSH
HOLY!
I BETTER GET SOME BETTER LINES IN THIS THING SOON OR I'M GONNA BE TICKED.
NO, THIS ISN'T THE WAY IT'S SUPPOSED TO HAPPEN. THOSE ROBOTS AREN'T READY YET. THEY'RE TOO DANGEROUS!
...AIR... PLEASE... AIR...
KASLAM

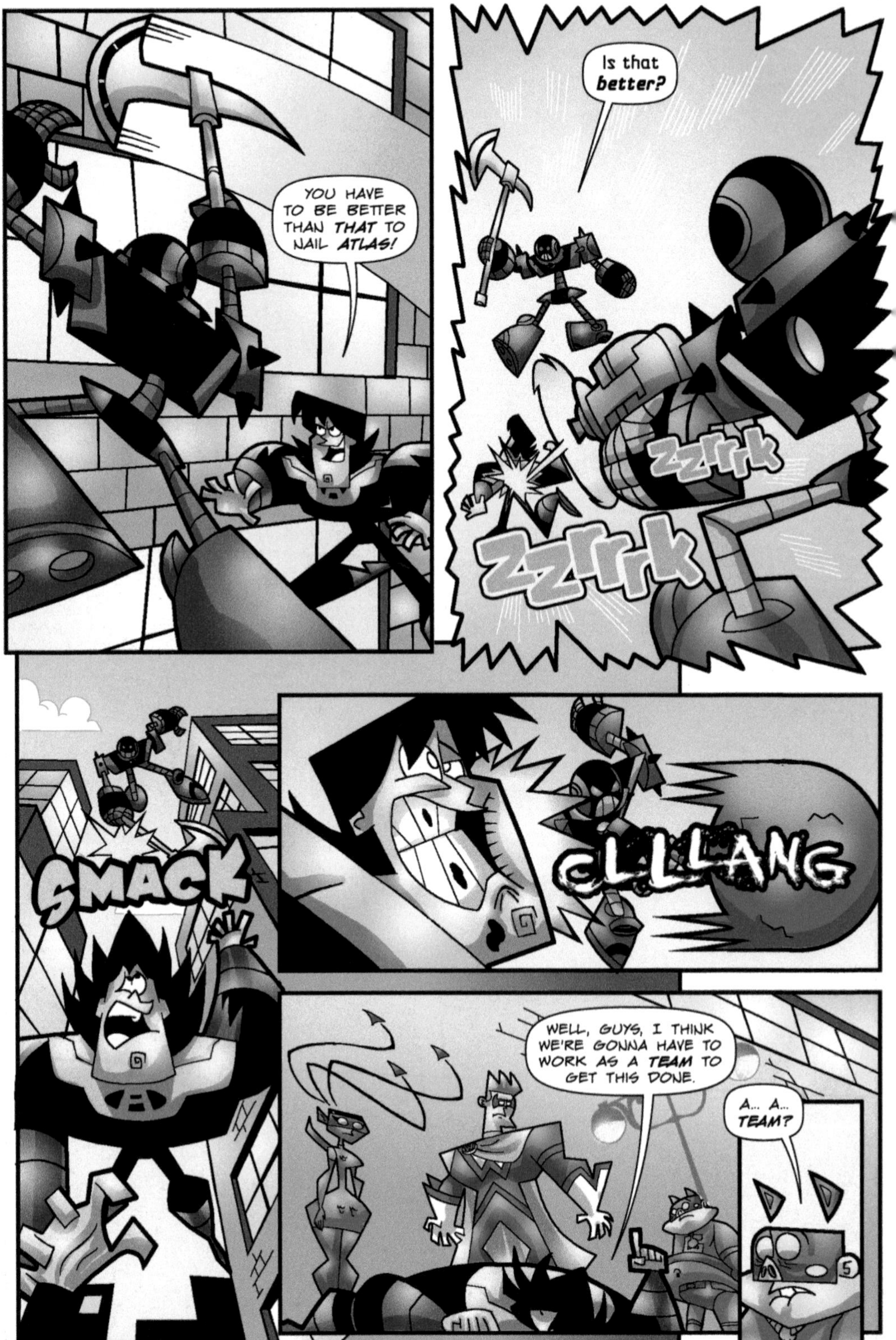
YOU HAVE TO BE BETTER THAN *THAT* TO NAIL *ATLAS!*
Is that *better?*
ZZRRRK
ZZRRRK
SMACK
CLLLANG
WELL, GUYS, I THINK WE'RE GONNA HAVE TO WORK AS A *TEAM* TO GET THIS DONE.
A... A... *TEAM?*

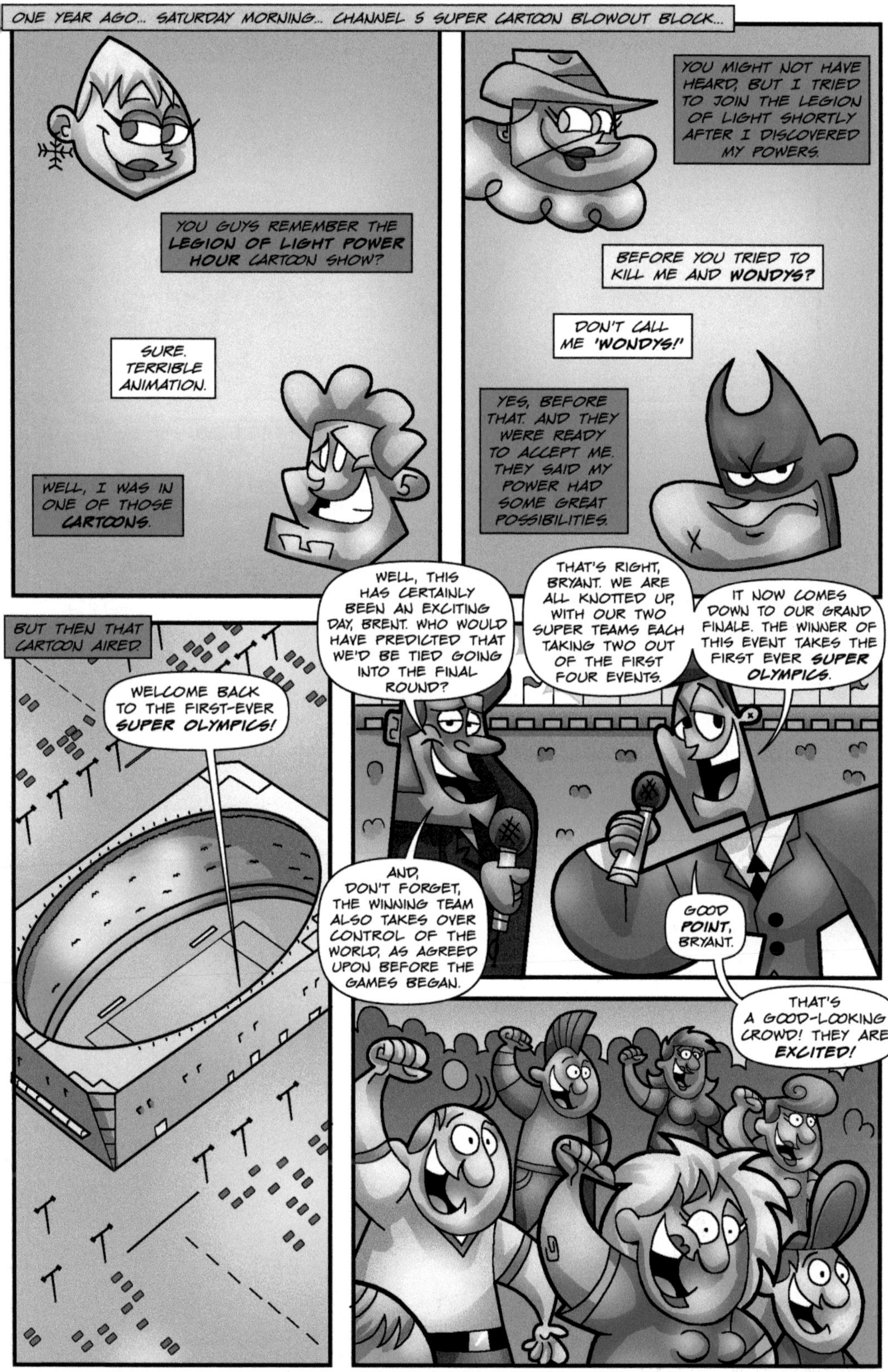
ONE YEAR AGO... SATURDAY MORNING... CHANNEL 5 SUPER CARTOON BLOWOUT BLOCK...
YOU GUYS REMEMBER THE LEGION OF LIGHT POWER HOUR CARTOON SHOW?
SURE. TERRIBLE ANIMATION.
WELL, I WAS IN ONE OF THOSE CARTOONS.
YOU MIGHT NOT HAVE HEARD, BUT I TRIED TO JOIN THE LEGION OF LIGHT SHORTLY AFTER I DISCOVERED MY POWERS.
BEFORE YOU TRIED TO KILL ME AND WONDYS?
DON'T CALL ME 'WONDYS!'
YES, BEFORE THAT. AND THEY WERE READY TO ACCEPT ME. THEY SAID MY POWER HAD SOME GREAT POSSIBILITIES.
BUT THEN THAT CARTOON AIRED.
WELCOME BACK TO THE FIRST-EVER SUPER OLYMPICS!
WELL, THIS HAS CERTAINLY BEEN AN EXCITING DAY, BRENT. WHO WOULD HAVE PREDICTED THAT WE'D BE TIED GOING INTO THE FINAL ROUND?
THAT'S RIGHT, BRYANT. WE ARE ALL KNOTTED UP, WITH OUR TWO SUPER TEAMS EACH TAKING TWO OUT OF THE FIRST FOUR EVENTS.
IT NOW COMES DOWN TO OUR GRAND FINALE. THE WINNER OF THIS EVENT TAKES THE FIRST EVER SUPER OLYMPICS.
AND, DON'T FORGET, THE WINNING TEAM ALSO TAKES OVER CONTROL OF THE WORLD, AS AGREED UPON BEFORE THE GAMES BEGAN.
GOOD POINT, BRYANT.
THAT'S A GOOD-LOOKING CROWD! THEY ARE EXCITED!

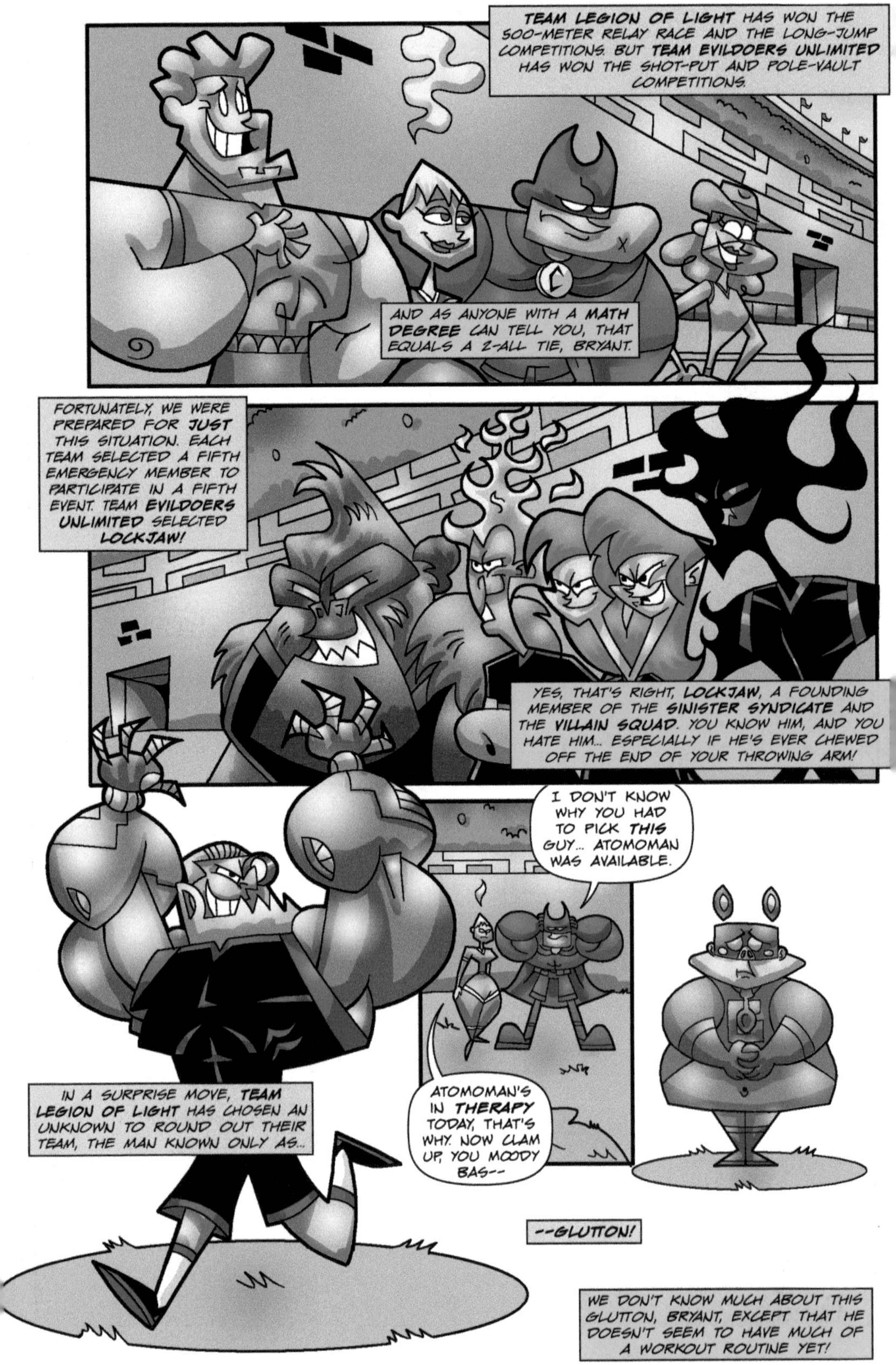
TEAM LEGION OF LIGHT HAS WON THE 500-METER RELAY RACE AND THE LONG-JUMP COMPETITIONS. BUT TEAM EVILDOERS UNLIMITED HAS WON THE SHOT-PUT AND POLE-VAULT COMPETITIONS.
AND AS ANYONE WITH A MATH DEGREE CAN TELL YOU, THAT EQUALS A 2-ALL TIE, BRYANT.
FORTUNATELY, WE WERE PREPARED FOR JUST THIS SITUATION. EACH TEAM SELECTED A FIFTH EMERGENCY MEMBER TO PARTICIPATE IN A FIFTH EVENT. TEAM EVILDOERS UNLIMITED SELECTED LOCKJAW!
YES, THAT'S RIGHT, LOCKJAW, A FOUNDING MEMBER OF THE SINISTER SYNDICATE AND THE VILLAIN SQUAD. YOU KNOW HIM, AND YOU HATE HIM... ESPECIALLY IF HE'S EVER CHEWED OFF THE END OF YOUR THROWING ARM!
I DON'T KNOW WHY YOU HAD TO PICK THIS GUY... ATOMOMAN WAS AVAILABLE.
ATOMOMAN'S IN THERAPY TODAY, THAT'S WHY. NOW CLAM UP, YOU MOODY BAS--
IN A SURPRISE MOVE, TEAM LEGION OF LIGHT HAS CHOSEN AN UNKNOWN TO ROUND OUT THEIR TEAM, THE MAN KNOWN ONLY AS...
--GLUTTON!
WE DON'T KNOW MUCH ABOUT THIS GLUTTON, BRYANT, EXCEPT THAT HE DOESN'T SEEM TO HAVE MUCH OF A WORKOUT ROUTINE YET!

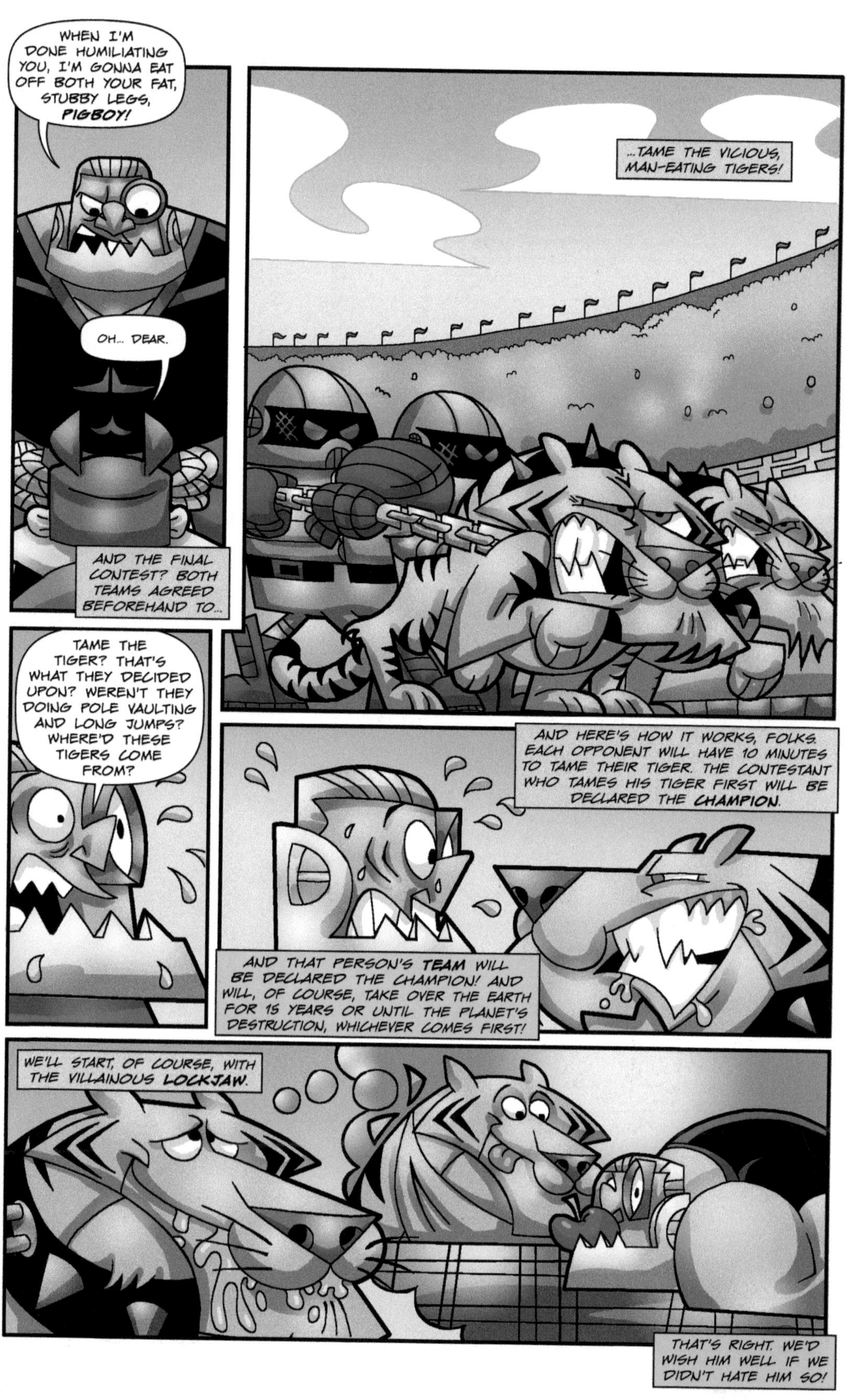
WHEN I'M DONE HUMILIATING YOU, I'M GONNA EAT OFF BOTH YOUR FAT, STUBBY LEGS, PIGBOY!
OH... DEAR.
AND THE FINAL CONTEST? BOTH TEAMS AGREED BEFOREHAND TO...
...TAME THE VICIOUS, MAN-EATING TIGERS!
TAME THE TIGER? THAT'S WHAT THEY DECIDED UPON? WEREN'T THEY DOING POLE VAULTING AND LONG JUMPS? WHERE'D THESE TIGERS COME FROM?
AND HERE'S HOW IT WORKS, FOLKS. EACH OPPONENT WILL HAVE 10 MINUTES TO TAME THEIR TIGER. THE CONTESTANT WHO TAMES HIS TIGER FIRST WILL BE DECLARED THE CHAMPION.
AND THAT PERSON'S TEAM WILL BE DECLARED THE CHAMPION! AND WILL, OF COURSE, TAKE OVER THE EARTH FOR 15 YEARS OR UNTIL THE PLANET'S DESTRUCTION, WHICHEVER COMES FIRST!
WE'LL START, OF COURSE, WITH THE VILLAINOUS LOCKJAW.
THAT'S RIGHT. WE'D WISH HIM WELL IF WE DIDN'T HATE HIM SO!

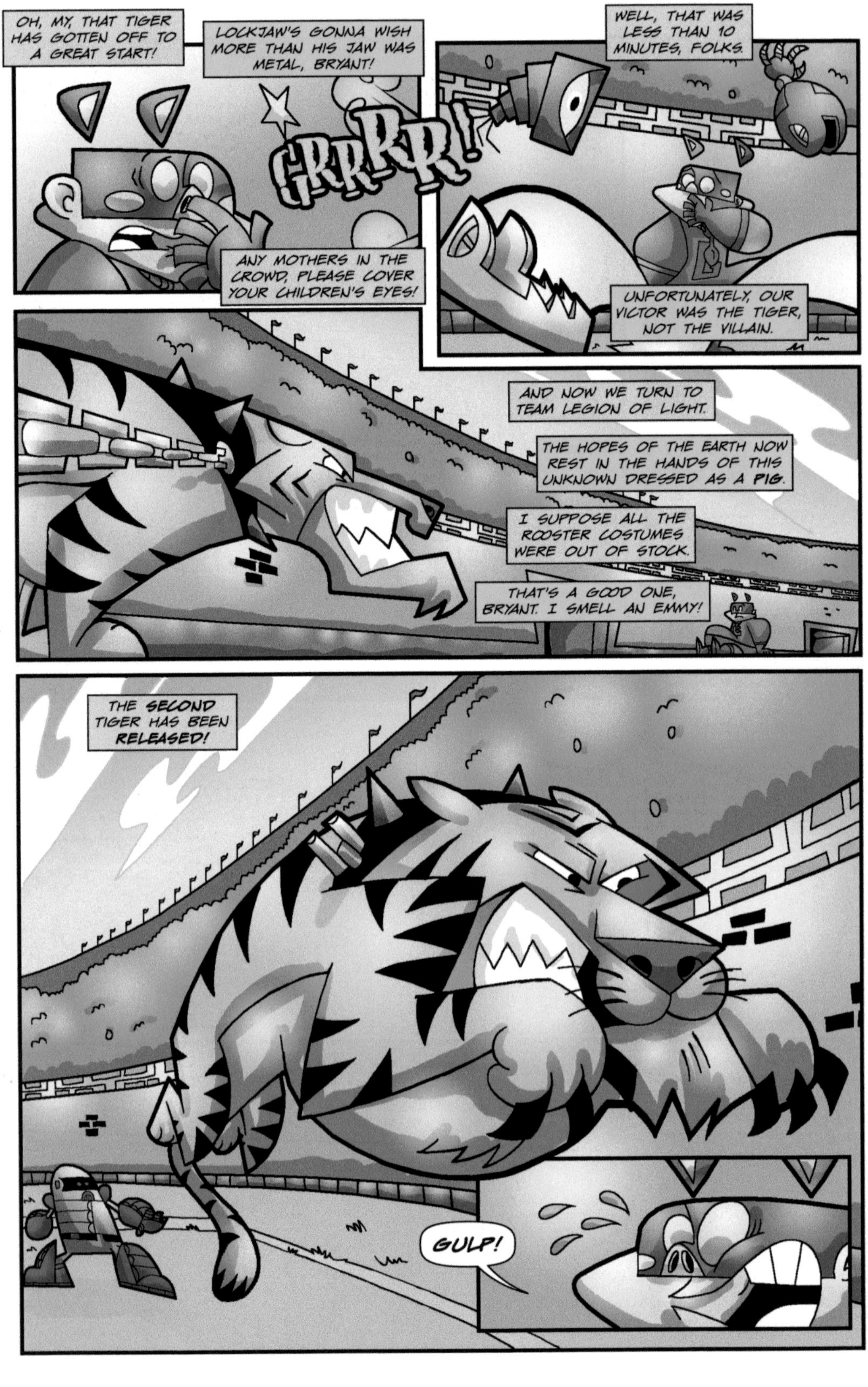
OH, MY, THAT TIGER HAS GOTTEN OFF TO A GREAT START!
LOCKJAW'S GONNA WISH MORE THAN HIS JAW WAS METAL, BRYANT!
GRRRR!
ANY MOTHERS IN THE CROWD, PLEASE COVER YOUR CHILDREN'S EYES!
WELL, THAT WAS LESS THAN 10 MINUTES, FOLKS.
UNFORTUNATELY, OUR VICTOR WAS THE TIGER, NOT THE VILLAIN.
AND NOW WE TURN TO TEAM LEGION OF LIGHT.
THE HOPES OF THE EARTH NOW REST IN THE HANDS OF THIS UNKNOWN DRESSED AS A PIG.
I SUPPOSE ALL THE ROOSTER COSTUMES WERE OUT OF STOCK.
THAT'S A GOOD ONE, BRYANT. I SMELL AN EMMY!
THE SECOND TIGER HAS BEEN RELEASED!
GULP!

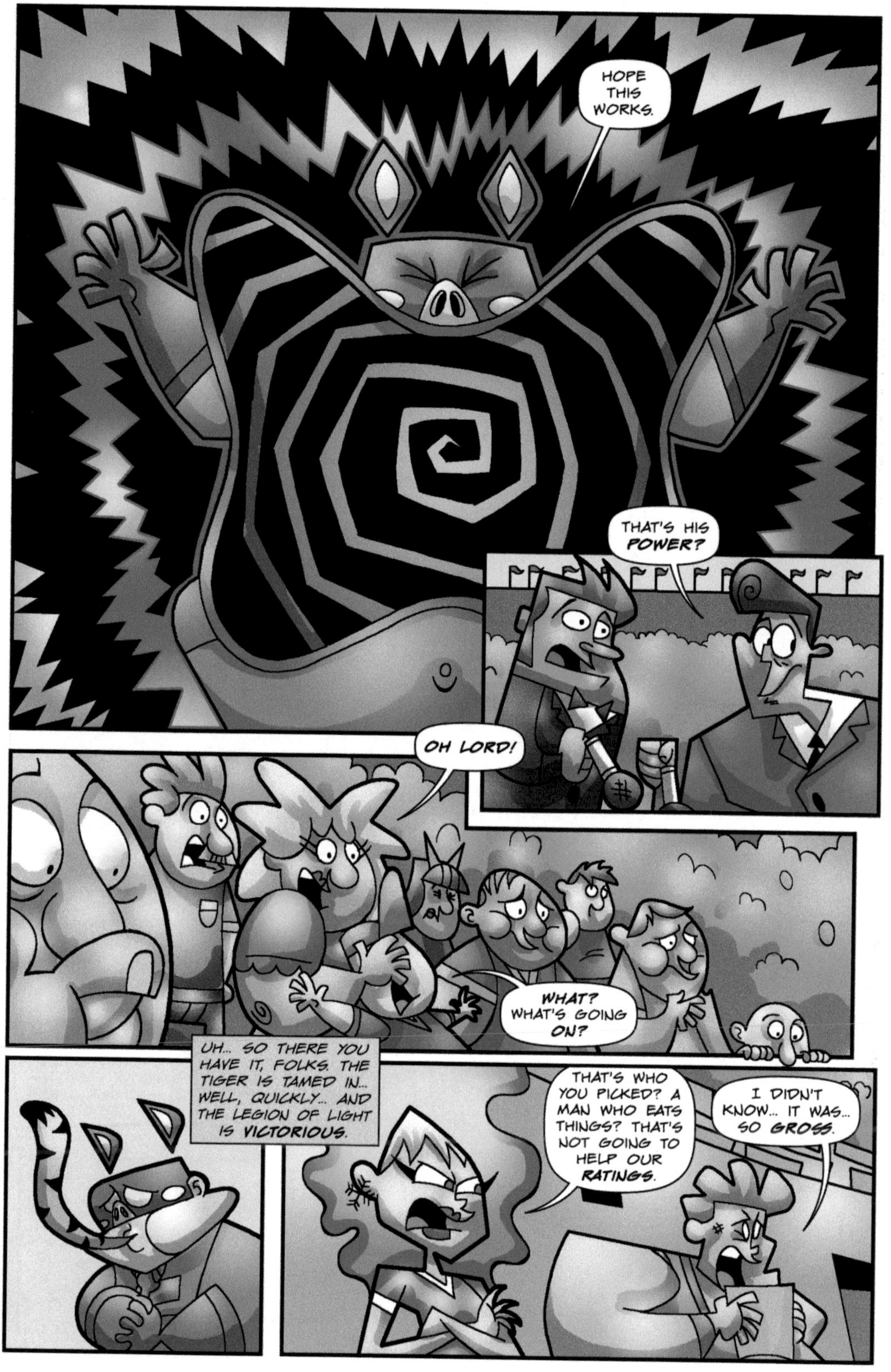
HOPE THIS WORKS.
THAT'S HIS POWER?
OH LORD!
WHAT? WHAT'S GOING ON?
UH... SO THERE YOU HAVE IT, FOLKS. THE TIGER IS TAMED IN... WELL, QUICKLY... AND THE LEGION OF LIGHT IS VICTORIOUS.
THAT'S WHO YOU PICKED? A MAN WHO EATS THINGS? THAT'S NOT GOING TO HELP OUR RATINGS.
I DIDN'T KNOW... IT WAS... SO GROSS.

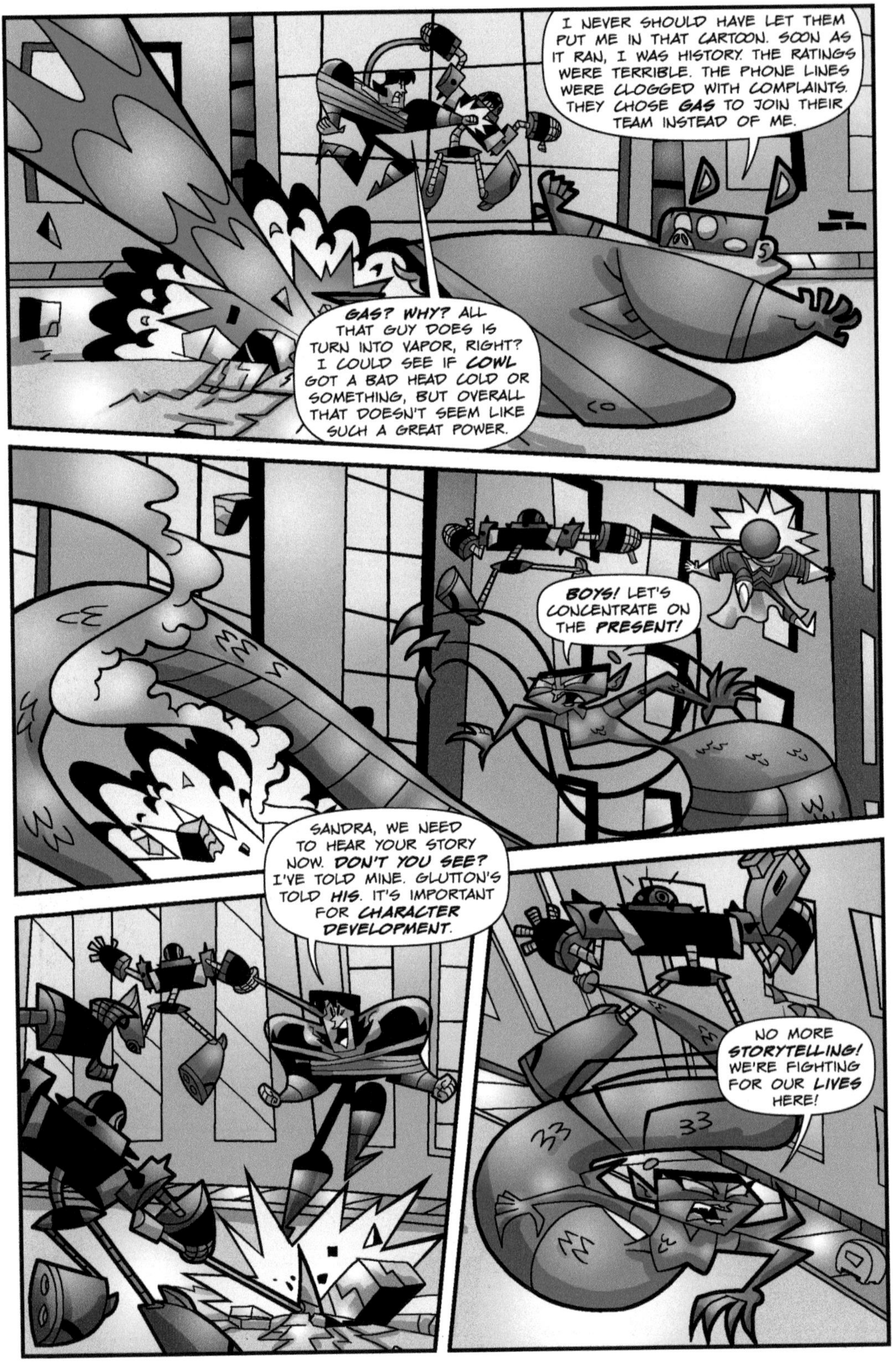
I NEVER SHOULD HAVE LET THEM PUT ME IN THAT CARTOON. SOON AS IT RAN, I WAS HISTORY. THE RATINGS WERE TERRIBLE. THE PHONE LINES WERE CLOGGED WITH COMPLAINTS. THEY CHOSE GAS TO JOIN THEIR TEAM INSTEAD OF ME.
GAS? WHY? ALL THAT GUY DOES IS TURN INTO VAPOR, RIGHT? I COULD SEE IF COWL GOT A BAD HEAD COLD OR SOMETHING, BUT OVERALL THAT DOESN'T SEEM LIKE SUCH A GREAT POWER.
BOYS! LET'S CONCENTRATE ON THE PRESENT!
SANDRA, WE NEED TO HEAR YOUR STORY NOW. DON'T YOU SEE? I'VE TOLD MINE. GLUTTON'S TOLD HIS. IT'S IMPORTANT FOR CHARACTER DEVELOPMENT.
NO MORE STORYTELLING! WE'RE FIGHTING FOR OUR LIVES HERE!

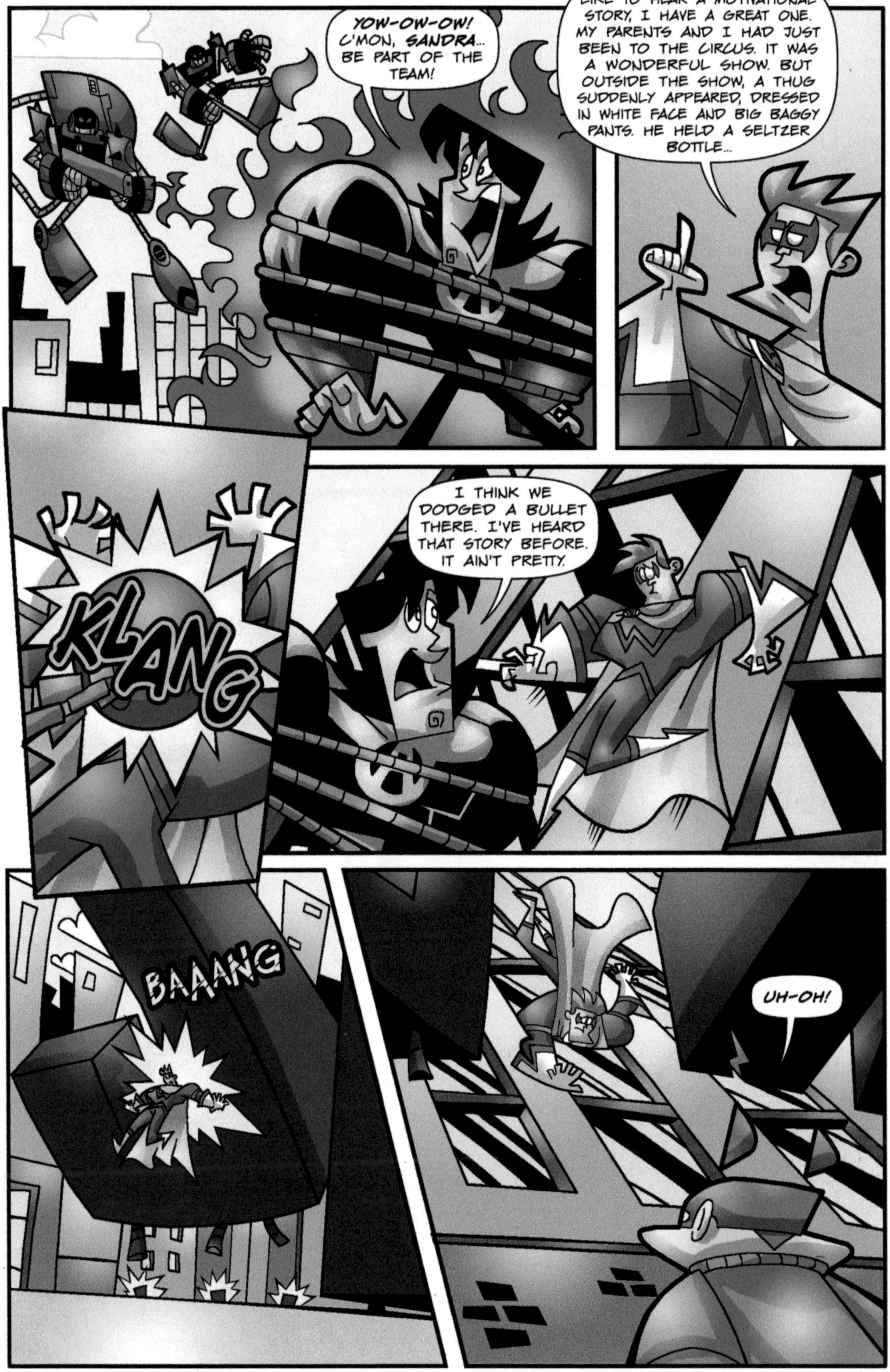
YOW-OW-OW! C'MON, SANDRA... BE PART OF THE TEAM!
ACTUALLY, IF YOU'D LIKE TO HEAR A MOTIVATIONAL STORY, I HAVE A GREAT ONE. MY PARENTS AND I HAD JUST BEEN TO THE CIRCUS. IT WAS A WONDERFUL SHOW. BUT OUTSIDE THE SHOW, A THUG SUDDENLY APPEARED, DRESSED IN WHITE FACE AND BIG BAGGY PANTS. HE HELD A SELTZER BOTTLE...
KLANG
I THINK WE DODGED A BULLET THERE. I'VE HEARD THAT STORY BEFORE. IT AIN'T PRETTY.
BAAANG
UH-OH!

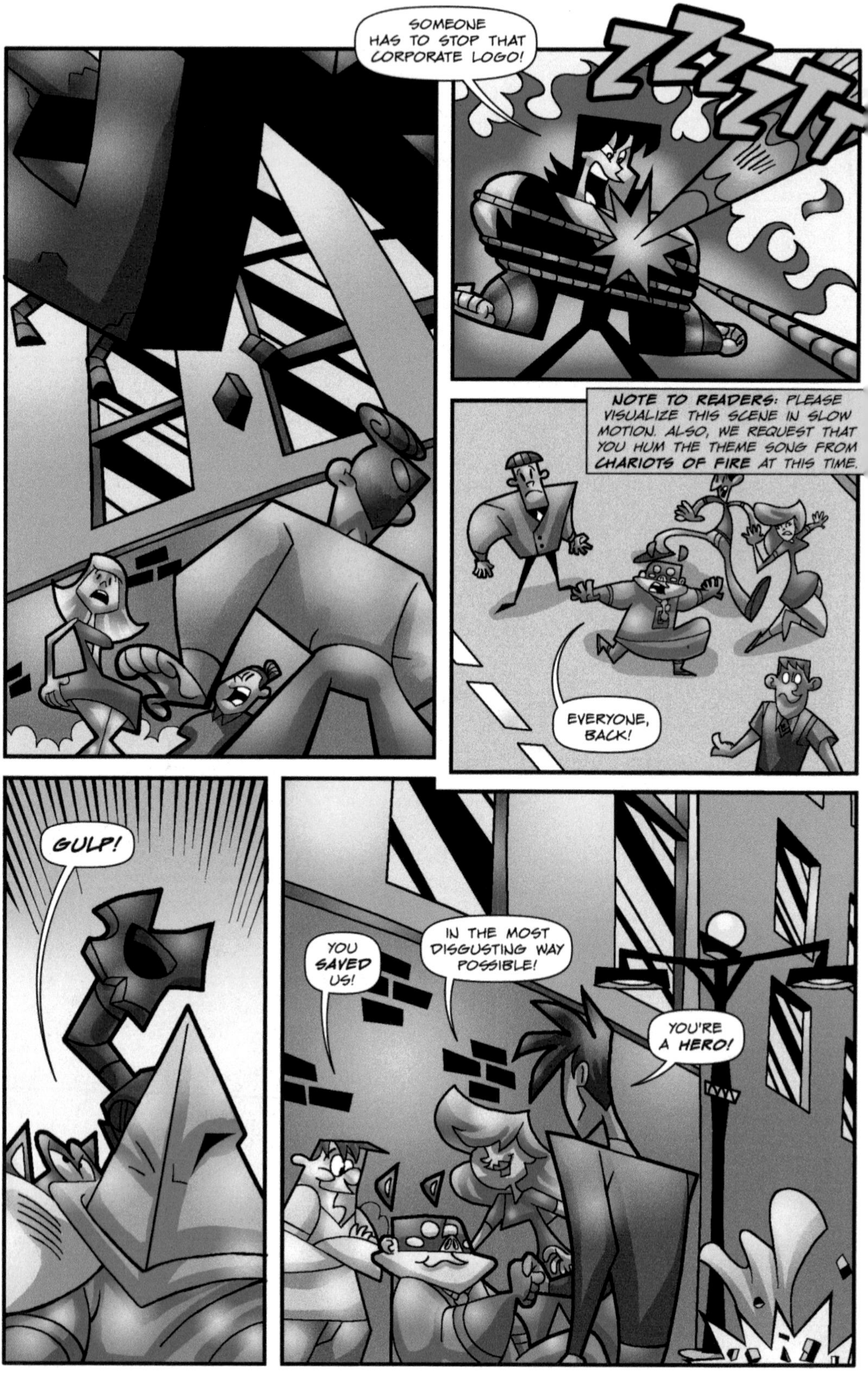

SOMEONE HAS TO STOP THAT CORPORATE LOGO!
ZZZZTT
NOTE TO READERS: PLEASE VISUALIZE THIS SCENE IN SLOW MOTION. ALSO, WE REQUEST THAT YOU HUM THE THEME SONG FROM CHARIOTS OF FIRE AT THIS TIME.
EVERYONE, BACK!
GULP!
YOU SAVED US!
IN THE MOST DISGUSTING WAY POSSIBLE!
YOU'RE A HERO!

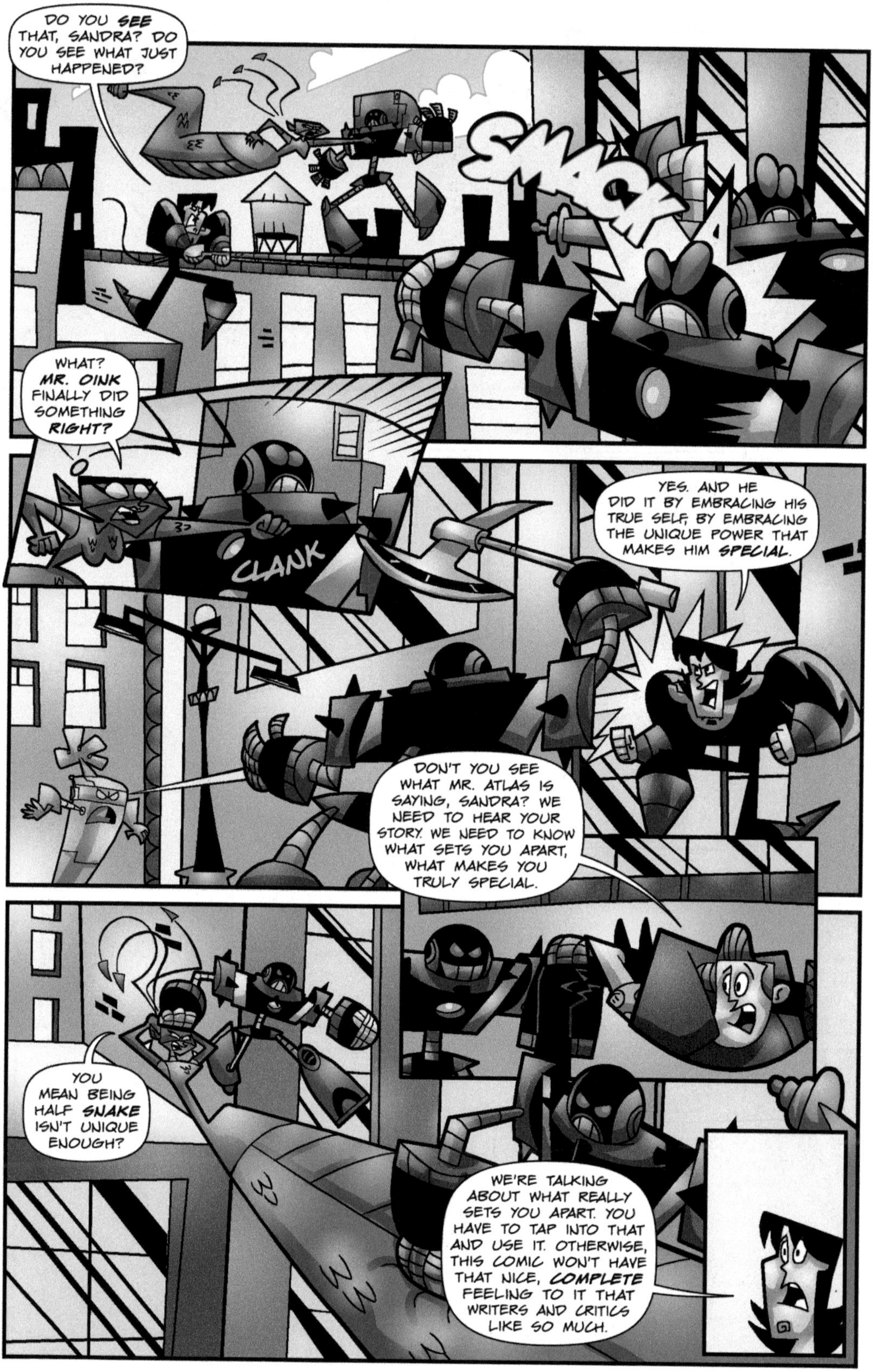
DO YOU SEE THAT, SANDRA? DO YOU SEE WHAT JUST HAPPENED?
SMACK
WHAT? MR. OINK FINALLY DID SOMETHING RIGHT?
CLANK
YES. AND HE DID IT BY EMBRACING HIS TRUE SELF, BY EMBRACING THE UNIQUE POWER THAT MAKES HIM SPECIAL.
DON'T YOU SEE WHAT MR. ATLAS IS SAYING, SANDRA? WE NEED TO HEAR YOUR STORY. WE NEED TO KNOW WHAT SETS YOU APART, WHAT MAKES YOU TRULY SPECIAL.
YOU MEAN BEING HALF SNAKE ISN'T UNIQUE ENOUGH?
WE'RE TALKING ABOUT WHAT REALLY SETS YOU APART. YOU HAVE TO TAP INTO THAT AND USE IT. OTHERWISE, THIS COMIC WON'T HAVE THAT NICE, COMPLETE FEELING TO IT THAT WRITERS AND CRITICS LIKE SO MUCH.

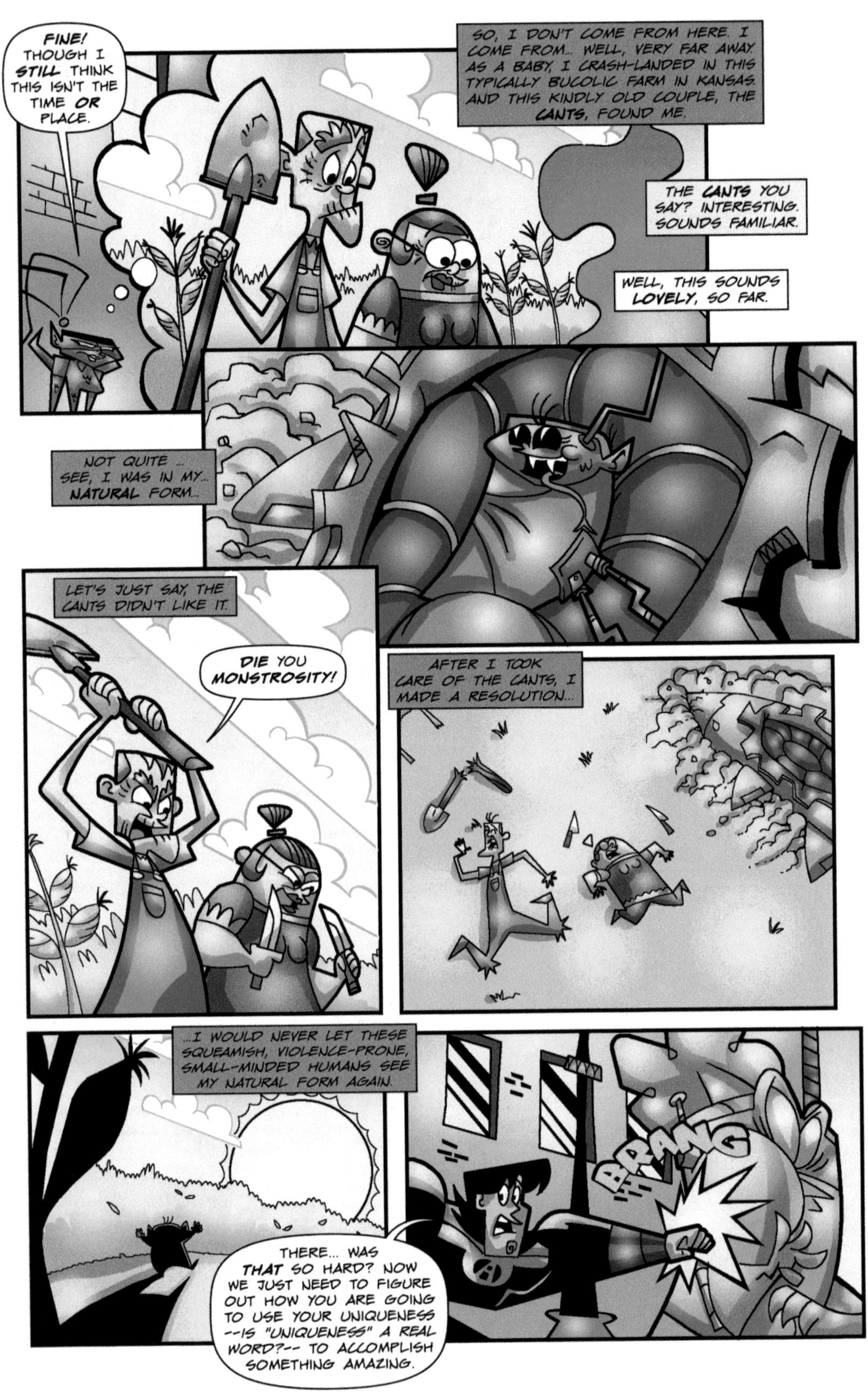
FINE! THOUGH I STILL THINK THIS ISN'T THE TIME OR PLACE.
SO, I DON'T COME FROM HERE. I COME FROM... WELL, VERY FAR AWAY. AS A BABY, I CRASH-LANDED IN THIS TYPICALLY BUCOLIC FARM IN KANSAS. AND THIS KINDLY OLD COUPLE, THE CANTS, FOUND ME.
THE CANTS YOU SAY? INTERESTING. SOUNDS FAMILIAR.
WELL, THIS SOUNDS LOVELY, SO FAR.
NOT QUITE ... SEE, I WAS IN MY... NATURAL FORM...
LET'S JUST SAY, THE CANTS DIDN'T LIKE IT.
DIE YOU MONSTROSITY!
AFTER I TOOK CARE OF THE CANTS, I MADE A RESOLUTION...
...I WOULD NEVER LET THESE SQUEAMISH, VIOLENCE-PRONE, SMALL-MINDED HUMANS SEE MY NATURAL FORM AGAIN.
BRANG
THERE... WAS THAT SO HARD? NOW WE JUST NEED TO FIGURE OUT HOW YOU ARE GOING TO USE YOUR UNIQUENESS --IS "UNIQUENESS" A REAL WORD?-- TO ACCOMPLISH SOMETHING AMAZING.

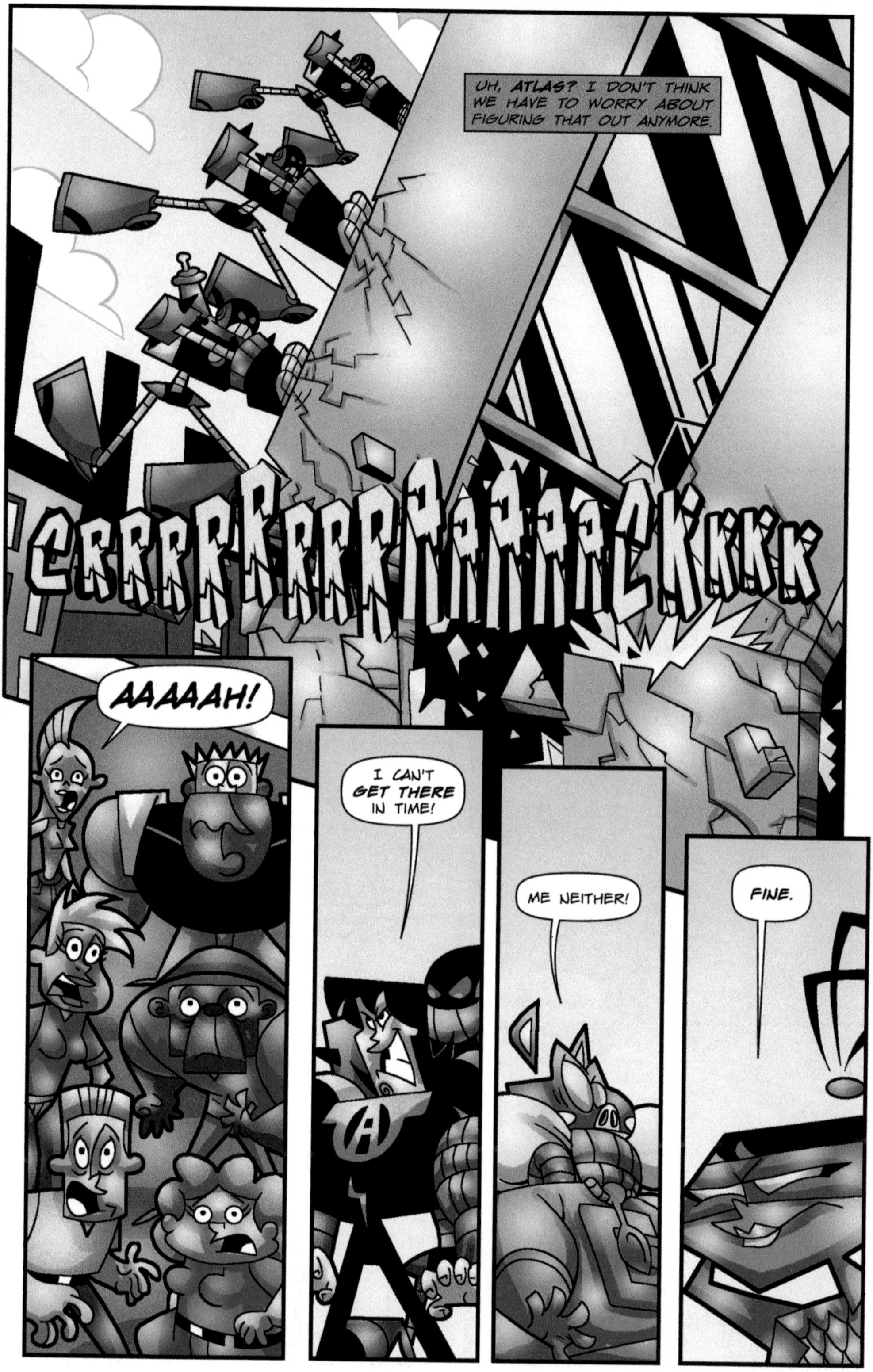
UH, ATLAS? I DON'T THINK WE HAVE TO WORRY ABOUT FIGURING THAT OUT ANYMORE.
CRRRRRRRRRAAAAACKKKK
AAAAAH!
I CAN'T GET THERE IN TIME!
ME NEITHER!
FINE.

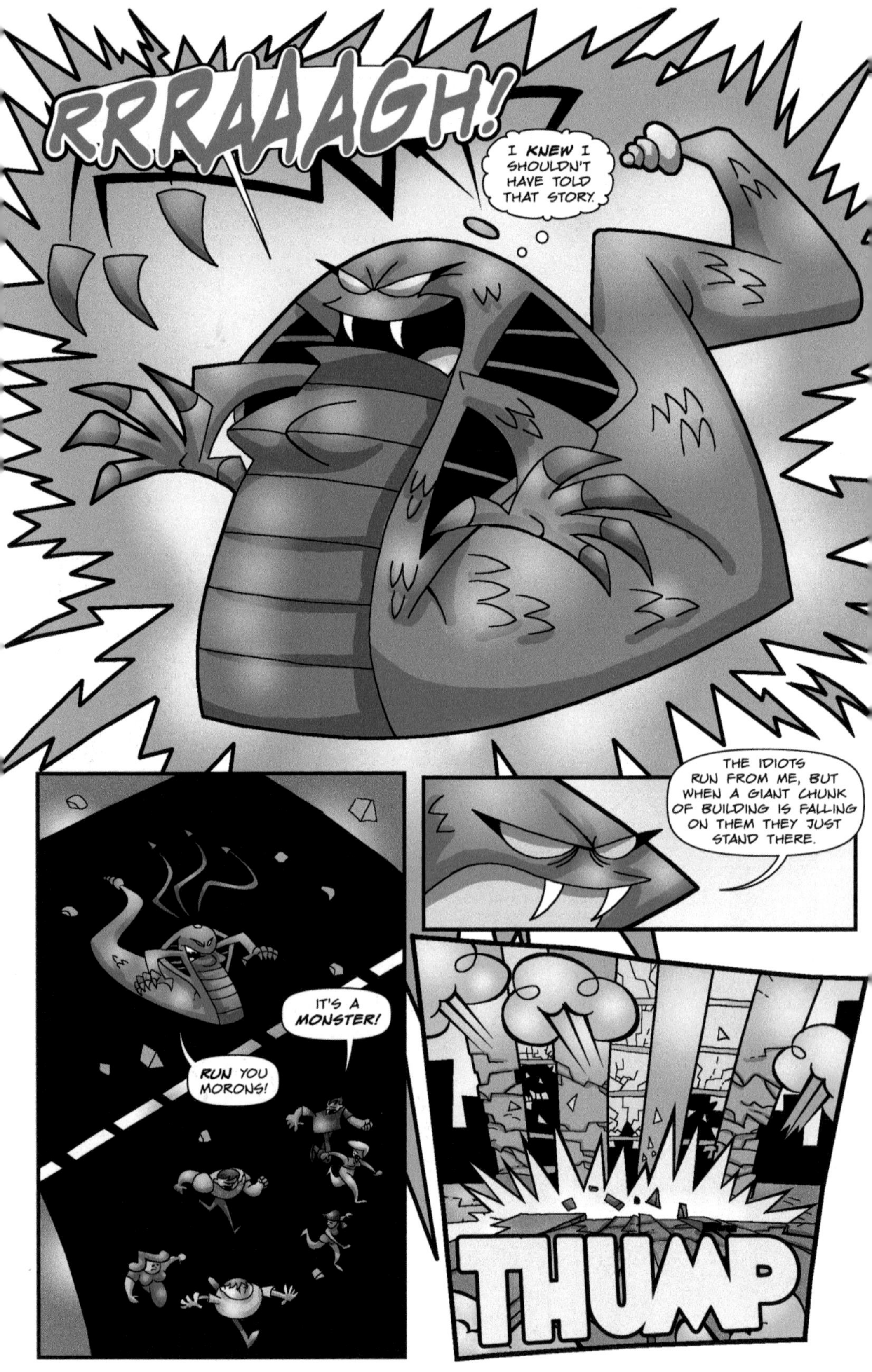
RRRAAAGH!
I KNEW I SHOULDN'T HAVE TOLD THAT STORY.
THE IDIOTS RUN FROM ME, BUT WHEN A GIANT CHUNK OF BUILDING IS FALLING ON THEM THEY JUST STAND THERE.
IT'S A MONSTER!
RUN YOU MORONS!
THUMP

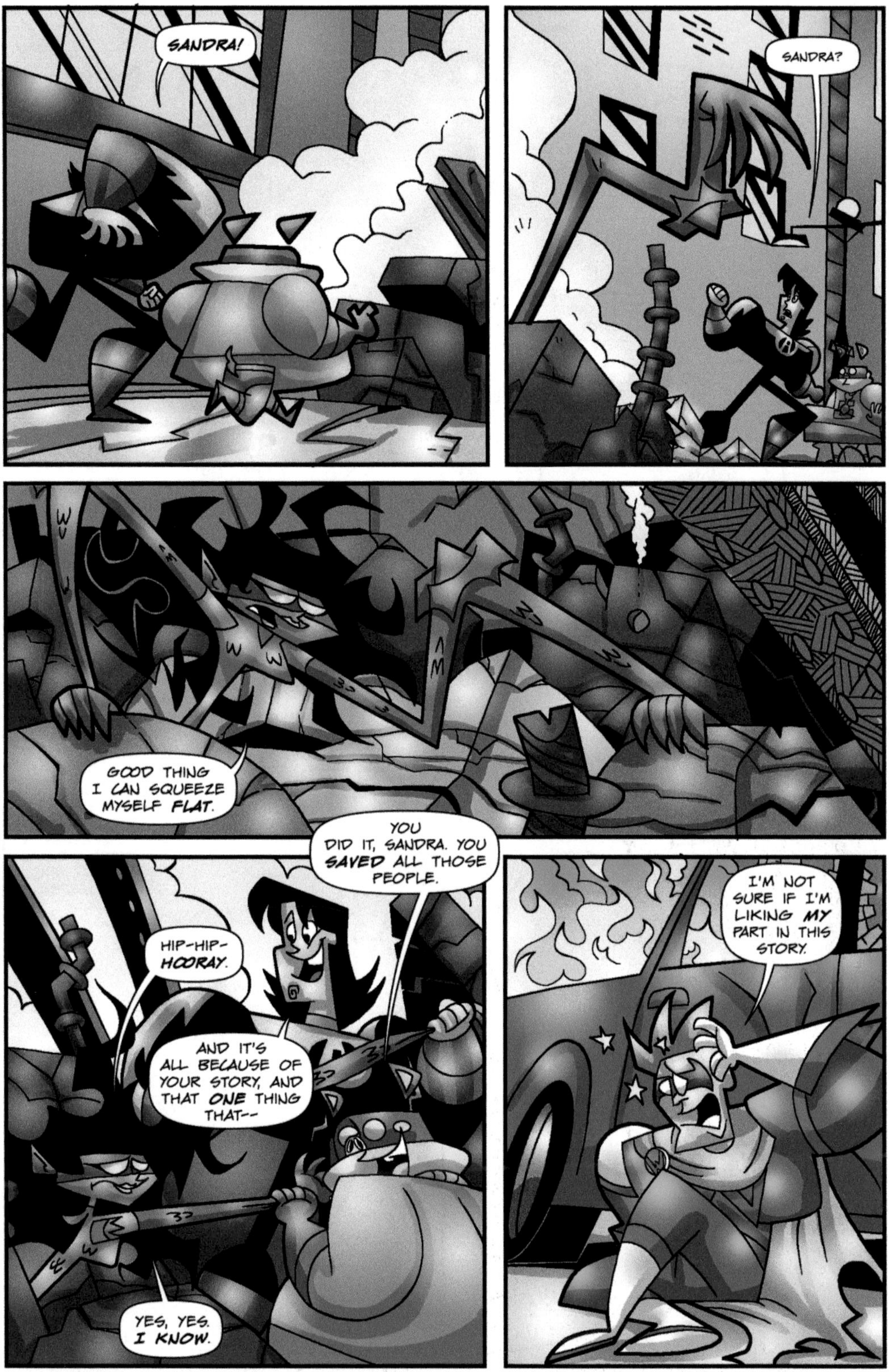
SANDRA!
SANDRA?
GOOD THING I CAN SQUEEZE MYSELF FLAT.
YOU DID IT, SANDRA. YOU SAVED ALL THOSE PEOPLE.
HIP-HIP-HOORAY.
AND IT'S ALL BECAUSE OF YOUR STORY, AND THAT ONE THING THAT--
YES, YES. I KNOW.
I'M NOT SURE IF I'M LIKING MY PART IN THIS STORY.

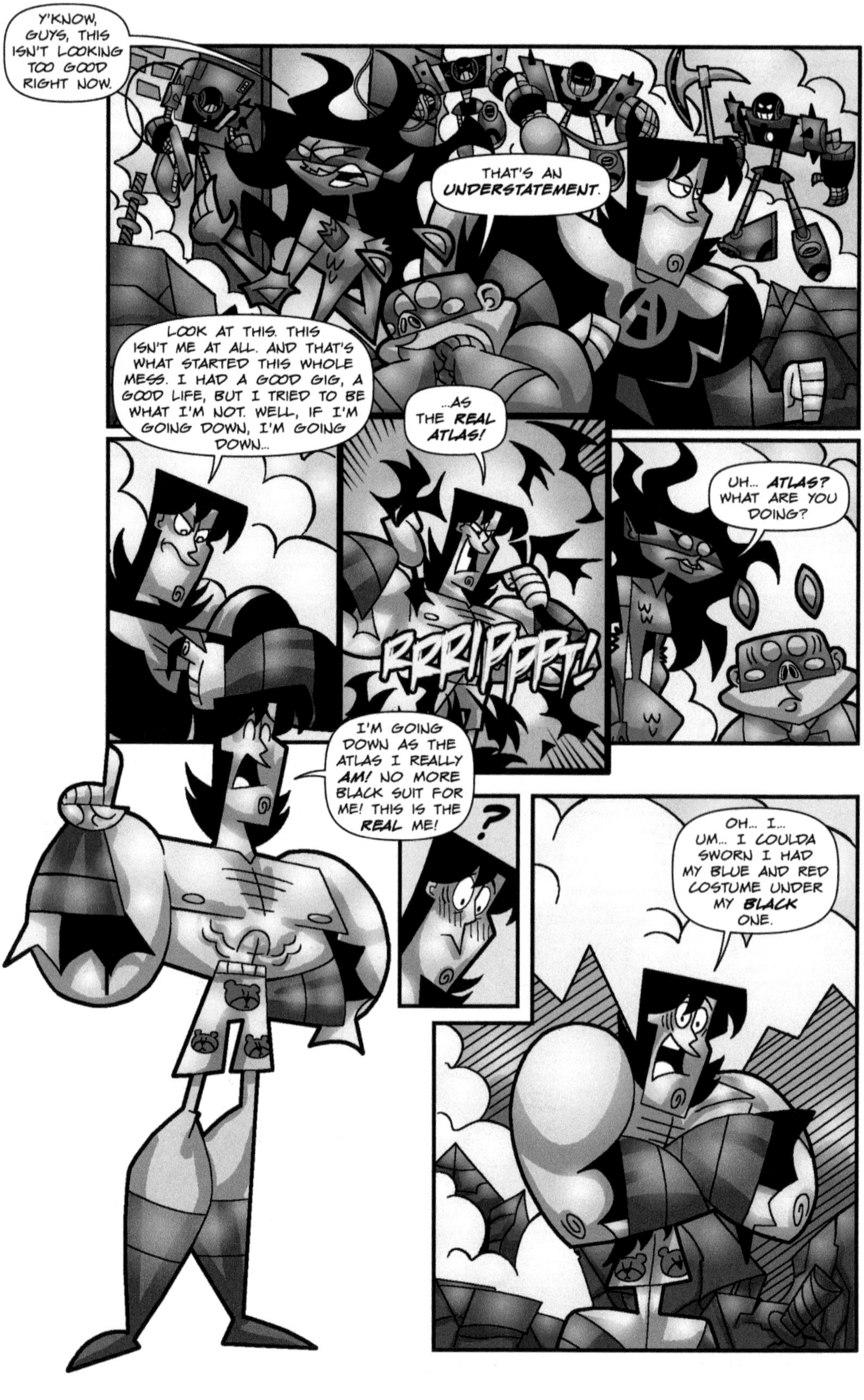
Y'KNOW, GUYS, THIS ISN'T LOOKING TOO GOOD RIGHT NOW.
THAT'S AN UNDERSTATEMENT.
LOOK AT THIS. THIS ISN'T ME AT ALL. AND THAT'S WHAT STARTED THIS WHOLE MESS. I HAD A GOOD GIG, A GOOD LIFE, BUT I TRIED TO BE WHAT I'M NOT. WELL, IF I'M GOING DOWN, I'M GOING DOWN...
...AS THE REAL ATLAS!
RRRIPPPT!
UH... ATLAS? WHAT ARE YOU DOING?
I'M GOING DOWN AS THE ATLAS I REALLY AM! NO MORE BLACK SUIT FOR ME! THIS IS THE REAL ME!
?
OH... I... UM... I COULDA SWORN I HAD MY BLUE AND RED COSTUME UNDER MY BLACK ONE.

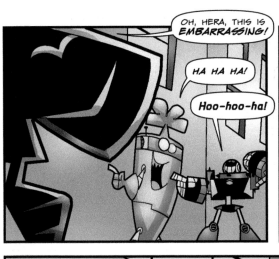

OH, HERA, THIS IS *EMBARRASSING!*

HA HA HA!

Hoo-hoo-ha!

WHAT... WHAT ARE WE DOING?

It feels... *nice?*

They call this... *laughter.*

I... I... I *like* it!

UH... ARE YOU GUYS STILL *INTERESTED* IN BLOWING UP CARS AND BUILDINGS AND THINGS?

OH, MAN. *NOT NOW.* THIS 'LAUGHTER' THING BEATS *ALL* THAT.

WELL, IT LOOKS LIKE THAT'S IT.

REALLY?

THEY'D RATHER LAUGH THAN FIGHT.

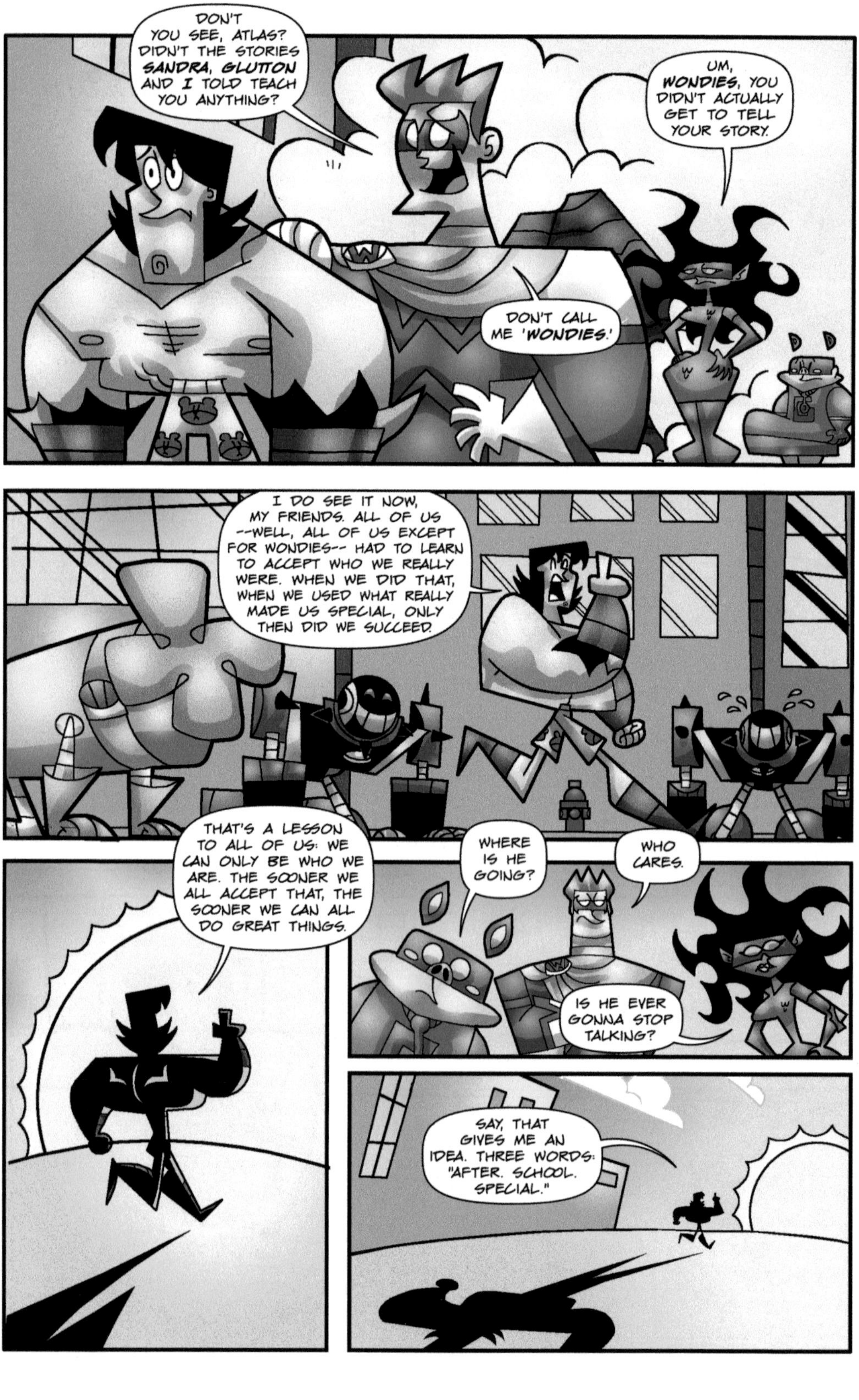
DON'T YOU SEE, ATLAS? DIDN'T THE STORIES SANDRA, GLUTTON AND I TOLD TEACH YOU ANYTHING?
UM, WONDIES, YOU DIDN'T ACTUALLY GET TO TELL YOUR STORY.
DON'T CALL ME 'WONDIES.'
I DO SEE IT NOW, MY FRIENDS. ALL OF US --WELL, ALL OF US EXCEPT FOR WONDIES-- HAD TO LEARN TO ACCEPT WHO WE REALLY WERE. WHEN WE DID THAT, WHEN WE USED WHAT REALLY MADE US SPECIAL, ONLY THEN DID WE SUCCEED.
THAT'S A LESSON TO ALL OF US: WE CAN ONLY BE WHO WE ARE. THE SOONER WE ALL ACCEPT THAT, THE SOONER WE CAN ALL DO GREAT THINGS.
WHERE IS HE GOING?
WHO CARES.
IS HE EVER GONNA STOP TALKING?
SAY, THAT GIVES ME AN IDEA. THREE WORDS: "AFTER. SCHOOL. SPECIAL."

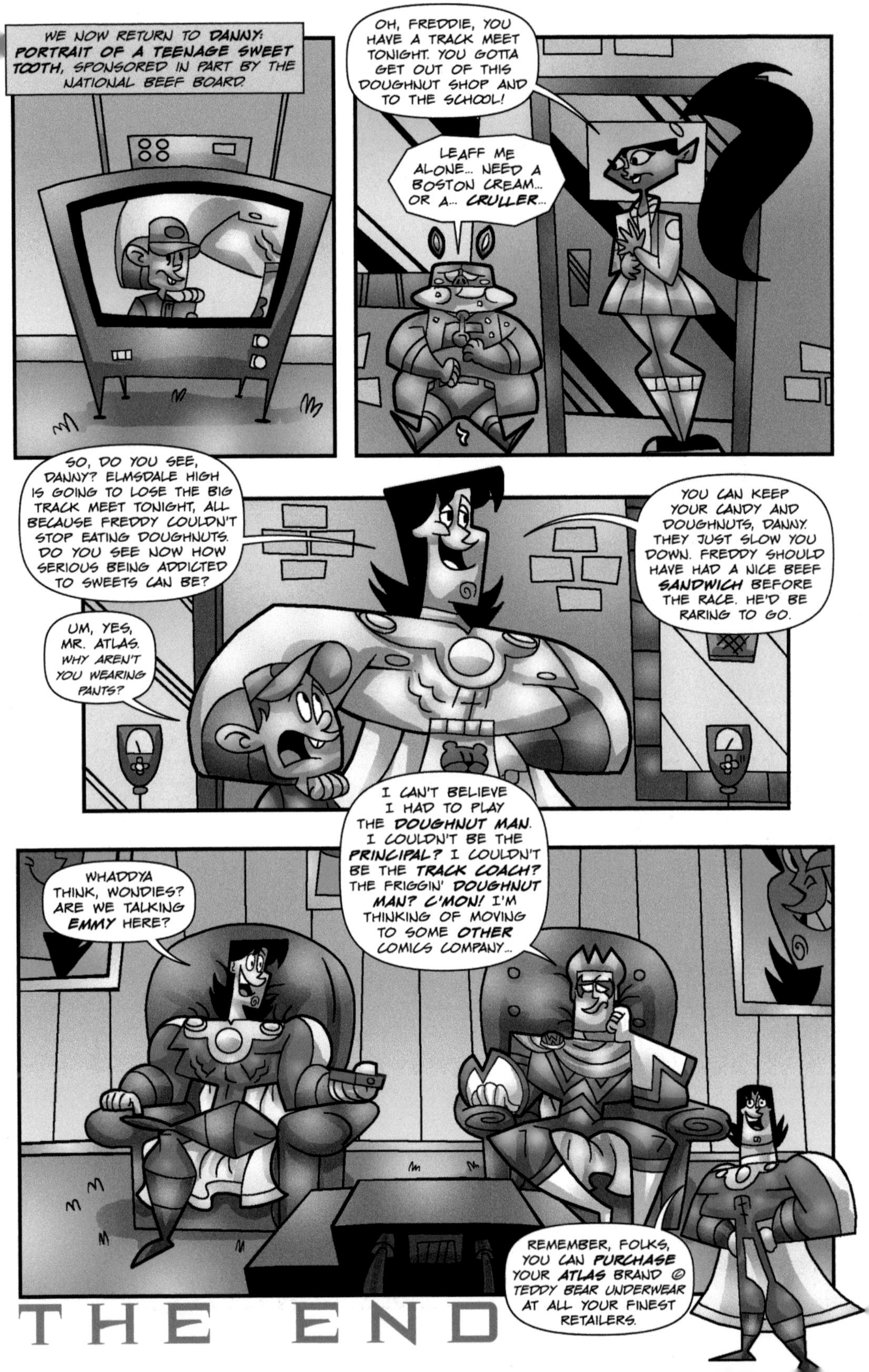
WE NOW RETURN TO DANNY: PORTRAIT OF A TEENAGE SWEET TOOTH, SPONSORED IN PART BY THE NATIONAL BEEF BOARD.
OH, FREDDIE, YOU HAVE A TRACK MEET TONIGHT. YOU GOTTA GET OUT OF THIS DOUGHNUT SHOP AND TO THE SCHOOL!
LEAFF ME ALONE... NEED A BOSTON CREAM... OR A... CRULLER...
SO, DO YOU SEE, DANNY? ELMSDALE HIGH IS GOING TO LOSE THE BIG TRACK MEET TONIGHT, ALL BECAUSE FREDDY COULDN'T STOP EATING DOUGHNUTS. DO YOU SEE NOW HOW SERIOUS BEING ADDICTED TO SWEETS CAN BE?
YOU CAN KEEP YOUR CANDY AND DOUGHNUTS, DANNY. THEY JUST SLOW YOU DOWN. FREDDY SHOULD HAVE HAD A NICE BEEF SANDWICH BEFORE THE RACE. HE'D BE RARING TO GO.
UM, YES, MR. ATLAS. WHY AREN'T YOU WEARING PANTS?
WHADDYA THINK, WONDIES? ARE WE TALKING EMMY HERE?
I CAN'T BELIEVE I HAD TO PLAY THE DOUGHNUT MAN. I COULDN'T BE THE PRINCIPAL? I COULDN'T BE THE TRACK COACH? THE FRIGGIN' DOUGHNUT MAN? C'MON! I'M THINKING OF MOVING TO SOME OTHER COMICS COMPANY...
REMEMBER, FOLKS, YOU CAN PURCHASE YOUR ATLAS BRAND © TEDDY BEAR UNDERWEAR AT ALL YOUR FINEST RETAILERS.
THE END

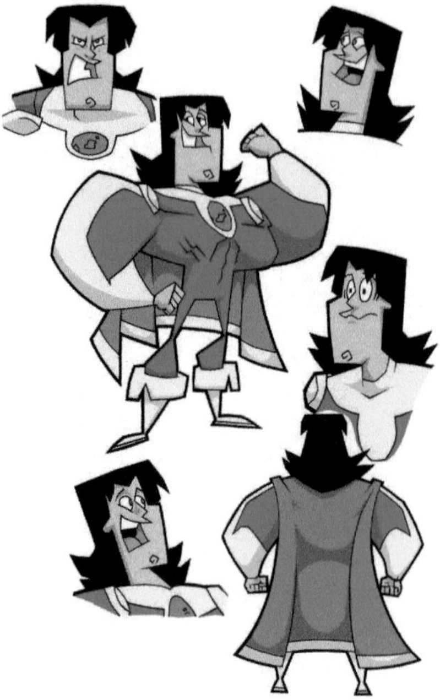

ATLAS

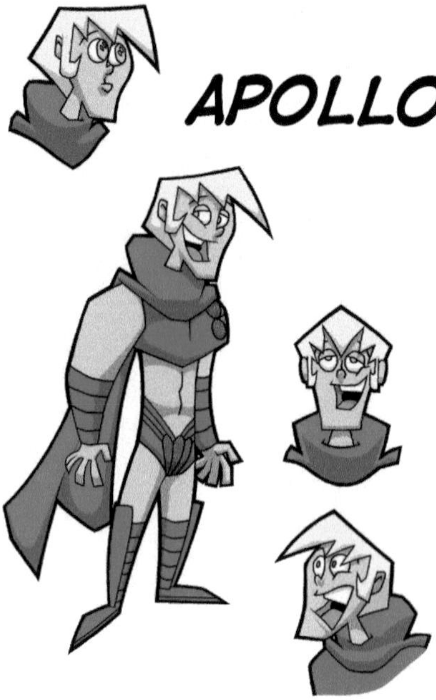

APOLLO

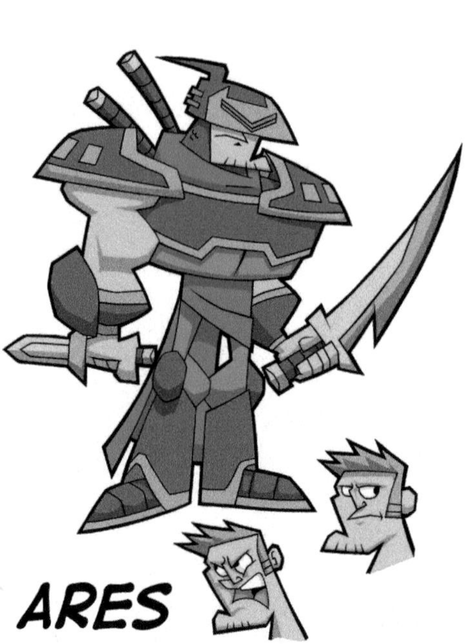

ARES

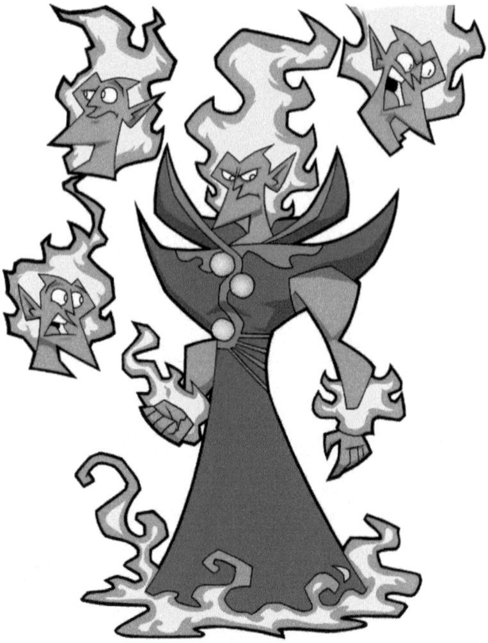

HADES

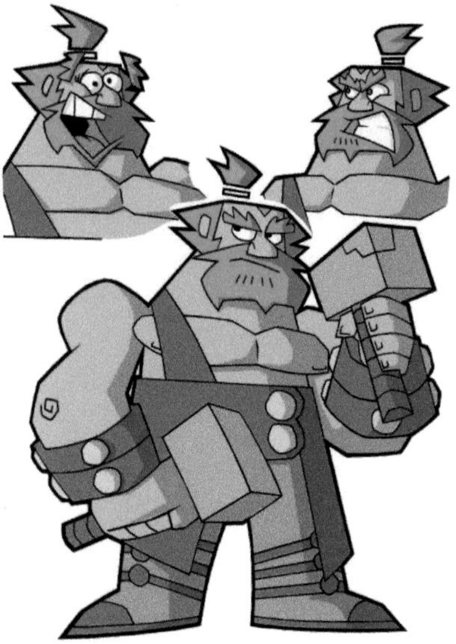

HEFESTUS

POSEIDON

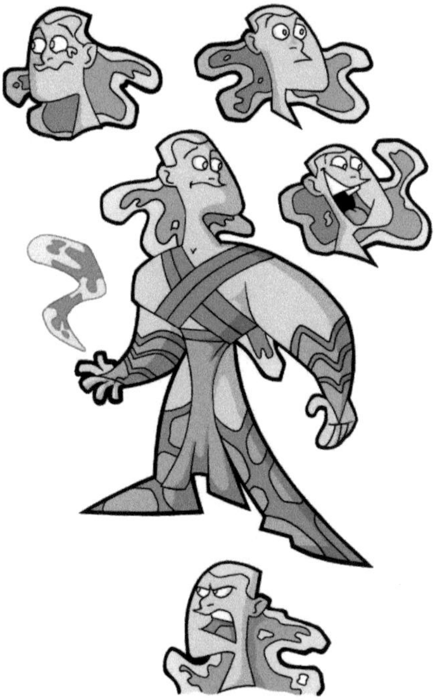

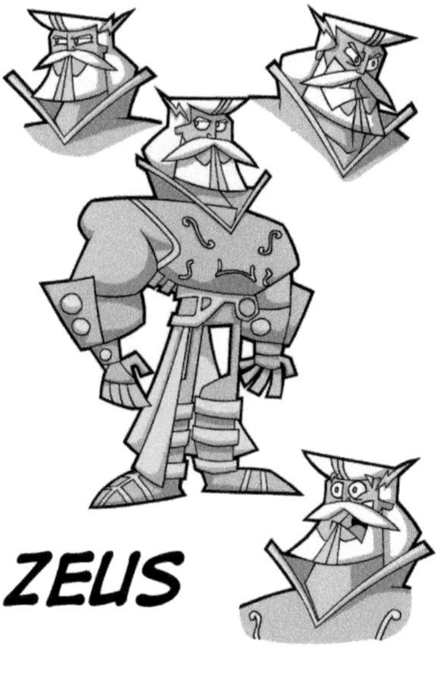

ZEUS

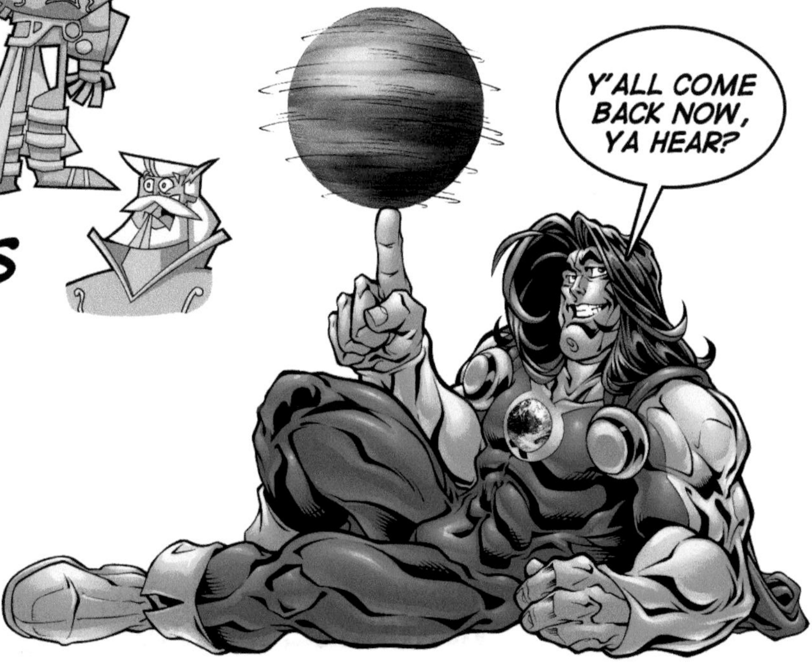
Y'ALL COME BACK NOW, YA HEAR?